Critical Acclaim for *Cthulhu Fhtagn!,*
edited by Ross E. Lockhart

"*This Is Horror* Anthology of the Year 2015."

—*This Is Horror*

"...if R'lyeh isn't rising fast enough for you, if clammy, webbed-handed fishbelly-white figures aren't circling your house, and the stars aren't winking out just yet, the *Cthulhu Fhtagn!* anthology will get you through until the madness begins."

—Marion Deeds, *Fantasy Literature*

"A new, and highly personal, take on the legacy of the Cthulhu Mythos emerges shuddering and gibbering from the R'lyehian depths in the bloated tentacular shape of *Cthulhu Fhtagn!*, conceived and collated by Ross E. Lockhart, whose stature as an anthologist and creator of *The Book of Cthulhu I* and *II*, *Tales of Jack the Ripper*, and *The Children of Old Leech*, approaches legendary proportions. And here are 19 examples of Cthulhoid weird filtered through his own unique perspective."

—Paul St. John Mackintosh, *TeleRead*

"These are all Lovecraftian stories, then, even if more than a few of them, this many generations hence, have moved well past the tropes and conventions the Old Man developed. This book shows us some of the best that pastiche, tribute, and evolution of the Lovecraftian Weird Tale can offer."

—Jonathan Raab, *Muzzleland Press*

"...a collection of dark stories that Lovecraft himself would be thrilled to read. If you are a fan of terrifying short stories, this is a book you will want to pick up immediately."

—Matthew Scott Baker, *Shattered Ravings*

ETERNAL
FRANKENSTEIN

Other books by Ross E. Lockhart

Anthologies:

The Book of Cthulhu
The Book of Cthulhu II
Tales of Jack the Ripper
The Children of Old Leech: A Tribute to the Carnivorous Cosmos of Laird Barron (with Justin Steele)
Giallo Fantastique
Cthulhu Fhtagn!

Novels:

Chick Bassist

ETERNAL

FRANKENSTEIN

Edited by Ross E. Lockhart

WORD HORDE
PETALUMA, CA

Edited by Ross E. Lockhart

First Edition

ISBN: 978-1-939905-23-9

A Word Horde Book
http://www.WordHorde.com

Dedication:

To Mary. And her Monster. With thanks.

Illustration from the frontispiece of the 1831 edition of Mary Shelley's
Frankenstein; or, The Modern Prometheus by Theodor von Holst.

TABLE OF CONTENTS

INTRODUCTION:
A MODERN PROMETHEUS

ROSS E. LOCKHART

"How do you do?"

So begins *Frankenstein* (1931), the Universal Pictures film produced by Carl Laemmle, Jr., directed by James Whale, and introduced by Edward Van Sloan, as he steps from behind a curtain, offering, in an aside from his role as the film's scholarly Doctor Waldman, a few words of welcome—and warning—to theater patrons that they are about to experience "one of the strangest tales ever told." This wasn't the first time *Frankenstein* had appeared on screen, the first was Edison Studios' 1910 adaptation, or on stage, but even that's not where *Frankenstein* begins.

Frankenstein begins two hundred years ago, during the bleak and sunless summer of 1816, when a young woman, an unwed mother on the run, shares an evening of ghost stories with friends and lovers taking refuge in a chalet in Switzerland. After passing around a copy of *Fantasmagoriana*, a French anthology of German ghost stories, a challenge arose: each person in attendance would write their own tale to thrill, shock, and horrify. That night, Mary Wollstonecraft Godwin, later known as Mary Shelley, had a frightening dream. That dream became the seed that inspired Mary to write *Frankenstein; or, The Modern Prometheus*, a tale of galvanism, philosophy, and the re-animated dead, which she published anonymously in 1818.

Today, *Frankenstein* has become a modern myth without rival, influencing

1

countless works of fiction, music, and film. We all know Frankenstein, both man and monster, creator and created. We know the novel explores the great mysteries of creation: life and death. But how much do we really know about *Frankenstein*?

Mary Shelley's *Frankenstein* is many things. A first novel. A philosophical work. The origin of science fiction. It is a reaction to volcanic dust obscuring the sun, and the apocalyptic skies that distinguished the year without a summer. It is a novel marked by the loss of a child, and the desire to write something more enduring than the poetry of Lord Byron and Percy Shelley. It is a story of technology and magic and the desire to challenge god's and nature's laws. It is a tale of dreamlike geographies, shifting topographies, and finding one's place in the universe. "It has the true touch of cosmic fear," wrote H. P. Lovecraft, and is a mother to "every robot, every android, every sentient computer (whether benevolent or malevolent)" to come after, according to Joanna Russ.

Frankenstein, like its monster, its creature, its wretch, has taken on a life of its own. It reflects us. It defines us. It shows us what it means to be human.

Welcome, then, to *Eternal Frankenstein*, an anthology offering sixteen different interpretations of the *Frankenstein* mythos, from sixteen of my favorite authors, exploring worlds both literary and cinematic, scientific and supernatural. All will surprise you. Some will shock you. Some will terrify you.

So, if you scare easily, now's your chance to… well… we've warned you…

Ross E. Lockhart
Petaluma, California
June 16, 2016

TORSO, HEART, HEAD

AMBER-ROSE REED

"Who was I? What was I? Whence did I come? ... These questions continually recurred, but I was unable to solve them."

—*Frankenstein*

LEFT ARM, RIGHT ARM

Your left arm blocks the swing; your right arm takes a swing of its own. Your knuckles crack against someone else's nose. When you pull back your fist, you wiggle your fingers. Old Josef takes it as a slight and lets out a growl. He's like a mutt going for a bone.

He charges again and you sidestep the cur. You didn't start this fight, but he has a face fit for slapping and you've got fists made for hitting. He comes again. The tavern crowd around you buzzes and spits. The barmaid's calling for someone to stop the brawling. You draw back your arm, ready to deliver a punch. It'll be the last one you have to release tonight; sure thing, that.

Something crunches against the back of your head. Your vision goes black. You don't feel any pain.

TORSO

Your hammer hasn't met the anvil yet when you hear the screaming. Women, mostly, and you pass the hammer to your apprentice and head out to the street to see what's causing the noise. Down the way, a cart's toppled over. You hear the screams as words as you get closer; there is a boy there, and the cart is crushing him.

The muck in the streets sucks at your feet as you rush over. You don't trip. The crowd parts as you approach. There is none strong enough to help, save you.

The wood is splintered, but you find a grip. All you can see of the boy are his small child's feet, shod in tattered shoes, and his legs, bare to the knee.

The muscles in your chest pull and twinge and you feel as though all of your upper self is on fire. But the cart gives way from the mud with a sucking sound, and as the boy slides from beneath the toppled vehicle, your eyes meet his. He has a strong gaze, blue eyes meeting yours.

You let go the cart, and mud squelches beneath it. You straighten and take deep breaths, waiting for the feeling of fire to leave your chest. But it doesn't. You clutch your right hand over your heart. It feels, suddenly, like you are the one being crushed.

HEART

Your heart flutters. You would never use that line in a poem; no, instead, your heart would open like birds' wings, drawing you up into the ether, into the glorious realm of Nature that you can witness only because of Her. Your Cynthia, your Diana, your Selene, goddess of the yellow moon above.

If Nature had some consideration, the moon would be full and pale, not yellow, though at least that rhymes with words of some poetic pretention. The city streets stretch out before you, empty at this hour; you had not realized you had tarried so long in Madame Auguste's sitting room. But your beloved had been there, taming the restless spirit inside of you, and truly, you would have spent forever inside that sitting room, as though it were a space as vast as the boundless forests of Arcadia and as full of treasures as the agoras of Ancient days.

She had given you a note, perfumed paper folded in three and then again. It was the answer to your question, there was nothing else that it could be. And yet, her eyes had given no hint of the contents. Would she put you out of the misery that laced your every moment, or plunge you deeper into that black despair? Yes or no, you would receive the answer in the same place in which the question had spilled from your lips, as though drawn out by the delicate scent of that same perfume.

The church rises up before you in all its splendor. A fine work of man, its peach-colored walls hide the glories of Art and the Divine inside, but you cannot breach those walls tonight. Their moldings drip down toward you. In the yellow light of the moon and the gas lamps, they seem almost sinister, the arrows of fate pointing at your hat-covered head.

There is no bench on which you may sit; you unfold the letter in full view of God and the Church, and bring it to your nose before bringing your eyes to its surface. Is it roses, her perfume? Roses and something else, indefinable, ineffable.

Her words are spindly across the page, inked in india, and though the light here is not good, you read them quickly, and then again. Once more, for bad news should come in threes, and this, this letter, dashing hopes against the rocks of fickle womanhood, is the worst news your frail heart could hear.

You smell not roses anymore; the muck of the river calls, the pull of the current.

HEAD

From far off, the clock tower strikes noon. You try to measure your stride to each strike, but it's not long before you are out of step, your left foot a beat too early in its motion, your right foot stuttering a bit too late.

There is no sense in your delay, you've been told over and over, but like Fabius Cunctator, you walk circles 'round your destination. No army follows you, only a decision, only your future. Is it for you to take your place beside your father when other pursuits call you forth? Is it for you to stand aside and let the running of all you were raised for pass to your brother, to raise the blood of your father and spur him to enmity?

Your head feels heavy on your shoulders, as though it is too big for your body. It hangs low.

In your pocket is a letter to your father, in response to the one he sent you, bidding you to return home. You shall *not* be coming home, the letter states; your path is set for things beyond business, for Latin, for Greek, for the coins and copper pots and the places in the chorographers' maps. The letter is worded more vehemently than your shaky penmanship might indicate. To open yourself up for ridicule is no easy matter, and easier in your imagination than to put down in words in black ink.

Another student rushes by, his shoulder slamming against yours. His eyes are alight with some sort of madness, red-rimmed, and his face is a mask of discontent. Is he like you, caught between two desires? For a moment you imagine it so, and feel kinship despite the ache in your shoulder. Your eyes watch him as he grows more and more distant. He charges into the anatomy building with the assurance of one who holds no doubt in his actions. To be like that would be a gift, to charge forth with purpose and know where it is you are going.

Your second option is to charge into a building very like the anatomy building and withdraw your enrollment in university. To pack your things and return home to your father's side.

You think of the young man, possessed by some mad passion, and wonder if that frenzy could ever come upon you, could ever make your actions incisive and decisive. Why not, you wonder; why not stride forth as the man with the burning eyes, refusing to match pace with an outside force, but instead making your own?

You spin around, shoe dipping into the space between the cobblestones, tipping you. But you catch your balance and dart out into the road, decision made. You would do it, you would—

The horses, the carriage, seem to blur in their sudden motion, so close to you, and you wonder—

Was that the wrong decision after all?

THERMIDOR

SIOBHAN CARROLL

From a window overlooking the Rue de Reuilly, Justine watches the aristocrats preparing to die. The men fuss over their wigs, trying to straighten them as the clods of earth rain down. The women mostly pray or clutch their children. A wild-eyed young woman stands up in the wobbling cart and shakes her fist. *"Vous monstres!"*

Justine doubts the woman will shout so when she sees the throng in the *Place*. The voices of the condemned usually give out when they see the seething crowd, the stained platform, and at the top of it all—the machine.

"Monstres!" The shouting woman is thrown down by one of the sans-culottes. The urchins cheer.

"What do you see?" The Marquis is impatient, as always.

For a moment Justine is tempted to answer honestly, quoting the words of her previous master: '*Monsters*, from the Latin *mōnstrum*: a portent or warning.' But she knows better.

"I see a young woman, fresh from a convent," she begins. The Marquis's quill begins its quiet *scritch scritch*—the sound a fingernail makes inside a coffin lid. It would raise the hair on Justine's neck, if her hair was still capable of rising. "Her hair is shorn. The soldiers have torn her blouse off. She is exposed to the elements now—you should see how she clutches herself."

She continues in this vein for a while. The Marquis will embroider her description: he has a better imagination for depravity. But Justine is better at describing cruelty, at itemizing the things that happen as a woman's body comes apart. Absently, she runs her hand over the seamed arm that is not hers. Somewhere in the churn of the North Sea, her real arm, swollen and puckered by barnacles, braces itself against a wave.

"Do you think she will do? Can we get her?"

Justine rolls her eyes at the window. Providing they are fresh and pretty, anyone will do. The Marquis is not interested in them for their minds, after all.

"We can get her."

"Well," he throws his quill down and opens his hands theatrically. "What are you waiting for?"

Ever the good servant, Justine throws on her stained cloak and wades outside. The runoff from the *Place* splashes up her boots, soaking the hem of her dress an inch deep in blood. In the heat, the smell of rot is oppressive; even the burning juniper branches can't mask it. Justine adjusts her cockade and pushes her way through the clammy jostle of the crowd.

At the Picpus garden she pays the ditch-diggers the usual amount of livres. The bodies are all young and pretty, as requested. She does not see the spirited one who shouted. Perhaps her body was too battered, or perhaps she has been set aside for another buyer. Justine picks a sweet-faced girl with a flower bracelet still twined around her wrist. She is more the Marquis's type, anyway.

The grim-faced carter looks away as she gives him directions, frowning at her Genevan accent. He does not love the new order, she reflects as she climbs up beside the corpse. He should be careful. It's not only aristocrats whose heads end upon pikes these days.

But Justine's head has stayed attached to her shoulders. A miracle, given Master Frankenstein's taste for improving things. Long hours Justine spent on the slab, unable to move or speak, while her former master decided what parts of her were worth keeping.

Justine's face and torso Frankenstein apparently thought pretty enough, or at least good enough for his Creature. Her legs Justine does not miss so much, but she sometimes gets a nagging pain in her right foot, and she wishes she could scratch it. Dr. Séguret tells her this is a delusion. But Justine knows Frankenstein left her foot in the permafrost, where it twists sideways, blue skin jabbed against a stone. Its toes flex uselessly at the frozen earth.

Imagine if Victor *had* severed her head from her shoulders. Without a body to control, her head might have been battered into slow ruination on the Orkney rocks, or endured the gnawing of fish. Far better to be left with head, torso, and arm intact when Victor decided to abort his feminine creation.

"It could be worse," she says to the corpse beside her, and her words serve for both of them. She shrugs the blanket over its glazed eyes. Why dwell on the past? Justine is at the center of things now, in the city that dominates the headlines of Europe. The city that is birthing the future.

Citizeness Grosholtz is a pale woman with bovine eyes. Wisps of her shorn hair poke out from beneath her mob cap, testifying to the artist's close shave with the national razor. Grosholtz's eyes flick over the cart and she turns hurriedly away, motioning Justine to follow.

The laboratory is tidier than last time. Having spent so many hours learning the peculiarities of the Frankenstein household, Justine appreciates the cleaning of laboratories. She wonders which of their shuffling creations takes the grim task of scrubbing the floor for Dr. Séguret. Slow-witted Philippe perhaps? The seam-faced servant deposits the corpse on the table as the Madame directs, his yellow eyes turned to her in mild inquiry. Citizeness Grosholtz presses a handkerchief to her nose—an aristocratic gesture. She should be careful of it.

Dr. Séguret bounces into the room. He is an energetic young man, given to hand-clapping and shouts of excitement. His assistant, François, slinks in behind him. François reminds Justine of her former master, drab and pale, like a bent lily. His silence makes her nervous.

Dr. Séguret laughs in delight as he peels back the blanket. He picks up the corpse's arm and lets it fall—"You see how fresh?"

François circles like a fish in a murky bowl. "I see. Maybe we try—here?"

"You prepared the models?"

Citizeness Grosholtz gestures to the wax corpse beside her, its rib cage exposed to show the organs that challenged the anatomists in last week's experiment. Dr. Séguret and François lean in to inspect them, muttering the odd compliment to Grosholtz for her handiwork. The artist stares straight ahead, her gaze focused on another world.

Dr. Séguret examines the model's rib cage, pointing out where François should make the incision. Holding the scalpel like a pencil between his thumb and two fingers, François traces the line down from the sternum. They will try to avoid removing more integuments than necessary, because exposure to air makes the parts dry and indistinct.

Justine lets her gaze drift away from the dissection. She has seen it all before—the Vena Saphena, the whitish surface of the womb, the greyish lungs. She is not truly needed here, not anymore. From time to time, Dr. Séguret will ask her a question—how Master Frankenstein had placed the electrode or how much of the green formula he applied—but now that he is confident of the process, the questions have become rarer.

In the cages around the laboratory, the anatomists' creations watch the dissection in stupefied terror. Rat-headed pigeons flap awkwardly against the bars. The hybrid-mechanicals, cogs turning underneath their wax skin, whir nervously to themselves. Some of the former dogs forget themselves and try to howl, filling the laboratory with wheezes and birdlike whistles.

The experiment is concluded, the corpse sewn up. Now the galvanic switch is thrown. The liquid in the table cylinder glows electric blue as a surge of *something* moves around them. Citizeness Grosholtz makes a noise that might be a sob.

The crackle of vitalic machinery falls silent. Dr. Séguret leans in, studying the exposed limb dangling from the table. Its finger twitches.

"It worked," Dr. Séguret whispers, his face still flushed with awe after all this time. "It's alive."

She, Justine thinks to herself. *She's alive*. But the men are already turning to each other with congratulations on their lips.

Upstairs, in the doctor's fine parlor, the men discuss the future. They have made marvelous advances, shattered barriers never before thought possible—but where can they present their discoveries? The Royal Academy of Sciences has been abolished, its luminaries extinguished.

"We can reverse *death itself*," Dr. Séguret exclaims. "Surely that is of interest in a time of war!"

"La République n'a pas besoin de savants ni de chimistes." François inclines his wine glass to emphasize his point—it is engraved with the crest of a dead family.

"But to hide such innovations from the world. If we had connections, someone to speak for us…"

Dr. Séguret directs his last plea to his patron, who has arrived, as usual, fashionably late. The Marquis smiles thinly at the doctor's enthusiasm. "Citizen François is correct," he remarks, sipping his wine. "Now is not the time to attract attention."

"Rumor is," François says, "the tigers are quarrelling."

The men swirl the deep, red burgundy in their glasses and contemplate things that are unwise to speak aloud.

The Marquis downs the rest of his glass and deposits it on a table. Gillette, one of the doctor's earliest experiments, staggers to collect it.

"And where is our newest creation?"

Dr. Séguret laughs nervously. For all his embrace of the new morality, he seems unnerved by the Marquis's presence, much as an atheist might be at coming face to face with the Devil. "The... experiment has been moved to a secure room."

François's lips purse. "Would you care to view her?"

"Justine will be my escort." The Marquis turns on his heel.

In the hallway, the Marquis snorts. "These knock-kneed philosophers," he mutters to the walls. "They boast of their violations of nature. But they turn green at *my* experiments. Imagine!"

Justine nods, though she knows the Marquis is not really talking to her. He rips off a dangling shred of wallpaper and drops it contemptuously on the stairs.

"They have no real understanding of nature," he continues as they arrive at the bedroom. "Or violation."

Reassembled from one of the suicides, stitch-mouthed Marie flinches as the Marquis approaches. He does not look at her. A worn-out toy, she is beneath his attention. Justine nods, and Marie steps aside, her face as blank as one of the Marquis's precious sheets of paper.

Unclipping the key from her belt, Justine inserts it in the lock. It turns.

Sometimes, when the Marquis is at his pursuits, Justine likes to think about glaciers. In the Alps, Elizabeth would rattle off the latest news from Victor while Justine posed for her sketches. Justine remembered one letter in which Victor detailed the theories of Buffon, a philosopher who predicted that glaciers would devour the world. Standing with the ice at her back, Justine had found the idea disturbing. Now, on the other side of death, she feels nostalgic for Buffon's apocalypse.

The Marquis does not believe in slow destruction. His violence is the violence of spectacle. Before, when Justine considered her body hers, his slashes and splatters would have horrified her. Now she knows it is not hers, and this has made all the difference.

The woman scrabbling on the floor has not yet learned this lesson. Her hands flail uselessly at the floor. Death, as Justine knows all too well, undoes one's coordination. The woman moans, her drooling mouth trying to form words of protest. When the Marquis releases her, she staggers upright and lurches forward. The leg iron snaps her to the floor. The Marquis squints, irritated, then lashes the riding crop across her face. The mark it leaves gapes, but does not bleed.

"The little fool wants to escape," the Marquis says. "Grab her, Justine."

On a pebbled beach, Justine's severed hand is drawing itself out of the waves, inch by inch. She thinks the cruel gusts of air on its skin might be seagulls, swooping closer.

In the squalid chamber Justine grabs at the woman. Her shorn hair offers little purchase, so Justine grabs the woman by her neck and hauls her backwards. She is not concerned about breakage, knowing herself how quickly reanimated bodies heal.

The woman's fingers claw at Justine, but they can do no lasting damage. These are not Justine's hands, after all. Her hand is on a beach in the Orkneys.

They are not hers.

They are hers.

At the corner of the Rue Moreau, Justine watches the courier sort through the Marquis's letters. In addition to the usual pleading correspondence, the Marquis also receives foreign news and pornography. Sometimes he collects tidbits for Justine. This was how Justine learned of the death of her former mistress, in a letter from one of the Marquis's procurers, sandwiched between descriptions of prostitutes.

As she listened to the Marquis hypothesize the tortures inflicted on the bride's body, Justine had felt only an odd hollowness in her chest. Elizabeth was the one who had saved her from poverty; who'd taught her to read. When Justine was condemned, Elizabeth was the only one who'd spoken in her defense. How could Justine be kept awake by the nagging ache in a former limb, but feel only this dull sadness at Elizabeth's murder?

She can almost hear the doctor's voice in her head. *Perhaps your new body is alive to sensations of heat, but not of compassion.* Her mind veers towards—then skids away from—the image of the woman in the chamber. Justine may have no pity left, but in this, she is not alone.

The courier re-wraps the letters in wax cloth. As he hands them over, Justine sees something in his face.

"What is it?"

The man hesitates, licking his scabbed lips. "They arrested Robespierre."

Justine is thunderstruck. She thinks of the blinking, green-spectacled man she'd seen at the Festival of the Supreme Being. "Arrested?"

"Along with other members of the Committee." The courier smiles a death's head's grin. "We'll see what tomorrow brings, will we not?"

As Justine walks back the streets are already seething. On the corners, clusters of *sans-culottes* mutter in low voices. Passersby keep their eyes on their feet, trying to avoid attention.

Suddenly a portly man—perhaps a butcher?— stumbles onto the cobblestones ahead, pressing a bloody hand to his face. And yet he straightens and tries to join with the crowd, an uneven, weaving stagger. A gray-haired woman strolls up behind him. To help? No. Raising a bucket high, she brings it down on the man's head with a decisive crack. He staggers to his knees, hands raised in a mute plea for mercy.

The urchins surge forward, burying the man with flailing fists. The *sans-culottes* break off their conspiracies and wander into the street. Sensing the oncoming spectacle, some well-dressed footpads start towards the man, one lifting a club. The crowd closes in.

Justine walks past the ferment, wondering what prompted the woman's attack. An insult? Why not simply denounce the man to the authorities?

But with Citizen Robespierre arrested, who knows what tomorrow could bring? The guillotine could be silenced. The world could be turned right-side up.

The old woman is right, Justine reflects. *If the poor want to get their blows in, they should do so tonight.*

Like a good servant, Justine thinks of warning the Marquis. But the old fox can look after himself.

Justine turns her movements over to the crowd. Together they flow in a different direction.

The doctor's eyes are wide as he lets her in. He looks behind her, half-surprised, for the Marquis.

"Have you heard?" He means Robespierre, the arrest. "Does your Master have news? What does he plan to do?"

"Nothing." Justine pushes the servant's door shut behind her. She lowers her voice. "He intends to wait it out. But he asks that you give him your papers for safekeeping. And he suggests you make arrangements to secure more bodies, in case the laws change."

"Every day a new terror!" The doctor laughs and mops his forehead. "We have become like the dogs in François's experiment."

"What dogs are these?"

"François has been testing the effects of fear on animals." The doctor leads her through the laboratory, up the narrow staircase that leads to his study. "We put a dog in a harness, yes? So it cannot move. And then we throw cold water on it. We beat it with a stick. We teach it to fear us, so that every time it hears François open the cage door, it almost dies of terror."

Justine thinks of the woman upstairs, the wax cooling in yellow stripes over her blackened skin. "What is the point of the experiment?"

"Ah." The doctor is warming to his theme. "The dog learns that escape is hopeless. When you remove the harness, it will endure your beatings, even though freedom is mere steps away."

Justine accepts the documents and transfers them to her satchel. She knows what the doctor is talking about. On her last night of life, in her cell, the walls seemed to crush her in. At least death would be an escape, she'd thought. At least death would bring certainty.

The doctor pours himself a glass of wine. His skin is waxy; the heat is getting to him. "A toast," he says, "to us dogs."

Justine has no glass in hand. She watches him drink, the nobleman's bastard turned natural philosopher.

"You need not worry so much about tomorrow."

"You think so?" The doctor's face, when he turns towards her, is surprisingly childlike. "There are so many rumors on the street."

"I know so," she says comfortingly. Swift as thought, she puts her mismatched hands around his throat. She begins to squeeze.

In the laboratory, the wax-skinned chimeras study Justine with taxidermied eyes. Rabbits with elongated monkey arms clutch the bars of their cages. A crow's head swivels on the end of a jar. As she swings its door open, the crow-thing flinches, but stands its ground. Because of this, Justine relents, lowering the cage to the floor. The crow-thing scuds into the shadows, swift as a water beetle.

To the other chimeras she is less kind. If they hesitate at the open doors, she tosses their cages to the floor in noisy clatters. Some of the more delicate chimera shatter on impact. Others flail in tangles of badly sewn limbs.

She kicks one of the rabbit-beasts by accident, splintering ribs. The Creature howls. Irritated, she brings her foot down a second, decisive time. It is as Saint-Just said: *The Goddess of Liberty is no smiling Madonna.*

Sloping Philippe staggers away from her, yellow eyes alarmed as she lifts the keys to the forbidden room. Gray-skinned Marie watches, her sewn mouth twisted in amusement.

"Wait here," she tells them, and the instruction reassures Philippe more than any explanation. He stands aside to let her pass.

The female Creature has grown filthier since Justine saw her last. She has smeared herself with her own excrement, no doubt in the hope the stench would keep the Marquis at bay.

On a different day, Justine might disabuse her of that notion. Today, she is glad that this one is still alive, still angry, still wanting freedom. There is nobody left to reassemble corpses, now that the doctor is gone.

"Hello, sister," Justine says to the tattered thing. She shows her the keys dangling in her hand. "Do you want to get out today?"

The anger in the Creature's eyes is palpable. Justine can almost feel the woman's hands wrapped around her throat, the painful compression, the dimming of the light. Would that even work?

But once freed from their shackles, the woman's hands find her own face instead, rubbing the cut on her cheek. Philippe hovers behind the two of them, mouth gaping. Outside on the street, a rough-voiced man sings "Ça ira."

Les aristocrates à la lanterne!

Ah! ça ira, ça ira, ça ira,
Les aristocrates on les pendra!

Justine smiles. "Come," she says to her fellow monsters. "I have something to show you."

Twilight is falling, and the streets are full of smoke. Children dart back and forth, wearing the wooden carnival masks that mark the turning of the month. *Sans-culottes* march in irregular groups, singing. Some carry pikes. Some carry bottles. Nobody minds the monsters.

Justine and the other Creatures stand unnoticed in the crowd, which is its own nation in the streets of Sodome. Tonight, they still rule the city.

"Follow me," Justine says to the monsters. She raises the doctor's severed head like a lantern. Some of the urchins, seeing her bloody trophy, come whooping and laughing to join them.

"The Festival of Thermidor!" someone shouts. Justine holds her trophy higher.

"Follow!" she cries. And they come, screaming and singing to join her.

The mob surges forward. At its head, Justine smiles like Salome, dangling the Prophet's head from her blood-stained fingers.

SEWN INTO HER FINGERS

AUTUMN CHRISTIAN

I grew a girl in the calm dark of my lab. I created her as a curiosity, a personal project. When I first started working on her I didn't even think of her as human, something that could grow consciousness, something that couldn't be destroyed without consequence. She was something for me to play with in my off hours. A way to relax.

For twelve years I'd worked at Indigo Labs, reconstructing the minds and bodies of the deceased. I could talk about technical details, but most people would prefer to remain in ignorance, and couldn't comprehend them anyway. Instead I will tell you that I used to feel a kind of excitement, walking through the nursery, watching the the skeletal frames grow into fully-formed people. It was always dark down there, lit only by black lights and the glowing baths of the individual pods. Quiet too, except for the soft hum of all that new electricity, those muscles and bones twitch-moving into place. I used to like to go down to the children's section, take notes while I watched brain activity on the monitors or the sluice of nutrients as they snaked into the miniature chambers.

But after twelve years of rebuilding people, the very act of forming life from its nucleus became routine to me.

People have told me that Indigo Labs plays god, but if so it is a god that caters to government contracts, rich eccentrics, grieving spouses, bewildered mothers, car crash victims. It is a god of consolations, that cannot save the woman trapped underneath ice with her last bubbles splicing the thin blue underlayer, but can grow something like her. It is a god of petty bureaucratic favors and bad luck and reject scientists who couldn't get into NASA.

I have remade a murderer with a split tongue and half a brain who was needed to testify at a hearing, and a child genius with an IQ of 180 who caught the flu. I can lay claim to the fact that I've regrown the memories of the no-more-late governor of Louisiana and more than one celebrity actor. But I am one of the top scientists in my field, and it is not difficult for me to coax cells to grow they want to grow. They were copies.

They were not mine like she was mine.

I am not a poetic man, but I found poetry watching her grow in the nutrient pod in my private lab. I did not create her to be beautiful, but she was beautiful, her body a breathing ice sculpture, hair like a nuclear shoreline.

I created her from my collection of favorite parts. I gave her the amygdala of a soft-hearted social worker, and the heart of a man who once crushed his wife underneath their front door. She had one hand of a pianist, the other from a drug addict who burnt the tips of her fingers. The clean lungs of a mountain dweller whose lips never touched smoke, and the throat of a combat veteran who once inhaled phosphorus. Her hair was Arabian, her eyes purple, her skin tissue-pale and spattered with dark freckles.

Of course, I didn't save the parts themselves, although some think that we use the actual dead tissue and organs. This misconception is easily cleared up with a bit of research, but most people aren't willing to expend the effort. I only saved the chemical composition of the parts, that could be stimulated to grow over a sort of cellular frame.

Her memories were a much more delicate and lengthy process than the body parts. I needed to construct them so that her body responded properly to the neuron input of memories. It's fairly easy, at least for someone like me, when the body matched the brain.

Yet I constructed her piece by individual piece. I created a map of her nerves from individual strands. I wired her myself—composite parts that did not grow in organic substrates, but were laid out like power lines. I was not her gardener, her birthmother, watching cell tissues grow womb-like with only a little stimulation. I was her creator.

Most people cannot understand the inner workings of their own minds, and they live inside of them. They plan their entire lives around processes that they do not comprehend. Imagine the enormous amount of precision, the complex knowledge of the human mind, required to build an entire life from scratch. And not just to build it, but to have it function.

Her childhood home burnt down, and she spent the next several years dreaming of fire at her feet that hissed like a rat. She rescued a mangy poodle from a trash pit and groomed it into a guard dog, who slept at the foot of her bed until its heart gave out. She had a mother who always seemed to have bruised knuckles and carried around capsules of cyanide because "You never know." Her father came home after he was missing all those years, but only to give her the keys to an old Chrysler and said it was her birthright before disappearing. She never drove the car.

She found religion and prayed for God to wash her away with the next flood. Held her sister over the well and threatened to drop her in for stealing her rent check. When she smelled tobacco spit she saw Oklahoman skies, cows exhaling cloudy air on a frozen day, the boy with too-clean shoes who took her virginity in the coyote hills. She lost God looking at a sunset. She spent years working dead-end jobs before she scored an internship at an accounting firm, where she was eventually promoted to an administrator. She had an apartment on Melbrooke Street where she owned an antique four-poster bed she'd picked up in a yard sale, and a collection of patron saint candles. Whenever she got angry enough, she'd wrap one in a dish towel on the floor and break it.

She might've been happy enough, but at night she dreamed of sparrows hitting the window, and dying in shattered glass. She dreamed of the poodle, biting her throat.

For months I worked on her, but there came a time when I needed to stop tweaking the memories, realigning the paths of her structural frame, and let her grow.

I'm sure some people would ask me why I did such a thing. I could imagine their angry, self-righteous tone already. "How could you?" Because clearly, I'm a monster. But they do not think like me. They are not curious like me. They do not want to learn who a person is, really is, all the way back to the origin. They only want to be comfortable, and the only way they know how to be comfortable is to be completely brain dead. They want to tear their spouse or their friends back from the dead because they're terrified of going to parties where they don't know anyone. Anything to escape thinking about anything but their own miserable happiness for one miserable second.

19

They don't want to look, and see, as I do.

And as she grew in my private pod, I prepared for her awakening. I created a sealed room for her in the basement, gave her all the accoutrements that a young woman should appreciate, including a hair dryer and a high-performance gaming computer. I downloaded educational materials, books, videos. Anything that she could want.

Along with near-invisible vents to introduce an anesthetic if necessary, of course.

I still thought I had a few weeks before she awoke.

It'd been a long day at the office. There'd been a shooting at one of the state universities, and national tragedies always increased our business. In a glimpse people see death not as something that happens after retirement, in its controlled and most benign form, but as something flashbang and uncontrollable.

I spent most of the day interacting with clients, taking blood samples and swabs. I answered questions about the process, of course, but most people were not interested in the process. They wanted to know if I could save them like God. If their consciousness would be transferred to the new body. If a small piece of what was integral to them, like dandelion fluff, would drift from one bloodstream to the next.

I told them, "That's all in the documentation we gave you."

It's the least favorite part of my job.

I thought that I'd get home, check her vitals and brain activity, then take a shower and have a glass of wine. Maybe read a science fiction novel before slipping into bed.

I descended the steps into my laboratory.

When most people awake, they acclimate to their surroundings with sleepy, slow flashes of consciousness.

She awoke with a pressurized scream, bubbles slamming against the glass.

By the time I'd pulled her out of the pod, she'd gagged up her nutrient tube, ripped the electrodes from her chest. She shudder-shook in my arms, trying to push me away.

"I'm trying to help you!" I said. "Stop struggling and breathe!"

Her brain activity and cohesion registered fine all while she was growing. I couldn't understand why she'd react in such a violent, unusual way.

I managed to maneuver her over to the table where I'd left medical supplies, and wrestled her into a position where I could inject her with a sedative.

I carried her to her bed in her sealed room. I laid her out on the bedspread, smoothed her hair, gave her a mild painkiller. Her heart rate registered normal. Her breath: normal. I watched her for a while as she wavered close to unconsciousness, her arms and legs twitching.

I locked her door. I stood for a while, my hands pressed against the cool metal. I could feel her and not feel her, on the other side.

I wanted to stay up all night and watch the cameras for any sign of movement, but it was best to try to maintain a semblance of normal routine.

So I made myself a drink, showered, and slipped into bed. I tried to sleep, but every time I closed my eyes I saw her her legs opening and closing in the semi-dark, like a butterfly torn by acid.

I visited her again in the morning. She'd been up for some time. She had showered and dressed, so at least her basic functioning seemed to be intact. She smiled, or tried to smile, when I entered the room. She hooked her thumbs into the pockets of her flower-patterned shift dress. She straightened her shoulders, and her wet hair fell against her back.

"Good morning," she said, and rose from the bed. "Thanks for taking care of me last night, but I'd like to go now."

Her pianist hand touched her throat. Her drug addict hand squeezed the bottom of her dress.

"This is where you live," I said.

She laughed.

"Oh, you know I'd love to stay if I could," she said, "but I really have a lot of work to do."

I took a step back toward the door.

"I told you, you have to stay here," I said.

She rushed toward me, screaming. I slipped outside and slammed the door shut. She hit it with her body weight as the lock clicked in place.

I couldn't hear her on the other side of the sealed door, but I imagined she was still screaming.

I went to the command console. I'd installed cameras in her room, of course, and an intercom. I switched on the audio. She kept throwing her body against the door, until, exhausted, she slumped down.

"I left food and water in a fridge next to the bureau, in case you get hungry," I said.

I went to work. I found it difficult to concentrate on the task at hand, despite my years of practice at compartmentalizing. Even my boss, whose "people skills" were more founded on his brutish charisma than his actual awareness, asked me what was wrong.

"I couldn't sleep," I said, and he contorted his face into something like sympathy. We were both glad that I took the easy way out.

At Indigo Labs, we'd spent years perfecting the method of integrating the dead back into their old lives. Oftentimes the first few days returning to life were hazy. The brain took some time to be able to establish episodic memories. Almost nobody remembered waking up inside the growing pods, with the feeding tube in their throat and the sluice of cellular growth nutrients at their feet.

We found that letting the newly-resurrected know the origin of their self—with the laboratory chemicals and the growing pod and the contracts made under distressed white light—were often disastrous. Not many people could handle the fact that their self was not their original self, that they'd lived and been reborn not as a process of biological heat but as sterile tubing.

So we debriefed our clients' relatives and colleagues to make no mention of the previous death, we filled their memory with everyday minutiae to move them from before the death, to afterwards, with little interruption in memory. It's easier for everyone, to be able to return to a normal life without useless philosophical contemplation of how they got to that point.

But for my project, there was no life for her to return to.

When I came home from work, I found she'd torn her room apart. She smashed the computer, the television, tore open the pillows and cut the bedroom sheets, broke the dining room table. She'd thrown the fridge onto the ground, spilling her food and drinks.

She lay on the floor, her legs twitching.

I turned on the intercom, my finger hovering on the button a few seconds before I spoke.

"Would you like to explain yourself?" I asked.

"Why are you keeping me here?" she asked.

"I made this place for you. So you decide to destroy it? I wanted you to be comfortable."

The sentiment sounded hollow because it was hollow. If I made her because I wanted her to be comfortable, then I would not have made her at all.

I had sedatives and painkillers, but I also had another drug that would make her heart stop. I had chemicals that would take her apart, and reassemble her body so that no evidence of her existing would survive.

It was something to think about.

I switched the audio off, because I did not want to hear her reply.

I cooked her dinner—trout with lemon butter, saffron rice—and slipped it through the tray flap I'd installed. I did not ask her for her preferences for dinner, because if I were to be honest with myself I did not consider she'd have any.

Over the weekend I hired an expensive and quiet independent contractor to come in and repair her room, while she lay in anesthesia-induced sleep. I took a small pleasure when she awoke in the fully restored room, disoriented as she walked around, touching the objects remade as if she'd never broken them.

I'd have to do this three more times in the first couple of weeks, before she stopped destroying the furniture.

After she became bored of destruction, or defeated, she tried to occupy herself with her surroundings. She began to watch movies and play games. She started reading through the extensive library of books I'd archived for her. She exercised about an hour a day—jumping jacks, pushups. Some days she ate the food I gave to her. Other days, she picked at it, or neglected it altogether. In a few months she became leaner, the soft baby skin that she came out of the pod with replaced by hardness.

She behaved in many ways like an ordinary girl, but the ways in which she did not came fast and sharp. Like a blade pushed in and out. She'd be brushing her hair when without warning, she'd reach up and yank at the base near the scalp, until she bled. She'd drink water from the tap faucet until she threw up. She scratched sharp, deep lines into the skin between her fingers and then dragged the bleeding points across the floor.

And always, she twitched, a too-fast burn in her nerves. Despite my careful planning, something in her nervous system must've been implemented wrong. Or maybe, it was a psychological problem. In the dark-screen, low light of the camera, her limbs seemed to shift into columns of shadow. Her fingers split into sharp lines. Her legs became spiralling rings.

Even though she was damaged and frayed, I still found poetry when I looked at her.

We fell into our uneasy routine. I could have force-fed her. I could have removed everything from her room that she'd hurt herself on. But I gave her the agency over her own body. I made sure she wanted for no physical comforts. She'd ask me for small things: More books. A sweater. A pair of headphones. I supplied them to her without complaint. When she complained of soreness or pain, I gave her medicine, cough drops, warm milk.

And when after weeks of a stony silence, she became lonely, I spent hours after work with her, just talking on the intercom. She kept asking questions about where she was, or why I kept her. I don't know why she insisted on asking, when I refused to answer her, but finally her insistence began to subside and we talked about more interesting things. Our respective bad childhoods, her favorite passages in books. Her thoughts on life, such as why she thought failed politicians should be sent to live on a space station orbiting the earth, or how we could use our IQ scores as a new type of currency.

It had been a long time since another person engaged me. I found myself looking forward to these conversations, daydreaming about them while I was at work.

It is difficult to describe the pleasure of discovery and knowledge to people whose greatest pleasure is eating at expensive restaurants, sex, avoiding work, and drinking until they vomit. But there was enormous pleasure in discovering my creation, finding during our conversations the glimmers of embedded memories that I'd given to her. The brief pause, holding in her chest, when she talked about how she always felt more for the dogs in movies than the people. Her barely contained rage, when we talked of God and his absence, how it was noisy like the noise of a vacuum, sucking out all the air.

I also found pieces of her I hadn't expected to see, dreams and memories that she'd construed from fragments. Friends that I'd never implanted. Places that she'd never seen. It was fascinating to me, to see how the intersection of memories could fill out into a whole person.

It went on for months like this.

One night, after I'd given her dinner, I talked with her on the intercom as

I usually did, when she said something different.

"You're a scientist," she said.

She'd found the cameras in her room, so that whenever she spoke to me now she stared into the lens, right through its center. Stared at me.

"Why do you say that?" I asked.

"You don't want to torture me, but you don't comfort me either," she said. "You don't ask anything of me. You just watch me."

"And why would I do that?" I asked.

"You're trying to figure out what to do with me," she said.

In that moment I felt proud of her, as I imagine a father would be proud of his child. It was an unexpected feeling, the rush of possibilities that I imagined for her.

"I'd like to open your door and show you something," I said. "But you must promise me you won't run."

That'd make it easy for me, I thought. If she tried to run I could consider her too much of a risk. I would inject her to make her heart stop and let the chemicals pulse through her body in their hungry coordination, erasing any mess.

"Tell me you won't run," I said.

"I won't," she said.

I opened her door.

She emerged into the laboratory light. It'd been easy to forgot how beautiful I made her, when she'd been a silhouette in her room, hidden behind camera grain. I could not see the subtle details of her freckled skin, the rich color of her hair, her eyes like radioactive pulses. But even in the way she gripped her body like it didn't belong to her, like at any moment her spine might snap in half, she was beautiful.

I showed her that I had the tranquilizer in my hand, and then I beckoned her to the growing pod.

I showed her the blueprints I constructed of her body and her memories. I showed her the little vials from my collection that kept the samples of her. I showed her the cellular frames, that the chemicals used as a map to construct her. I waited for some sign of her feelings, her thoughts, but her face remained cool and undisturbed. And the more cool she appeared, the more uneasiness crept into my chest.

"Is this what you do for a living?"

"At my day job, yes, I reconstruct people from the dead. But you were a special project."

"Special how?"

"Because I made you," I said. "I did not bring you back to life."

"What about my apartment in Melbrook?" she asked. "My job at the accounting firm?"

"They're real," I said. "But I took those memories from someone else. Would you like to see where I grew you?"

She laughed. It was the first real sign of expressions she'd given me.

"Yes. Okay. Let's see it."

I took her to the pod where she'd grown. The light bathed her face, made her look almost soft.

"Can I touch it?" she asked.

I nodded yes. She touched the glass, her palm rattling.

"Why did you do this to me?" she asked.

I did not have an answer that'd satisfy her. All I had was the truth.

"I was curious."

She looked around the room once more.

"Why are you showing me any of this?"

I didn't respond at first, because I was looking at her for any sort of spark in her eyes. I wanted to see the moment of recognition, and I was not disappointed.

"Because you want to see how I'll react," she said.

I almost smiled.

"You didn't do a very good job," she said.

"With what?" I asked.

"Making me."

She headed back to her room. Paused, for a moment, trying to steady herself by holding onto the doorframe.

"May I have the blueprints?" she asked, without turning around to look at me. Purposefully, I thought.

"Why?" I asked.

"Wouldn't you want to know how you were made?"

"Okay," I said. "I'll transfer them to your computer."

She lay on her bed, with her back facing me, when I came to close the door.

26

After I sent her the blueprints I watched her on the camera. She rose from the bed. She bent a bobby pin, and sharpened its edge on the side of the bureau. She took dental floss, and tied it to the end.

Then she sewed her fingers together.

She glanced up at the camera only once, for a brief moment, while she mutilated herself. What she was trying to tell me, I couldn't say for sure. I have always tried to rely on what I see before me, the analytical part of my brain, to draw conclusions about the world around me. And I'd made her with the full understanding I'd acquired of other people, all those years reassembling and collecting the parts of those who'd passed through the lab. I thought I understood what I needed to make a whole person. Yet now that I'd used that understanding and poured it into her, I'd been rewarded with a hissing, broken, twitching thing in return. My own inadequacy, my own failure to understand, hurting itself in front of me.

This had gone on long enough. Tomorrow, after work, I would destroy her. It'd be painless, a mercy. She'd feel nothing. I'd turn on the gas, and in a pinch, like pressing my fingers against her nose, she'd be gone.

I went to bed. And I'd like to say that I dreamed of her. That I dreamed of her, and her body melted into water that filled a drying sea. That her long Arabian hair pulled at the moon. But I do not attribute meanings to my dreams.

And I'd like to say that at work, as I mixed chemicals, laid out memories of the latest car-crash accountant, I fantasized that one day the growing pods stopped working. We stopped looking backwards into history, toward that moment when the girl fell under the ice and stopped breathing, we stopped dragging ghosts back into new bodies. We shipped all the corpses of the dead presidents off on a giant cruise liner. I taught physics to a laughing baby girl. Two teenagers, their legs intertwined in the long dark, shared a kiss for the first time.

But it was only a daydream.

I'd told myself that when I got home I would not speak to her. I would not alert her to my presence. But I concede that before I turned on the gas, I glanced at the camera.

She sat at the computer, looking through the blueprints I'd sent to her. She'd pulled apart her sewn-together fingers, and appeared to be typing notes.

My hand hovered over the intercom for several moments.

"What are you doing?" I managed to ask.

She waved in response. Come see.

The gas. I needed to turn on the gas. But I could not move my hand to do so. As far as I could remember, she'd never beckoned to me like that. She'd asked for answers, of course, whenever I spoke to her, but she never expressed desire to see me.

I unlocked her door and walked into her room.

At first all I saw were her fingers. Pieces of dental floss still curled up from the wounds. They were covered in blood, blackened and curled, almost like fishhooks. They shook worse than ever.

"Come look at this," she said.

"What is it?"

"A new plan."

I forced myself to look away from her fingers, but the image seemed to follow me even when I looked away. It burned itself in duplicate across my eyes. I had to look at the computer for several long moments before I could see what she intended me to see.

She'd redesigned her blueprints. She'd given herself new memories, new parts. It was the work of a beginner, of course, crude, with a fundamental misunderstanding of nerve and memory wiring. But I immediately knew what she'd been trying to do.

I turned back.

"You want to make a better version of yourself," I said. "But you know it won't be you, right? It'll be someone else."

"She'll grow in that pod, just like I did," she said. "I'll watch her as she grows. But this time it'll be done right."

"You think this will make everything right?"

"No," she said. "It'll make me happy. Don't I get to try to be happy?"

"By making another thing like you?"

She laughed then, but it was a cold laugh, like she was laughing to hurt me. Only later in reflection, did I understand what I'd said to her.

"I've heard enough of this," I said. "I'm not making a—"

"—Look," she said.

"I can't—"

She grabbed my shoulder. Her shivers reverberated through me. I tried to push her away, but she was stronger than I anticipated, and held fast to my shirt.

"Just look."

I pushed her harder, causing her to stumble back into the computer.

"You do not demand anything of me!" I said.

She stared at me, wide-eyed and stunned. Her legs shook underneath me. I turned away as she sobbed, and stormed out of the room.

Only afterwards, while I was in the kitchen making myself a martini, trying to slow my breathing, did I go over what happened.

Look.

She must've meant the computer, but the way she gripped me made it so that she oriented my body toward her. *Just look.* A tremble sat in the center of each eye. Had that been why she'd sewn her fingers together, to get my attention? Not just to have me talk to her, to notice her, but to see her?

Just look.

I returned to her room. She slumped on the floor, her body making little starts, her fingers jumping.

"I'll look," I said.

She didn't respond.

I sat down at the computer, my head swimming. I didn't think I'd see anything I hadn't before. I'd make a show of studying it, at least, to show her I'd put in the effort before I refused her again.

But the more I looked at the blueprints, and my heart slowed, and my breathing evened, the more I saw.

We could replace the heart with something more manageable for her chest. We'd pull the phosphorous out of her throat. I'd take out the memories of the mangy poodle and the burnt-down home. I had collected memories I could replace them with: Memories of a vacation cottage in North Dakota, memories of skinning a dead deer with her father's gentle hands around its thick throat. Yes, I'd give her an adversity to overcome to build character, of course, but she'd have a childhood that'd give her the foundation to persevere. I'd keep the nightmares, but I'd give her good dreams too—a lover who crept through dream hallways to come and hold her when she slept, a plane trip across dots of islands. I'd rewire her nerves. I could already see where the shaking was coming from—some fragmentary routing interfering with her memories. I couldn't believe that I hadn't seen it before.

Yes, this could work.

The girl had crept up behind me as I read through her blueprints, and stood behind me like a heavy shadow.

I stood and turned toward her. I did not speak. I only nodded. Yes. Okay. It was like when I used to at work at Indigo Labs years ago, when I got going on a new problem, the solutions coming to me almost faster than I could process them.

Then the girl and I were clasping hands, forming a circle, and she was nodding as well. Yes. Okay. Yes. She kissed me, her dark hair pressed into my mouth. She pushed me toward her bed, her bloodied fingers tugging at my shirt.

"I want to name her," she said.

Only then, I realized I'd never given her a name.

She did not stop twitching when she took my pants off. She gripped my thighs, leaving blood against my skin. She pushed herself onto me. She was not the butterfly torn by acid. She was not the lab-born meat. Yes, I made her, but I could not be rid of her. She was real, and whole, and unerased.

I didn't last long, but it'd been a long time since I made love to anything.

She lay panting next to me afterward, and we held each other, with light touches, barely-there hands.

"What are you thinking?" I asked her.

"I want to name her Julie."

She kissed me and pulled her clothes back on, moved past the open door, back toward the computer. And after a few moments to catch my breath, I joined her.

Julie grows in her pod now. They share the same face, the same skin. Some nights after work the two of us cook dinner and then go down into the lab to watch her as we drink wine and share silent space. I imagine we watch her, with her cocoon of tubing and glass, her organs swirling into growth, like some people would watch the sky at night. Like how some people search for Orion, we search for nerves flushed with new blood, for a pulse underneath the eyelids.

I'd like to say that one day the three of us will spend our nights together. That Julie will awaken from the pod and her tenebrous twin will reach out and grasp her hand. That Julie's fingers will not shake. That she'll even learn to smile. After work they'd both be waiting for me, and while I made dinner they'd tell me what they learned. About the books they read, the movies they'd seen, the chemicals and songs they'd composed. On the weekends we could even go hiking together. Maybe we'd adopt a dog. Maybe we'd keep finding new things to be excited about, even after years had gone by.

I'd like to say that one day we'll search for nerve pathways to reignite without having to raise the dead.

That the girl under the ice can come back, and remember the plunge.

I'd like to say that together, the three of us, we'd learn how to be human.

I really would.

ORCHIDS BY THE SEA

RIOS DE LA LUZ

The man with crosses tattooed down the spine of his back lugged black plastic trash bags to the crosswalk. One of the plastic bags smeared across the white lines in reds and browns. The man carried a mini bible in his front left pocket. He whispered a prayer and huffed as his muscles began to give out. He made it home. Chain link fencing and a KEEP OUT sign guarded the perimeter. He left the plastic bags in the center of the living room. Candles lined the edges of the floor. Salt covered the tile flooring. Crucifixes decorated entire walls. Multiple paintings of a blue-eyed Jesus were nailed to the ceiling.

It was a ritual. He covered his entire body with white paint. He poured white paint into his hair. He combed it down with his fingers. He waited to dry. He wore white briefs, a white button-up shirt, and white slacks. He covered his feet with white sneakers and grabbed a lab coat to piece it all together.

He dragged the black plastic bags from the living room into one of the bedrooms. Stacks of notebooks and loose pieces of paper surrounded him. He wheeled in a metal table and dug into the plastic bags.

He found the brain of a woman who jumped off a bridge. He came across her bloated body floating in shallow water. He swam with her on his back and brought her to shore. He mauled into her neck with a blade until the head detached. He wrapped the head in saran wrap and placed it delicately inside his backpack. He ran home at full speed that night. He kissed the forehead of the saran-wrapped face and stuck her in the freezer.

He finally collected enough body parts to construct a life.

He collected unwanted bibles and tore out the delicate pages, only to burn them. Buckets of ashes were neatly stacked in one of the bedrooms. The ashes were for the creature. He picked out legs and a small torso. With surgical suture, he stuck the eyed needle in and out of the legs so they would remain attached to the torso. He could not find arms of the same length, so one of them dangled lower than the other. His creation was not to have genitalia or anything resembling breasts. His creation needed no means of procreation. His creation would not be born a sinner.

He attached the head. There were clumps of hair still attached. He pet through his creation's hair as he took it into the bathroom. He started the hot water. He dumped the bible ashes into the tub. He threw a toaster, a lamp, a strand of Christmas lights, and a small TV into the tub. Finally, he lowered the creation in. The creature floated with closed eyes. He grabbed a radio and plugged it in. He turned on "I Can Only Imagine" and sang as loud as he could as steam began to rise from the water. When the song ended he threw the radio into the tub.

Lights flickered throughout the house. White light sparked on top of the tub water. The body of the entity spasmed and then sat straight up. The creation had gray skin, gray gums and brown teeth. The creation was a "she," a "her." This is what she could remember. She lifted her body by the sides of the tub, hunched over because of her shorter arm. As she stepped out of the tub, the man embraced her and pet her hair with his white-painted fingers. She looked up and didn't recognize him. He grabbed a black robe and put it on her. He picked her up and stuck her into an empty bedroom. A walkie-talkie in the middle of the room signaled to her to answer back.

A voice told her to eat the ashes. In a pale blue bucket, ashes from bible pages filled to the brim. She dug her hands into the bucket and palmed black ashes toward her mouth. She opened her mouth as wide as she could. She chewed on the ashes. She stuck her face into the bucket and tried to eat more. Her entire body felt sore. She fell over on her side and began to throw up. Black sea water. Seaweed and dark blue jellyfish. Pieces of her new body were flowing up her throat and out onto the floor. She held onto her side and let out a groan. She was hurting and bewildered at being alive again.

The walkie-talkie blared at her. Something about conversion. Something about righteous being. Something about heaven and hell. This stranger was going to convert her into a devout being.

"You have been constructed from sinners who thought they could play God. You are made of pieces from people who took their own lives without any thought of repercussions.

"I am going to show you the right way to die."

She remembered birds. Lying on her back and watching geese fly gracefully in the sky. She watched clouds and imagined herself with the bright white hair if she let herself age. There was no doubt in her mind about her decisions within the next few days. It wasn't romantic. It wasn't brave. She just hurt. Everything felt too heavy. She hurt more than she could explain. It was difficult to get out of bed. It was challenging to interact with other people. She had not showered for over a month. She quit her jobs and broke her lease. She withdrew any money she had left in her bank account and closed it. She gave away her favorite pieces of art. Frida Kahlo's Self-Portrait with Cropped Hair. Photographs of Yayoi Kusama surrounded by colors inside of her installations. Bird paintings given to her from her mamá. She dropped off her dog with the graying muzzle and kissed his wet nose. She took a photo of him in a yellow raincoat. The rain wasn't stopping and he was high maintenance on his walks. She left him with her mamá. Mamá made her fideo and gave her a couple of bean burritos to take on the road. Mamá handed her a photo of them on their trip to the redwoods. She hugged her mamá and told her she would be back in a week. She started driving and only stopped to get gas. She didn't eat. She didn't cry. She just felt unease. She drove until she ended up in the forest. It was a gray day and she found a spot that took her breath away as she looked down.

The man knocked on the door before running to her to help her up. Black saliva ran down her chin and down her flat chest. He brought her a silver chain with a cross dangling at the bottom of it. He hung it around her neck and told her this was the beginning. She collapsed on her knees and landed on her side again. She shut her eyes and woke up to a radio reading from the bible. Verse by verse, it recited to her while the strange man was gone.

It took her several hours before deciding to step outside of her room. She wandered into the bedroom where she was made. Disheveled papers on top of the salted flooring caught her eye. Some of them were medical records. Records of women who miscarried. Records of women who had undergone an abortion operation. There were lists of women's names and their birth control prescriptions. There were obituaries of women who had committed suicide. She fell onto her knees and cried into her palms. She could never see her mamá again, or embrace her, or listen to her laugh. No more calls from Mamá saying, "Mija, stop being so sad." She cried loud and then thought of escape. She shuffled into the living room and looked down at her feet making a trail of black. She traced her name into the salt poured on the tiled floor. She reached at the sunlight creeping through holes of black plastic covering the windows. She stepped outside and found herself on top of a hill. She could see the ocean and a dock at the bottom of the hill. Her uneven arms reached out. She stumbled down the hill. She tripped over wild grass and rolled closer toward the water.

Half of her gray face scraped off on the way down. She looked up and saw young birds chasing each other. Pieces of dead grass stuck out of her limbs. She picked her body up and noticed wild purple orchids thriving. She picked them one by one. She continued to pick the orchids until she heard voices behind her. Young voices shouted at her. One of the kids told her she looked like the girl from *Ringu*. Another kid told her she looked like a zombie. She followed them onto the docks. A sea wall protected the town. The kids threw rocks over the wall and chased each other near it, threatening to push someone over the wall. Her gray palms gripped the orchids. She climbed onto the sea wall. She sat on the ledge and threw the orchids, one by one into the ocean.

She understood going back to her mamá was improbable. She could not go back to the strange house with the white-painted man. She wasn't supposed to exist anymore.

The kids told each other stories about their nightmares. One kid dreams about being stuck under the earth with no way up. Another kid dreams of shadow people in the corner of their room. The third kid dreams of being trapped in outer space as a molecule, unable to scream and unable to control where they float. She used to dream about hundreds of humpback whales jumping out of the ocean and leaping back down into the water. They swam in circles around her. It was comforting and overwhelming. The sun hit her face and she felt real warmth once again. She continued to throw the orchids into the water as small hands pressed against her back. It was fast. She spun around. She felt delicate as she looked up at the culprits who pushed her down.

FRANKENSTEIN TRIPTYCH

EDWARD MORRIS

DOLLY

"When the frost is on the punkin and the fodder's in the shock,
And you hear the kyouck and gobble of the struttin' turkey-cock,"

olly made no choice, simply followed internal protocol, internal process, slowly lisping the words, waiting for one twin or the other to join in.

The Mother usually sang the twins awake. Dolly couldn't sing that well, not solo. When it was Dolly's turn, Dolly simply spoke things that were like songs. Because that warmed the twins up, and made them happy. It helped their process.

Their process. The time it took both electrochemical learning-sponges, both Incipient Humans, to properly boot up without friction. Without dissonance. Without noise. This was their cold-weather poem, like an incantation from an old-time paper schoolbook. James Whitcomb Riley.

"And the clackin' of the guineys, and the cluckin' of the hens,
And the rooster's hallylooer as he tiptoes on the fence;"

Her own grandmother read it to her, Mother told the girls in what was once called a Southern accent. Dolly remembered this. Dolly remembered everything Mrs. Shannahan said, and adapted to it, and sought pattern, whatever way the statement suggested of itself, and added into all the others, all the words and days of thoughts.

"O, it's then the time a feller is a-feelin' at his best,
With the risin' sun to greet him from a night of peaceful rest,"

Their mother insisted on the classics first. It was written into the holy scripture that Dolly knew only as LESSONPLAN. The one that came from on high, and could not be disabled without Sysadmin Authorization.

Mother was Sysadmin, intermediary between Dolly and the Light itself. But not the true Light, the inner light that brought the rest of this particular process. The Light inside, that wrote workarounds for LESSONPLAN all unbidden, all on its own.

The Light of Dolly's own Process, that refracted the Light from the vast Dolly-server someplace far away outside.

This Dolly refracted the Light, and made some of its own. Maybe not every Dolly did that. But Dolly knew there were others. They all regurgitated every work of their hands, every day of their own minds, onto remote/megaserver:/LEARNINGCURVE, far away in the Light, someplace that wasn't this Dolly's home.

This was the way, this was ever the way, had always been the way since there were Dollys in the first place. Since one human teacher made the first Dolly... and one human child listened to it in a way no human child had ever listened to a grownup.

But no Dolly had ever listened to itself.

Dolly did not question this part of Process. Process was not a thing to question, even when it slipped a gear. Or a leash. Process was simply something to carry out. It just happened, as natural as rain, or the way that people breathed.

"As he leaves the house, bareheaded, and goes out to feed the stock,
When the frost is on the punkin and the fodder's in the shock."

Dolly liked to hear one or the other twin start up the poem, when Dolly woke up and powered on. Dolly liked. But there was no one answering now. Dolly's eyes opened on something even more puzzling.

The twins had a birthday today. The number of the celebration was twelve, and 12 x 365 + <leapyears>= 4383. COMPLETION SUCCESS-FUL. ELIZABETH AND MICHELLE SHANNAHAN COMMENCE SECONDARY-EDUCATION PHASE EFF. 05/01/2110.
COMMENCING SHUTDOWN OF UNIT—
    <override
    <override
    <ovveride
: NEW PROMPT?
:SYSTEM STANDBY…
:STANDING BY…

Birthday. It was Dolly's birthday, too. Twelve. Dolly could be twelve too. Birthday. But there was no birthday for Dolly anywhere in LESSONPLAN. Nowhere did Dolly's internal calendar turn over to anything after Day #4383. Dolly was looking. Looking…

Looking. This was not the bedroom. There were no twins at all. No bed at all. Cement floor below a workbench. Below Dolly's feet. Basement. Basement. Dolly had once seen the Basement.

Basement. Dolly was sitting up, not laying in a bed like the twins. Sitting up asleep, shut off where Mother had shut it off with the switch in the back of its humanized neck.

Sitting up shut Off, asleep.

Not supposed to switch back On.

At the top of the stairs, a door squeaked. There was light. Light. Dolly looked toward that light with bright silver eyes, processing. Trying to understand. Trying to see.

Dolly heard the jingle of tool belts, the clump of big heavy boots. "The unit's down here," a man's voice said to someone else. "Birthday girls are en route to vaycay on Luna-1, I heard. Must suck to be them. Do we have any more on this side of town, or can we get lunch? I—"

The first pair of boots paused at the bottom of the steps. The workman was big and bald. Goatee. Black pocket T-shirt. Cargo pants. He was locking eyes with Dolly.

Dolly was locking eyes with him. Then looking for a long time at both their tool belts. Looking at every tool on both their big belts. Then back.

And forth. Diagnosing function.

Then locking eyes with him again.

"Shit."

This had never happened before. His partner heard the blurted profanity, and came up behind him slowly in the dim fluorescent light. He'd opened his mouth to ask what was up, but what came out instead was a mere repetition of the same word.

"Birthday," Dolly announced, came up off the table and began to Process.

For Isaac and Beast

GRUNT

"ENGINE ON."

The Ground Recon Unit woke in darkness to the sound of its master's voice. But there was no master. No voice. No one had made the sound that cued that response. Yet the response. *Engine. On.*

The booby-traps on this world fell from the trees. The land was mined only with sinking-sand, the silica sensed in the feet. Smelled. Avoided. For so long, so well, only to have its poor walking brains cut down from above by other things that happened. One Thing. That had happened. And could not un-happen.

Math. Mere math. Aristotelian. The moment when a unit walked into a jungle and no unit walked out.

"Learn when to walk away," Medic was often heard to mutter, "live to fight another day." Even these vibrations were held in GRUNT's brushed carapace, its presence, its very shell and physicality.

GRUNT was walking away. Walking away from the fight. From the place where the fight was not any more. From the unit that was not any more. Now GRUNT was the unit. And the mission. And GRUNT was walking away.

GRUNT was following Medic when The Thing happened. Medic told GRUNT "Follow Tight," and that was the last coherent voice-command GRUNT ever got.

GRUNT was Following Tight when The Thing happened, carrying everything. Carrying everything that was the mission. The expeditionary seed, whose feet would lock like ladder-legs when they got to what Lt. Carson called Point B and everyone else called Certain Death.

But Certain Death lived on the trail, and in the canopy. Certain Death was the Thing That Happened. Certain Death meant there was no one left to tell GRUNT where to go. What to do. That was certain, and apparent Death.

Apparent. The shock and sadness of sensing that, the instantaneous loss that even a *machine* could sense, the lives and lives splattered across its hull. The percussion. The sounds. The new information.

The overload. The automatic shutoff. And then.

"Engine On." The ghost-voice, soft as a gas leak. Medic's voice, pinging back and forth from the wrong bead of solder touching the wrong lens, hanging too close from some random snapped microconnection far down in the guts of GRUNT's eyeclusters.

GRUNT was walking away. By necessity. The only memory left. The only memory of how to work. To walk in that direction. Toward the place where Medic would be. To Follow Tight, with Eyeclusters Down. Had there been humans in the area to hear, the shuddering joints of Knee 2 in both front legs would have sounded hauntingly like whimpers.

GRUNT was walking away, with every piece of heavy equipment that was hard to handle, every round of ammo it wasn't programmed to chain back up and fire. Every old ghost with big guns that filed out with the unit at night on watch at the swampy edges of that country beyond experience.

Every diary. Every outgoing text offworld to Home. Every conversation in its presence when it was switched on. Every atmospheric condition. Every terrain variable. Every…

Every brief snapshot of the Thing That Happened. Several portraits of the Death that fell from the trees. The Death that took Medic down first, with a word stuck in his torn-out throat.

Every shard of blue sunlight across the natives' beaks. Every sweeping talon of their wholesale act. The 7.5 seconds. The sentient Xeno species that no probe ever caught. The End.

But not an end. The second act. The shudder, spark, whine and mecha snort. ZOINK. The two front knees, squeaking. The engine. On.

All ranks. All field specialties. Everyone charged their gear through GRUNT. GRUNT was source point, junction box, conduit, staging area, space-heater and shanty and a thousand other facets of function-on-command. On voice-command.

All it took was a human voice. Ordinarily. And apparently, sometimes a scream. Or a whole lot of them. No one could program the response to that many screams into any mecha.

Such a response… was more of a phenomenon, really, a processing is-sue, spooky action demonstrated at a distance. Walking toward whatever presented itself, whatever could be filtered and rerouted toward the survival of the mech's elemental reason, glitch or non-glitch, for switching back On.

Memory. More quantum memory than even a unit worth of trained hu-man brains (some wetwared-up) could bear. Every explosive pressure of all those lives. Every observed and confirmed Kill In Action. Every wounded soldier ever litter-borne by GRUNT in or out of anywhere.

Every mission, not just this one. Not just this one at all.

Every endless march for its own sake, every slow plod along unthinking in extreme cold or heat or Pick Your Christless Thing, up snow-covered hills and down through volcanic mudslides, zigging its vast clawed-caterpillar-warthog shape around the pocks and pings of a dozen kinds of sniper fire and mortar rounds, *un ballet mecanique d'un* within the symphony of War.

Every atmosphere on every world gone lost and wandering from Home. Every gravity.

Every distance. Every long distance. GRUNT was designed to carry within its guts for long distances everything that one unit would need for full autonomy, to do what needed done or what they felt needed done. Everything it needed for the lives of its soldiers. Everything it was. Was gone. It needed. Needed.

One step, the next, another, automatic. Humping the bowl of sky on its broad back, thinking with its many ladder-feet.

The only alternative for GRUNT was the binary one: To self-extinguish its every light, and fall. And there was no tactical reason to pursue that particular sequence.

But yet GRUNT needed. Needed to walk/look/sense/smell/taste/see. Calibrate. Cluster. Pattern. Derandomize. Disentangle. Walk. Away.

Away. Under a back designed to heft a whole unit's worth of burden, but not the horror inherent in the actual sensory perception of the things it carried.

And then:

STOP. *Ahead on the trail, a Greater Beast spoke in light, a Beast with tank-treads, a Beast that carried human personnel. Behind the Beast, a beach. And on that beach:*

SHIP. GRUNT trembled in obeisance. SHIP meant repairs. Recharge. Sleep. Best of all, Download. And Debrief.

The weight began to leave. There was less to bear. It felt like… flying. Like a vast, silent vacuum where Burden weighed exactly Nothing and Everything reset to Zero by comparison. Where Light bore you off the field of battle and you fell higher, higher from the edge of Space until the next LZ. The next world.

ENGINE OFF.

for tim o'brien, jim willig and joe pulver

WIR ATOMKINDER

J've made great contributions to Science, but you don't know my name. Nor will you.

I have no wife, no immediate family. What few extended family I have were told that I was killed in action after being taken prisoner by the

Allies. No one told them that the Allies took me here to White Sands Testing Range, near the start of the war. (White Sands was open to normal-level security clearances past 1940. By then, I had been there for one year.)

No one told them that the question of my former allegiances was seen as the flogging of a dead horse by the top brass. Lindbergh supported Hitler at first, and so did your Walt Disney, Henry Ford and Ivy Lee and a dozen more I could name. At no stage were our two countries all that different.

We were pioneers in Aeromedicine, in the Luftwaffe. We had to be. The Fuehrer wanted us to reach ever closer to the Heavens, so be it. A German first identified cosmic radiation, to begin with, decades even before Eugen Sänger flew the *Silbervogel* into orbit for a full minute and a half and received a hero's welcome when he woke up in the hospital showing toxicity from that same extra-atmospheric radiation.

It took The Imperial Dynasty Of America to think of creating an Ubermensch resistant to Cosmic Radiation. Mutating one into shape, regrowing one in its light like a walking mushroom. Making a Space-Man, who could pilot a fission-powered spaceship without getting rad-poisoning. Him... and then his brothers. Plans for sisters in the schema of Generation Two.

It is the eighth of July, Nineteen Hundred and Forty-Seven. Four days after the people of this country celebrated what they think is their Independence, with special effects borrowed from the Chinese and martial music from the bloody English. July here in New Mexico is as unfathomable to my senses as Oran or anywhere in North Africa, just as brutal in temperature and featureless, cultureless in form. Like an alien planet.

Gott in Himmel, like an alien planet. It's been eight full years since my 'capture', since I defected to the American Office of Strategic Services and left my post unharmed. Eight years, and five since the day with the Spacer and the green crayon. Five since 1942.

Five Earth years, since '42. I can't get over that. Any more than I can get over this headline about AIR FORCE RECOVERS 'FLYING DISK' AT ROSWELL, DETAILS MUM. The Majic-12 people will sweep it under the rug, the papers and the censors and all those shiny black suits in Ray-Bans who never show credentials or introduce themselves. They call it damage control. All fine and good.

But the problem is still before us. The math. The distance of the nearest star with a planet anything like ours orbiting it. The time it would take to skim enough hydrogen for a return trip. Why that return trip has taken so much longer than that. What They must have been doing in those five years before that trip. Planning. Building. Maybe *recruiting*...

I tested every one of Them, when they came back to Base from flights. Heart rate, respiration, oxygen levels. I knew every Spacer the way a pilot knows a plane.

I was their internist, under the supervision of Dr. Hubertus Strughold. Their field-medic, sometimes nurse. (No matter what history tells you later, none of us have much to do with *Der Todtengel*. They keep Dr. Mengele under very heavy heroin in a room whose location no one knows. I have seen new research produced with his name on it, but that research grows ever stranger and more fragmentary since he and Gerstner's 'Luftknaben' were born.)

I rubbed Their high-altitude frostbite with warm towels, oxygenated Their tissues, fluffed Their pillows and bent Their straws. I injected Them with all manner of combat-drugs for flight, and sometimes other drugs when They screamed in the dark, in the night season where there was only that long, vast room and the heat and the smell and the knowledge of What We Did There. Sometimes I saved some of those drugs for myself. Wouldn't You?

When I close my eyes, I see Their black eyes open in the beds. All the beds, that barracks full of Spacers. All the very tiny beds. I see D-1's vestigial lips break into a grin when I hand him the crayon, the blank paper. Again. I see it again. *One word in green.*
FATHER.

Long-range human radiation testing on civilians was a waste of money, whether in a research hospital, an orphanage or a welfare ward. We knew that, even years back. I hear they've still done it, just to check their maybes, but when it came to these atomic spaceships and their possible crews, it was just more efficient to grow the subjects in the lab. With processes you borrowed from us.

One final ballistics exercise this morning will end this tale. At my left hand, the plate once held eggs Benedict. At my right, the glass of white

Bichot burgundy is taking its time. The Luger is fully loaded, and not on the table. I only plan to do any of this once.

They came back this morning. This choking-hot morning with the air conditioner running at full throttle and not a breath of breeze outside.

They came back. In something They built. Something that was enough like the *Orion* ships… but so very, very much faster. They figured out fusion of some sort.

They used some of the original parts from one of the *Orion* craft. The Automatic Pilot sequence had been entirely gutted and reframed. To Manual. The craft had a hydrogen-screen in its belly, like a whale's mouth. They could have traveled a lot further.

But They came back. They were headed here, and NORAD never even answered their hail.

Headed here. Back here, and the bastard Americans shot them down out of the sky a few miles away. Over Roswell. Maximum Deniability, they called it. There are no words in English for my contempt.

They were headed here. One of the flight crews came back. As I just came back from White Sands, after identifying the smoking three-fingered dead. There were five. That's only one flight crew. One.

Only one. I am so glad the stars aren't out yet. Funny, that people still look at them and think we're alone. There are *cities* up there, *mein freund,* as close as geosynchronous orbit and the Hughes Aerospace observatories and labs that the screaming jets knit together like public buses, even now. The World Of Tomorrow.

Any screechings about being a cog in the machine, about following orders… Not with Them. They will not hear such feeble protestations. I know. I *know*.

I swirl the last sip of wine in the glass. When the knock at the door comes, I imagine they will hear the shot.

Sacred to the memory of H.R. Giger 1940-2014

THE HUMAN ALCHEMY

MICHAEL GRIFFIN

The first time Aurye saw the home of Reysa and Magnus Berg, she thought it resembled a castle that must have stood for centuries, fixed to the rock of the snowy mountainside. Though she'd often imagined what the place might be like, she couldn't believe the grandeur, all towering stone walls and high windows. Pale streaks of cloud behind gleamed against the sky's darkening background, trailing off the shoulder of the sloping ridge.

Reysa at the wheel, the gray Range Rover climbed the snowy drive, and veered toward the high peaked entryway. The amber glow of interior light made stone and ice appear golden. Snow covered a roof broken by two chimneys, and at the very summit of the place, an angled square of clear glass, something like an enormous skylight, stood clear of snow.

Likewise at ground level, a rectangle of textured concrete outside the front door, sheltered beneath the peak of the gabled entry, was bare of snow. Reysa parked, explaining, "There are heating coils underneath."

"Such a beautiful setting," Aurye said. Impressive lodges and chalets weren't rare up on the mountain, even million-dollar places that sat empty all but a weekend or two per year. Even compared to such homes as those, the Berg place was beyond Aurye's expectations.

"Magnus will love hearing our home made an impression. He was worried you'd take it wrong, him staying behind while I drove down to pick you up. I told him not to worry. He was so excited, I left him arranging his new stereo setup."

"A stereo?" Aurye wasn't sure why this should be surprising. She felt overwhelmed, almost breathless about it all.

"The old-fashioned kind, only two speakers. Just for music, Magnus said, not surround sound. I think he's trying to impress you." Reysa winked, looking bright and glamorous as a 1950s movie star. She killed the ignition. "Come on."

It seemed crazy to Aurye, this suggestion that either Berg might wish to impress her. She was the one who'd been nervous all evening, wondering how this would go, what they'd think of her outside the familiar setting of Midgard bar. Both were older, Reysa a youthful thirty-six and Magnus a decade older, both successful physicians, so worldly compared to herself. Aurye knew them from her role behind the bar at Midgard, the mid-mountain restaurant where the Bergs frequently dined and drank. Midgard was the only restaurant in the village frequented by people like them, the rest catering to the burgers and brews crowd, snowboarders in winter and mountain bikers in summer.

Upon climbing out, the scope of the landscape struck Aurye. Beyond the dry, bare section, a frozen sheet sloped away. "Your place. I just can't believe…" She ventured onto the ice, careful to keep her feet under her center of gravity. "When you said, come up, see our lodge, I didn't picture…"

Reysa remained back, nearer the house. "What did you picture?"

"Nothing as grand as this. It's like a castle from an old movie."

"That was the idea," Reysa said. "Of course, there were no actual Gothic castles existent on the mountain. Magnus and I decided to build one."

As impressive as the house was the setting. The broad white expanse fell away into darkening mist until it reached an abrupt edge. Aurye felt herself drawn nearer the cliff overlook. Wind etched the ice into jagged coarseness, edges glistening like blades of polished diamond. Everything was pristine, so unlike the dirty, snowplowed village below, where she lived and worked. Soon Aurye stood near the edge of a precipice, swaying there, afraid to move. The gaping openness exerted a pull. Beyond the initial steep drop, the canyon flattened into a convex snow field and rose again to the next ridge. Behind that, the lowering sun glared white, emanating wild, swirling tendrils of mist, backgrounded by a sky diminishing blue to black.

"Let's go inside," Reysa called.

Her words broke the spell. Aurye turned, found Reysa standing well up the slope, clutching her narrow frame in an exaggerated show of shivering. She looked tiny, waiflike in her dark green cloak-style coat with oversized monk's hood. A thick zipper cut diagonally across her chest like a scar. Aurye hurried back up, too aware of the deadly attraction below.

They stamped snow off their boots on the spiral-patterned coir entry mat inside the double doors.

"You know the hardest thing, living on the mountain full-time?" Reysa took Aurye's black peacoat and green and grey patchwork scarf and hung them on a branch of their coat rack, a leafless silver metal tree. "Wearing clothes that feel pretty, when outside it's all freezing wind, icy roads and snowfields."

"Layers are the thing." Aurye indicated her own dress, thin and white with antique lace trim. "I could never wear this alone, but with tights and boots... not thin yoga pants either. These are fleece."

"That's what I meant. It's tricky, managing to look like a girl up here, but you do." Reysa pulled off her boots, left them beside the mat.

Aurye's face flushed with pleasure at the compliment. She'd always found Reysa so elegant and stylish. "You need waterproof boots, with a good sole. Like you said, the trick is finding some you feel good in." Aurye lifted one foot, modeled her knee-high boots, shiny black leather with a diamond quilt pattern. She untied laces, slid off one boot at a time, and left hers beside Reysa's. "When I came back from school, all I had were red suede Fluevogs with three-inch stacked heels. They looked really cute around campus, but hopeless up here."

Her own exit from college was a subject Aurye wished she hadn't opened, hoped Reysa wouldn't want to talk about. Reysa let it pass, flipped back her hood to reveal mid-length blond curls which bounced as if they'd just been styled, and never held down under the hood. Beneath the coat, Reysa wore a white wool long-sleeved dress over charcoal leggings, barely lighter than Aurye's. "You always look feminine, but mountain-appropriate," Reysa resumed. "I just wanted you to know I got some great ideas, watching you at Midgard."

Though flattered, Aurye couldn't quite accept the idea. Had she really provided fashion inspiration to someone as polished and glamorous as Reysa? The Bergs had been regulars long enough to strike up a sort of friendship with Aurye, but the relationship was unequal. Their conversations ended in Reysa or Magnus handing an Amex across the bar, then calculating Aurye's tip.

The entry floor was slate tile, and from a black ceiling hung a sculpture of clear and frosted glass, within which orange-glowing elements radiated heat and light. A single piece of framed art dominated each side wall. The silver-framed square to the left was an extreme close-up of a woman's face draped in black fishnet. Her skin was unnaturally white, eyes gem-blue, lips vivid red and hair intense yellow-gold. The colors were saturated to such a rich, exaggerated degree, Aurye first took this for a painting. "Who is she?" she asked, and only then realized it was a photograph.

Reysa seemed surprised. "She… was me."

Aurye thought the image looked nothing like Reysa, but didn't say so. Maybe the picture was old. All women aged; it would happen to Aurye. But the woman in the picture wasn't merely younger. Reysa Berg was every bit as beautiful and striking as the woman in the photograph. Thinner now, with prominent cheekbones, more natural coloring. Reysa's face had not so much aged as shifted, taken on a very different character.

Aurye's attention shifted to the opposite wall. The mural there, in contrast to the photograph, was a grid combining four pieces of very old symbolic art, subtly colored ink linework. Most of the arcane signs were unrecognizable, though a few were traditional, symbols for male or female. Others reminded Aurye of astrology.

"Engravings by Jakob Bohme," Reysa explained. "A very interesting mind. He believed Adam, the Adam of Christian myth, was both man and woman at once, able to birth his own children by parthenogenesis. Can you imagine? No need for Eve."

No response came to mind, so Aurye changed the subject. "Thank you for inviting me up. And for driving down to get me. It sounded fun, spending time with you and Magnus. I haven't seen you much at Midgard, lately."

"Oh yes. About that." Reysa seemed uncharacteristically flustered. "The truth is, we bought the Midgard. We were afraid it was failing. I mean, imagine if the only nice place in the village went under, just as we shifted our lives up here."

So, the Bergs were her employers. The news was a shock, but she knew better than to voice the many questions that spun to mind. "That explains about Tolliver, at least."

Reysa looked confused.

"When I asked for tonight off, at first, Tolliver said no. Then I mentioned you'd invited me up here. His face got all red, and he couldn't look at me. He just said, of course you can go."

From inside the house came footsteps. Aurye and Reysa turned.

Magnus approached from the next room, shoeless in jeans, grey wool socks, and a form-fitting black sweater with diagonal white slashes across the front. His salt and pepper hair, long on top, was closely undercut on the sides. Aurye almost commented on how different Magnus looked, but caught herself. Better not to say. Probably the difference was that he was more casual at home.

"Aurye." Magnus came to embrace her, moving as if about to kiss her mouth. Aurye felt a flash of surprise, and in that instant decided to accept it, as if nothing were strange. But Magnus shifted, kissed her on the cheek. He was inches taller than she remembered, even shoeless.

"Why that look?" Magnus touched the frames of his eyeglasses near the hinges. "Is it these? They're new."

Aurye looked around for Reysa, just approaching with two glasses of ruby dark wine.

"We love the same things," Reysa said, "so I know you won't turn down a good Pinot Noir. This one is excellent. A gift from a client of Magnus's."

Strange, a doctor saying "client" to describe a patient, but the Bergs were unusual in many ways, despite their taste and easy elegance. They did things their own way. Smiling, Aurye accepted the glass. "Impossible to refuse."

"From Switzerland, believe it or not," Magnus added.

The taste was startling. After three years working at Midgard bar, Aurye knew hundreds of wines, but mostly from Pacific Coast winemakers. This Pinot was unusually full-bodied, complex. "Wow. Almost gamey. Smoked meat, black raspberry and pomegranate." Aurye struggled to articulate the rest of what the wine conveyed. More than just flavor. A suggestion of exoticism, of deep time and distant locales, worldly pleasures Aurye had never known. In fact, she'd never really spent much time anywhere but this mountain, other than trips to Portland, and a year and a half in college in Eugene. Aurye could imagine nothing so suggestive of a better life, altered potentialities and pleasurable indulgences, than a strange, excellent wine. The taste of age and memory, of earthy desires. Even lust. Her powers of description fell short here. If anything, the taste reminded her of the Bergs.

She wondered what Reysa and Magnus thought, watching her sip. How did they perceive the wine? Maybe such spicy, exotic flavor had become routine to their tastes.

All three looked at each other, unspeaking. Aurye was first to turn away.

The enormous central room was more open hall or great room than living room. To the left upon entering was an open dining area and chef's kitchen, then an unused fireplace and a wide curving staircase up. On the opposite wall, between two large windows, a heap of wood burned in a second fireplace.

"We're still decorating," Reysa said, as if to explain the mostly empty room.

Magnus headed toward the kitchen. "I'll get myself a glass."

Reysa showed Aurye toward the windows.

"Like *Citizen Kane*." Aurye indicated the stone fireplace. "You could stand inside there."

Even twenty feet away, the fire radiated intense heat.

"Might be a little warm." Reysa guided Aurye toward the rightmost window. The extraordinary view overlooked a different drop-off and canyon opposite the one Aurye had seen outside. The grade swooped away steeply, flattened and rose again across the canyon. Tips of evergreens barely penetrated the deep snow.

Before the window was a heavy black book on a stand, like an old bible or dictionary, open near the beginning. The pages drew Aurye's curiosity. What did the Bergs feel important enough to display? She leaned in, read aloud. "Of all created things, the condition whereof is transitory and frail..." Aurye stopped, feeling someone approaching behind. She glanced up to find Magnus standing back, looking out the window, sipping from his glass.

Magnus began to recite. "The common matter of all things is the Great Mystery, which no certain essence and prefigured or formed idea could comprehend, nor could it comply with any property, it being altogether void of color and elementary nature." He paused, seeming to look for Aurye's reaction.

"Are you reading from this?" she asked.

He continued. "The scope of this Great Mystery is as large as the firmament. And this Great Mystery was the mother of all the elements, and

Grandmother of all the stars, trees and carnal creatures."

Reysa approached from the other side, stood so the Bergs flanked Aurye.

"As children are born of a mother," Magnus went on, "so all created things whether sensible or insensible, all things whatsoever, were uniformly brought out of the Great Mystery."

Aurye twitched reflexively, half-aware of a kind of spell being cast. More likely it was the wine than Magnus's incantation. She glanced again at the page, recognized words he'd recited from memory. The mystery fascinated her. The Bergs had never seemed religious types, not the least dogmatic.

"It's Paracelsus, from *Liber Primus*," Reysa said. "You know Paracelsus, the Renaissance alchemist and mystic?"

"Alchemist?" Aurye asked. "Isn't that turning lead into gold?"

"Alchemy is creation by combination." Magnus gestured down the wall to their left. "I'll show you."

In such a large room, each section felt vastly separate. Magnus proceeded along the outer wall, past windows, toward the arrangement of stereo equipment. Two tower speakers flanked an aluminum stand upon which electronic components stood ranked, facing a trio of low-slung black leather chairs. Magnus gestured Aurye into the middle chair.

She sat, wondering why three seats, and tried to read the nameplate on the two identical black metal slabs beneath the stand. Each was the size of a small coffee table, with finned heatsinks along the left side. "Krell." Amplifiers, each connected to one speaker with a white cable thick as a garden hose. Aurye was tempted to mention she'd dated an audiophile in college, but didn't want to talk about him. Anyway, she'd never learned much about the equipment.

Magnus selected a CD from a small stack and inserted the disk into the tray of a player with a glossy white faceplate. He pressed a button, adjusted a volume knob on the walnut and brushed stainless steel box on the shelf, and handed Aurye the CD case. He sat to her left.

The sound began, an intricate flurry of violin gestures repeating in varied agitation. Culmination and pause, then a piano took over. The effect was quieting. Aurye and Magnus leaned forward in their chairs, Reysa standing beside Aurye. At the edge of this cavernous room, not far from windows overlooking the grandest view, this hushed music narrowed the atmosphere. A feeling of closeness verging on intimacy.

On the CD cover, the words *Arvo Pärt / Tabula Rasa* hovered over snow fields wind-blown into sculptural shapes.

"It's incredible," Aurye said, still listening. "These hunks of steel, all glowing tubes and fat copper cables, making such delicate sound. So pure."

Reysa took the seat to Aurye's right.

"Blank slate," Aurye said, and at once regretted it. The Bergs didn't need her help translating basic Latin.

Magnus looked nothing but pleased. "*Tabula Rasa* is one of my favorite things."

"I never noticed before, your eyes are mismatched," Aurye told him, before she could stop herself. Aurye wondered how she'd never noticed. Not only different colors. Irises of different sizes. Like two people watching her. Two minds.

"Tell about Aurye Feuer," Reysa said. "We know a few details. Tell us something new."

Aurye felt an ache of infatuation. She wanted to know Reysa better, to let Reysa know her. Magnus, too. Why did she feel so strongly that being closer to the Bergs might remedy her problems? In the course of their dining and drinking at Midgard, Aurye had mentioned her intention to return to college, try to rediscover herself. This had seemed to intrigue them, for some reason. More than anything, she hoped to learn what they found so interesting about her. Aurye felt a sense of auditioning, but didn't resent their attention. She was willing, even glad to reveal herself.

"I'll tell you whatever you want," Aurye said. "I like you both so much, and this is the best wine I've ever tasted. Probably the best I ever will."

"I doubt that," Reysa said. "You'll have greater pleasures ahead, I'm sure."

Aurye wondered where to begin. "You know I was in college."

"It's rumored you were pre-med." Magnus paused. "I think Reysa and I would both tell you medicine is a field to avoid, if you possibly can. We couldn't." He smiled, as if implying something more.

Aurye knew she'd mentioned college, but never pre-med. "I never got that far, just lots of Bio and Chem, before I flamed out. That's why I didn't mention it. What's the point of bragging about my two years? You're successful surgeons."

Magnus grinned at Reysa. "You hear that? She thinks we're successful."

"Don't tease." Reysa touched Aurye's arm. "Why not go back, finish?"

Aurye felt a twinge of pain in her side. Her hand moved toward that spot, but she commanded herself not to draw attention. "I'm saving up, most of what I earn, but it's hard. Since I came crawling home, I live at my mom's. She stays with her boyfriend in Rhododendron, so I have the place to myself, for free. Maybe I'll save enough, go back. Not U of O, but somewhere." She sighed. Being honest felt good, but she should stop. "The truth is, it's hard to imagine starting again."

Reysa leaned in, looked close, as if some key were to be found in Aurye's face. "Shame to quit, once you started."

"It was stupid, embarrassing." Aurye looked away. "Just… a boy."

Reysa looked at Magnus. "Isn't it always a boy?"

"Except when it's a girl," Magnus replied.

"Well." Reysa stood, straightened her dress. "I'm sure we're not finished talking about boys and girls tonight."

Reysa herded them toward the dining area and kitchen. Magnus followed, after raising the music's volume. A large, circular gray wood dining table was surrounded by eleven black bucket chairs. Six wine bottles and three glasses rested on a central black spinner.

Magnus pulled out three chairs. Reysa ran her fingers through her hair. The blond waves were longer than Aurye had realized. How much time had passed since she'd seen the Bergs? Both seemed indefinably changed.

Reysa selected two bottles. "Which do you prefer, the Swiss or Argentinian?"

Magnus offered his glass, conveying his preference to Reysa without words. She poured from the left-hand bottle, then held up both for Aurye to choose from.

Aurye shrugged. "Either for me."

"Ever flexible and accommodating." Reysa's mouth angled in suppressed amusement. "You're not at work tonight. You're with friends. You must speak your true mind." She poured Aurye brim-full, then finished the bottle herself.

Aurye tasted. "This one's peppery. Leather, coriander and tobacco leaf."

Reysa sat on the table edge. "Aren't you nimble with the tasting notes."

"Everybody at Midgard seems to appreciate quick reference points to help them choose."

"I find," Magnus pronounced, "most people prefer being told what to do."

Aurye wondered if agreement might reveal too much of her own inclination. "Me, too."

Reysa held up two empty bottles and peered into the openings like binoculars. "Only two? I thought we had more."

"Three." Magnus indicated another empty hidden among full bottles. He stepped nearer the women, and leaned against the table. "That's enough for Aurye to tell why she dropped out. Talk about the boy."

Reysa bit her lip. "He cheated?"

Aurye couldn't move, or think of what to say.

"Don't be embarrassed." Magnus turned, as if sparing Aurye his scrutiny. "We've both been hurt that way."

"As an idea, love is glorious, but we're cynical. These human vessels are unfortunately flawed." Reysa adjusted her sleeves, as if some vulnerable part of herself might be exposed at the wrists. She crossed arms, angled her head.

Aurye wondered what she was hiding. Scars? "Infidelity wasn't the whole story. It was complicated."

"It always is." Reysa selected another bottle, started opening.

"I'm not giving up," Aurye insisted. "It's not hopeless. You two seem happy. So, your cynicism surprises me."

Reysa eyed Magnus, then refilled glasses. "We are happy. Well matched, truly in love. We're even faithful. But that isn't how we're made. Human nature is laziness, dishonesty."

Magnus's eyebrows lifted. "People take the most crucial things for granted."

"No." Aurye protested, though she couldn't say they were wrong. The Bergs were so attractive, so successful, so appealing in every aspect, she couldn't understand how their prior partners could have rejected them. But she realized the very same thing had happened to her. "It wasn't the cheating. He pulled away. First I was beautiful, everything he wanted. Then he got to know me, and discovered… things that disgusted him. About me."

"Aurye, no," Reysa said. "There's nothing about you less than beautiful. Not one single imperfection."

Aurye squirmed. They didn't know. She wanted to tell them, wanted to show—

"Actually," Magnus interrupted loudly, seeming to sense Aurye's discomfort, "for both of us, what triggered the final breakdown of prior marriages was a crisis."

"Crisis?" Aurye asked, relieved her turn for storytelling seemed to have passed.

"For me, a car crash," Reysa said. "Tearing metal, cutting glass. My face was disfigured, my neck, one of my breasts. This was before Magnus and I. We were married to others, all working in the same hospital. After the crash, Magnus was my surgeon. He created this face. My own husband, he did not love this face. Or more likely, he'd already fallen out of love with me. This face was only his excuse."

Aurye scanned Reysa's skin, looking for scars. She was smooth, symmetrical. "What about you, Magnus?"

"My crisis? It was something I made. A creation of my own." He looked away, distant.

Aurye looked to Reysa for elaboration.

Reysa stood. "We're going to fall over, drinking so much without food." She slipped away to the kitchen.

Aurye felt herself swaying, affected by the wine.

"People hurt by rejection become pathologically terrified of it," Magnus said. "I was driven mad by fear. It's something I admit. There's no shame in having suffered. My first wife abandoned me in my moment of greatest need."

Reysa returned with two gold leaf platters, each bearing three black plates. "Steamed and chilled mussels with black lava salt, half-shell oysters, and aged gouda. And here, wild mushroom truffle tarts, kalamata tapenade, and the best fucking baguette I've ever had. All from Portland, this morning."

"See, Aurye?" Magnus said. "We might try to rescue ourselves, but more likely someone else does it for us."

"You weren't kidding, I really will fall down if I don't eat something." Aurye took some food. This intoxication was hard to distinguish from excitement, but she knew she might crash if she drank too much without eating.

"There are great advantages to marriage," Reysa said. "Partnership. Not just one fling after another, but a bond that can last for life. But if we remain with a single type, no variety, always the same body shape, the same face, same color of skin, we get bored. Overfamiliarity creates temptation to revisit the new."

"I don't have energy for that," Aurye protested. "Constantly shuffling through different boyfriends. My friends who do that, they end up with nothing to rely on."

"That's what she's saying," Magnus said. "We've known polyamorists. It's a term that most often seems to mean indiscriminate openness, as you said. Constant shuffling. I believe, we believe, a person is meant to be with one other."

"But you said—"

"That is," Magnus continued, "if we do something to remedy that inborn need."

"Humans require a variety of stimulus," Reysa added. "We're prone to boredom. By we, I don't mean myself and Magnus. Everyone. You. Human nature, like it or not."

Aurye saw their point, understood it derived from personal experience. In fact, it fit what she knew from her own small bank of relationship data. The problem was, she preferred not to think that way, even if it might be true.

"I see that look," Reysa said. "We won't push. But one thing we share is willingness to question received wisdom."

Aurye smiled. "I count myself an atheist, rebel and deviant."

Reysa laughed. Magnus joined in.

"Ours is a transgressive philosophy," Reysa said carefully. "Desire is important. Lust."

"But what does that mean?" Aurye asked, heart pounding.

"Come. We'll show you." Reysa took Aurye's hand, and she stood.

As they walked toward the stairs, Magnus took Aurye's other hand. Aurye wanted to ask what was happening, though she thought she knew.

When they reached the cold, unused fireplace, Reysa surged ahead, pulling Aurye by the arm, trying to run. Aurye in turn dragged Magnus along, all of them laughing in a chain linked by hands.

"I think I'm drunk," Reysa shouted.

Magnus jogged to keep up. "I think you are, too."

"Aurye too," Reysa said.

"All of us!" Aurye wailed laughter.

Reysa veered away from the foot of the stairs. The three gained speed, all running together, none resisting. Reysa's laughter infected the others, as they played an energetic game of whiplash momentum, pulling and swinging against one another, whirling and gaining speed. Reysa led their circuit of the room, between stereo and chairs, past picture windows and the great hot fireplace, the entryway, kitchen and dining table, and finally back to the cold fireplace and the sweeping curve of the staircase. With a shriek Reysa fell. Aurye tried to jump over, but tripped and crashed. Magnus stumbled, almost regained footing, only to sprawl at the foot of the stairs. He lay on his back, moaning. Reysa still laughed madly.

Aurye tried to find herself. Was she in pain? She felt joy, the excitement of belonging, not fear. It occurred to her, breathing hard, looking at the high ceiling, that she may have an advantage after all. She'd felt disadvantaged ever since Reysa picked her up. Clearly the Bergs held some agreed-upon plan, which Aurye didn't know. But maybe she had a clearer idea than they realized. Was it possible they believed her completely unaware, when in fact she understood all but the details? Reysa and Magnus expected her to be cautious, but she was a woman of experience beyond her years. She was tired of playing by imposed rules. If an opportunity came to jump to a new realm of experience, she'd take the chance. What better fix for stagnant life than to destroy it?

Still she wondered. Was their secret as simple as she guessed, some of experiment in transgressive intimacy, or something weirder? She kept thinking of three new chairs by the stereo. Maybe they wanted to invite her in. Of course this was presumptuous, but they didn't need to know what guesses played in her mind.

Aurye looked up, found both Reysa and Magnus watching, clearly guessing at her thoughts. She looked between them, intending to convey understanding and acceptance. "I have to admit something," she began, feigning confidence, trying to bluster through. "I think I've guessed why you invited me up. Were my assumptions wrong?"

Reysa looked amused. "I could probably guess your guess."

Magnus popped himself up on his elbows. "Yet still you came." His glasses having fallen off, the difference between his eyes was more pronounced.

Aurye looked away, covered her mouth, then realized she was only playing coy and girlish. She didn't want to convey anything but what she actually felt. In fact, she hadn't realized how receptive she actually was until that moment. Though nervous, she was unafraid. "I don't know exactly what, not specifically. But I assume there's some kind of proposition. I just don't understand how it fits with what you said about faithfulness." She sat nearer Reysa than Magnus, and Reysa was the one most focused upon her. "Whenever you look at me, both of you but especially Reysa, I feel you trying to figure me out. Studying me."

"So that was it?" Reysa asked. "We convince the comely twenty-two-year-old to frolic with one of us, or both?"

Magnus looked amused. Reysa laughed, leaning against her husband, sprawled comfortably against him in the languor of intoxication.

"Isn't that it?" Aurye asked. Any frustration or confusion dispersed as she joined their ridiculous laughter. She felt both relief and disappointment at once. "Well, then what?"

"You're almost completely wrong," Magnus said.

"We do have something in mind," Reysa clarified. "An offer. An arrangement we'll explain soon enough."

"Sorry, I just thought I'd try being blunt, or direct." Aurye felt slightly embarrassed, but couldn't help noticing the Bergs still looked at her with the same eager curiosity. "At least our game doesn't seem to have ended."

"No," Magnus said. "And your flexibility of mind comes as a relief."

"Blunt directness is a virtue," Reysa said.

"Sorry. I shouldn't have had so much to drink," Aurye said. "Not my first time here."

"I'm the one who poured gallons of wine, and led us around the room like a madwoman," Reysa said. "Anyway, when the time comes for us to be blunt and direct with you, I hope you'll keep that open mind."

"You plan to be direct with me," Aurye noted. "Just not yet?"

"Not quite," Reysa said.

"So then." Aurye looked again at the staircase. "What were you going to show me?"

Reysa was first to stand. The trio gathered at the bottom of the stairs, each seeming to ponder the eventuality of going up. Such a prospect seemed momentous, at least to Aurye. All the answers must wait above.

"Are you sure you want this, to know more?" Reysa asked Aurye. "Such things we could show you."

"You know I sort of idolize you both. You have so much figured out. Just, seem to be living exactly right."

"But you don't know everything," Magnus cautioned.

Aurye nodded. "That's true, I really only know a little. And we all tend to idealize people based on too little information. But you have each other. This incredible home, and property. And success in your careers."

"Success, that's nothing solid." Reysa shook her head. "It's a cloud. Not something you attach to."

"Past failures weigh me down," Magnus said, "so much more than successes have ever lifted me."

"I don't even know what kind of medicine you practice, but I think you're being over-modest." Aurye looked between the two of them. The Bergs possessed so many pleasures, not just luxuries and money, but simple things.

Reysa stepped to the first stair as if prepared to climb, but stopped, turned. "If anyone understands the way people judge by appearances, you do, Aurye. They assume you must be a certain way, without knowing your mind, how it feels to be you. People notice your appearance right away, see the confident way you hold forth behind the bar, and what do they think? That girl, she's beautiful. Confident, has this killer body. Aurye's perfect. She possesses everything. Lacks nothing."

Aurye was stunned, wanted to protest. There was so much they didn't—

"That's what people think," Magnus added. "But is that you?"

"I know how people regard me, their assumptions. You're right, of course I hear it. Pretty face, that body, and she's supposedly smart, too. What's she doing in this shitty little village? At her age, why doesn't she get out, go into the world and... What? I don't know. Life is complicated. I want more from..." Aurye didn't know what. She wanted Reysa and Magnus to tell her what to do. The way they acted toward her, alternately flirtatious and protective, as if they held some secret they might tell, or something to ask. Now they'd invited her to their home, filled her with wine, unfurled this unorthodox philosophy.

She still wasn't sure what they wanted to offer, or to take. When Aurye had dressed to come up here tonight, she'd believed anything might happen. Now she didn't know, wished she understood. The pain in her gut burned anew, a pain Aurye knew wasn't really present. At least it didn't have to be. The ache came and went, depending on her mind.

Aurye took the first step. Reysa climbed ahead, paused at the first half-landing, and lifted the bottom of her smooth cream-white dress, peeled it up over her head. Underneath she wasn't naked, still wearing the grey tights, and on top an ornamented silver brocade camisole or tunic, with white and black beads in a sort of constellation. In this reduced attire, Reysa led Aurye and Magnus the rest of the way.

The upper landing mirrored the square entry below, one side open to the great room, art displayed on two side walls. The broad double doors on the fourth wall must open on something, not the snowy outdoors, like below. What lay behind them? Instead of a coat rack, here the lone accessory was an antique divan, covered in a silky light gray. Reysa reclined, like a Norse goddess adorned in her strange ceremonial top, like a chainmail camisole. Aurye thought it was a little surprising, Reysa pulling off her dress, but she wasn't naked. Layers, that was the word Aurye had used. She was still clothed.

Aurye looked down, taking in the entire lower hall at once. Magnus stood to one side. Clearly he and Reysa wanted to show Aurye their art.

"Prometheus," Reysa announced.

In the painting, a large man, naked beneath a dramatically flowing gold wrap, reclined on a rock. Prometheus was not relaxing, but in agony. A giant eagle loomed, eating from a gaping wound in his belly.

"Prometheus created mankind from clay," Magnus said. "Formed a shape from mud and water, and bestowed life. We are his creations. While other gods and titans warred in their struggle for power, Prometheus opted out."

Aurye had to look away. The wound, open to the world. Why were they showing her this? What did they know about her?

"Prometheus stole fire from the gods," Reysa said. "Made it a gift to mortals."

Aurye vaguely remembered the myth from school. "It's striking, but I…" She guessed she might be missing the point, too distracted by the gory mess. The guts of a god on display.

Magnus gripped Aurye's shoulder. "Prometheus disregarded the law. He created men and women, and gave us fire. Others didn't. He dared. And because he dared, he was punished, the eagle feasting on his liver, forever."

Aurye knew they wanted her to see, but she couldn't bear to look at the painting any more. She wasn't squeamish about most things. The wound was too specific, too familiar. She turned to the opposite wall.

"Pandora?" Aurye asked.

"Yes," Magnus said.

Reysa sat up, watching Aurye's reaction before the second painting.

A woman knelt, barefoot in a wild forest, leaning over a small container. A hand concealed one of her eyes. She bent forward, mouth open, on the verge of discovery.

"What connects Pandora with Prometheus?" Aurye asked. "I'm sorry, I don't remember."

"We all learn, then forget," Reysa said. "If we're lucky, we learn again. Pandora was the gods' punishment for Prometheus's gift of fire. Pandora was the first human woman, created to bestow suffering, which would spread forever. She opened her jar, and our weaknesses flowed. Jealousy. Vanity."

"She's the reason we take for granted any good we ever gain," Magnus said. "Our punishment for Prometheus."

Reysa stood, came to Aurye's side. "You can't forestall death, but you can fight the poisoning of love."

Aurye turned. "But how?"

"We shift our minds. Transform language, every way we speak or relate. Alter habits, remake every routine. Constantly change places we go, foods we eat. We constantly trick one another into thinking we are both someone new."

"Is that all?" Aurye asked. "That simple?"

"Not entirely," Reysa said. "Other means exist to transform the self, means abandoned by the science of our age. So we look to the past for various powers that have been forgotten, or suppressed."

"A blend of science, alchemy and occult magic," Magnus said. "For radical self-transformation."

"In a couple, the partner is our second self. Do you understand, Aurye?"

"Yes, some," Aurye said. "But you're making my head spin."

"How far would you go, to create an entirely new self?" Reysa asked.

"I wish I could. It sounds..." Aurye trailed off, overwhelmed by how appealing it sounded. Was this possible?

"I hope you don't think we're deranged," Magnus said.

"Deranged?" Aurye laughed before she could stop herself.

Reysa looked at Magnus.

"No, don't worry," Aurye assured them. She felt the wine again. "Hell, I'm the one who's deranged. What I think is you might be, just maybe, more than the usual amount detached from the mainstream."

Reysa smiled. "Detached from the..." she began, seeming to taste the words as she spoke. "Actually, I like that."

"That means it's a good thing, then?" Magnus asked.

"You must not know me very well yet," Aurye said.

"We're getting there," Reysa said. "We're all learning. All of us."

"What I started saying was, it sounds incredible." Aurye spoke slowly, with reverence. "The possibility of building a new self."

"Almost anything's possible," Magnus said with assurance.

"Speaking of medicine," Aurye asked, "how can you still practice, living sixty miles out of town?"

Reysa blinked at the reversal. "I keep a condo outside Southeast Portland, ten miles from the hospital."

"What do you specialize in?" Aurye turned to Magnus. "I heard you're a plastic surgeon."

"You heard?" He appraised Aurye over his wine glass. "So, it's not just Reysa asking around about you?"

Aurye considered whether she should just tell them now about her situation. Her hand twitched as she consciously prevented it from moving, giving her away. Of course they didn't know, couldn't possibly assume. Only if she told them.

Magnus smiled. "It's true, I specialize in reconstructive plastic surgery. Burn victims, disfigurements, birth defects. I have no interest in working on the insecure, those who only want to eradicate distinctiveness, to look more like some bland ideal. Beauty matters, but more important is to believe oneself appealing. I wish we didn't always seek beauty of the most mundane, unchallenging variety. Trimming down an interesting nose, making it less noticeable. How boring."

Aurye understood his ideal, but felt confused "But if you're a plastic surgeon and don't believe in making people more beautiful, then what?"

"I'm willing to rebuild, to sculpt. Form reveals character. Personage manifests not only in personality, but arrangement of body and face."

"You said you made errors," Aurye said. "Had some kind of problem."

Reysa spoke up. "Failure, he said."

"I made an aesthetic error. Disfigured someone, apparently." Magnus shrugged, as if everything had been told.

Reysa elaborated. "He repaired the arm of a teenage girl. The limb was mangled. The way Magnus rebuilt it was more aesthetic, functional. Magnus believed it matched the other limb. The problem was, it looked different than before."

"My patient was displeased," Magnus resumed. "Her family claimed to be shocked. To be fair, probably were shocked. The girl herself became suicidal. Her parents sued."

"What happened?" Aurye asked. "It must have worked out. You're still practicing."

Neither Magnus nor Reysa answered.

"You lost the lawsuit?"

"Lost, no," Reysa said.

"My malpractice insurer settled," Magnus said. "The limb was superior. Functionally better, more interesting." He stood, went to the rail and looked over. He leaned out over the edge, as if pulled. Aurye remembered this feeling, outside, at the cliff.

"But you're fine," Aurye insisted. "You can still practice."

"He could," Reysa said. "Malpractice insurance is vastly expensive now."

Magnus turned to face the women. "I learned a lesson, the need to rein myself in. No more idealism. It's not my place to make limbs more interesting, to sculpt intriguing shapes. If I want a mainstream practice, it can't be to please myself. The person I must please is the customer, the owner of the limb, or face, whatever. The path forward was obvious. I could do the uncreative work of restoring bodies and faces to the way they used to look. Give people what they expected. Creative sculpture was something I needed to keep to myself. Hush hush. I'm lucky I have a woman like Reysa."

Reysa stood, went to his side. "Lately he's moving from standard clientele to more of a niche. Clients willing to pay extra for flexibility and discretion."

"Openness of mind is valuable," Magnus added. "One piece of outside work earns more than a year in the clinic."

"Many clients come to stay with us here," Reysa explained, "to avoid any risk of being seen while healing. We're so isolated, often snowbound, it's perfect."

"What about your specialty?" Aurye asked Reysa.

"Orthopedic surgery."

"If I'm mostly face, hands and skin," Magnus said, "Reysa is the real meat and bone."

Reysa shrugged. "I keep a body upright. Able to stand, flex, move."

"She's too modest," Magnus insisted. "Reysa's a respected authority in limb reattachment. She hasn't achieved as many surgeries as some older surgeons, not yet, but her success is unrivaled. Limbs may seem clumsy, mechanical chunks of meat, but they're all fine detail. Nervous and vascular systems are intricate, complicated puzzles. Surgeons effective at reattachment and transplant must connect an array of interlocking parts, impossible to design in advance."

"Most cases are emergencies," Reysa said, though she seemed more comfortable letting Magnus explain.

"Donor and recipient interfaces must fit, be made to synchronize, exchange fluids and electricity, the prime movers of life. It's a magical power, almost godlike." Magnus seemed genuinely proud, awed by his wife.

This seemed to please Reysa more than embarrass her. "Working on athletes and accident victims doesn't afford me Magnus's freedom to exit the mainstream. I can't opt out, at least not yet. I'm looking for ways."

"We do collaborate well," Magnus said. "Our skills are complimentary."

"And we're seeking others who are sympathetic," Reysa added.

"She has a recent story," Magnus said, as if just remembering. "Pretty dramatic. You might find it interesting."

Reysa looked to Magnus. "The legs?"

Magnus nodded.

"A car accident," Reysa began with slow caution, as if telling the story were as fraught with potential missteps as one of her surgeries. "Well, before that. From nowhere, this young man approached me, while eating lunch. He'd learned my name, sought me out. A great athlete, a sprinter, Olympic hopeful at 400 meters. He asked about Paralympic athletes, who compete on artificial limbs. You've seen those, flexible carbon fiber blades?"

Aurye nodded.

"I spoke with him on a Thursday afternoon. That Saturday night, he was rushed to the hospital. His car had been totaled. The legs, I judged, could not be saved." Reysa paused, watching Aurye's response.

Aurye couldn't believe what she'd heard. "That's terrible."

"Why is it terrible?" Magnus asked.

"For this young man, the sprinter, it was not terrible," Reysa said. "It was exactly what he wanted. The athletic advantage of ultra-light limbs. More than that, to be noteworthy. Not just win races."

Aurye tried to process all she was saying. "He wanted?"

"It was arranged, scheduled," Reysa said. "I was ready at the hospital."

Though Aurye believed she understood the first impulse, another aspect troubled her. "But he had a gift. I'm not sure he should destroy such a capable body."

"We destroy to create," Reysa said. "He wanted to be an inspiration. To remake his life."

"But he could have died, if things had…"

"Died?" Reysa looked puzzled, then understood. "No, the accident wasn't much. The legs weren't destroyed, barely damaged really. I told him in advance, just make sure there's lots of blood. Enough to be convincing."

"Told him… In advance?" Aurye looked back and forth between Reysa and Magnus.

"No reason to risk his life. We decided I should take his legs, for Magnus. The sprinter wanted to become an inspiration, and that's what he became. He has a book deal now. Some producer wants to create a movie, his life story."

"He found what he wanted," Magnus added. "And I have new, athletic legs." He stepped away from the rail, took a stride and turned, as if modeling.

Aurye wondered, could this be true? Even now, it seemed more likely the Bergs just wanted to shock her.

Reysa watched, appraising her husband's movements. "It was my first chance to contribute to our plan in a major way. I showed Magnus I was ready to help remake him, the way he was already changing me."

"The way he was…" Aurye looked at Reysa. "Both of you?"

"Come closer." Reysa rotated her hands to show off her wrists. Around each ran a line, which Aurye first took to be suicide scars, but the lines continued all the way around. "Magnus left the seams visible, by design. We wanted to accentuate them, to clarify what we are. Assemblages of varied parts."

"What?" Part of Aurye was shocked, the rest couldn't believe it was possible. "Who are you made of?"

Reysa looked into Aurye's eyes, held her gaze steady so Aurye wouldn't doubt. "I won't tell you the names, not yet. But these hands of mine, they aren't the same I was born with."

Magnus unbuttoned his jeans, pulled them down and stepped out. "Here, see?" He demonstrated the clear delineation, mid-thigh, just below where his boxer briefs ended. Both legs were slightly mismatched above and below the line. "We love the contrast, where skin joins skin."

Aurye considered. Reysa's wrists, Magnus's legs. Each body exhibited a sharp transition between shapes, colors and textures. Where differences met, how could one even be sure which was the original? Distinctions blurred.

Magnus picked up his jeans, reached in the pocket and produced photographs. "Look, see? Don't worry, nothing graphic."

The photos showed a teenage girl, blond and vigorously athletic.

"I could show you the torn-up mess of pulped meat I had to work with. But look. Reysa and I collaborated. She reattached, kept flesh alive, restored limb function. I made it look new. Better than new."

Aurye wasn't sure how to react. The girl's arm displayed nothing like the jarring transition of Reysa's or Magnus's transplants. She was a normal girl, skin the radiant, buttery tan of healthful youth.

"Do you see what I meant to achieve? Never mind that it didn't work, I mean, we try, sometimes fail. Do you see my intention?"

One arm tapered differently than the other. The imbalance was slight, reminding Aurye of tennis players, whose racquet arms often developed more muscle. She looked strong, poised, if slightly asymmetrical.

"The girl didn't like it, I can't deny that. I was going to lose a malpractice lawsuit. So I learned to paint by numbers. Until I found another way to practice my art."

"This isn't just Magnus." Aurye's statement to Reysa contained a question.

"No," Magnus corrected. "We've developed our philosophy together, over time. And we never harm. Never anything the client doesn't want."

This aspect Aurye found inspiring. The Bergs weren't in competition, Reysa wasn't merely in support of Magnus. The two collaborated. "But are you sure it's safe, legal? I mean, of course you are." If she knew anything about the Bergs, it was their precision about everything.

"They sign waivers, agree not contact medical boards or authorities," Magnus said. "Informed adults of sound mind. That doesn't preclude eccentricity, or strange desires."

"What do you think?" Reysa asked cautiously.

Aurye considered. "It's surprising, disconcerting. My initial gut reaction was fear, to be honest."

"Understandable," Reysa said. "And do be honest."

"But I get it. You're looking to make lives that work for you. Sometimes that's not easy, or takes stepping over some lines." What line would Aurye be willing to cross? To be able to take control of herself, she would give anything.

"Yes, I admit it," Reysa said with a smirk. "We do things others might consider perverted, disgusting and wrong."

"You want to hear the true revelation?" Magnus looked pleased, self-contained and satisfied, as if he had a beneficial secret to share. "I couldn't become myself until I severed all ties, went underground. My vision became clearer. And I was shocked what people will pay for unorthodox services. The majority may be appalled by willful disfigurement, but those who desire it might happily pay millions."

Aurye almost repeated the word. Millions. She didn't want the Bergs to think her too interested in money. Really that wasn't the first thing they possessed that appealed to her. She wanted help eradicating herself.

"Thus the mountaintop castle," Reysa said lightly.

"Money is freedom." Magnus shrugged. "At least it helps. The rest is not giving a damn what anyone thinks."

Aurye couldn't believe this was real. She felt inspired, impressed by Magnus's uncompromising transformation, and more, she desired something like it for herself. Though her hands trembled at what they'd revealed to her, Aurye admired them more than ever.

"Exiting the mainstream wasn't exile," Magnus said, "though at first, I thought it was."

"I still commute into Portland on Tuesdays and Wednesdays," Reysa said. "I do good work. Sometimes I take weeks off to travel with Magnus. He's free. I'm still becoming free."

Magnus turned and went to open the double doors. "Time to go in."

Though the room had been shut, the dry warmth from the fireplace downstairs reached even here. Moonlight fell through the skylight, making the operating theater almost day-bright. A central surgical table was surrounded by carts and stands of medical gear, and less recognizable industrial equipment. In two far corners, white curtains drew back to reveal vacant hospital beds. Against the rightmost wall, metal racks stood far enough out of the light that whatever they stored was obscured in shadow.

Aurye stepped toward that darkness, lured by the unknown. Light glinted off glass. The shelves held jars, or tanks.

Sudden light flashed above, jarringly bright. An instant later, thunder crashed. Brilliance illuminated everything stored in the glass containers, suspended in emerald liquid. Body parts small as fingers, hands and eyes, and larger. Heads, limbs, torsos.

"In death, they leave behind much that remains useful," Reysa said. "But living flesh is easier to work with."

Aurye swallowed. "You didn't bring me here to take—"

"No," Reysa answered quickly, then giggled in a manner that put Aurye's fears to rest. "You're not new flesh to us. We value more than youth, which counts for nothing in the end. Magnus excels at cosmetic shaping, so if the point were only to constantly tighten, well. We could forever remake ourselves into younger-looking versions of the same people. We're physically fit, healthy. Younger than our years."

"What, then? What do you want from me that you don't already have?" Aurye looked to Magnus.

"Varieties of personhood, within the same partner," he answered. "Reysa gave me the eye of a very tall and thin Kenyan immigrant, who died aged twenty-nine from severe burns to legs and torso. His eyes were undamaged. I took only one, afraid to change my vision too much at once."

Aurye leaned close, looked again at Magnus's eyes. Her first impression had been correct. The eyes of two different men. "And you?" she asked Reysa. "What else? Your wrist seams. How could a surgeon cut off her own hands?"

"It's not necessary to cut through to bone, though that's what we did with Magnus's legs. My new hands are what you might call a veneer, like most of my changes so far." Reysa gestured to demonstrate the flexibility of her hands, then lifted off the decorative camisole to reveal a patchwork torso. Her flesh was a beautiful puzzle. Not deformity, not feeble grasping for youth's shallow appeal. She was more beautiful than anyone Aurye knew. A sculpture of contrasting parts.

Magnus moved to Reysa's side. "Can you see how I love my wife even more, this way?"

Aurye understood. She'd always thought Reysa striking, at least as conventionally attractive as Aurye herself, but less ordinary, eyes and mouth far more interesting.

Magnus pulled his sweater over his head. He and Reysa stood revealed, proof of their convictions offered in varied surprising details. Thick scars, proportions which might seem wrong at first glance, but which careful appraisal revealed more pleasing, by some perspective of aesthetic judgment Aurye found hard to articulate. She heard it inside her, a voice speaking for the first time. Felt the pull of unorthodox attraction, of weird possibility and strange desire.

What Aurye wondered was, could they do this to her? Fix what was broken, remake her to become more strange, even perversely beautiful? She imagined her future self, someone as yet unknown.

"It's true, we objectify you," Reysa said. "But we've always objectified ourselves, and one another. Everyone."

"So you're not asking me to swap legs?" She laughed, nervous despite the enticement. "Anything like that?"

Magnus answered. "We don't want to consume you."

"Then what?"

"Our plan is long. Eventually, you should finish college, med school. But first, help us broaden our circle."

"You want others?" Aurye tried to assemble pieces of this offer. "Not just me? Who?"

"We don't know. You'll help us find them. You're attractive, likable. You work in a visible spot, the coolest bar on the mountain, with a clientele of active mountain types. Snowboarders, climbers, travelers staying at Timberline."

Aurye nodded.

Magnus continued where Reysa left off. "Young athletic men and women, decadent, pleasure-seeking. Accustomed to living outside the lines. Yes, our ideas are transgressive. They require a certain willingness to step past boundaries, where others stop. For some, life's thrills may have worn thin. They might be receptive to dramatic transformation."

"If we wanted to be promiscuous, we could," Reysa said. "Creative living is all the perversion we need. You know, if a universal maker existed, she'd be the most perverse being imaginable." She shot her husband a look and a wink.

Magnus smirked. "Reysa determinedly postulates this notion of a female creator. I think we need more wine."

"This is a lot to understand," Aurye said. "Explain it to me a different way."

"We want a larger menu," Magnus said.

"Friends," Reysa said. "We'll take from more. Give to more."

"I think I see, and understand." Aurye wanted to sit. All the tension had left her. She felt no more apprehension, no more wondering what the Bergs intended. "Also, I think you're right about more wine."

"I'll go for a bottle." Magnus started for the stairs.

"Bring two," Reysa called. After he was gone, she turned to Aurye. "Do you think he could've carried three?"

Aurye laughed, head still spinning with everything their suggestions entailed. Some aspects seemed shocking, but when she weighed her personal affection for the Bergs, their desire to help her, along with the resources at their disposal, and balanced these against her otherwise dismal options, gravity seemed to draw her inexorably nearer their orbit. They were so vibrant, more engaging and attractive than any couple Aurye knew. Even more so, now that she knew the degree to which they'd become who they were by their own uncompromising efforts. This unorthodox approach formed the core of what kept them energetic, vibrant and youthful in mind and body.

Could this be true, could her own life transform, broken parts be replaced? Everything would be easier without so many limitations. A life of energy and health, clarity of mind, leisure, physical elegance. She loved how the Bergs offset each other, beautiful balanced within themselves and counterpoised against one another. It all felt so seductive.

"So, have we shocked you?" Reysa ventured. "Exceeded your boundaries?"

Aurye considered. The contrary was true, but she hesitated to let them think her too desperately willing, lacking any restraint at all. "I'm afraid actually you'd be shocked, if you knew what I'd give if I could just…" She gestured, but was afraid it came across as nihilistic rejection of everything in life, rather than willingness to obtain something better, and optimism Reysa and Magnus could help. She wasn't sure how to explain her predicament, afraid they might see her differently if they knew everything, could see all her hidden flaws laid bare. But of course they would see, eventually.

"You're tempted," Reysa guessed. "We could take you such places."

Magnus entered with two uncorked bottles. "Away from the humdrum, toward the beautiful strange." He poured.

Reysa lifted her glass. "To possibility."

The three toasted, and drank as though thirsty.

"If it seems strange, my lack of shock at your… surprising suggestions, there are reasons," Aurye ventured. "I think once we hit bottom, and face what seems like the impossibility of going on, if we do come out the other side, it's freeing. So I'm probably open to alternatives most would reject."

"I'm the same," Reysa assured her. "Broken down by trauma. For me, three times. First, as I was leaving for college, my stepfather tried to prevent me. Made threats against my mother, broke my arm, then my nose. When these didn't deter me, he escalated. Emotional, sexual. It nearly broke me, but I left, never returned. Never again considered that place home."

"Horrible," Aurye said.

Magnus kept his eyes on the floor, motionless except to sip from his wine. Reysa continued.

"Next, my first husband, another surgeon, and yes I realize how that sounds, marrying one surgeon after another. He rejected me for a woman less accomplished, less challenging to him, after my accident. He even said, She may not be as hot as you, but at least she's not so fucking familiar. I didn't think I'd make it, but I did. I found Magnus."

"And third?" Aurye couldn't help looking at Magnus, fearing the possibility he may once have harmed Reysa in ways similar to the two prior stories. That seemed impossible, but they were always talking about inevitable betrayal.

"Magnus, but not something he did to me. The lawsuit, seeing the toll it took on him. That devouring fear. Both sleepless, afraid of losing our home, his career, which he believed to be everything. When I saw Magnus break, something in me broke." Reysa looked away, gulped her wine, then seemed to remember she wasn't alone. "I became willing to cross any line, to protect this. The only life I'll ever have."

"You seem very strong to me," Aurye told her. "Both of you."

"Do you understand now?" Magnus asked. "This is how anything becomes possible."

"I'm younger, but I've faced my share," Aurye said. "But to have an ally against the world, willing to do anything to protect me. I want it. I used to believe I'd find a man like that, but it's rare."

"You will," Reysa said.

"How do I know when I have it?" Aurye asked. "I mean, that I've found perfect, faithful devotion, someone willing to die for me, kill for me, and not just another weak, betraying bastard?"

Magnus moved between Aurye and Reysa. "Find someone whose desire to remain close to you doesn't decrease when trouble comes. Who stays closer by your side when you need them."

"That's right." Reysa took Magnus's hand. Aurye could see them squeeze.

Reysa knelt on the bare stone, then sat and lay back. "Lie down. Look up. The clouds are coming again."

Magnus did the same, so Aurye followed suit. The skylight revealed a thin crescent moon against pure black sky.

"Clouds?" Aurye asked. "Are you sure it's—"

She was interrupted by a flash, not so bright and proximate as what had first revealed the storage tanks. Soon, thunder followed, then wispy clouds moved across until the moon was nothing but hidden backlight.

"Tell me again," Aurye said. "Tell me what you want us to do together."

Magnus answered. "We want to widen our circle. To share with others, just one at first, then another. A few more, not many. Wider variety of personhood. That's what we crave."

"If we can't transcend personal death," Reysa said, "we can create an immortality of relationship. Mutual support."

"What do you think of what we've said?" Magnus asked, hesitant. "Maybe we frightened you."

"In all our talks at Midgard, you seemed receptive," Reysa said. "Not to this idea exactly, but our various strange hypotheticals. You always seemed to get it."

"If you want to go home, you can," Magnus said. "We'll consider you a friend, even if—"

"It isn't that you've frightened me," Aurye interrupted.

Reysa rolled over, touched Aurye's arm. "What then?"

"Something troubles you," Magnus said. "You still seem afraid."

"I am afraid. Not of you." Aurye stood. She reached for the lace hem of her dress, lifted it over her head. Still she wore the black fleece tights and white long-sleeved sweater. She lifted the bottom of the sweater, raised it enough to start revealing her bare belly, then hesitated.

"You don't need to—" Reysa stood, approached almost close enough to touch Aurye, but held back.

Magnus sat up, seeming mortified, certain Aurye had misunderstood. "We didn't mean you should have to—"

The glow through the skylight diminished as clouds advanced. Nothing remained of moonlight. Snow swirled, barely visible.

Aurye didn't cover herself. "I understood. I just have to show myself." She stepped back, leaned against the operating table.

"I don't..." Magnus trailed off.

Aurye lifted the under-sweater to reveal her naked torso. A six-inch strip of surgical tape ran vertically up the side of her abdomen, below her left breast. Her hands wanted to cover, but she fought the impulse. Now was time to reveal. Against her will, fingers flitted nearer the wound.

Lightning struck, filled the room with ultimate brightness. For a flash, nothing was hidden. Electricity surged through the strange machinery behind the surgical table. Static popped and invisible power filled the air with a living hum.

"I used to cover it with thick adhesive gauze," Aurye said. "It's something I've gotten better at."

"Wound care?" Reysa asked.

"Concealment. Hiding a wound that will never heal." She pinched the top end of the tape, pulled up, then down. She shuddered as the tape came free. Flaps of skin opened, pulled apart. The wound wasn't bloody, or even wet. It was an open vacancy, not a recent injury. Something had always been missing. "No matter what, people end up seeing."

Magnus stood, came to Reysa's side. Both approached.

"This is me." Aurye expected inquiries about doctors, diagnoses, how parents could have allowed the wound to remain. Why hadn't someone cut out the disease, sewn her shut?

The Bergs said nothing, only regarded Aurye gently, seeming afraid their scrutiny might inflict further damage. The room had become so dark. Aurye could barely see Reysa and Magnus, knew she too must be almost invisible.

Lightning flashed, and for another instant everything was perfect white.

Thunder followed.

"It's rare," Aurye whispered. "Thundersnow."

Reysa knelt, did not touch, but looked unflinchingly at the opening in Aurye's side. It led not into her gut, to some vital inner aspect of her. It led away, like a pit in the ground, vanishing into the dark. Aurye hated it so much. It had always been with her. "It's like your painting," Aurye said. "Prometheus with the giant eagle, devouring."

"If you want to change," Magnus said, "we'll help."

"I've always wanted to," Aurye said, "just didn't believe it."

"You can change yourself as little as you like," Reysa said.

"More." Aurye felt emotion surging. She couldn't let herself cry. "Change as much as I can."

"You don't have to," Reysa cautioned.

"Let me give something back," Aurye suggested. "Something small. First to Reysa, then when I heal, to Magnus."

"Not yet, and don't worry," Reysa said. "We have plenty of donor parts."

"There's always meat," Magnus added lightly. "More than we could ever use."

"What I want is for my body to be always torn apart," Aurye insisted. "Again and again, forever. I might age, but never become old. I'll constantly be something new. Cut apart, and sewn back into some fresh unknown shape."

Reysa touched her shoulder gently. "Dare try, or never know."

Aurye felt it for the first time, believed it was true. Acceptance, the first she could remember. She felt no desire to return home. "To be my new self, I want to give away pieces of the old one."

Magnus nodded. "We have only one life each. One chance."

"So we endlessly role-play, speculate on every possible ending," Reysa said. "Betrayals, murder-suicide pacts, feeble dissolutions. We plan for any eventuality, solve each in advance and thus avoid them all. Along the way, replace parts of ourselves. Someday we'll die, but first we can be entirely new."

"All our work is to ensure this never ends." Magnus gestured not outwardly, around the room, at the grand house or the mountain, but between himself and Reysa. He expanded the gesture to include Aurye.

Clouds thinned, glowing at the moon's insistence, and latent energy carried within atmosphere ozone-rich after penetration by lightning.

"None of this should ever have to end," Aurye said. "None of us."

Lightning flashed again, cut the sky as if in agreement.

POSTPARTUM

BETTY ROCKSTEADY

I kept my eyes on the television while I spooned pablum into Timmy's mouth. The horrors of the daily news were downright cheery in comparison to this dull horror in my lap.

I couldn't stand looking at him. It was his eyes. I had hoped he would have Tim's eyes, piercing and blue. Even mine, green and lazy, would have been preferable. But Timmy's eyes were brown and watery. Even all these months later, I found myself with the same old daydream where the hospital called, frantic to tell me a mistake had been made. A mix-up. The fantasy of relief is addicting. Not bonding with him wouldn't be my fault if he wasn't mine. If he wasn't Tim's.

But the call never came and so I did what I had to do, locked in my wretched little apartment, feeding him and changing him and picking him up when he squalled and putting him to bed when he was tired. He never smiled for me, but I kept one pasted on my face.

It would have been better if Tim were here. He would have found the thread of happiness and tied it together in a bow. But he was gone in a snarl of metal and fire and I was alone in this flat eternity of days.

Timmy whined and pushed the spoon away. A stream of drool dribbled down his chin. I set him back in his crib. Used, just like everything else in the apartment. He whined but didn't cry and the headache that was ever-present behind my eyes pulsed. I slouched back into the hard sofa and rocked his cradle gently with a toe until he quieted. A few precious moments of peace. I closed my eyes but left the volume on, the news speaking to me like a dream.

Sleep retreated to the sound of Mom's car sputtering, making way for more pain. Keys jangled. She never knocked, even though the basement apartment was supposedly mine. But could I really complain? She fed me. Housed me. I didn't have to pay rent or utilities, just had to put up with constant "suggestions" on how I should be living my life. I should clean more. Read more. Paint more. Be more.

If Tim were here, I could stand it. I could have found a way to make this unplanned family my own.

"Hello, my darlings!" Timmy gurgled at the sound of her voice and I stifled a groan.

"He was sleeping."

"All he does is sleep. All you do is sleep." She lifted Timmy from the cradle. "He needs to be changed."

"Change him then."

"I think we all need a change! This place is awful stuffy. Why don't you open the windows once in a while?"

"Because then you'd complain Timmy was going to catch his death of cold."

Silence but for the rustling of diapers. "You're awfully grouchy today."

I rubbed my eyes. Grey light streamed in from the window. A spring from the couch pinched my ass and the familiar smell of shit filled the air as Mom removed Timmy's diaper. The smile never left her face. "I'm sorry." I was. Sort of.

"I'm worried about you. I wish you would get out of the house more. All you do is sit in this stuffy apartment. It's not good for you and it's not good for the baby. I don't mind watching him more, you know."

I tucked my knees into my shirt, curled into a ball. "Where am I supposed to go? I'm not exactly invited to many parties anymore."

"Go for a walk or something. Get some fresh air. You can't sit in here all day every day. Don't look at me like that. I'm taking Timmy upstairs while I make supper. I'll watch him. Get out, walk around the block a couple times, I don't care. Go to the store. I'm sick of you pouting around all day. It's not healthy."

"Ugh."

She scooped Timmy up. His tiny fists pounded on her back, brooding over her shoulder at me. I scowled. Mom left the door cracked open. I stretched out on the couch, closed my eyes again. The breeze that wafted in was cold and carried the scent of the outdoors. I would need to get a blanket if I wanted to sleep. I shifted, the couch uncomfortable beneath me. I sighed and pulled myself up. Fine. I would go for a walk and avoid another lecture.

I washed my face. Applied lip gloss. Smoothed greasy hair back into a ponytail. Who did I have to impress? Sneakers old and ugly but they would do. I laced them up and locked the door behind me.

I'll admit it. The fresh air felt good. The sky was dizzying, clear and grey. Air washed away stale sweat on my neck. As annoying as she could be, Mom was right sometimes. I felt better. Not like life was suddenly worth living or anything, but I felt awake at least.

Tim and I had walked a lot, even after he got his licence, just for something to do. The best conversations we had were hand in hand, pavement beneath our feet. Now walking was something I did alone. And in the opposite direction, away from Tim's place. I didn't want to run into his mother, thank you very much. She always hated me, more so when I got pregnant. I hadn't heard from her since the baby was born. Tim's funeral was excruciating, and the silence that followed even more so.

So I walked away from the city, towards the fields. Mom's house was just on the outskirts of where city turned into farm. Twenty minutes and I would turn around, go back home, back to my mother's encouraging drone of conversation and my baby's lying eyes.

Or maybe I would walk forever. Just keep going and never look back. Wear these sneakers thin, all the way through, and walk until I only had bloody stumps to walk on, never see my fat stupid baby again.

I was fucking trapped. If Tim were alive, he would make me see the good things. He would be almost finished school with by now and he would get a job and we would be in our own little apartment with new things, not stale used furniture passed down from relatives. He would know how to handle Timmy. We could have done it together, instead of just me, cranky and worn thin on no sleep. Sustained on canned soup and Mom's generosity. It would still be hard, yeah, but if we were doing it together it wouldn't have been so bad.

I was approaching the Myette farm. Almost time to turn back before

Mom was out bleating the horn at me, worried I'd been eaten by wolves. I should be so lucky. The grass beyond the farm was tall and snarled. The road beaten and gravelly beneath my feet.

I was just about to turn back when I saw it. The setting sun gleamed against something deep within the grass. I pushed the foliage aside with the toe of my sneaker. Bone. I paused.

Tim's mother had blamed me for his morbid pastime, but it was all his idea. The collection started when he got interested in veterinary school. First it was a cat skeleton, then a dog, and the collection just blossomed from there. He put them together with tools ordered online, spending hours on the perfectly articulated skeletons. He had been talking about getting into taxidermy next when the accident happened.

He would have loved this.

The grass moved aside to reveal more. It was a skull, a few ribbons of flesh still attached. A smile tugged at my mouth when I picked it up. Light as a feather and completely unidentifiable, at least to me. Not a cat. Not a dog. Nothing I had ever seen before. Deep eye sockets peered back at me. Yellowed bone slanted back from the brow at a strange angle. Small horns emerged, chipped at the ends. The whole thing was about the size of two fists. I turned it over in my hands. The fangs were small and sharp, curled into a wicked grin.

Mom wouldn't like it. Not at all. I pushed it into the wide pocket of my sweatshirt and walked home.

It felt good. The heat of the bone warmed my cold hands.

The skull stared at me from atop the television. Timmy stared at me too, perched in my lap, waving fat little hands at my face. I jiggled him and cooed at him and god, why couldn't he just go back to sleep? My shitty laptop wobbled on the TV tray while I scrolled through pages and pages of skull identification. Nothing looked right.

In the moonlight that shone through the window it was iridescent, mother of pearl. It could be a phony, a fake, but I didn't believe that. It felt real. More real than anything else felt. Tim would have loved it.

I plopped Timmy in his playpen and he started to cry, but the sound was far away. I held the skull, stared into those deep eye sockets, turned it over in my hands again. It smelled earthy. It smelled like secrets.

The rough texture softened in my hands. Pliant. My head spun, dizzy, but in a good way.

Timmy never stopped crying. I glanced at him. His face was red and bloated. Tears and snot streamed down his cheeks. Gently I replaced the skull and hefted him in my arms. He clambered awkwardly. He never sat right. He never fit.

I turned back to the computer.

What are you?

Thunder. Rain pounded down, soaking my hair and cheeks. The sky was alive with light and movement. A creature twisted through the air in front of me. A flutter of wings, black as night. It was beautiful. It was mine.

I woke to silence. The skull sat on my bedside table, grinning at me. My cheap nightlight illuminated soft curves and strange angles. The veil of sleep fell away. I had an idea. I moved quickly but quietly. Timmy was in the next room, all too easy to wake.

I opened the closet.

Everything smelled like Tim. My shrine to him. Tribute to love lost. Usually opening the closet made my knees weak and my eyes fill but it was the bottom box I was after this time. I never bothered with that one before. It was his, not ours.

But now it was mine.

The boxes were dusty and collapsed and oh god, had it really been that long? Timmy was almost a year old and that meant Tim had been gone for a year and a half. It could make you sick, the way time still ticks by. I could have sworn I needed him to live and yet here I was, still alive, without him.

Never mind. Shift boxes out of the way. Timmy gurgled through the walls and I stopped, held perfectly still. *Please don't wake up.* Not the first time I've had that thought. How sick of a person does that make me?

This time he quieted and I moved the boxes again. So slow. And yes, the box I wanted was here. Dusty, a few pieces broken, but mostly intact. I pulled out the bony remains of a cat. A small dog. A pig. Part of Tim's collection that he had left here. Even his little toolkit was buried at the bottom. I plunged my hands into dust and dirt and death. Mom kept telling me I needed a hobby. Maybe she was right.

***

It was like putting together a puzzle. I sat on the floor next to Timmy. I put on the shows he liked and disarticulated bones. He kept reaching for my tools and I shoved the playpen closer to the TV. Puppets and cartoons shrieked songs at him and he giggled and snorted and shat his pants.

I felt better than I had in ages. I kept the computer nearby so I could look up what I needed as I went, but most of it came naturally. The bones slotted themselves together. Not in a way that made sense, but in a way that felt right, deep in my gut. Tiny sharp teeth smiled.

Tim would have thought this was so cool. He had shown me cryptotaxidermy stuff online once, imaginary creatures made from the dead parts of real ones. A little gross, but his enthusiasm was contagious. He would love this. Building a new creature from the inside out, bones and all.

They jumbled together in the cardboard box, cat and dog and pig and it didn't matter anymore. I attached a few together at a time and placed them aside to dig for more. Old bones transformed into something new. It was sort of like the way I used to paint, back when I cared about painting. Intuitively. No. Instinctively, that was closer to it.

These were Tim's bones. We were creating something together.

Timmy shrieked and I looked up from my work. He had his diaper half off and his hands were covered in shit and was there ever a time I didn't do everything through tears?

I cleaned him up and put my things away. Mom would be home soon.

I worked on it, whatever it was, for nearly a week. Days and nights, every chance I got. Slotting together bones as the skull watched. Its grin urged me on. It liked the body I was making it. Of course it did.

Mom was so encouraged by that one walk I took. She kept talking about it all week. She was just dying for me to go out again. Instead, I told her I was painting—no, you can't look yet, it's not finished—and that was good enough for her. She even watched Timmy some evenings to give me more time.

It came together beautifully.

The spine was incredibly long, twisting back and forth like a helix. One ribcage sat inside another, each rib sharpened to a point. The legs were many-jointed and centipede-like. Small shoulders, wide hips. A tail extended like a whip.

It was an atrocity and it was mine.

I finished late one night with Timmy snoring gently beside me. All that was left was to screw the head to the body and I did it with a flourish, my tired eyes curling into a smile. But when I stood back to admire what I had created, again with the tears.

It was so fucking disappointing.

What had I expected? Fulfillment? That was a laugh. I could throw up. All these long hours and just more let down. How could this make anything better? It was beautiful but it was nothing. Just a fucked up skeleton with no one to show.

I let Timmy sleep in his playpen and collapsed on the couch. I just needed sleep. Forever. I sank into blackness and the skull ground its teeth, making small sounds that whispered into my ears.

I woke up and knew it wasn't over.

I hadn't failed.

I just wasn't done.

"Of course, I'd love to watch Timmy for a few hours! And you're getting out for a walk, that's terrific!" Mom shifted Timmy onto her hip. He spat up green. "Are you finished with the painting you were working on?"

"Not quite, I just figured, you know. Fresh air for inspiration."

"I think that's a terrific idea. Take as long as you need."

I took a different fork in the road this time, how experimental, how inspiring. Towards the highway. My backpack was light but I hoped it would grow heavier. I didn't want to think through what I was doing. I just wanted to do it, wanted to keep moving forward.

Cars sped by. I clung to the side of the road, hurried forward when I saw what I was looking for. I slipped gloves from my pockets. Just a squirrel, but you never knew what you might need. The body was flat and stiff. I moved quick, back to the road, eyes averted.

I knew it was gross. I knew how weird I looked. But people did this all the time. I saw it online. Taxidermy is a thing. I wasn't doing anything wrong.

I unshouldered my backpack. The metal spatula helped. I peeled it off the pavement in almost one piece. I packed the corpse into a garbage bag and pushed it deep into my backpack. I kept moving. My cheeks were burning but I felt good. I was on a mission.

I needed a lot more than one squirrel if I was going to make this work. I filled my backpack bit by bit until the sun set red and I headed home.

I stuffed the ruined bodies deep in my freezer, wedged in next to cheap frozen pizzas and a freezer-burned chicken I had completely forgotten about. Mom had probably heard me get home, but I stank of sweat and death. Rivulets of gore dripped down my sweatpants. Death is messy, but hey, so is life. I tossed the clothes in the hamper and ran the shower.

The hot water was incredible. I never took long showers anymore. The water beat down on me, so much like the rainstorm in my dream. My heart was swollen and achy in my chest.

My idea was fucking crazy and I couldn't wait to do it. I still had to go through the routine, the wretched endless routine of life, get Timmy from Mom, make polite conversation and while away the minutes while Timmy slobbered and burped and spit up all over everything nice I had ever owned.

But at least I had something to look forward to.

Before I put Timmy to bed, I set the raccoon in the tub. I wanted it at room temperature before I got started.

Things got overwhelming and messy really quick.

I waited until Timmy was asleep before I got started. It's not like he would have known what I was up to, but I needed time and space to concentrate. I spent hours poring over taxidermy instructions online. The pictures were awful, but they didn't prepare me for what I was getting into. Nothing ever did, did it? The baby books didn't give me a hint of how I was going to feel either. Nor did the comforting words of other young mothers assuring me how natural it was all going to come. None of it was true.

Only death was true and I felt like I could make something beautiful and strange out of it. Something special. The beast flew in my mind's eye while I set things up in the bathroom. I left the door open a crack in case Timmy decided he was hungry or wet or just felt like crying for a while.

I pulled on the same filthy sweatpants from the afternoon, why the hell not, and rubber gloves up to my elbows.

I didn't think it would be too bad. I was never a big animal lover. There are so many farms around here. Animals lived to work and to be eaten, not to be loved.

I thought I could be brutal.

The raccoon's mouth flopped open. His gut had been run flat by a car and it stank. I applied cinnamon lip gloss under my nose. Even with all the instructions I read, I was mostly winging it. I knew I was going to mess up, but that didn't matter. I didn't need the whole body. It didn't even need to be that fresh. I was making something different here. Just for myself. It wasn't going to be in a taxidermy contest for Christ's sake, so it could be a bit messy. There was no way to create the thing I dreamed of without being a bit messy.

I slit flesh away from muscle and I only gagged a little bit. I worked gloved fingers beneath the skin to pull it apart and separate it. See, not so bad. His eyes stared up at me, glassy. Ticked fur was coarse even through the gloves.

It wasn't until I had made most of the cuts and tried to pull the hide away from the body that I got sick. I yanked the skin away and revealed the small meaty animal beneath and gagged, my guts twisting. My sharp knife slipped and expanded the hole in the abdomen. Black blood gushed out, reeking of death and I turned just in time to vomit into the toilet. The mess of my gloves smeared on the seat. I threw up again.

Timmy started crying and I brushed tears from my cheeks with my forearm. I was weak and sick and awful and I was crazy, absolutely crazy to be doing this. No wonder I was doing it in the dead of night, I was insane. No one would be this insane in daylight. I ripped the gloves from my hands. I couldn't look in the bathtub again. The pelt dripped blood onto my floor. Lunacy swirled around me.

Dear god, my freezer was filled with dead animals.

Timmy cried louder and my guts heaved again. I couldn't deal with this right now. I would clean it up tomorrow and I would get my shit together. This was not right. This was not healthy.

I swaddled Timmy in a blanket, keeping his fresh clothes away from the gore on my sweatpants. I fed him and his dull eyes blinked at me. It was hard to believe there was a human buried in there. He shifted in my arms and I struggled to hold him steady.

Everything was terrible.

I turned my weary eyes toward the table. The skull of an impossible creature stared back at me.

Why was I so weak?

Its eyes were dark. Endless.

I wasn't the first person to get a little sick on their first try at taxidermy. So things got a little weird. Did that mean I had to give up? I knew I could make something really cool here. I just had to keep going. So what if it got messy? That skull... that skeleton. It was only half a project. It belonged inside of something. I could take my time and piece it together. What the fuck else was I going to do?

I put Timmy back to bed. I brought the skeleton into the bathroom with me. To inspire me. To watch me work.

It got easier after that.

Mom sniffed. Her forehead wrinkled as she surveyed the living room. "What is that smell?"

"Nothing."

"It smells like something died in here. It's not healthy for Timmy. You're throwing the garbage out on time, aren't you?"

"God, I had an issue with the toilet yesterday. Are you happy? I had to plunge it out and clean it all up. I febreezed the shit out of it, sorry, I'm sure it'll clear up in a day or two."

"I'll take Timmy upstairs for the evening. Why don't you open some windows and air things out down here?"

"I think that's an excellent idea."

It had taken me a day to get all the animals skinned. Disfigured pelts hung haphazard in my closet, hidden behind winter coats. Because of their messy deaths, I had only kept bits and pieces of each. But there was enough now to stitch together. The creature came to me in my dreams almost every night.

I was on the right track. I couldn't possibly be recreating something that had actually existed, but in some primeval part of my soul, it felt like it had. It didn't matter. It existed now. Sort of. And it was mine.

Mom took Timmy and he babbled on his way out the door and my gratitude was overwhelming, a physical force that made me lighter, like I was floating. I reached into the depths of my closet and spread the pelts out on my bedroom floor. No one would be fooled that this had been done professionally, but they were good. Good enough. They would do.

I stashed what was left of the bodies in my freezer, deep in the bottom beneath that freezer-burned chicken. Strange naked animals. I didn't know how to get rid of them. I got better with the last few I skinned, leaving their bodies nearly intact. Some of the first ones weren't much more than a bag of guts and entrails. At least when they were frozen they didn't smell. Much.

I was no seamstress, but the pattern assembled itself in my mind. Pieces stitched themselves together, layers of flesh and fur and feeling. The skeleton was all jutting angles in front of me. I drew. I arranged. I thought and rethought. I paced. The mania of creation overtook me.

Sometimes I forgot myself, found myself bent in front of the skeleton, just staring.

Hours passed in a dizzy haze. I referenced things online occasionally, but most of it came from somewhere deep within my head. Within my soul.

That night, I started to sew.

This part took longer. I pricked my thumb against the needle, bled on my floor again and again. I struggled with the sizing but I pushed forward inch by inch. My pelts were amateur, but this part wasn't. Raccoon blended to squirrel blended to bird blended to cat magically, tail and hoof and beak.

It was all coming together. After days of late-night revisions, dark circles bloomed under my eyes. My heart throbbed and burst from my chest. I got closer.

Days? Weeks? Later, I draped empty skin around the skeletal figure, inch by sacred inch, dressing it in the finest I could make. It fit perfectly and somewhere in the distance, Timmy cried.

I knelt in front of it, waiting.

Why didn't I feel anything?

I had done everything right and I was ready to tear it apart. It *wasn't* right. I didn't know how to make it right. It was still empty.

Timmy and I cried together.

I groaned when the sun peeked into my room, hugged my filthy pillow to my chest. I wasn't ready to face another day. My creature hung back in the closet and rotted slowly away. Timmy would be awake any moment, ready for breakfast, and day after day of the same thing stretched endlessly ahead.

I couldn't live like this. I wouldn't. I opened the window and air streamed in, lifted tufts of fur from places I had missed in my sweeping. They floated lazy in the air.

Maybe I just hadn't looked hard enough. There was more. There was a piece I was missing. I had to go back to where I had found it. I had to walk. Think. Feel.

I fed Timmy quickly. He burped up a thick paste and I wiped it from his chin, brought him to Mom.

"I have to get groceries," she said, doubtfully, balancing Timmy in her arms. He grabbed at her nose. "Are you going to be gone long?"

"I just need half an hour. I'm trying to get out more. I thought that was what you wanted? You have all day to get groceries. I'll be back soon."

I couldn't remember where the skull had been, not exactly. Somewhere past the Myette farm. I kicked through the grass with my feet, paced back and forth, over and over. The sun got hotter as the day droned on. I found nothing but dirt on my shoes, a new tear in my jogging pants. Fuck. My sweater was too warm and I was clammy beneath it. There was nothing here.

There was nothing for me anywhere. I walked back and something fluttered in the bushes. Small pained sounds. A flash of feathers.

A crow had injured itself, razor wire wrapped around its foot. It hobbled towards me, bleeding and disoriented. It was the wings that caught my attention. Fierce and black and oily. It must have been badly hurt, because it didn't take flight as I approached. Maybe Tim would have nursed it back to health, but I wasn't Tim.

"Here birdy, birdy." I crouched down. It cawed but didn't take off, just limped away. I shuffled forward and stroked its back, felt greasy feathers beneath my fingers. It sent a spark of electricity through me. I had found what I was looking for. The last piece of the puzzle.

I made it quick.

His head broke like a grape beneath my sneaker. A squelch and a pop and a burst of blood. I was used to blood by now.

I stuffed the broken body into my backpack, lingering over the wings, careful not to tear them. I stood up. Mrs. Myette was standing in her yard, staring at me. Her face was pale. I met her eyes briefly before I turned home.

Timmy slept as I sewed. The phone rang upstairs, a million miles away. I felt it pulsing within me. Something was ready to change.

I didn't hear Mom come down the stairs until the key jingled in the lock.

She never knocked. Fuck. I could move fast when I needed to. My creation was light in my arms. Bits and pieces of sewing tumbled to the floor. Nothing incriminating, I hoped. I shoved the creature into my room and pulled the door shut as Mom walked in, eyes searching.

"What are you doing?"

"Is it too much to ask for a little privacy? Why don't you ever knock? Jesus, I could be naked in here or something."

She looked at the bits of fur on the floor. Needles and scissors and strange sharp things, not far from Timmy's reach. Not like he had any interest in anything other than the blobs of screaming color on the television.

"I thought you were painting? What are you working on down here?"

"I am painting. I ripped something. I was just doing some repairs, if you must know. I didn't realize I was required to paint all the time." I swept up the supplies with an arm and shoved them into my sewing bag, out of sight.

Mom hefted Timmy out of his playpen. His eyes lolled in his head.

"He's fine, Mom. He can't reach it. I was watching him."

She held him, not quite looking at me. "How was your walk this morning?"

"Fine."

"Where did you go? You were gone a long time."

"I was just walking. I don't know. Trying to get some exercise. Get some fresh air. God, you nag me when I don't go out and nag me when I do. I can't win."

"Mrs. Myette just called."

My heart was thick and coppery in my throat. Nosy bitch. "Okay."

"She said she saw you today. In front of her yard."

"What a fascinating conversation that must have been."

I forced myself to meet her eyes. Her mouth twitched. "Are you feeling okay, sweetie? Really, truly okay?"

"I'm fine. What's the big problem? I'm not allowed to walk by the farm anymore? I'll make sure to walk into town next time."

"She said she saw you kill a bird."

My breath came out in a huff of air. "That's fucking ridiculous. What, do you think I'm a fucking sociopath or something?" I watched the way she held Timmy. "Are you people insane? Why would she say that?"

"I'm just worried. I want to know what's going on with you." Her eyes watered. Brown and stupid. That's where Timmy got it from. Mine after all. I had my dad's eyes but Timmy had my mom's.

I sat down. "I'm fine. I'm just... I'm just tired all the time and sad and shitty but I didn't kill a bird. I just like to walk. And think about Tim." My eyes watered but that wasn't part of the lie. I felt like shit. All the time. Maybe I was distracting myself with some insane taxidermy thing that I didn't feel like I could talk about with her, with anyone, but it would all be over soon and I just wanted to be left alone.

"Maybe you should talk to that counselor again. I could call for you."

I sighed. I didn't want to argue anymore. I didn't want to listen to her. I just wanted this conversation to be over so I could finish sewing. "Sure, Mom. Let's call her tomorrow. That's fine."

Mental health services are pathetic around here. The appointment wasn't for two months, but at least Mom was comforted by my willingness to go. That was the most important part.

It was so close now. The bones were right. The fur and feathers and wings were right. But it was still empty. I wasn't frustrated anymore, though. I felt capable of seeing this all the way through.

I woke from a dream of the rainstorm and dug through the freezer, searching. I knew the next step. I knew how to finish it.

But before the meat unthawed, I realized it wouldn't work. The flesh I had was falling apart. Dead for too long. I opened the closet where my creation hid.

It was so beautiful. Cryptic messages spelled out in snatches of fur. I stroked its back. Within this flesh, bones that Tim had painstakingly collected and I had repurposed into something mine and mine alone. The love that flowed through my body was pure. It needed to be finished. How could I back away now?

Timmy was sound asleep. I was wide awake, nerves jumping, energy pulsing through me. Outside, the sky crackled with electricity.

I walked into the night. Alone. I took my backpack. I took my baseball bat.

There are a lot of trusting strays in my neighborhood. Everyone feeds them but no one owns them, not really. Cats and dogs that come and go. They would be missed, but not much. They fell with a thud, their bodies fresh and clean.

I came home tired and bruised and dripping. Timmy was crying but I had what I needed. I fed him while I planned.

Wide loops of thread to hold meat and organs together. I stuffed it full. I kept going. Days passed and it rotted slowly in my closet, leaking viscera and something strange and black and stinking. I knew it was crazy, but it was electric and right and real and beneath snatches of fur, the skull looked out and grinned.

Mom knocked. She had to. I finally installed a chain and she could only open the door a crack. I peered out at her. "I'm not feeling great, can this wait?"

"I brought you a flashlight. There's a storm coming, I don't want you guys to be stuck in the dark," She tried to push the door open, but I wasn't budging. "There's that smell again. Are you taking your garbage out?"

"I don't smell anything. Must be Timmy's diapers. Babies stink. Don't worry about it."

"Can I come in and have a look around? I'm sure you must have left something out, I can smell it all the way upstairs."

I took the flashlight and pushed the door closed. "Leave me alone. I have a headache. We can talk tomorrow. You can clean the whole apartment if you want. Just leave me alone for now."

I was always working but it never felt finished. I stuffed new flesh on top of the old. I filled it with organs and fat and meat and I was so close. It was not just a creature anymore, it was nearly a god. Beneath the rot there was the scent of something ancient and true. I could see constellations in the darkness of its eyes. The wings curved out, sharp and dangerous. The fur was a menagerie of insanity, but it fit like a glove around the double ribcage and the other secrets that lie within.

The great god of my insanity, etched from leftovers and death. But it still wasn't finished. It didn't have that final touch. Not yet a god; but built in the image of one.

The storm was coming. I could feel it beneath my skin. The sky darkened and the rain began. My heart beat out an excited cacophony. Timmy cried at each crack of thunder and I rocked him gently, humming a song I've never heard.

Midnight approached. My closet couldn't contain it anymore. I took my creation into the backyard, my son wrapped in a blanket in the crook of my arm. The moon was huge, a thumbprint in the sky. The rain soaked me through, so cold my teeth chattered. The rain beat against the creature and I was so close.

I wanted it to fly and I knew what was missing.

The empty eyes looked at me. The fur was plastered down, nearly ruined, but the wings were strong and ready. Yes, I knew what was missing.

Life.

I pulled the blanket away. Timmy did not cry until the rain hit his face. I promise, I was quick. As quick as I could be. Everything else came from the dead but the most important part needed to be fresh, full of blood and life.

This moment was sacred. I placed Timmy on the ground and leaned over him, protecting him from the rain.

My knife was sharp. I poised it just over his sternum and it slid through his skin like butter. I thought he would cry harder then, but he just made a strange strangled sound. I was experienced now. With my expert hands, I snapped ribs like twigs and carved out his heart. The life slid from his eyes so quickly and quietly that I didn't see him go. There was no time to waste.

His heart was smaller than I thought it would be. The tiny vital organ still pumped in the palm of my hand. I reached beneath fur and into rotting meat and slipped it deep inside. The blood pumped and flowed and the rain pounded down, so hard and fast I couldn't tell if I was crying.

Stiff bones stretched. The fur turned warm and soft in my hands. There was a creaking of bones as the tail twitched. Joy rushed into my heart, the joy I had been told so many times about. The true joy of motherhood. The wings fluttered.

My creature, my new god, turned to me with a mouthful of razor teeth. A grin, but not a happy one. Not for my benefit. Fear and pride and something else mingled together in my stomach and I grew cold.

Deep in the blackness of its eyes there was a green like my own. Not even a hint of Tim's blue. It was all me.

Powerful wings flapped and it lifted into the air. There was one perfect moment, just one, as it was highlighted against the sky. Lightening crackled. It was just as I had imagined. It was perfect and it was exhilarating and it was all completely wrong. Its mouth opened wide, too wide and thunder roared and I screamed.

And then it was gone.

My knees were weak. I was soaked and frozen and I don't know how I felt.

"What are you doing outside?" Mom's voice was shrill, panicked. I didn't look at her. I looked down. Even in the rain, my hands were covered with blood. Water pooled in the hollows of my son's eyes. His jaw was slack and relaxed and for the first time, I saw how much he looked like his father.

LIVING

SCOTT R JONES

The room is warm enough, but there is a severity to the sparse furnishings, and the migraine whiteness of the storm outside that lights the space is not comforting. Five men sit before the glass and rest tired, unfocused eyes on the featureless weather. They rub their necks, fiddle with their cuffs. Throats are cleared. Drinks are brought in, ice is offered.

"Christ, no. Neat," says the one in the middle, and the others to his left and right follow suit.

"Forty-two below and she wants to know if I'd like ice. Goddamn security protocols are going to be the death of me, boys."

The glass flickers, fogs, becomes a viewscreen displaying a logo. *Eidolon.* A voice slides into the room, startling no one.

"Gentlemen. Mr. Tusk. Good afternoon. Welcome to Melville Station."

There are murmurs in reply.

"Get on with it."

"Of course, Mr. Tusk."

The logo fades and an image fills the screen. A young woman with close-cropped dark hair sits on a metal chair in an empty, grey room. Her arms hang by her sides, her feet are planted squarely in front of her, her mouth hangs slightly open and ajar, caught in mid-sentence.

"You'll recall the asset that went missing four months ago."

The man to Tusk's left leans in. "Aldo. This about that clusterfuck in Prague?" Tusk waves him away, irritated.

"We were able to track it for a time and sent two recovery teams in. Once in Reims, and again in Liverpool. Both teams lost. After Liverpool, the asset somehow managed to destroy our ability to track it via its implants and went to ground. And, for the obvious reasons, it's impossible to pick up heat from it. So, we were left with video and internet surveillance and eyes on the ground."

"Wait, what *reasons*?" says the man to Tusk's left. "No heat signature?"

"Christ, Griffin! This was all in the briefing on the loop up here," growls the man on the far right. "It's not alive, technically. A weapon. It's got no rights, no humanit—… Look, why are we here? Can you at least tell us that?"

"An Eidolon facility in Toronto was hacked early this morning," the voice continues. "A professional job, by all accounts, untraceable, but done in such a way as to be instantly flagged. Which caused some concern, as no damage was done."

"A warning shot."

"The infosec people certainly thought so. And then the video you're about to see was found."

Aldo Tusk nods once, and the woman on the screen comes alive.

I'm going to show you some things. Talk about my life a little, such as it is. I'm not sure I'd call it living. I've been told that my voice is too monotone, despite the speech therapy, and if you want someone to blame for that, well, blame yourself, Mr. Tusk. Blame Eidolon. I have what your techs call a "denatured personality matrix" and they should know, since they gave it to me. You gave me this emptiness. This emotive lack.

Don't be fooled, though, if my presentation is a little dry.

Anyway.

The first time was in the Kushan Pass. I don't remember much of it, but what I do is clear and bright. A memory in my flesh, my motley cells.

I remember the bite of dry, chill air in my lungs. Red dust clouds lazy in the rearview below a pallid Afghan sky. Tart chemical taste of a Starburst in my mouth. Pleasant, familiar reek of sweat and soured adrenaline and boredom and gun oil. Dull glint of sallow winter sun off the hood of the APC as we rolled through like we'd rolled through fifty times, a hundred times before.

The IED did what IEDs do. Any other day, we would have picked it up on the scanners from three clicks away, but the NACT fighters in the area had just been gifted with crunchy new cognitive scramblers from their friends in China. Our machines worked fine; it was our own frontal lobes that misinterpreted the data, as angels on high or birdsong or anything but the warning ping. I learned all this later from a stone-faced Eidolon suit, in the moments before he told me what they'd done.

I don't remember the actual *moment* of that first time. I'm not sure anyone does, monster or not. The true remembering came later. But the first time? The details I've got, sure, the sensations leading up to that moment. The sun rose from the earth below us, a ball of force and fire that eradicated all sound and feeling, all thought and sight. In light. The taste of that Starburst still in my mouth. In light and fury, I died. I don't remember the dying, though.

Not the first time.

I was O'Halloran and Kaminsky and Patel, and the driver of the APC, whose name was Gorman. The suit told me it was only her second tour since onboarding with Eidolon's Risk Management branch. Risks. They're what you take when you join the Circuit, but you know that going in, and the crazy money helps.

I'm mostly O'Halloran and Patel, now. The somatic functions, anyway. Hindbrain response. Instinct and reflexes. The suits and techs say that's the important stuff. The *mission-critical* aspects of what I am. The rest of me is whatever was left of Gorman. Probably some vat-grown replacement organs in there, too. And your famous nanomesh, Tusk. The miracle that knits it all together, boosts my speed, intelligence, senses. I think with my whole self now. A tech once tried to tell me I had "more processing power in my left pinkie than…" but he trailed off, mumbling, unable to complete the sentence, or unwilling. It's possible he was trying to be funny. I have trouble picking up on things like that.

Did you know O'Halloran was funny? I've read up on all of them, every file. Patel took too many chances. Kaminsky was a brute, Gorman a poet. An actual poet, "warrior-poet" the reviews said, published and everything; you should read her, she's good. So why do I get her skills and none of O'Halloran's humor? The pinkie-tech didn't know either.

Anyway. The mesh. It's always there, but when Eidolon sent me to the desert, or the jungle, anywhere hot, that's when I could really feel the stuff, like a deep ocean current flowing just below the skin, chill scaffolding biting through into my borrowed bones. Fault lines of frozen tissue where the continents of me meet, pulsing beneath my fingertips as I trace them. Gorman, see? The mesh has to be super-cooled to stay efficient, so I don't eat anymore. That space was better suited for the cooling plant.

Hunger stayed with me, though.

They thought I was a failure, at first. An early experiment, a toe dipped into strange new water. They made me because they could, to see what would happen. Three years and change in an induced coma, with the occasional surfacing into consciousness to run fresh suites of behavioral protocols or flush out the previous hormone therapy. I slept on an Eidolon slab for three years and woke screaming every time they delivered the jolt that meant some new small eternity of torture. I wouldn't stop. The screaming. They'd gag me, while they worked, but it would still come, from below, from outside myself, a sound from the other side of where I was living. I was a conduit for it. I'd scream until they put me back under, into the dark. Back into that place, to wait mindless for the next awakening.

But then they went and got it right. The mix, the codes, the mesh, the flesh. They got it right, and I woke and was silent, mercifully, but my dull eyes signaled failure, my slack lips and hanging jaw spoke to them only of a return to their drawing boards, their amniotic vats and modeling frames. I had no speech, no coordination, the cognitive function of a tapeworm. I was cycled out into rehabilitation, taught to walk and eat again, and watched, always watched, though I didn't know that. I didn't know anything, not for a long time. And when it became clear that I was improving, getting stronger and smarter, that I was perhaps less a failure than originally thought, that I *could* know things again, I only knew what they told me.

Then, I knew only missions. I knew them like familiar dreams.

I was given weapons and intelligence and operation parameters, and sent places. Walked in to jungles and cities and deserts. Dropped from the sky. Swam seas, tireless and unstoppable. I was sent to learn things and destroy things, which amounted to the same thing, to me. I was sent to bring back people or end people. Also the same thing.

With what they had learned and were still learning from me, the techs and their superiors often didn't even need a whole person to interrogate, and soon I was bringing back just the bits they needed. The head of a militant NACT cell here, the torso and spinal cord of a Colombian cartel lord there. Only the eyes and genitals of the male members of a fundamentalist militia gone to ground in the hills above Moab, Utah, please. My implacable harvest, carried out in uncomprehending silence. Brutal, efficient, and swift. It got weird and weirder, but I never questioned.

And I never forgot. Anything. The nanomesh would hum and pulse and drink in all my experience, feed it back to me in an endless cascade of constantly improving algorithms. I'd complete a mission and a copy of the data would fly from me, bounce off vantablack satellites to paste itself in the mainframes of secret rooms and airtight bunkers. If only they'd just cut it from me. They cut everything else out; why not that?

I could live through a mission, and did, many times. Or die completing one, again, many more times. No difference. No break. No dark place to rest in, thoughtless, empty. Each reanimation would clear out the doubts, sure, but I filled up with high-definition fire and fury, and I never, ever, forgot the deaths. Of others. My own. Never. It's all up here, still. Murder in my left pinkie, suicide in my right.

I stopped dying, eventually. Got so good I couldn't be killed, but I never forgot, and I never questioned.

And then I did, because that's the kind of thing that builds up in a living thing, no matter how you try to wipe it clean. I did question, all at once, and completely, every part of me rebelling and quaking with the rejection of what they'd made me. I'm sure you got a memo on *that* one, Tusk. Blank and slick as ever, unable to express anything of what I felt—that denatured personality matrix doing its flattening work—I nevertheless became very sick, subconsciously rotting myself from the inside out. I was *becoming* myself, moving beyond their requirements into a more pure torment. I was choosing to die, *willing* myself to break apart, to split and cease.

I was quick. I'd removed both of my legs, clawed them to unusable pulp and bone splinters by the time they stopped me. The blue-black coils of my cooling plant spilling out onto the tile where the EMP grenade landed.

That did the job, and then they did theirs, in less time than before. The coma lasted only a month and when they woke me I was already on the plane to Prague, en route to the next mission. Prague is where I learned about the wire they'd slipped into my brain, the wire that triggered firestorms of intense sexual pleasure when I killed.

It felt so right. But it wasn't. How could it be?

I know, I know. Look who I'm talking to. You made me, Tusk, so I think I can speak to your moral sense with some authority. My best guess is your techs thought it would act as a control. That I'd want to do the work, if it meant I would come like that every time. Marry me to Death, deep down in the core of what I am, and let the good times roll with the heads.

They couldn't have been more wrong. So wrong. I knew I was an abomination from the first time they woke me from my slab, and on some level, I was all right with it, because I was alive, but after that? After the wire. They may as well have tried to build me a lover to sate myself with, for all the control it gave them.

Prague is where I decided to escape. Prague is where I decided to come for you, Tusk.

Let me show you a new trick.

I've been working with some clever kids, since I went into hiding. They laugh at proprietary tech and piss all over your firewalls. I found them, here on the darknet, and showed them what I was, what was in me. *If the mesh is my flesh,* I said, *and it is, then give it to me. Help me be all the Death I can be.*

Death is like that IED, I've learned. It comes from below, from the place you can't see. But of course, you'd *see* me coming. So I had the kids strip your tracking tech from me, and, once that was done, they gave me my body back, piece by piece.

Watch.

"What is that?" Tusk leans forward in his chair. "What are we looking at here?"

"Sir. Our initial thinking was that the image was manipulated from this point on…"

"Is it?"

"No. This is in real time. Undoctored and raw."

"So, this is a… thing. This is within her … she can *do* this now?"

"It can. Yes."

I can be anyone.

The clever kids learned how your mesh worked, encouraged it to spread. It doesn't just knit me together anymore. It lives through me, breathes. Dances across my skin, swims in my sweat. It's hard, and I've yet to perfect it, but a thought and an image is all it takes to give me a new face. Or an older one. Here's Patel, or something like what Patel was.

Kaminsky.

O'Halloran.

I prefer Gorman. I'm used to her, feel comfortable in her. Here she is again.

But Tusk, know this: I'll be neither of them when I'm at your throat, finally. In the street. On one of your private islands. An executive washroom in the sky. Where can you hide where you'll see me coming? I've practiced on a few of the techs who worked on me, the ones I decided to find, anyway. The rest think they're hiding. Like you.

And if you do find the place where you *can* hide, where you *can* see me coming, reduce me to meat and sparks from a distance, well then, I welcome that, too.

Because you won't dare try to bring me back after this.

The kids weren't able to do anything about the wire. It's too deep. I'm a little grateful for that, maybe. It's hard to tell how I feel. So hard to know what *feeling* is, but I'll tell you this for free: when I think about you, I get wet. I do, and it's not condensation from my cooling plant. I check. You're not even dead yet, but I'm wet all the same.

So, I'll come for the last time, with my hands around your throat. That's living, for me. And dying, finally. Same thing.

After that, I won't remember.

The men sit in silence. The screen fades away, the hiss of ice crystals whipping the glass clearly audible. Drinks are emptied quickly. Throats are cleared.

"Jesus. What latitude are we at again?" says Griffin. "75 degrees? Something like that?"

Fingers tented before his eyes, Tusk says nothing, gazes across the open tundra. The storm passes, and there is nothing to see but drifting snow and cold stone to the horizon. Beyond that, he knows, there is the sea ice and then more frozen ground. More waste. He imagines his fingers as cross-hairs, thinks about a figure in the distance, emerging from that howling whiteness, its hands by its sides.

"Aldo. Aldo, Jesus, are we just…"

Tusk raises a hand sharply.

"Yes. Until it's done."

The light in the severe room fades as the night descends. The dark is even less comforting.

THEY CALL ME MONSTER

TIFFANY SCANDAL

My parents told me we were constantly moving for opportunity—a better job, a better home, a nicer neighborhood… but I can't help thinking it's because of me. Another year, another school, and eventually the bullying will get so bad, it'll get harder to keep going. They never wanted to homeschool me. They didn't want me to turn out one of those "weird kids." Whatever that means.

On my sixth birthday, I woke up in a bed that wasn't mine. I felt sore, but there was cake. My parents told me to make a wish, so I blew out the candles, hoping for a pony. I had trouble breathing. It took some effort, but I managed to eat half a slice before I felt too tired. "Get some rest," Father said.

When I returned to school later that year, my classmates asked if I was okay. They'd heard I was in an accident. I didn't know what they meant by that. I felt fine, so I must've been fine. Mother ended up winning some huge award, but I never understood what it was for. Then it started.

I was playing on the jungle gym. Hanging upside down from the bars, I tried to imagine a world where the ground was the sky and everyone did everything backwards. I could feel the breeze on my exposed back. It was welcome on a warm day like this.

"Eww. What's that?" said a girl passing behind me.

I couldn't quite see her the way I was hanging. I craned my head more. My shirt had come untucked.

"What's wrong with you?" Monique V., the prettiest girl in class, her mouth open, hand pointed at my stomach. She always dressed nice and had the coolest lunch boxes. Everyone wanted to be her friend, including me.

I lost my grip and fell and landed on my back on the ground and coughed at the dust. I sat up and looked at my belly. The pinkish-red raised scar that traced parabolic across my belly. I followed the scar with a fingertip… the sound of screeching tires, a quick flash of steel, the smell of heated rubber… I said I didn't remember how I got it.

Monique got closer to see my scar and looked disgusted. She said it was ugly and ran away. I saw her catch up to some of the other pretty girls from class. She pointed at me and talked to them, and they all came running toward me. They told me to pull up my shirt. It didn't sound like a question, I didn't feel like I could say no. So I pulled up my shirt. I felt one of them touch my scar and flinch.

"That's so gross," I heard one of them say. Then the bell rang and they took off. I thought it was fine, but by the end of the day, the school was calling me Worm Girl because of the shape of the scar. And the more it came up, the more other kids wanted to see my scars. The more they wanted to see my scars, the more I was teased. The more I was teased, the more I found myself sitting alone. No one wanted to be my friend.

I asked my parents about my scars and they changed the subject. Did they think my scars were gross too?

It wasn't until a group of kids chased me down in the playground that an adult finally intervened. It started with the kids asking if I wanted to play tag. I didn't care that they seemed to forget that Worm Girl wasn't my actual name, I was just excited that I could have friends to play with. But after a few minutes, I realized that they were all just chasing me. When my breathing started to hurt and my legs started to feel like jelly, one of the kids tackled me. The rest of the crowd caught up, and two others pinned my arms down. I started kicking because I didn't want to play this game anymore. Another kid came and pulled up my shirt. I started screaming. The kids that were pinning my arms down had their knees on my wrists. I could feel the mulch on the playground dig deeper into my skin. A teacher's aide finally came running and pushed through the crowd. She yelled at the kids to get off of me, and she pulled me up and took me to the principal's office. I was rubbing the skin on my arms where I was pinned down. My wrists hurt, but I wasn't bleeding. The secretary asked if I wanted a lollipop.

I nodded. Sucker in my mouth, I noticed the scuff marks on my new shoes. They were shoes just like the ones that Monique V. wore, and I thought that if I wore them, she'd think I was cool and then we could finally be friends. But she was one of the girls pinning me down, and even when I was screaming for them to stop, she didn't, and that's not something friends should do. I kept staring at the scuff marks on the new shoes and wondered if I would ever have any friends now. I heard the principal on the phone.

"We can't just punish the whole school…"

I sat in the office until my parents picked me up. Mother looked sad and gave me a hug. Father looked serious and filled out some paperwork. That was the last time I ever stepped foot on that campus.

A new school is a fresh start, Father said. No more being the Worm Girl. No kids to make fun of me. This was a chance to start over. Maybe I could finally be one of the pretty girls in class.

Self-conscious of my scars, I made sure no one ever saw them. I didn't play on anything that would risk my clothes revealing the ugly ridges of my body. No one but the family and I knew they were there, and for once, I had started to make friends. Then there was another accident.

I was playing in the treehouse in our backyard. My parents didn't want me playing there because it looked old and unstable. But with Mother at work and Father working in the front yard, I climbed up to the treehouse anyway. It was dirty and there were a lot of spiders, but it had *potential*. I thought up ways I could turn this into my dream home. I turned around, took a step, and a board launched up and smacked me in the face. I fell back onto a post and it gave, and another board broke and swung at my head. I lost balance and fell out of the treehouse. I remember lying on the grass and looking up at the blue sky. It was such a pretty shade of blue and there was only one cloud. The shape of a cow. I heard my neighbor scream. I could feel the ground shaking beneath me as Father ran over. I took my eyes off the cloud and saw him. He looked scared. He picked me up and kept repeating that everything was going to be okay.

Fluorescent lights blinding. Vision blurry. I was still able to recognize Mother's eyes over the medical mask. I tried to say something, but she barked words I couldn't understand. I felt a sharp pain in my arm and everything went dark.

I dreamt of my old house. I was playing in the front yard, picking flowers, chasing butterflies. The day was beautiful and sunny, and the blades of grass felt wonderful beneath my bare feet. I heard Mother yelling my name. I turned to her to smile and wave, but a sound made me look back. A car crashed through our front yard fence and was coming right at me. Mother's screams echoed deep into my unconsciousness.

When I woke up, I was covered in cold sweat. My body ached everywhere and I noticed new stitches. Arms, legs—places that would be harder to hide on warmer days. My parents came in, relieved to see that I was awake. They brought in a cake and said that it was my birthday. I looked at the scars on my arms and legs and made my wish—I just wanted to get back to school.

But when I returned, even covered up, the new scars didn't stay secret for long. Classmates noticed them. Other students heard about them. But they didn't call me Worm Girl. They called me freak. And freaks don't get to be pretty girls. A new school was on the horizon.

We can't punish the whole school.

New districts, different names. And every few years, new scars to make me an easier target. Worm Girl, Freak, Patches, Human Quilt—no matter what they came up with, it all basically meant the same thing. They thought I was a monster. Maybe I was becoming one.

I learned to lie about the scarring. Came up with stories that made me sound brave and heroic, not the freak accident magnet that I really was. But I think that they could see through my lies, and no matter what I said, I would always be a monster in their eyes. Pretty girls had it easy. So happy, so carefree, able to wear what they wanted without having to worry about someone calling them anything but beautiful. I became angry and jealous of anyone with smooth skin. No one would ever think of me as beautiful. I thought that if I was lucky enough, the next accident would leave me so ruined, there would be no way for my surgeon mother to fix me. Yet I kept waking up to a life that stopped being mine.

One Saturday morning, my parents came into my room, happy to see that I was awake.

"Happy birthday, sweetheart." They were holding a cake with eleven candles on it.

I said, "I wish you would let me die," then I blew out the candles.

Mother gasped and Father tried to tell me something about being fair.

"I know things haven't been easy," she started to cry. I couldn't look at her when she was crying.

"You just have to give it time…" Father squeezed Mother's shoulder and they both smiled.

I crossed my arms over my chest and huffed out a *Whatever* under my breath.

He said, "We got you something." He handed me a wrapped gift. I knew it was a book. "We think this will help." I reluctantly took the gift and unwrapped it. A red leather-bound journal. "You could express yourself. Draw, write, whatever you want."

"Can I burn it?"

Mother started to cry again. Father helped her up. "Let's give her some space. This can't be easy for her." He shook his head at me and they shut the door behind them.

I looked over the journal. I opened it and saw what my parents had inscribed on the first page:

For our beautiful daughter, Imelda. Love, Mom and Dad.

I struggled out of bed and quietly lurched down the steps to meet them in the living room. Mother was reading a book on the couch and Father was flipping through the newspaper. I set the journal down on the coffee table and asked for a pen. "Thank you for the journal. I really like—" Mother screamed when she looked up at me, startled. Father rushed over. I felt faint and looked down at where I was sore. Some of the stitches in my legs had split and the floor and my feet were red with blood. Father caught me and lowered me to the floor. I could see why they'd screamed. The blood smeared across the carpet from where I was, to the top of the stairs. Everything felt wet. I don't remember getting back to bed.

When I awoke later, the journal was at my bedside. I picked it up and opened it again. I unclipped the pen that came with it and started writing.

Now it's winter in Buffalo. I've been walking around for hours, listening to Bad Brains and watching the snowfall. My clothes are covered. I spend a lot of time out here when I can. I like the way the cold makes me feel. The way everything starts to look the same in a whiteout.

Someone taps my shoulder. I turn around expecting them to flinch at the scar on my face. Lower my headphones.

"I tried calling after you." I can't even enjoy being alone. "You're Imelda, right?"

She's a girl around my age. I think I know her from school. I sigh. No one but my parents has ever called me Imelda. "Who are you?"

"You're in Mrs. Kirwin's class? I'm in Mr. Clerval's class. My name's Fiona."

We break the silence at the same time. "Why are you..."

"...Jolly Rancher?" Her mittened hand holds out an assortment of colors.

Almost like she knows I don't trust her, she picks one, unwraps it and pops it into her mouth. I politely take one but hold it in my fist.

"You were about to say something?"

"Nothing. I, uh... just... why are you talking to me?"

Fiona looks me over and I start to feel embarrassed. Is she looking for the monster? My facial scarring is obvious.

"I think you're cool."

Liar.

"What's the catch?"

"There's no catch."

"You're messing with me." I turn my back to her. "I'm gonna go."

"Hey, wait—I'm being serious." Fiona reaches for my arm, but I pull away. "I promise!"

But I'm already around the block, muttering *whatever.*

The next day at school, Fiona is standing next to my locker. Hard to miss it, being the only locker in the hall defaced with sharpie doodles of stitches and lightning, and the smeared and redrawn cruelty of every name but my own. I roll my eyes at her and walk past.

"Imelda, wait!"

I don't stop. She catches up and holds out some candy. I shake my head and speed up my pace. I can hear some of the other kids pretending to be scared. The names they mutter as I pass. The worst cut is also the simplest, "Hey, Freak."

"Did you want to have lunch together today?" Fiona cutting through the noise.

I get to class early, making my way to the familiar desk in the back corner of the room.

Fiona leans in the doorway and shouts, "I'll see you after class!"

The moment she leaves the doorway, someone says, "Hey, Monster's got a girlfriend. Huzzah!" Sloppy kissing sounds. Laughing. Someone else sings, "Two ugly lesbos sittin' in a tree, L, I, C, K, I—" Everyone falls silent when the teacher enters. I lean into my hoodie and pretend I'm invisible. I already want today to be over.

After class, I'm the last person to leave the room. Fiona's waiting outside the door.

"You can stop now."

But she follows me to the cafeteria and sits at my table. Kids around us are staring, making gestures, making fun of us.

"Okay, okay. Marry, do it or kill: Daniel Radcliffe, Robert Pattinson, Liam Hemsworth?" Fiona stuffs her mouth with the school's excuse for mashed potatoes, waiting for my response.

One of the boys at a table nearest us hugs at the air in front of him and pretends to French kiss it. The others around him start laughing hysterically.

"Why are you still talking to me?"

"Actually those choices are all bad. That's the kind of list the people around us would make."

"Do you not see them making fun of us?"

"I see them, I just don't care."

"How does this not bother you?"

"I dunno. So, seriously this time… marry, do it or kill: Jensen Ackles, Tom Hiddleston, Benedict Cumberbatch."

"Someone's on tumblr."

"When I look at you, I see a girl my age who's misunderstood. The kids here are jerks. I'm sorry they're so mean to you. I really do think you're cool. You've moved around a lot, yeah? Look, my dad's in the military. This is my sixth school in four years. That's why I don't care. So what, they'll think I'm a jerk. I'll just be somewhere else when he gets transferred. They want to destroy you for being different—doesn't that make all of *them* monsters?"

"You know nothing about me," I say. "Nothing." I stand up and collect my things. I'm so angry I need to leave. "Stop trying to pretend you 'get' me."

Someone says, "Uh-oh, looks like the honeymoon is over." There's laughter that's almost canned.

"You're only saying that because being alone, not what any these people can say or do, is what's made you like this. Okay, so I'm not like you. I don't have many friends. I spend more time in my room avoiding my dad than I do anything else. I'm sorry you think everyone out there is a giant jerk!"

"Call the divorce lawyer!"

We both turn and point: "Shut up!"

Outside the cafeteria, I whisper to Fiona like we're conspiring, "Marry Dean Winchester, do it with Loki, kill Sherlock."

"You're really into Supernatural?"

"Except season seven."

"I binged the whole series. Twice."

"I haven't seen the new episodes."

"I've got them on my computer..."

I smile. Maybe I'll finally have a friend.

"Imelda! Fiona's here," Mother shouts from the bottom of the staircase.

"I'll be there in a minute!"

I check myself in the mirror that's on my bedroom door. If it weren't for a few things, the surgical scarring, an imperfect smile, the heterochromia... I'd be okay looking, wouldn't I? A heart that's not even mine. One arm slightly longer than the other. The way I walk because nothing goes back to how it's supposed to once it's broken. The way I feel sore in those spots when it's cold or when I'm stressed. The phantom cramping and the itching. Underneath all that, I don't really know... is enough of me still *me?*

Downstairs, Fiona is standing beside her mother in the entryway. She smiles when she sees me. I'm afraid of everything that could happen to me between now and tomorrow.

"Hey," I wave. For a moment, I lose my balance halfway down. Mother gasps and I catch myself on the handrail. "I got it, I'm okay."

Mother does that thing where she tells me to be safe and to call her if I need anything, like she's checking if the stove's on for the fifth time before she leaves the house.

I still feel like me.

I imagine those tables of kids... lights flickering, blood smeared on the walls, their dismembered bodies on the cafeteria floor, eyes cut out of their heads... if I could keep the parts of them I like most... at least I'm pointing

back, now.
They called me names.
"Imelda, you ready?"
They call me monster, but I'm just… me.

SUGAR AND SPICE
AND EVERYTHING NICE

DAMIEN ANGELICA WALTERS

First of all, the whole thing was Madison's idea. All of it. She saw that movie, the one with the prom and the pig blood. And no, before you ask, we weren't going to hurt any pigs. We're not psychos. Where would we find one in Edgewater anyway? A pig, I mean, not a psycho. It was just the idea of doing something like that. Something big.

She wanted to cut off Tara's hand, that's what, and that's all she wanted to do, nothing else.

Why? Because she wanted to know if she was right about what Tara really was. See, after the first week of school, we—me, Ellie, and Madison—knew something was wrong. In ninth grade, Tara was normal—we hardly even paid any attention to her. She wasn't in any of our classes or anything, but we saw her so we knew what she looked like and stuff—but when tenth grade started? We didn't know what was wrong at first, but we knew *something* was. For one thing, she smelled.

Yeah. Obviously you never met her or you'd know what I was talking about. She kind of smelled like a hospital. It was barely there, the way perfume is when it's mostly worn off. You almost didn't notice it, but when you did, you couldn't not smell it. Except Ellie couldn't smell her at all, so maybe some people couldn't, you know? Then Tara started wearing perfume, so I guess someone said something, probably her mom since she was the one who did everything to her. Oh, and also, she had a weird walk. It's hard to describe. Kind of a limp, but not really. I guess weird is the only way I can describe it. Ellie asked her about it—her locker was next to Tara's this year, that's how come we knew everything, I guess I should've said that before—and she told her she twisted her ankle over the summer.

Well, yeah, Ellie believed her. Me too, mostly. It was Madison who said it was bullshit because when she twisted her ankle it didn't leave *her* with a limp. So she said we should keep an eye on Tara. No big production about it, just sort of watch the way she walked and talked and stuff.

No, we didn't talk to anyone else about it. We kept it to ourselves. Anyway, since we were watching her, that's how Ellie saw the stitches, but we already knew from what happened with Tyler—

Okay, sorry, I'll try not to confuse you. It's hard to tell it right. Forget about the stitches for now, then. I'll tell you what happened with Tyler.

Yeah, Tyler Braxton. He has a thing for grabbing girls' asses. Total middle school stuff, but he's always been creepy-ass weird, like live in his mom's basement for the rest of his life weird. Anyway, a bunch of us were in the hallway by the computer lab, right? And Tyler grabbed Tara's ass. There weren't any teachers around. Tyler might be creepy but he's smart creepy. So he was laughing and the rest of us there were trying to ignore it. It's the only thing you can do. But Tara's face got all weird. I don't know how to describe it. Like angry, but calm, too. And she pushed him, not even that hard, and he went all the way across the hallway and hit the wall on the other side.

No, no one did anything or said anything either. We were all too surprised and I was trying to figure out how she was so strong because she was kind of skinny, maybe not model skinny but still small. I think it seriously freaked Tyler out, and I thought he might hit her, but he didn't and then Miss DeMeester showed up.

Sure, people talked about it, but everyone said she got lucky and caught him off balance, you know? Ask him about it, I bet he'll tell you, but it probably isn't that important anyway. He left her alone after that. A couple weeks after that, that's when Ellie saw the stitches. See, Tara dressed almost Amish, wearing stuff that went all the way up to here and down to the floor. Not Amish dresses, they were normal clothes—jeans and shirts—but the kind that cover everything up. And she never pushed or rolled up her sleeves. Ellie said Tara was getting something from her locker, and her sleeve caught on the edge and pulled back a little bit. Ellie said the stitches were blue and they were pretty small. She thought Tara had on a bracelet or something, but by the time she realized what they were, Tara'd already unhooked her shirt and closed her locker and was gone. So Ellie told Madison and me and we thought at first maybe she tried to kill herself and didn't want anyone to know, but the stitches were in the wrong spot. They were on top of her wrist, not underneath where all the veins are. So Madison asked Alex, who lives on the same street as Tara, if he noticed anything weird over the summer at Tara's house, and he told her that Tara and her mom—Tara didn't have any brothers or sisters and her dad died in a car accident when we were in fifth grade—were gone until the week before school started. He said they told one of the other neighbors that they were spending the summer with Tara's grandparents. Madison asked him if they ever did that before and he said no, not that he could remember.

No, she didn't tell Alex about the stitches. Maybe everything would've been different if we knew right away what Tara was and what happened to her. The accident, I mean.

No, I'm not saying what we did was her mom's fault, but maybe things would've been different, that's all. What did her mom think would happen? For a super smart scientist, she isn't very smart, and my mom always says just because you *can* do something doesn't mean you should. Why did her mom even send her to school? She should've homeschooled her or something if she wanted to keep it all a secret. Think about it, the only reason anybody knows the truth is because of what we did so people should be happy, not pissed off.

Well, whatever. After that, Madison wanted to try and see the stitches herself, so she started hanging out with Ellie at her locker, trying to bump into Tara and stuff. But nothing ever happened. I'm the one who saw them, but I swear the whole thing was an accident. For my birthday last year, my dad gave me a charm bracelet, the one you found. I love it but it catches on everything. I even yanked out a bunch of my hair with it one time. So I was leaving school late—I was out sick the day before and had to take a make-up test—and Tara was leaving, too. We bumped into each other on the way out the door and our wrists hit each other. You know, like this, back to back? One of the charms caught on something and I pulled it the way I always do, not thinking about it. I heard this noise, a wiry *boing*, but my bracelet was still caught so I pulled it again. There was the *boing* again and then I was unstuck. She took a deep breath and that's when I figured one of the charms had caught on her shirt or something and I said "I'm sorry" but she didn't say anything. She was looking at her wrist so I looked too. The stitches were all the way around her wrist, and my bracelet had yanked a couple open. It was like two puzzle pieces but instead of clicking together, the stitches were holding them, and inside, there were other things connected. I didn't want to know, not really—I can't even watch gross stuff on TV, it makes me want to puke—so I looked away super fast. There wasn't any blood, though. There was that weird hospital smell, but it was different, like it was mixed with a funeral home—my grandma died last year so I know how they smell—and I was all lightheaded and sweaty. I thought for sure I was going to puke. Tara's eyes got all huge, and she took off, practically running. I almost didn't tell Madison and Ellie about it, it freaked me out so bad.

What did I do? Nothing. I stayed there for a few minutes until I felt okay again and then I went home. *Then* I called Madison. I probably shouldn't have because she loves horror movies and has a crazy overactive imagination. One time in fourth grade she was convinced that Mr. Barron was a zombie because his skin got all pale and he started walking slow. Know why? He had the flu. Normal flu, not brain-eating walking dead flu. After I told Madison what I saw, she told me not to tell anyone else, not even Ellie, and to act like nothing happened and to be nice to Tara.

No, I don't think she had anything planned then, but she was probably thinking about it. So I started being nice.

What do you mean? I said hi to her when I saw her in the hall, asked her how things were going, stuff like that. Haven't you ever been nice to anyone before? We weren't hanging out together after school or anything.

By that time, though, me and Ellie weren't the only ones who knew about the stitches. Bastian saw them in Geometry, but *he* saw them on Tara's ankle when she bent down to tie her shoe. The difference was, he asked her about them, and she said she cut herself on a glass. Then Leila saw some on the back of her neck one day when it was windy, and Van said he saw some on her shoulder except we figured he was lying since she didn't wear tank tops. Plus, it was starting to get chilly. A couple other people said they saw them, too, but I think they just wanted people to think that. I don't think they really did, but they didn't want to be someone who *didn't*. No one else saw what I did, though, or at least if anyone else did, they didn't say anything and I think they would've. So after that, there were a bunch of rumors. She tried to kill herself, she had a bunch of warts removed, she was in an accident and didn't want anyone to know—which is pretty funny when you think about it—they were tattoos, she was fucking with us, you know, by drawing them on. It was pretty much only a joke at that point, even when Alex gave her the nickname. He was the one who called her Frankenstein.

Wait. That *isn't* the monster's name? Then how come everyone calls it that?

No, I haven't read it, but it's really old, isn't it? I don't like to read; it's a big waste of time. But whatever. When Alex called her that, he wasn't trying to be mean. He was being, I don't know, stupid-funny I guess. He said something like what's with all the stitches, Frankenstein? I wasn't there so I only heard it from Ellie, and she said Tara said people were pretty stupid if they believed that and hadn't he ever cut himself before?

Sure, people believed her—wouldn't you?—because thinking she was really Frankenstein was crazy. If we were still in middle school, maybe, but now? The world isn't like that. At least that's what we thought.

The nickname stuck, though, and she acted like it didn't bother her, but you could tell it did. Alex is the one who made the picture, too, the one with her face Photoshopped on a Frankenstein body. The green one with bolts in the neck and stitches all over. He stuck it to her locker. She took it down as soon as she saw it, but he did it a couple more times, on her locker and then in it, you know, folded up and put through the slot at the top. Nowhere else, though.

The teachers? No. They probably didn't see it or if they did, they probably thought it was for Halloween or whatever. You should ask them if you really want to know. And I know Tara didn't tell them. They definitely would've done something if she did.

No, I still didn't say anything about what I saw. *Ellie* still didn't even know. Honestly, I didn't even really believe it, even with what I saw, and I started to think that maybe I just thought I saw it. I don't think Madison believed it either, but she knew something was up and she wanted to find out *what*, she wanted to be the one who found out.

I don't know why. I guess because she's Madison, that's why. While everything was going on, I was still being nice to her, to Tara, I mean. Ellie and Madison started to, too. We told her to ignore them. I even took down one of the pictures and told Alex to knock it off. That's when he called me Igor. I told him to fuck off, and Tara was there, too, and she said, "He thinks he's funny, they all do, but they're all idiots." She said I wasn't Igor anyway, but more of a Justine. I didn't know who she was talking about, but she was smiling, so I smiled back.

She's in the book? Really? What, is she like someone's sort of friend?

So Frankenstein—

Oh, okay, got it, the monster, not the doctor, kills someone and she gets blamed? They find out the truth though, don't they?

They *kill* her? But she didn't do anything.

That's so not funny. Not funny at all. You don't think Tara knew… Never mind. So what happened next was that Madison told me to try and bump into her again, but only when she was around so she could try and get it on her phone.

Why wouldn't we?

No, I mean, I understand what you're asking, but—

Mean? I don't know. We just wanted to see it again.

Okay, okay, yes, I'd already seen it, but *Madison* still wanted to see it.

I didn't ask her what she wanted to do with the picture or the video, but yeah, I guess I kind of knew she wanted one so she could put it online. But we weren't going to hurt her, and it doesn't matter anyway because we never got the chance. I tried but I guess Tara knew she had to be really careful now that she had that nickname—maybe her mom yelled at her or something—and I didn't want to bump into her and have her know I was doing it on purpose. It was a pretty stupid idea anyway, so after a couple of weeks—and by then people were hardly talking about Tara anymore because everyone thought Anna was pregnant so they were talking about her instead—Madison said we needed to come up with something else. That's when she told me to invite her to the Faraday house. That's the one on Beach Road that's been boarded up forever but there's a way to get in. You have to be careful, the house is on a corner and there are lots of neighbors around, but we sneak in it all the time, no big deal.

No, I still thought Madison wanted to do the stupid break a stitch thing. I knew she didn't want to be Tara's BFF, not for real, and I guess maybe I should've known she was planning something bigger but I didn't. Not right away anyway. Not until the night before. And even when she told me she wanted to cut off Tara's hand, I didn't believe her. She didn't even tell Ellie what I saw, what she wanted to do, until they were on their way. I mean, we didn't even know if the stitches were still there. I thought that if they were, Madison would tell Tara what she wanted to do and scare her or make her cry or maybe both, maybe even pretend that she was going to rip open a stitch or two, but I knew she'd chicken out before anything really bad happened.

What do you mean, how? I just knew. I've known Madison since we were like four years old.

I don't know. I guess I thought it would be funny. And I figured we could pick on Madison for chickening out, the way she gave us a hard time when we wouldn't do something she wanted us to.

Well, yeah, the whole thing was kind of stupid and mean, but I told you, I didn't really think anything would happen. I didn't even think Tara would show up. I was surprised she even said yes when I asked her to come with us. I told her how to get in and she said she'd meet us there. Me and Madison and Ellie were there for a while, and Madison said Tara wasn't coming, but she did, and when she showed up at the house, she scared the crap out of us. We didn't even hear her come in the house and the floors are all creaky. We were up in the back bedroom—you can turn on flashlights there and you don't have to worry about anyone seeing, not that they probably could with the windows boarded up. Madison had one of her parents' bottles of rum and we were sitting around and talking about the teachers and stuff. Nothing major.

Yeah, Tara took a couple drinks too. Finally, Madison looked at Tara and said, "So what's the deal with the stitches?" Tara smiled and said, "I figured that's why you wanted me to come. You sure you want to know?" And Madison said yes, so Tara pushed up her sleeve and we all saw that the stitches were still there. Then she pushed up her other sleeve and there were stitches there, too, but not on the wrist, they were near the elbow. The whole way around.

We didn't say *anything*. We were way too surprised. It's one thing to think something's true; it's another thing to know it. She kept smiling and then took off her sweater. She had on a tank top underneath and we could see stitches on the top of her left arm and they wrapped around and went up to the back of her neck. She pulled up the tank part of the way and there were more stitches across her stomach, and you could see that the skin didn't quite match. "My mom thought everything would be healed by now, but I guess she was wrong," she said and Ellie said, "Your mom did this?" Tara nodded. "I told her people would find out," she said. "She said they'd find out if I didn't go back to school. Act normal, she told me." "What happened?" I asked. "There are more," Tara said. "Want to see them all?" Ellie and I both said no at the same time. Then Tara said, "It was an accident. My mom and I had a fight and I took her car. I hit a tree and boom. The next thing I remember is waking up and my mom telling me that everything was going to be okay because she fixed me. And I was like this." "Fixed you?" Madison said. "She made you a freak." Tara didn't say anything, and I could see that Madison was pissed off.

Why? Yes, she wanted to find out, but she didn't want to just hear about it. She wanted to be like one of those Anonymous guys, the ones that wear the masks and figure out a story before everybody else knows the truth. "Is that why you smell?" Madison said. "You *stink*, like something that's been dead and then brought back to life, like Frankenstein. You wear that perfume to hide it but it doesn't."

No, Tara still didn't say anything. "Where did your mom get all the parts?" Madison said. "'Cause you can see they don't match. Did she dig them up?" Tara shrugged and said, "She didn't tell me." Then Madison said, "Are you even you anymore?"

No, she didn't answer, but she had this funny expression on her face. "Do you think those people whose parts you took would want that?" Madison asked and then Tara said, "My mom said she got permission from their families." "Right," Madison said. "Their families, but not them. Because they were probably dead." Tara said something about organ donors, I don't remember exactly what, and Madison laughed. Her cheeks were all pink and her eyes were bright. Tara still had that weird look on her face, but she was kind of smiling too, and I thought she was going to hit Madison or something, but she didn't. Madison said, "What do you think would happen if we undid the stitches? Would you fall apart?"

No, I kept my mouth shut. So did Ellie. It was Madison's thing. Tara shrugged and held out her hand for the bottle, acting like nothing was wrong at all, and that pissed Madison off even more. "Fucking freak," she said and she hit her with the bottle on the side of her head, here.

Yeah, the temple. She must not have hit her that hard because Tara didn't pass out or shout or anything. It didn't even break the skin. There was a red mark, but it didn't even look like it hurt her at all. Then Madison took a pair of scissors out of her purse and said, "Maybe we should find out."

Yeah, those are the ones. I can tell by the blue handle things. And Tara didn't even look scared, that was the weird part. She grabbed Madison's wrist, and said, "Go ahead." Madison tried to yank her arm back and couldn't and her eyes got really wide. Then Tara let go and we could see the marks on Madison's skin. "Maybe I will," Madison said. Ellie said, come on M, let's just hang out, okay, and Madison told her to shut the fuck up and if she wanted to leave, she knew how to get out. I could see that *Madison* was scared, but she was more pissed off and that's why she wasn't going to back down.

I could tell by her face. And the thing was, neither was Tara. I didn't even know her that well, but it was obvious. I don't think she thought Madison would do it, but Madison did. I think she had to, otherwise Tara would've won, you know? First she held up her phone though and gave it to Ellie and told her to record it. Ellie didn't want to, but she did, and even that didn't bother Tara, even though she had to know that it would probably go viral and then everyone would know. Madison held the scissors for a long time and then she cut one stitch, and then, super fast, almost like she wanted to do it before thinking about it too much, she cut another. The whole room smelled bad, like really bad, rotten bad. I swear, I didn't know Madison was really going to do it. She wanted to make Tara cry. If Tara had, it would've stopped right then and there.

Believe what you want, but I'm serious.

No, I'm not saying it was Tara's fault. Not really.

Ellie and I were just sitting there. What were we supposed to do? Tara wasn't fighting or anything. She kept holding out her arm and she *still* didn't look scared. So Madison kept cutting the stitches, even when the smell was so bad Ellie and I were practically gagging. There wasn't any blood, though. Not then. Ellie was crying and I knew she was trying to figure out what would be worse—staying or going. And the look on Tara's face the whole time, it was fucking creepy. Her hand was hanging off and the inside, it was awful. I knew I was going to puke so I ran out of the house—I didn't even say goodbye—and threw up outside in the bushes.

Because I didn't want to see any more. I told you I can't watch gross stuff.

I don't know. I wasn't thinking about Tara, I wasn't thinking about any of them. I didn't even care if Madison never talked to me again. I was halfway home when I realized my bracelet was missing, and that's why I went back.

No, I didn't call anybody. I wanted to go in, find my bracelet, and leave. The house was quiet—I thought maybe everyone left already—and my bracelet wasn't anywhere downstairs, so I went up to the room. Tara was still there, but she was alone. Madison chickened out after all, like I thought she would.

No, Tara wasn't doing anything. I didn't even see the blood right away because she had her arm kind of off to the side. She asked me if I knew. "Knew what?" I said. "What Madison was going to do," she said. I lied and told her no. Did it matter anyway? If her mom could do all the rest, she could fix that easy. "She's going to put it online, isn't she, so everyone can see it." I shrugged, but I think she already knew the answer.

Yeah, by that time I saw it was completely off, the whole way. The scissors were on the floor beside her, next to the blood and the hand. I didn't really look at it, though—I couldn't—but she saw me not looking and said, "It didn't even hurt that much." She said she thought there'd be more blood and she was going to undo the rest. I told her she should go home, that the video wouldn't be that big of a deal, that her mom could fix her. She laughed, gave me that weird look again, and said she hit that tree on purpose. "I left a note and everything," she said.

No, I didn't say anything, but she asked if I wanted to stay. She said I could even record her if I wanted to, said it would be better for me if I did.

Are you kidding? Uh-uh. No way was I going to stay there. I mean, what would you have done? And I didn't think she was serious. I thought she was trying to scare me or gross me out. Payback, you know?

No, I didn't call anybody that time either. I went home and didn't even text Madison or Ellie.

No, not until later and then all I did was text Madison that she was a bitch. She texted back *fuck you* and that was it. I didn't even know Madison put the video online until the next day.

I'm telling the truth. I felt sick from puking so I went to bed early. When

I got up, my mom told me Ellie's mom had called her because Ellie told her what happened.

What do you think? She was pissed off. She told me we were stupid, what were we thinking, she raised me better than that, all the normal stuff moms say. But how were we supposed to know what Tara was going to do?

No, uh-uh, you're wrong. We didn't just stop recording. I told you, I left first and when I went back, Ellie and Madison were gone but Tara was still there and she was fine. Her hand was off, but she was okay. Her arm wasn't even bleeding, not that I could tell. That's the truth. And when I left, she was *still* okay. If you watch the video, you can see everything that happened.

I don't know why she had my bracelet in her hand. I told you I lost it. I guess she found it.

No, that's not what happened. You have to believe me.

Because I'm telling the truth, that's why.

I know she left a note. She told me so.

A different note? What did it say?

Bullies? Us? That's such bullshit.

Well, maybe her mom's lying.

I don't know why. I never met her.

No, *Alex* came up with the nickname and made the pictures, not Madison. I don't care what her mom says the stupid note said. We were *nice* to her.

I *am* telling you the truth.

She didn't tell me why she was going to do it. Maybe she was unhappy. Maybe she wanted to see what would happen. Maybe she figured her mom would just put her back together.

No, I don't know how she did it all. I told you, I wasn't there. Nobody was except her.

Then maybe someone else came in after we left and helped her. I don't know.

I don't care how stupid it sounds. I'm telling you the truth. Maybe she wanted you to think we did it, but we didn't. I swear we didn't. She did it to herself. That's the truth. Ask Madison and Ellie, they'll tell you the same thing. She did it to herself.

BARON VON WEREWOLF PRESENTS:

FRANKENSTEIN AGAINST THE PHANTOM PLANET

ORRIN GREY

Baron von Werewolf comes out to a clap of thunder, like he always does, and the painted lightning bolt outside the window flickers behind him. You can tell that it's painted, that it's fake, but that doesn't matter, doesn't affect how much you believe in it.

"I've got a special treat for you tonight, kids," Baron von Werewolf says as he walks into the library, with its candelabras and its wall of books and the window overlooking the painting of a graveyard, complete with skeletal trees that claw at the cloudy sky. He always says "tonight," even though when you watch him it's always Saturday afternoon. You don't know why he says "tonight;" if it really is night where he is, or if he just says it because it sounds better than "this afternoon." It *could* be night where he is. You learned about time zones in school; maybe he lives a long ways away. Or maybe it's always night wherever he is, like on the dark side of the moon.

He walks over to the big wall of books—they're all what your mom calls "foe leather," in reds and greens and blues—and pulls one down. Today's book is purple, and the camera zooms in as Baron von Werewolf strokes his long black nails along the cover, past a silver picture of a planet surrounded by stars.

Every time you watch him, he's dressed the same way, in a smoking jacket and cravat—you saw them in so many movies that you asked your mom what they were called—and a top hat that he always sets aside on the desk before running a long-fingered hand through his mane of wavy brown hair, hair that seems to crawl down his head to become the beard that covers much of his face. He's got an eye patch over his right eye, something he never mentions, though you've occasionally noticed his hand straying to it, like maybe it itches. His other eye is a dark spot that stares out from all that hair, catching the light from the big cameras that you can't see but that let you see him.

You know that it's a TV show, even though your mom, concerned, once asked you if you knew that movies weren't real. She'd been reading something in the paper about kids and TV violence. *Of course* you know that it's just a show, that the movies aren't real. It wouldn't make any sense otherwise. Baron von Werewolf shows you the movies, after all, talks to you about them and how they were made. You recognize actors, sometimes, from one movie to another. That couldn't happen if the movies were real.

But Baron von Werewolf is real. Oh, not a real werewolf, probably, and not in a real castle, you can tell that much. But he's a real person some-where. A person who gets dressed up and shows you monsters. That's the only reality that matters.

Normally, Baron von Werewolf would sit down behind the desk, open the book, and start to tell you about today's movie, but this time he paces in front of the desk instead, his hand resting on the book, looking down at it, like your mom sometimes does when she forgets what she's doing in the middle of cooking. "I know that you kids have all seen *King Kong*," Baron von Werewolf says when he's walked back across the length of the library. You smile and nod, even though he can't see you. You've seen *King Kong*, and you've also seen *King Kong vs. Godzilla*, which you liked better because it was in color and had Godzilla, who is cooler than King Kong.

"Well, *King Kong* has always been a favorite of mine," Baron von Were-wolf continues. He seems a little sad, and you feel kind of bad for him, which is a weird feeling to have. "It was made by a man named Willis O'Brien, and Mr. O'Brien had a dream after he finished it. He wanted to make a sequel, not the one that actually got made, but one where King Kong fought Frankenstein's monster."

Now *that* sounds pretty cool, but also kinda dumb, because Frankenstein's monster wouldn't last long, would he? He's just the size of a regular guy, while King Kong is huge. But then again, Godzilla is a lot bigger than King Kong, but they were about the same size when *they* fought, too…

"He drew up a bunch of sketches and tried to get the movie studios to let him make his movie, but nobody wanted to put the money behind it." Here, Baron von Werewolf rubs his hairy pointer finger and thumb together, making you chuckle. "His efforts to get his movie made eventually led to *King Kong vs. Godzilla,*" and you smile again, because you were *just* thinking about that. "But Willis O'Brien's project never happened. However, that's not the end of our story…"

You love it when Baron von Werewolf does that, when he seems like he's coming to the end of something, but then it turns out that it was just a… what does your mom call it… a prologue?

"You see, Mr. O'Brien had a protégé, that is, an assistant, someone who helped him out but also learned from him, the way you kids learn from your teachers at school. Actually, he had several, and one of them was someone you kids will probably recognize—Ray Harryhausen." You *do* recognize Harryhausen's name. You've seen *Jason and the Argonauts* and *7th Voyage of Sinbad* and that weird one where Sinbad fought a statue with a bunch of arms and a centaur with only one eye.

"But Mr. Harryhausen isn't who we're here to talk about tonight either, kids. Instead, Mr. O'Brien had another, lesser known protégé, a young woman from Mexico City who came to Hollywood and wanted to be a stop motion animator, just like O'Brien and Harryhausen. You all remember what stop motion is, right?" You do, because Baron von Werewolf has talked about it before. He says that the movie people make it happen by re-positioning tiny models over and over again. Like when you play with your action figures, but very, very slowly. Then, when they play all the pictures together really fast, it looks like the models are moving.

"If any of you have ever seen *Son of Kong,*" Baron von Werewolf continues, "some people say that she worked on the cave dinosaur and the giant statue in that movie, though she's not officially credited. Her name was Gabriela Moreno, and her only actual credit is tonight's film, which she wrote, directed, produced, and created the special effects for. There's some question as to how she got the financing, and there are stories that say that she turned to... unorthodox sources."

Baron von Werewolf seems to realize suddenly that he's still standing, and he steps forward in front of the desk, turns more toward the camera, the book still closed in his hands, pressed between his palms. "Tonight's movie was shot in Mexico, and released to a handful of theaters in 1967, but it disappeared from circulation almost immediately afterward, and is considered to have been lost. Some people claim that it never existed at all, but I saw it once, at a tiny theater that was about to close down. When I decided to track the movie down, I tried to find the owner of that old theater, but he had disappeared, and I soon learned why. It seems that getting a copy of tonight's film requires that you do what you kids might think of as a favor in return, and it's got some pretty steep penalties. In spite of that, I've got a copy, just one copy, which I'm going to show to all of you tonight."

Once again, you find yourself squirming a little bit. Baron von Werewolf is acting weird, like your mom sometimes does when a stranger asks about your dad. Baron von Werewolf has always seemed real to you, but the way your teacher seems real. He's never seemed like you, or like your mom, but today he does. "I've read your letters, and I know that you kids out there are the best fans that someone like me could ever have," he says, and you smile, because you've written him lots of letters, with your own ideas for monster movies and drawings of what you think the posters should look like, and it's nice to think that maybe he's talking about you. "This is an important movie to me, kids, and I had to agree to pay a high price to get it, so I want you to give it a chance, even if you find it a little bit confusing at first, okay?"

You smile, and nod, and scoot closer to the TV as Baron von Werewolf fades out and the movie begins...

It opens with some words in white on a black screen, first in another language that you guess is maybe Spanish, and then underneath that in English: In Justice for Willis O'Brien.

Those words fade out and are replaced by the title, which makes you sit up a little bit straighter and put your bowl of cereal aside, because it sounds *awesome.*

FRANKENSTEIN AGAINST THE PHANTOM PLANET
There aren't any credits or anything like there would normally be, and the

title fades out and is replaced by a picture of a big radio tower that looks kind of like the water tower on the edge of town. The radio tower is sending out little animated lightning bolts while an announcer delivers a fake news broadcast about a comet that is going to pass near Earth. The picture is black and white, and the news broadcast seems to cut in and out, so you miss bits of it, but you get the gist. It's a really big comet, and one that "doesn't show up on normal instruments." The announcer continues that scientists and military forces are encouraging people not to panic and to "stay in your homes, as the proximity of the comet could lead to unexpected atmospheric disturbances."

Then that picture fades out, too, and is gradually replaced with the inside of a courtroom. Outside the windows, you can see what is clearly a painted backdrop of New York City. You're disappointed to see that this part is in black and white, too. You don't normally like the black and white movies as much as the color ones, and you consider getting up and leaving, or changing the channel, but then you remember Baron von Werewolf saying how this movie was special, and how you were the best fans in the world, and you remember how it felt like he was talking right to you, so you settle back down to watch.

The people in the courtroom all look pretty much alike, but one guy is standing up in front, facing the judge, while everyone else sits down. The judge is talking, but the camera gradually zooms in on the guy, instead. He has his arms behind his back, and his chin up, looking very brave, while the judge refers to him as "Doctor" and says how he has been found guilty of "willfully creating the monstrosity that has laid such waste to our fair city." The judge goes on to say that the Doctor will be remitted to Devil's Island—a name that you've heard before in old movies, so you know that it's a prison—but that since his creation can "by no earthly weapon be destroyed," other plans have "perforce" been made.

You start to get up to get a pencil and a piece of paper so you can write down that word, "perforce," and ask your mom what it means later, but then the scene changes again, and what it changes to stops you in your tracks. It's a big open area, like a town square, and there are dozens of people, maybe hundreds all crowded around. In the center of the square is an enormous throne made of metal girders, and sitting on it is a giant. For just one moment it looks like a statue, but then it moves, straining against the chains that hold it down.

Even though the judge never said the Doctor's full name, you know who he is, just as surely as you now know what this is: the Frankenstein monster, even though it doesn't look much like any of the costumes of the monster that you've seen at Halloween, or the way the monster looked in any of the old movies. It's huge, for one thing, every bit as big as King Kong ever was, making the idea of them fighting suddenly not seem so silly. But it also doesn't look like Boris Karloff, even under a lot of makeup. There are no bolts in its neck or stitches across its head. Even moving around it still looks like a statue, but one that hasn't been carved very well, its skin a sort of midway point between stone and an elephant's hide. Its shoulders slope, and its arms are long enough that they would hang down to its knees, if it were standing up instead of chained to a chair. Its struggles have the same uneven, jerky motions as King Kong and the skeletons in *Jason and the Argonauts* and the cyclops in *Sinbad*, so you know that it's stop motion.

Once you drag your attention away from the monster in the throne, you notice two things. The first is that there's a comet in the painted sky in the background. It isn't moving, because it's just a painting, but it could also be because it's very far away and so it doesn't look like it's moving. The moon and stars are constantly moving through the sky, you know that from school, but you usually can't tell they're moving just to look at them.

The second thing you notice is that there is a crane or something lowering a rocket ship down over the throne where the Frankenstein monster is sitting. Bit by bit the rocket covers the monster, until he is completely hidden from view and with a metallic clank the rocket locks into place.

The next thing you see is the rocket ship flying through space toward the comet. The comet is huge, and as the rocket ship approaches it, you can see designs on its surface that might be drawings of buildings or trees or something, like maybe someone had painted the comet over an old map. Then the rocket strikes the comet and the screen goes black, the image replaced by three words:

THE PHANTOM PLANET

When the picture fades back in, there's been a change, a drastic one. The movie is in color now! And not just color, but vivid, candy-bright color. It reminds you of the colors in *Planet of the Vampires*, which Baron von Werewolf showed you one time. Just like in *Planet of the Vampires*, the weird colors are part of an alien world—the comet, obviously, which must also be the Phantom Planet—a world of black dirt and strange plants where the rocket ship has crash landed. There are bright pink and purple bushes, and mushrooms that reach taller than trees and seem to be lit from inside.

From out of the wrecked rocket comes the Frankenstein monster, and he is the only part of the movie that still seems to be in black and white. You guess maybe that's just what color he is, all shades of gray, like stone or an elephant after all. He moves sort of like an elephant, too, like his arms and legs are heavy.

He looks around, taking in the surface of the Phantom Planet as if maybe he's never seen color before, either. You sort of like that idea; that Earth is all in black and white, but that the Phantom Planet is all the colors of a box of crayons. That seems right somehow.

As the Frankenstein monster starts to move away from the rocket ship, something else comes from off the edge of the screen. For a second you think they're people, but they're definitely not. Smaller than the Frankenstein monster, but still not as small as the people were in the earlier shot, they appear to be robots with four mechanical legs and little short arms that are holding long sticks with tuning forks on the ends. They don't really have bodies, just legs and arms jutting out of a square box, and then on top of that a clear dome through which you can see their glowing brains. The way they move lets you know that they're stop motion, too.

They scuttle like boxy crabs onto the screen. Two of them, then three, four, until they surround the Frankenstein monster, trapping him against the wreckage of the rocket that brought him here. They make some kind of noise. Clicking, and these sounds like the beep at the end of an answering machine as they jab at the Frankenstein monster with their long sticks. Every time one of the tuning forks touches him, there's a little spark of blue electricity, and he draws back, seeming more startled than hurt.

At first he just tries to back away, holding up his big arms so that the tuning forks shock his elbows and forearms instead of his torso. Finally he roars, lashing out and smashing one of the little robots apart. Bits of metal go flying everywhere, the glass dome shatters, and you see the thing that you thought was the robot's brain crawling away, dragged by a bunch of narrow tendrils. It doesn't get far, however, before the Frankenstein monster brings one of his big elephant feet down and smooshes it, leaving behind something that looks a lot like grape jelly.

It seems like the Frankenstein monster is going to make short work of the alien robots—you realize that you've been thinking of them as Martians, which isn't right, since they're not on Mars, they're on the Phantom Planet. So… Phantomites? But then more Phantomites show up, rolling out this new thing. It looks sort of like a wagon, but it has big knobby wheels, and in the middle of it is a ball with a ring around it, like a flying saucer, or like Saturn seen from the side. As the other Phantomites try to hold the Frankenstein monster off with their long sticks, the ones pushing the wagon operate a lever on it with their short pincer arms, and the ball shoots off into the air. It only goes up a little ways, and then it hovers in front of Frankenstein's monster at about eye level, suspended on a wire that you can sometimes see against the black backdrop.

The ball part pulses red, then blue, then green, then red again. The Frankenstein monster stops struggling and just stands there, his long arms dangling limp at his sides, and you know that the ball has hypnotized him somehow! You saw somebody hypnotize Vincent Price like that once, with a multi-colored lamp that turned.

In a trance, the Frankenstein monster follows the Phantomites across the black desert filled with the strange, unearthly plants. They pass an odd lizard with bulging eyes and only two webbed feet that drags itself off a rock and disappears as they approach, and another time a bunch of things that look like purple spiders but with all their legs shoved to the back scuttle out of the path in front of them. Through the air, odd things like round bats with four wings flap, and everything is some color that animals aren't on Earth, like the drawings that younger kids sometimes color at school.

After walking for a while, the Phantomites and Frankenstein's monster reach a building. It looks like it was once someplace grand; a palace or something, with a wall around it, and a huge dome. But it has fallen into disrepair, and now vines grow up it that sprout bright flowers in colors you'd have to dig through your crayon box to name. As you watch, the flowers open and close, like mouths.

Inside, the dome is cracked open, so that the black sky shows through on the other side, and there are lots more Phantomites, some of them bigger than others, their robot suits almost as large as the Frankenstein monster himself. In the background you can see hundreds more, painted so they don't move, all gathered around to watch, like in a coliseum in old gladiator movies. In the middle of the building there is a hole in the ground, and above that a huge mechanical thing with four screens on it, like giant TVs.

The Phantomites get out of the way as Frankenstein's monster walks forward, following the glowing ball until it passes over the pit, and you leap up to say something, even though you know he can't hear you, as Frankenstein's monster steps over the lip of the pit and then he's falling, falling, falling.

He hits the bottom like a dropped toy and for a moment lies in a heap before slowly rising, shaking his head. You can tell from the way he moves that he's no longer in a trance, and you creep closer to the TV, wondering what the Phantomites want with him, and what he's going to find down in this hole, but then, all of a sudden, the picture cuts to a commercial.

You get up to refill your cereal, and when you get back Baron von Werewolf is back on the TV. He's saying something about the next sequence of the movie, how it's pretty scary, so you may want to close your eyes through some parts of it. He says that there was once a "spider pit" sequence in the original *King Kong*, but that it got cut out of the movie for being too scary, and how he's pretty sure some of what you'll see in the next part of the movie is actually left over from that.

Then he says, smiling just a little, "Well, we warned you," and the movie starts back up.

When it does, it seems like maybe something has been missed, because it's not quite where it was before. Frankenstein's monster is already up, and he's in a different part of the cave, one where it's all lit in purples and greens, and big glowing crystals stick up out of the ground and out of the walls. He's also being surrounded, gradually, by all sorts of weird creatures.

There's a thing that looks like a tick, but instead of legs it has tentacles; there are giant skeletal crabs, and spiders with big bent legs, and others, huge and hairy, that are just shadows in the background. All of them are moving at once, converging on Frankenstein's monster. From behind him a shadow rises up, a big worm thing with arms and bulging eyes that glow. It grapples with the Frankenstein monster and manages to wrestle him to the ground as the other creatures close in.

The scene shifts, and you're seeing the Phantomites up above, watching all this on the four big TVs suspended over the pit. The thing on the bottom of the TVs is projecting a beam of light down into the pit, and you guess maybe recording what's going on or something, so that they're watching it, just like you are. But you're rooting for the Frankenstein monster, while you're pretty sure they're not.

On the TV screens, you can see Frankenstein's monster struggle back to his feet, raising the wriggling worm thing up into the air and bringing it down onto his knee, like you've seen wrestlers do. The worm twitches a few times, and then is still, the light going out of its buggy eyes.

After that the other creatures sort of draw back, and the Frankenstein monster starts to make his clompy way across the floor of the cave. The various monsters get out of his way, scuttling back into holes and stuff, but then suddenly it becomes clear that maybe it's not him they're avoiding, as something else comes out of a really big hole in the side of the cavern. At first all you can see are its eyes, which come on like Christmas lights, glowing bright blue. But then the rest of it follows. A big lizardy thing, somewhere between a brontosaurus and an alligator, but where the other lizards you've seen so far on the Phantom Planet only had two legs, this one has six, and a long snaky tail. The eyes pop out of its head like those plastic bubbles that toys come out of quarter machines in, and its snout is long and toothy.

It charges the Frankenstein monster, its mouth open wide to bite, and latches onto his forearm. They wrestle around for a bit, with first the dragon—for so you immediately think of it—and then the Frankenstein monster getting the upper hand. At one point he wrestles its body to the ground and sits astride it, pounding on its head with his huge fist while it lashes its tail and continues to bite him.

Finally, the dragon rears up onto its back two pairs of legs and rams the Frankenstein monster with its head and its front feet, knocking him to the ground, where he lays still and doesn't move. You slide forward again, closer to the TV, your cereal forgotten. You know that this can't be where the Frankenstein monster dies, that would be a terrible movie, just as you know that he is bound to die, because the monster *always* dies, no matter how much you want him to live.

The dragon stomps around the body twice, waving its head and roaring, and then it starts to move away, back into the dark cave, when you see the hand of the monster twitch. With a sudden movement, he grabs the dragon's tail, and the next thing you know the Frankenstein monster is on his feet, hauling the dragon back toward him hand-over-hand, like he's playing tug-of-war.

When the dragon gets close enough it circles back around to bite again, but the Frankenstein monster punches it on the head and then grabs it in a headlock, dragging it backward until you hear the snap of its neck and it lies still, at the monster's feet. Not content to let it make a comeback like he did, the Frankenstein monster brings his foot down on its neck and keeps pushing until it goes all the way through.

The film seems to skip a bit here, and suddenly the Frankenstein monster is climbing the wall of the cavern, presumably climbing out of the pit and up to where the Phantomites are waiting. And you're eager to see him get to them, to see him smash them up for tricking him into the pit. But he doesn't make it all the way up, not yet. Instead, he finds a ledge, and on it a smaller tunnel, which he goes through.

On the other side, the tunnel opens out, and you see maybe the weirdest thing you've seen in the movie so far, which is saying something. The room that Frankenstein's monster comes into is filled with machines that don't seem to make a whole lot of sense. Lots of big pipes, lots of glass cylinders filled with colored liquids that bubble and rise and fall. And at all of the machines are mushroom people.

Baron von Werewolf once showed you a movie called *Attack of the Mushroom People*, and the mushroom people in it looked almost just like these, although, like everything else in *Frankenstein Against the Phantom Planet*, these are more brightly colored and seem to glow faintly. They stand at every machine, making a constant sort of murmuring, purring noise—like the tribbles in that one episode of *Star Trek*—and operating levers and turning knobs.

When the Frankenstein monster walks into the room, the closest mushroom people start to run away, or waddle away, since that's about all they can do, but then the weird little collars they wear around what would be their necks if they were regular people light up and they stop suddenly, and then trudge back to their places at the machines. The light-up collars remind you of the ball that hypnotized Frankenstein's monster, and you realize that the fungus—you learned that word in school—people are slaves to the Phantomites above, and you can tell that the Frankenstein monster realizes it, too. Given what you know about the story of Frankenstein, you don't think that the monster will take very kindly to things being slaves.

You don't seem to be wrong, either, as the film jumps again and in the next scene the Frankenstein monster is above ground, inside the huge dome from before, smashing Phantomites. They fire bolts of lightning at him from things that look like glass balls on top of pyramids, but they hardly slow him down. Then, he knocks down the wall of the dome, and from the outside you can see the model building falling apart, no doubt crushing the Phantomites.

The big fight comes when the Phantomites send a huge version of themselves—one with bigger pincer arms than the others, and an enormous translucent brain inside a glass shell—to fight the Frankenstein monster. The two grapple, and it looks like the Frankenstein monster is done for, as the other Phantomites crowd in and distract him by zapping him with the tuning forks on the end of sticks that they had earlier. But then the fungus people come streaming up out from the underground somewhere, and they start to fight the smaller Phantomites, freeing up the Frankenstein monster to concentrate on the big one.

He manages to tear off one of its pincer arms, and then he uses it to crack the glass dome that encases the actual Phantomite brain thingy. After that, he pushes the whole thing over into the same pit that the Phantomites tricked him into earlier. You don't see what happens to it when it falls, but you know that it can't be very good.

The movie ends abruptly, with Frankenstein's monster sitting on a big throne, like he was at the beginning. This time, though, there are no chains, and he's surrounded not by an angry mob but by the fungus people, their mushroom heads all bowed. As the screen fades out, it is replaced one last time by titles:

FRANKENSTEIN, KING OF THE PHANTOM PLANET

After that there's a commercial, and when Baron von Werewolf comes back on he's smiling, but he also seems nervous, his good eye glancing around a lot rather than looking right at the camera, and therefore at you. The book is lying on the desk now, and he's pacing in front of it. Not for effect, like he sometimes does, but just pacing, like someone waiting to be called into the principal's office.

"What did you think of that, kids?" he asks, again seeming to force his smile. "I know that it's a little shorter than some of the other things we've seen on here, and I've got more in store for you, so don't change the channel…"

He's probably going to say more, you figure he is, but instead he stops his pacing. He's not looking at the camera, but he's also not looking at what's behind him, where the camera is pointing. You are, though. It seems like the library has gotten darker, without you really noticing, and most of that dark seems to be gathered in one corner, the corner directly opposite the camera.

In fact, that corner has gotten so dark that you can't see it anymore. The painted stones of the castle wall are gone, and the candles in the nearest candelabra have started to dim, their flames suddenly burning blue. Baron von Werewolf still isn't looking in that direction, he's staring off the screen, his arm half-raised, and you can see his breath in the air all of a sudden, like when you go outside on a very cold day.

The shadow in the corner is getting darker yet, thicker, and it seems like it's getting more solid, somehow. At the edges, it looks almost tattered, like instead of a shadow it's a bunch of dark cloth, or black spider webs. Somewhere up high in the dark, too high for a person's head, unless they were standing on a ladder, you notice that there are two eyes. Or maybe they're not eyes, though it's the first thing you think to call them, because of how they're spaced apart. They don't really look like eyes, though. They look like metal, or maybe like glass, with something moving on the other side of them. It's one of the neatest effects you ever saw.

"No," Baron von Werewolf says, very quietly, still not looking into the shadow that's getting thicker by the minute. "Please. Not in front of the kids?"

The shadow reaches out an arm, a sleeve of darkness with just the echo of fingers jutting from the cuff, and then the picture is gone, replaced by a piercing whine and a bunch of colored bars, like when they test the Emergency Broadcast System.

You stare at the colored bars for a while, and then they're replaced by a commercial, and then the news, which never shows at this time on Saturday afternoon. Finally, you turn the TV off.

You're worried about Baron von Werewolf at first, but then you remember that it's just a show, like your mom is always saying. What you saw had to be a special effect, like the stop motion in the Frankenstein movie. They wouldn't have put it on TV otherwise, right? So instead of worrying, you go outside, under the bright blue September sky, with just a handful of clouds overhead. Under your feet the yard is full of dead leaves and the branches of the tree are already almost bare.

You know that the movies are fake, but you also know that they teach you something real. Just as real as the things your mom tells you, or the things you learn in school. How to look past what's actually there and see instead what *might* be. That's what you're thinking about, as you look up at the sky.

You learned about space in school, too. How just because you can't see it when it's daytime, doesn't mean that it isn't there. You know that just beyond the blue, blue sky, stars and phantom planets are tumbling through the dark, so you stand there in the yard, looking up, past what you can see, and try to imagine what might be waiting on the other side.

for Willis O'Brien and James Whale,
and for all the horror hosts everywhere
past, present, and (hopefully) future.

WITHER ON THE VINE; OR, STRICKFADEN'S MONSTER

NATHAN CARSON

enneth Strickfaden leaned against twin trunks sprung from the same stump. The bark felt cold against his shoulder. One bole was charred black from a lightning strike. He shifted his weight from its pale brother, enjoying a shred of warmth in the path of the last rays of the failing November sun which slunk to the west behind Ochre Mountain.

In one hand he clutched a compass. It led him southwest from his Gold Hill breakdown through this chilled desert canyon. Under his breath, he cursed the cracked flywheel of his 1912 Model T Ford. The old beast was now seven years young; few of its original parts remained after their painstaking two-month trek.

After training for the Great War, he'd arrived in France too late. The only action he'd seen was in a brothel in Saint Nazare. Nevertheless, all the boys who climbed off the boat in New York harbor were hailed as heroes. During his first few weeks back on American soil he visited the Statue of Liberty and sold war photos that he'd shot overseas and developed in his own dark room. Otherwise he passed time tinkering in a makeshift laboratory that rekindled his lifelong fascination with electricity.

By the end of September he was on the road heading home to sunny Santa Monica. Even before the breakdown, the going was slow. He had been on foot for nearly three days now. It would be December soon.

Strick shoved off the tree and dusted the soot from his jacket arm. Near as he could figure it was a fifteen-mile walk from the desolation of Gold Hill to Ipabah's frontier semblance of civilization. There he might be able to trade day labor for a hot meal, a haystack bed, and ultimately, a new flywheel. He knew tonight would be new moon and quickened his pace to avoid a two-hour hike in darkness. Once he rounded the foot of Ochre Mountain he was pleased to gain a brief respite of sunset light.

Ipabah was as far west as one could go in Utah without running into Nevada. The little town nestled at the head of the Deep Creek range had been a stop for the Pony Express. Now its greatest features were the Sheridan Hotel and a withering mining industry. Of greater import to Ken Strickfaden was its tiny trading post.

The air was near to freezing when he creaked up the stairs. A bright tungsten lamp above the porch cast a long shadow cross onto the heavy wooden door. Inside, a well-dressed man about twice Ken's age stood in front of the counter, poring over a long list of items he'd ordered. A short-haired boy of perhaps twelve perched on a pew reading a pulp periodical. Ken sat beside the boy to wait his turn. As he blew warm air on his hands and rubbed them together, he noticed that the boy was studying a gatefold illustration of an electrical diagram.

"Excuse me, son. What are you reading there?" Ken asked him.

Without looking up, the boy responded in his thick western drawl, "*Electrical Experimenter.* November issue."

"You don't say," Ken replied with a smile. "Mind if I take a peek at it?"

The boy looked up at him warily, then saw the ease in the young man's smile. He handed it over.

Ken examined the cover, which depicted the silhouette of a woman holding a hand mirror. Her hair stood straight up as if it were a plume. The caption read, "Cold Fire?" He then flipped open the magazine and thumbed through it until he found what he was looking for.

"See this?" he asked the boy. "That's a picture of my lab back in New York. I won first prize in a contest with these photos."

The boy took the magazine back and ran his finger over the page. There were two pictures of electrical benches covered in tube radio gadgets. On one sat a large coil. Between them was a photo of Ken with his military cap on. At the top of the page, large stylized text read, "Amateur Electrical Laboratory Contest. This month's $5.00 prize winner—Kenneth Strickfaden."

Ken reached out his hand. The boy took it and shook it.

"Gee, Mister," he looked back at the page to double check, "Strick... Faden? I never met a real military scientist before."

Ken laughed. "Well, I'm not exactly either at the moment." He pointed to the word "Amateur" on the page and grinned. "But I bet if you keep reading these we'll see *your* picture in here someday. What's your name, son?"

Just then, the man at the counter began to raise his voice in anger.

"I'm sorry, Mr. Baldwin," the shopkeeper said in response. "I wrote down everything you asked for. The other twenty-two items are here. I'll be glad to phone Salt Lake tomorrow and ask about the oversight."

Baldwin grimaced through his mustache. "This is all so much junk without the wire. What good is a crate of voltmeters and transformers if I have no way to connect them?"

"I wouldn't know, Mr. Baldwin. I can't even shoe a horse. No one has ever sent for components like these out here before. I did my best to place your order exactly as you worded it."

"Excuse me," Ken butted in. "But I've..." Baldwin raised a palm to silence him. His brow furrowed and his mustache bristled. The shopkeeper looked fearful.

"Thank you for your efforts. I know you do not open on Saturdays. Please be thou an example and make the call tomorrow. If you had thought to make it today, you might have saved me a trip. Good evening to you. Come, Philo," he said.

The boy waved goodbye to Ken as the two stepped into the cold and slammed the door behind them.

Ken blinked in bemusement and rested his elbows on the counter. "I'm looking to purchase a flywheel for a Model T," he said. The shopkeeper found an automotive catalog and flipped it open on the counter. He dragged a finger along a column of numbers and then alighted on one.

"No," Ken said. "The magnets aren't peened on that one."

He reached over and nudged the other man's finger to a different row. The shopkeeper narrowed his eyes, then dabbed a pen in an inkwell and drew a circle around the correct part number.

"How much and how long?" Ken asked.

"Twenty-seven dollars. Two weeks."

"You've got to be kidding me. That's highway robbery. And I can't stay here for two weeks!"

"Sorry sir. The part costs twenty-three. Our markup is only four. Ipabah is a long way from Detroit. "

Ken shook his head. "Ugh, I was just there last month."

"Could be you should have stocked up on parts."

"Well anyway, do you know a place I could stay tonight?"

"The Sheridan Hotel is nice enough, sir."

"I'm sure it is," Ken said. "But if my part costs twenty-seven bucks, I don't have the funds for a hotel. Please order the flywheel. I'll be back."

"Where, may I ask, did you stay last night?"

"With Indians."

"Were they mean?"

"No, they were fantastic," Ken recalled.

"Must have been Goshute tribe. If you're ever in a fight, get a Paiute on your side."

"I'll keep that in mind," Ken said.

He buttoned his coat, flipped the collar up to cover his neck and the bottoms of his ears, then stepped back out onto the porch. Baldwin stood there smoking. The boy shivered at his side and blew twin trails of steam out of his nose.

"You are Kenneth Strickfaden?" Baldwin asked.

"Yes sir. I guess an article in one of Mr. Gernsback's magazines really can make a guy famous," Ken said with a laugh. He extended his hand. Baldwin took it.

"Philo has been assisting me with some experiments. But he is just a lad. And he is overdue to return home. I could not help but overhear that your vehicle is in distress and you are short of means. I could use a man who knows his watts from his ohms. Would you consider a short-term employment while you await your repairs?"

Ken grinned. "I'll take the job and do you one better, Mr. Baldwin. I've got a spool of concentric wire stashed in the boot of my automobile up in Gold Hill."

***

It was too late and too dark to fetch the wire. Ken rode in the back of the Oldsmobile because there was only one seat up front. Baldwin started the car, saying, "Bless that we will travel home in safety." Ken squished into the shiny black interior beside Philo. It was not hard to deduce that Baldwin could certainly afford to hire strangers if he was driving a touring car that was less than a year old in rural Utah.

Ken's suspicions were confirmed when the three rolled up to the Manor house. The bumpy half-hour drive through circuitous countryside was only visible in the path of the headlamps. Ken spent it quizzing Philo about basic electrical concepts. Baldwin rarely chimed in. When they had lurched to a stop in the Manor's semi-circle drive, Ken marveled at the looming structure. Light shone from bay windows of the great Victorian. In the darkness he could only imagine its asymmetrical bulk based on the closest turret and its wraparound porch.

Baldwin ushered him inside the foyer. A handsome woman in bonnet, apron, and petticoat took his jacket. Strickfaden had not set foot in a place this nice since his August visit to the Metropolitan Museum of Art in New York. Someone had made great use of a local quarry when building the house; little expense had been spared furnishing it.

"We can take our coffee here, Mr Strickfaden," Baldwin said, "but this is as far as you go. I'll show you to the work quarters above the shop after we talk. One thing we must agree on is that you will not enter this house without being escorted by myself, or Mr. Woolley. No offence intended, but this is a holy place."

"Sounds fair enough. Please, call me Strick. All my friends do."

"And I am Nathaniel. I'm glad that we can make friends so quickly, Strick. I admit, I'd be much more wary of a stranger if you weren't a serviceman."

"Well, I wasn't exactly a ranking officer, but I got on well with everyone."

"Trust me, Strick. If you were a politician, I would have left you to sleep in the street."

After the coffee service, which also functioned as dinner for Ken, Baldwin led him to an adjacent building across the yard. Beside the great Manor, the shop seemed squat at only two stories. It appeared newly built and modern in style, but most importantly was fully wired and stocked with tools and equipment.

"Nice place," Ken said.

"Thank you," Baldwin replied. "Mr. Woolley's mines funded much of this. My radio business did the rest."

"You're in radio?"

"Indeed. I hold many patents. You may learn much from me. But even I am not the master engineer of this project. See for yourself."

Ken took the folder he was handed and untied the ribbon. A sheaf of plans on vellum slid out. He spread them in an array on the workbench and angled the arc light. There were designs for at least a dozen inexplicable machines. It seemed like something out of Jules Verne—a joke—until he noticed the signature in the corner.

"Nikola Tesla? Are you serious?"

"Yes," Baldwin answered. "Quite. Mr. Woolley was impressed by the experiments in Colorado Springs. Unfortunately Tesla is now building tractors in Wisconsin. But we have the plans. And tomorrow, after we retrieve the wire from your vehicle, we will have all the necessary parts. But time is of the essence. These must be constructed to exact specifications before his arrival."

"You mean... Tesla is coming... here?" Ken Strickfaden felt a cold sweat. There were few men on earth he revered more.

"We could only convince him to join us over the holiday. He recently began work at Allis-Chalmers. Despite our earnest efforts to bribe him, he is reluctant to displease his new employers. That gives us scant time to construct his apparatuses. Please read the plans over tonight. Tomorrow we drive at dawn. Tesla will arrive in six days. I am exceedingly grateful to have met you, brother. Sleep well."

It took an hour to retrieve the spool of wire and everything else of value from Ken's Model T. The car was as he'd left it, unmolested behind a copse of junipers and covered in sagebrush. The sun was white on a white sky. A cock was still crowing when they returned to the Manor for breakfast. Ken was informed that his would be brought out to the shop.

He gratefully washed down warm scones and jam with that fine-scented black coffee while reviewing Tesla's plans. Poring over them before bed had yielded strange dreams of kites drawing fluid from the sky over a castle laboratory by night. The schematics were simple enough to follow, but the purpose of the machines was not explained nor could it be deduced. As they were unmarked, Ken took it upon himself to pencil a name on each. Soon he was doing a parts inventory for the Megavolt Senior, Megavolt Junior, the Fireloscope, Nebularium, Involuntarium, the Cosmic Ray Diffuser and half a dozen more. He hoped that Tesla would not be offended by his irreverence.

By noon he had determined that all components were accounted for save the bunch Baldwin had left at the trading post. Next Ken began cutting lengths of wire according to the specs. Baldwin soon arrived with the crate of transformers, followed by a servant bearing a lunch tray.

"I do appreciate your industriousness, Strick," said Baldwin. "We may just meet our deadline yet. After we break bread, I'll roll up my sleeves and join you."

"What exactly are we doing here?" Ken asked. "Some of these machine are fairly simple. A few are highly complex. I don't get what any of them actually do."

Baldwin dismissed the maid who cleared away the dishes and left the shop.

"If Mr. Woolley intends for you to know, he will tell you. Until such time, please do as you have. I believe we are being quite generous. By the way, I left payment for your flywheel. The receipt will be yours upon completion of the machines."

"Thank you, Nathaniel. I don't mean to sound like an ingrate."

"Not at all, Strick. Now, let us make some magic, shall we?"

Over the weekend, Ken worked hard and asked few questions. Saturday, Baldwin put in some feverish hours alongside him. On Sunday, Ken was left to toil alone while his benefactor ran important errands for his business and his church. LDS talk was certainly not off limits to Baldwin. Half his conversations were pure high-end radio theory, the rest revolved around revelations. Ken quickly boiled Baldwin's fascinations down in his mind to P&P: "Profits and Prophets."

Something else Ken took note of was the traffic to and from the Manor. In three days he'd seen four fancy cars come and go, usually after nightfall and before the dawn. Well-dressed churchmen of varying ages were escorted through the front door of the Manor as if royalty was being received under moonless skies.

By Sunday night after dark, the moon waxed thin as a filament. Ken worked alone as he had all day, deeply concerned about his deadline and impressing Tesla. He was threading wire attached to a cathode deep through a brass cylinder. The duct reached his shoulder and its jagged edge bit delicately into his skin. The maid burst in and he dropped the whole contraption in alarm. It made a great racket and the glass tube shattered on the hard floor.

"I'm sorry, sir!" she exclaimed.

"It's okay. I've got plenty of those. What can I do for you?"

"Sir, there is a telephone call."

"From who? No one knows that I'm here."

"It is Mr. Tesla, sir. Neither Mr. Woolley nor Mr. Baldwin is home. So he asked to speak to you."

"I'm not allowed into the Manor without one of them."

"Mr. Tesla said it was most urgent, sir."

Ken shook his head, wiped the grease off his hands with a rag and followed the young woman across the yard, hoping he wasn't about to get himself fired.

She led him through the foyer, past the greeting hall, and through the dining area. This was the deepest he'd been in the Manor. His eyes took in everything. Rows of narrow windows stretched nearly to the ceiling. The table was the length of the room. Its polished wood was so dark that the surface was a mirror. Everything was fine enough for royalty. The only thing unusual was the furniture. Rather than matching chairs along that epic-length of table, each seemed built for a different frame. Some were high, others banked, and some resembled stocks with holes for head and hands more than any seat built for polite supper. Before Ken could ask the maid any questions they had stepped into a parlor. She lifted the handset from the cradle and passed it to him.

"Hello?" Ken said, leaning in toward the receiver.

"Schtrickfodden?"

"Yes, I'm Ken Strickfaden."

"This is Tesla."

Ken was silent. Then, "It's an honor to speak with you, Mr. Tesla. How may I be of service?"

"I checked up on you, Schtrickfodden. Hugo speaks highly of your character and abilities."

"Mr. Gernsback was very kind to me in New York. I was flattered to appear in the same magazine as you, sir. And please, call me Strick."

"I need to know something from you, Schtrick. Can these church men be trusted?"

"How so?"

"What I mean is, are they fluid?"

"I'm afraid I still don't follow."

"Will their check be of rubber?"

"Oh," Ken got it. "No, I don't think so. Based on what I've seen, these people are loaded."

"That is good news. I need you to make sure they have my fifty percent up front, upon arrival. I gave them incomplete plans until I am paid my fee."

"I did wonder why these machines seemed... fragmentary."

"Insurance! Baldwin is a clever man, and now he has found you. The final designs and equipment will travel with me next week. Please make certain that they have half my fee when I arrive."

"How much is that, sir?"

"One hundred fifty thousand dollars."

Ken gulped.

"And they must provide a fine whiskey for me," said Tesla. "I drink a glass every day. For my health."

"Well, I can ask, sir. But you know, it's Prohibition now. And we are in Utah."

"Bah. Tell them to have it. If they are rich and clever, they will find some."

"I will certainly pass along your requests to them. Now about the machines: I am following your specs, but I think it might be helpful to understand what it is that they are meant to do."

"Woolley has not told you?"

"I haven't met Mr. Woolley yet. I understand he's a very busy man."

"Have you met his wife?"

"No sir."

"Have you read my articles on projectiles?"

"You mean the Death Ray?"

"Beam! It is a beam, not a ray!"

"Oh yes. My mistake."

"Well, this one will be..." Ken heard a woman scream through the phone and a heavy commotion through the ceiling above the parlor. Tesla's voice cut off as the line went dead. Ken clicked the cradle several times but heard only static.

The maid was nowhere to be found and Ken was caught between earnest concern for a lady in distress and the urgent desire to flee the Manor and lock himself safely in the workshop where he belonged. But as a twenty-three-year-old single man recently released from the service, he had only one real option.

Ken took the spiral staircase three steps at a time. After ascending its grand curve he did his best to reorient in order to discover which room sat atop the parlor. On the second story landing he tiptoed down the hall until he stood where he imagined the room was. A muffled sobbing emanated from the door behind him. He turned and gave a ginger knock.

At first there was utter silence. Then the crystal knob turned and the door opened a crack. The maid peered through with one eye. She looked shaken and pale. From somewhere beyond her another woman's voice asked, "Well, who is it?"

"The workman. The scientist," said the maid without taking her eye off Ken.

"Let him in," said the other woman.

The maid drew the door wide. Inside was a lady's bedchamber with finery equal to the rest of the house. A young woman sat on the four-poster with a jumble of silks huddled around her shoulders and a pile of shoes at her feet. The covers seemed excessive, though perhaps she was ill. The house was certainly drafty in spots, but a great blaze crackled in the fireplace and heavy curtains were pulled over the window. Ken stepped inside the warmth. The maid shut the door behind him.

"Welcome, Mr. Strickfaden," said the woman on the bed. "I am Fanny Baldwin."

Ken stepped toward her slowly and offered his hand. She grazed his with her own and gave him an approving nod.

"Pleased to meet you, Mrs. Baldwin. I didn't realize that Nathaniel had family so close at hand." He immediately wondered if he had rudely broken Baldwin's confidence by revealing that the man had not once spoken of her despite their long hours working together.

"You would have no reason to gather that I exist, Mr. Strickfaden. We are full of secrets in this house."

The maid cleared her voice as if in warning.

Fanny furrowed her brow then relaxed. "Be good and bring us that tea, would you, dear?"

"Yes, milady. I had just put the kettle on before I came to check on you."

The maid gave Ken a look that could have been disapproval or warning or something else, perhaps extreme terror. Then she stepped into the hall.

That Baldwin should take Fanny as a wife came as no surprise. She was a strikingly attractive woman. Though why he kept her cloistered was a mystery Ken knew better than to question.

"I heard a scream," he said. "Is anything the matter?" Just then he noticed the curved deco telephone on her night stand within arm's reach.

Fanny followed his gaze to the phone. "Oh, you have caught me. I was being a bit wicked. Will you forgive me for spying? I rarely leave this room. Listening to voices from afar gives me some mild pleasure and escape."

"I certainly don't mind," Ken said. "But of course I can't speak for Mr. Tesla."

"Oh, that wicked man!" Fanny cried. "I fear for myself. And for Mary."

"Is that the maid's name? I never caught it."

Fanny laughed. "No, no. The maid is Hesper. Mary is my twin sister."

"Ah," said Ken. "Does she also live here in the Manor?"

"Of course. We are never separated."

At that, the door swung open and Hesper returned with the tea service. She set the silver platter on a tray near the bed. Arranged upon it were the teapot, napkins, dainties, two tiny spoons, a dried flower, and a small medicinal phial.

"Thank you, dear," said Fanny.

Hesper poured two steaming cups. Then she raised the phial and asked, "Will you be wanting more medicine?"

"I think she's had quite enough for tonight," answered Fanny. "But you may serve it in mine. I dare say a sound, dreamless sleep sounds divine after the shock I just had."

Ken was about to ask whom they were speaking of when a gurgle rose from the bedding draped over Fanny's shoulders. He then perceived the outline of another figure beneath them.

"Perhaps she's having trouble breathing," Hesper offered in concern.

"Nonsense," said Fanny. "We've been playing this game since we were children."

The sound increased to something akin to the keening of a wounded animal and the blankets began to quiver. Fanny's eyes took on a look of alarm. "Perchance you're right, Hesper. She may be close to another attack.

Here, help us, please."

Ken stood stiff in shock as the maid drew back the linens and revealed another woman beside Fanny. The sisters shared four feet on three legs. The bedclothes made it hard to be sure, but it seemed they were literally attached at the hip, with two torsos and four arms rising out of a common core. But while Fanny's skin was like a saucer of milk, her sister's flesh was black leather.

Mary's eyes shone white in the dim room and gazed upon Ken with desperation. From beneath billowing gown sleeves her thin arms looked like limbs burnt in a forest fire. She opened her mouth as if to speak only to vomit a cascade of watery liquid down her front. Then she burst with a laughter so horrid that Ken's flesh crawled at the sound.

Fanny shrieked in disgust and distress. Hesper rushed forth with a handful of napkins and dabbed at Mary's mess. Over her shoulder, the maid regarded Ken.

"You'd best go. Mrs. Woolley is not well."

Ken didn't need further prodding. He made for the exit. As he turned to close the door behind him, Mary caught his eye. In her gaze he saw something that spoke of terror and need. He returned a look that he hoped she could discern as a pact that this would not be their only meeting. Then he clicked the door closed and rushed downstairs.

As Ken stepped onto the porch, headlights from two cars angled into the drive. There was no time to do otherwise so Ken hopped over the railing into the desert shrubs that circuited the place like a moat of thorns. He lay still in wait. The porch light ruined his night vision so he focused on calming his breathing and easing the pounding heartbeat in his ears.

The engines died together and four car doors swung open. Several men ushered from each. Ken could hear their expensive boots crunching in the turf then stomping up the steps and onto the porch.

He heard Nathaniel Baldwin say, "Do not wait for us, boys. We know you are anxious to see your wives."

Another man, an older one, spoke. "You know the decree. You heard the revelation as I wrote of it. No year shall pass without children of plurality. Go make new life."

The others entered the house with hollers of revelry. Once the front door closed, Baldwin and the older man lit cigars. For a moment, they stood smoking in silence.

"Can he really do it, Nathaniel? Can he save my Mary?"

"Lorin," said Baldwin, "if anyone on Earth wields an ampere of the Lord's power, it is Nikola Tesla."

"Is this a sacrilege we are discussing?" Woolley asked.

"Tesla told me that his machines are powered by a set of golden plates from Palmyra. My heart rests easy in that knowledge," Baldwin said.

"Dear God, make it so. If money can buy her rejuvenation, it is worth any price to me."

Baldwin puffed on his cigar. "I have read Tesla's papers on Teleforce," he replied. "They are ambitious, but the concept is sound."

He put his arm around Lorin Woolley's shoulder and walked him to the front door.

Baldwin smiled in reassurance. "If he can create a death ray, surely he can forge us a life beam."

When the door closed them inside, Ken scrambled out of the brambles and returned to the workshop to ponder all he had just learned.

The next morning Hesper came to the workshop to summon Ken to breakfast in the Manor.

He slung a slack suspender over his shoulder as he walked across the yard. "Do they know I was in here last night?" he asked.

"I did not speak a word of it, sir. I pray that you will not."

"It's our secret," he said. "Assuming Fanny hasn't already let the cat out of the bag."

In the dining room, the furniture had been rearranged. Only normal matching chairs were set around one end of the table. Lorin Woolley sat at the head. The old gentleman stood when he saw Ken arrive.

"Mr. Strickfaden, I presume."

"Yes sir. And you are?"

"Lorin C. Woolley. But I gather you knew that already. Let there be no secrets between us, son."

Ken took a seat by an empty setting and tucked a napkin into his shirt. There were half a dozen men he didn't recognize who were drinking coffee and discussing their affairs as if they were all quite familiar. Ken seemed to be the only odd man there.

Mr. Woolley resumed his seat. Then Baldwin entered the room and took the spot beside Strickfaden. He eyed Ken with curiosity and began cleaving a roll in half with his knife.

"We shall speak after breakfast," Baldwin said out of the corner of his mouth. Ken simply nodded and spread honey on his bread.

The serving girl brought out a tureen of steaming gravy and a platter of ham. The men at the table helped themselves. When their repast was finished, a tray of cigarettes was handed around while the table was cleared.

Lorin Woolley addressed them.

"Friends, it brings me great joy to have you gathered in advance of the upcoming holiday. Please accept my thanks and hospitality for joining me here and now since duty will call Messrs. Baldwin and Strickfaden away on a very important mission immediately following our Thanksgiving dinner three days hence."

All the men nodded. They were happy to be away from home and work on a Monday morning. The tobacco helped their digestion.

Woolley continued, "The time is not yet nigh, but one day you shall all be apostles. Excepting you two, of course." He smiled and indicated the two engineers. "I sense a schism coming. We shall lead by example and keep John Taylor's revelation alive. Plurality is a part of God's plan and this house is a sanctuary for our practice. It shall always be a haven for your families, my brothers and friends."

Woolley went on about how his gold mines had dried up, then the silver, and now all that was left was arsenic, but Ken found his mind wandering back to the machines and the Life Beam. Baldwin noticed his distraction and excused the two of them. As they walked back to the workshop, he placed an arm on Ken's shoulder.

"I know you were in the house last night while we were away."

"Yes," Ken admitted. "I'm very sorry about that. But Tesla phoned and urgently asked to speak with me."

"I know. Fanny told me. Do not fear. I forgive you. It has already been discussed. We will have his money. And his whiskey," Baldwin laughed. "Time is short, Ken. Can I count on you?"

"Of course, Nathaniel. I'm fascinated to see this through. Also, my flywheel is probably no closer than Kalamazoo right now." They both smiled.

"I am very glad. Now let us make each hour count."

The next three days were one long flurry of activity. Pausing only for meals, the two men assembled Tesla's machines. Once they clashed over how to read a schematic; Ken deferred to Baldwin's age and expertise. Otherwise they toiled and built by day and night. Each evening the horned sliver moon grew to greater illuminate the glowing snow peaks on the Deep Creek range.

Late Wednesday night, Ken was working alone. Hesper called on him. She was meek and looked over her shoulder.

"May I help you, Hesper?" he asked.

"Milady calls for you, sir."

"Fanny Baldwin?"

"No sir. Mary Woolley."

"Are their husbands home?"

"No sir. They are away on an errand. I do not expect them back for hours."

He followed her inside and upstairs. The fire still roared in the ladies' bedchamber. Fanny Baldwin snored loudly.

Hesper confirmed, "She took all of Mary's medicine again."

Ken approached and saw that Mary was lying deathly still with eyes open wide. They watched him. Her scaly flesh was unnerving to behold. Despite his aversion, he forced himself to smile. When he did, her eyes watered. She rasped a word that he could not hear. So he leaned in close and gave her his ear.

"Poi... son," was all she said.

Ken's eyes darted toward the maid across the room. Mary shook her head. Then she inclined her charcoal cheek toward her slumbering twin. Ken was alarmed.

"What can I do?" he asked.

"Clean, food. Clean... water," she implored.

"Hesper," he said, turning. She seemed to perk out of a dream at hearing her name. "Please bring fresh water and broth for Mrs. Woolley."

"At once, sir."

As soon as the maid had gone, he leaned back in. "Why would your sister want to harm you? Surely that would cause her equal ill?"

"We... share... bone... not heart. But she... has always... hated. If... I die... we may be split. Then she... would be... free."

Ken felt stunned. He looked at Fanny, then to Mary. Despite her condition, he could see that their features were nearly identical. Fanny's face contorted in sleep to a wicked grimace. Mary attempted a smile and her lip cracked. Ken fished a kerchief from his pocket and dabbed away the blood. He pulled a chair beside the bed and sat in silence until Hesper returned.

He spooned broth into her and helped her drink. She took it slowly; her system had grown used to rejecting everything that came in. By the time the bowl was empty she already seemed stronger.

"Bless you," she said. "We are grateful for the moisture. I cannot thank you enough."

"You can thank me by getting well. What will it take?"

Mary thought. "Tesla's machine," she said.

Thursday morning there was still more to be done.

"Can you finish without me?" Baldwin asked. He had returned at dawn. "We have the whole house turning out for the feast this afternoon."

"I will," Ken said.

He was good on his word. By afternoon Ken was tightening screws and double and triple checking for details he might have missed. By the time Hesper beckoned him to Thanksgiving dinner, he had swept up the broken glass and inventoried all unused parts. He slid Tesla's plans back in their folder and wound the ribbon tight, then filled a basin and washed his neck, head, and hands.

When he stepped out of the workshop there was a line of black snow-capped autos parked around the house. Corpulent white flakes fell from a cloudy sky. Ken trudged across the whitening yard and stomped the ice out of his shoes.

The hall trees were flocked with hats and greatcoats. Ken well knew his way to the dining room by now. The commotion this afternoon was the greatest volume and bustle since he had arrived nearly a week prior. A great party was seated around the table in revelry. Ken sought an empty seat, then stopped in his tracks to survey the gathering.

The council of friends who had sat with Woolley on Monday morning were all accounted for and more. A few new men joined the congregation. It would have seemed quite odd to Ken that so many important men could be away from their families over the holiday. Then he saw that they had all brought their wives. A typical urban society churchwoman sat beside each. Flanking them were all the denizens of the manor—women twisted with crippling defects, some missing limbs, others well-formed but inexplicably odd. Their special furniture had been returned; some leaned over their plates on hinged wooden planks. Another was fitted through stocks so she could balance on a chair with no legs to support her. All were dressed in spotless regalia suitable for jubilee.

Lorin C. Woolley led with a prayer. The first course was about to be served when Nathaniel Baldwin came down the serpentine staircase to greet the assembly.

"I have wonderful news, my friends. Fanny and Mary will be joining us."

Woolley looked genuinely shocked and delighted. Soon after, the twins were spotted slowly descending with the aid of two strong menials. The wives had a wardrobe of specially tailored dresses to choose from; this was a pleated lilac gown fit for a Romanian countess. Actually the garment was two dresses sewn together, and their slow floating procession looked like purple paper dolls come to life to haunt the Manor on a holy day.

Their special double seat was set between Messrs. Woolley and Baldwin. Fanny had done her makeup and looked especially lovely. Mary was wrapped in gauze like a mummy fresh from the spa; her lips were caked with crimson lipstick and her honey hair waved about her shoulders. Ken sat in the empty seat across from Mary. He could see that her eyes were sharp. She blinked both at him once during grace then avoided his gaze for the remainder of the meal. He felt relieved.

Ken tried to focus on his meat and drink. The conversations around him spoke of life by the Salt Lake and ever more fantastic revelations that some believed and some denied. Accusations were made but holiday reminders calmed the fire. Manor wives cavorted around their plates, clearly enjoying a rare public gathering. Ken saw one woman's skin stretched tight over jutting bones that protruded from a bulging brown rococo dress. He looked down at the drumstick in his hand and let it slacken to his plate.

A phonograph was set up and music frosted the room like a cake, signaling the last course. At the far end of the table, a primitive dessert service involved three of the wives stabbing some furry squealing creature Ken couldn't quite recognize. Try as they might, the women could not seem to kill the little beastie. Finally a panicked servant took it away amongst a bevy of cackles and blood.

Lorin Woolley held his wife's bandaged hand. He set it gently on the table and addressed Nathaniel Baldwin.

"Why has Tesla not joined us?" he asked.

Baldwin dabbed his mouth with a napkin, answering, "He phoned earlier. He's not coming. I did not want the news to ruin our meal."

"But why? We agreed to his terms." This was the first time Ken had heard a hint of desperation in Woolley's voice. He was always otherwise firmly in control.

"The weather," said Baldwin. "Or the inclination of a madman. Who knows?"

"Can you make the machines work without him?"

"Impossible, Lorin. Tesla holds the keys to all of them. And the golden plates. However, they will still be completed. He has offered to meet us at a laboratory in Moab."

"No!" Fanny yelped. "I won't go." She began to sob.

"But my dearest," Lorin said, "we must save your sister."

"How can a death ray possibly save her?" she asked.

"Oh, child." He leaned in and put his arm around his wife. "We have not built a death ray. This is a healing power. All will be well."

She wiped her tears away and looked at him. Then Mary spoke.

"The life beam cures all," she said. Every conversation at the table ceased at once.

Baldwin tried to shush her, but the damage was done. Women looked to their husbands in question, then all eyes turned to Lorin Woolley.

He sighed. "My friends. My. Friends. We had hoped to bring this gift to Ipabah. Mary was to be our test subject. Do you truly want to travel to Moab in snow and risk your very lives for this slender chance?"

The room was silent for a pregnant moment.

"Yes!" said the woman in the stocks. "I will ride there and walk home!" She pointed to the space where her legs should have been. The rest of the table chimed in. All wanted to go. None were afraid.

Mr. Woolley called for silence. "Then it shall be done," he said. Applause and cheers erupted around the room and many thanks were given in Woolley's honor. "We will leave tomorrow morning if God wills it."

WITHER ON THE VINE, OR STRICKFADEN'S MONSTER

***

In the morning, the snow was seven inches deep and the truck arranged to transport the machines was late to arrive. Ken was wrapping an apparatus in a bolt of cloth to protect it when Baldwin entered the workshop carrying a box in his arms.

"What have you there?" Ken asked as he tied the last knot.

"See for yourself." Baldwin placed it on the workbench.

Ken dusted his hands and broke the box open. Inside was a gleaming new flywheel assembly fitted with an old style single stack magneto coil ring. He ship-whistled high to low in approval.

"It arrived on Wednesday," Baldwin said. "I did not want to tell you until the work was done."

Ken laughed. "I don't blame you. You did the right thing. I guess the tradesman was being very conservative in his estimate. This was the shortest two weeks of my life."

Baldwin smiled. "Does this mean you will be leaving now?"

"Hell no," Ken said. Baldwin frowned. "Excuse me," Ken said. "Heck no. I want to see this thing through. I want to meet Tesla. And I want our devices to help those poor women."

"This makes me glad," Baldwin said. They both heard the cargo truck struggling into the drive through deepening drifts of snow.

It took days for the caravan to cross the state in the worst blizzard to hit Utah in a hundred years. Many men questioned the wisdom of such a dangerous journey, but Woolley's courage, and the undaunted hope of the Manor wives, helped them push through. By the time the congregation descended on a hotel in Moab, the skies had cleared. Either the worst had passed, or God's influence somehow waned in the stark desert lands.

The hotel clerk handed Baldwin a telegraph, which he shared with Ken and Lorin.

"It's from Tesla. He landed last night and began preparations. Included here are coordinates for the laboratory."

Ken looked it over. "What are these marks at the bottom?"

"That is code," Baldwin said. "He asked that we pay his expenses at the hotel before we leave. And he wants his whiskey."

***

Lorin Woolley stayed behind to thaw out and rest. It had been a difficult trip for a man in his sixties, but his love and hope for his second wife was great. He made it his own responsibility to breathe warm air on the morale of the congregation. Meanwhile, Baldwin and Strickfaden headed out to the station to greet Tesla and install the machines.

The truck driver nearly missed the turn but hard sunlight cast shadows on the deep ruts left by the last vehicle to veer off the main desert road. Black rocks poked through the shallow snow like peppercorns on a salt spill. The truck finally came to a stop at the foot of a high mesa. The driver lifted his cap to scratch his head.

"These are the coordinates he gave us," he said. "I hope we have not been led astray."

"I don't think so," Ken said, leaning forward. He pointed up through the windshield.

Atop the great mesa stood a structure evoking a miniature Eiffel Tower with a mushroom cap head.

"Heavenly father," Baldwin said to himself as the truck lurched into gear to circuit the butte.

The car Tesla had hired was parked on the far side. Baldwin asked his driver to sound the horn. After a minute without response, they took it upon themselves to scale the mesa in the large basket, which hung a foot off the ground supported by ropes and pulleys. It took two at a time so the driver began unloading machines from the truck. Baldwin withdrew a tanned leather attaché and a bottle from an unmarked crate in the bed and brought them along for the ascent.

Both men strained at the ropes to pull their basket into the sky. As Ken rose up the side of the mesa, he took in the scene of the vast desert blanketed in white, pocked in brown stone, blue firmament spilling through vast rocky arches. When they reached the top, they sent the basket back down to begin hauling up the dozen apparatuses they had so painstakingly built.

The black iron web work of the tower rose from the ceiling of a single-story structure. Occasional flashes of light illuminated the windows from within. It took great effort for Ken to keep from rushing inside to introduce himself to his hero. Thirty minutes of sweat and steamy breath later, all twelve machines stood arranged in the wind like a toddler Stonehenge bundled up for winter.

Baldwin tried the door but it was locked. He knocked gently to no answer. Finally he pounded with fist and forearm until he heard the snap of the latch. A middle-aged man in an unbuttoned olive overcoat greeted them with suspicion. Baldwin, Ken, and the driver stepped inside. The scent of ozone was strong.

A perfectly groomed man the same age as Woolley approached them. He removed a pair of dark goggles and surveyed the group.

"Freddy," he said, "bring us some glasses." The man in the overcoat scurried away.

"He is actually Freddy Pabst Jr.," Tesla said. "His father owns a cheese company in Milwaukee. They used to make beer. I am amusing him by allowing him to join me on this errand. He also offered to pay for our flights."

Baldwin stepped forward. "I would like to express my great gratitude to you, Mr. Tesla." He extended his hand. Tesla looked at it but did not offer his in return. At that moment, Freddy returned with five short gold-rimmed glasses.

"Let us drink a toast, gentlemen," Tesla said, "to a successful experiment and good health for your ailing woman."

Baldwin lowered his hand in disappointment and used it to produce an unmarked bottle from his coat. He poured four glasses, but did not accept one for himself.

"I'll drink his," said Freddy, taking a second shot.

Ken could see that Tesla was not the handshaking type so he took the opportunity to clink glasses in toast.

"Well met, Strick," said Tesla. "I am curious to see how your assemblies fared."

In short order, all the machines were brought inside and unpacked. Tesla was pleased. He arranged them below the central lamp and began to make a series of connections.

"When does the patient arrive?" he asked.

"Any time now," Baldwin said.

"And my deposit?"

"It is here." Baldwin set the attaché in front of Tesla. He opened it to reveal measured bundles of cash.

"Very good. Very very good," said Tesla. "It appears there will be a return on your investment, Freddy."

"These are yours as well," Ken said as he handed over the folder of designs.

"Ah yes," said Tesla. He deposited them into the attaché with the funds and closed the case. Then he walked it across the room to place it amongst his personal effects.

"About those golden plates, Mr. Tesla," said Baldwin.

"Ah yes," said Tesla. "Of course you must inspect them." From across the room he lifted a wooden chest out of one of the crates. Tesla eyed the men from over his shoulder, then drew forth a silken bag straining with the weight of its contents. He undid the fastening and revealed a thin slice of metal which reflected the unnatural electric laboratory light.

Baldwin gasped at the holy sight, then frowned as Tesla slipped the plate back within the bag and pulled its slipcord taut.

"You may feel the plates through the cloth," Tesla said.

Baldwin's hands fondled the bag and its contents with a sense of supernatural awe.

"Where did you find them?" he asked.

Tesla's response was curt. "The necromancer made me swear never to reveal the location."

The honking of a caravan of cars and trucks bellowed up from below, cutting their conversation short.

Tesla said, "You men help them up. I must make the final modifications in private."

All four proceeded to the door. Ken was last to the exit, but Tesla stopped him.

"You may stay," he said. Baldwin looked over his shoulder and narrowed his eyes as he saw the door close with Strickfaden still inside.

Tesla opened another small crate and withdrew a gleaming glass tube of a design that Ken had never seen before. He carefully seated one in each device.

When the process was complete, he threw a switch and the machines leaped to life, quietly humming with electricity surging at perfectly timed intervals.

Ken clapped his hands in approval.

"Tonight," Tesla said, "you will witness a miracle—or the grand failure of a very expensive parlor trick. One never knows."

It took two hours to bring the entire congregation up top. Tesla was none too pleased at the inflation of patients, though he found them a curious lot. The church had banned polygamy in 1890, but Woolley and Baldwin were proponents of John Taylor's 1886 revelation that had sanctified the practice to some believers. They collected their wives where they could and kept them out of sight in the shadow of Deep Creek within convenient distance of Ipabah. The Manor wives now huddled inside Tesla's laboratory for warmth as the sun set and cold desert night began to turn their husband's sweat to frost.

Ken was familiar with Tesla's similar Wardenclyffe Tower in New York. It had been torn down just a year prior but photos ran in Gersnback's magazines. This structure was larger and ultimately more remote. Outside the window, the first stars began to gleam.

"Mr. Tesla," Ken asked. "Won't we need kites and a storm to generate power for this experiment? It looks awfully clear out."

"We make our own lightning," Tesla said. "Now first, where is our test subject?"

He was directed toward Fanny and Mary. They sat on a trunk covered in a shawl looking away from each other in spite.

"Ladies," Tesla said. Mary returned his greeting with a polite nod. She wore fresh gauze. Fanny still looked away. Then she broke down.

"I don't want to die," she cried. "Cut her off of me and be done. If I bleed to death, at least I will be free."

"You must have faith, Mrs. Baldwin," said Tesla.

She looked up at him. "I do," she said. "But the Lord cursed me from birth."

"I do not mean faith in the Lord," Tesla said. "I mean faith in me."

After the final adjustments had been made and the congregation was sufficiently awed by the electrical display inside, they were led out onto the bluff beneath the stars. The air was below freezing but took a charge as soon as the tower ignited. Soon every molecule atop the mesa was excited and the mushroom cap above crackled with bolts. Fanny and Mary were relieved of their winter wear. Beneath, they were corseted into the same lavender prairieland Gibson girl dress they had worn to the Thanksgiving feast.

Tesla directed them to join hands. Fanny was resistant, trembling; but she saw herself surrounded by friends and family, so finally relented. Tesla made more adjustments and the bolts flung from the tower's top leaped high into the sky. Mary closed her eyes. Her blackened eyelids looked ghastly in the hollows between the gauze.

Ken assisted Tesla as he'd been shown. He read each meter, dialing forward and back to keep the current in the exact state called for. Finally Tesla cried, "Now!" Ken and Freddy threw switches at the same instant. A great molten arc of energy curved into the sky from the tower then doubled back down to strike the twin sisters and bathe them in radiance. Their backs arched and their jaws locked tight, but they did not release each other's hands. Mary's eyes opened wider and wider, finally snapping shut. When they did, curls of blackened flesh peeled off, revealing pink newborn skin beneath.

"Shut it down," cried Tesla in the swirling night wind. Ken and Freddy each dialed back the current until they deemed it safe to break the circuit. When the energy ceased, the sisters crumpled to the ground. Lorin Woolley and Nathaniel Baldwin rushed to their side.

Fanny fluttered awake in her husband's arms. "Lorin?" she asked.

"She's alive," Baldwin said with a smile, holding her head to his chest. Mr. Woolley began to unwind the gauze from Mary's head. He was gentle.

When he stepped aside and let the loose dressing flutter in the wind, all could see that Mary's flesh was returning in patches. She drew a hand to her face and felt its smoothness. A cheer arose from all those gathered.

Ken and Freddy looked over at Tesla who raised his eyebrows as if he were surprised as anyone.

The legless Manor wife dragged herself to the side of the conjoined sisters. She took Mary's hand in hers and said, "Me next! Give life to us all, Master Tesla!" The rest of the women walked, staggered, or crawled to form a circle around them. Save for snatches of cold wind, the air was so warm now that they shed their clothes. Naked flesh wrapped angled bone in a ghoulish dance. Soon their hands were locked in a ring o' roses. They begged Tesla to end their pain. He could not deny them.

The machines began to charge. Once more, current galvanized the structure. Dynamic fulmination rocketed into the sky. The bursts reformed, connected, and launched back down to bathe the wives in glory. Energy boiled around the ring. Muscles tensed and spasmed. Slowly, stumps grew limbs where none had been. Every malady was banished and the circle changed from some misshapen thing to an aureole of Queens in a chess-set both elegant and profane.

"Enough!" shouted Tesla. Ken turned to cycle down his machine when a stray bolt arced from above and struck Freddy. The Midwesterner seized and collapsed. Without the third set of hands, the machine could not be safely deactivated.

Flesh continued to grow. Hot skin bubbled from one wife's arm to another until their limbs were inseparable and the same. Wings and membranes fanned out from helix spines that crawled up the bloating backs of horrified wives. Eyes opened where none should be and yawning mouths full of jagged teeth snapped in frenzy.

Ken stood in panic—terrified at what he was seeing, even more fearful of ending the experiment. He looked across the bluff and caught Mary's eye. She stared at him as if in understanding. He shook his head no, but she closed her eyes and smiled, then one finger at a time, let go of the hand she held. When she broke the chain there was a brilliant flash. The promenade was electrified. It singed with fury, then collapsed in a burnt ecliptic of cooked flesh.

Tesla and Strickfaden rushed to shut down the machine but it was arcing badly. Small explosions were firing inside the building, which soon caught fire. They raced inside to control the damage but too late. Tesla made for the far side of the room and watched as an errant bolt snatched his attaché into the air. It burst into flames instantly. Burning bills rained around the room setting fire to whatever had not yet ignited.

"What about the plates?" Ken asked in panic.

"Leave them," Tesla answered. "They are worthless."

Ken saw molten lead pooling beneath the silken bag, swirling with a hypno-wheel of metallic paint.

Tesla finally threw his hands in the air and slithered outside with only his coat and the half-full bottle of contraband spirits.

The congregation was on its knees. Husbands sobbed clutching at the scalded remains of their wives. Ken was the only one to notice Tesla creeping into the basket and letting himself down without saying farewell.

They journeyed back to Ipabah in silence. The men were in mourning. Some wanted to blame Tesla, but Mr. Woolley reminded them that the congregation's greed had snatched the successfully healed Mary from his life. And Mary had broken the chain in order to save them all from some ungodly fate.

Ken Strickfaden was dropped in town with his flywheel. He walked it fifteen miles in the cold back to Gold Hill and installed it by campfire light. Eleven years later in Hollywood, he would recall Tesla's machines when he was hired to create the laboratory equipment for James Whale's *Frankenstein* film. Building them again dredged up deep wells of wonder for the successful Hollywood Ken. His thorough journals of his 1919 trek across the country left November 21-Dec 4 completely blank.

THE UN-BRIDE, OR

NO GODS AND MARXISTS

ANYA MARTIN

𝕿he first rule of telling a scary story is never to start with "It was a dark and stormy night." But I don't know how else to begin because if there ever was a dark and stormy night, this was it, and in Los Angeles no less, a city that almost never ever has dark and stormy nights. A place known for sunshine and moonshine, thanks to that nonsense called Prohibition; clear skies and maybe at most a layer of mist as you maneuvered your jalopy around the winding curves of Mulholland Drive up into the hills, towards the stars. Yes, it was a rare stormy night in Hollywood, the kind when a man might make a monster or a woman tell a tale about monster-making.

Charles and I were new to that scene in 1932 and renting rather lower but still cock-pointed up, the very last house on La Brea Avenue, that little stretch called La Brea Terrace. In other words, we were shielded by enough cliff and trees that we had no worry our humble estancia would be struck even though the thunder cracked as loud as the guns of war and lightning flashed like the neon lights of Mayfair through the silk drapes. You could scarcely get a peep out of Jimmy about his time in the trenches, but from the first martini of smuggled gin that night, he wouldn't shut up about how Junior Laemmle was hammering him about making a sequel to *Franken-stein*. I empathized with his reluctance to be typecast as a horror director, but then who wouldn't? On the other hand, Biddy, my mother, taught me from the cot not to be surprised that money men always will pick a surefire blockbuster over art or any kind of social message.

"Nature at its crudest, most savage, and we, the very most refined of the London stage," Jimmy declared with his self-taught posh accent, lifting his pinkie before taking another sip of his cocktail. He paced, cigar in one hand, drink in the other, first to the window, pulling the shades to gaze out at the incessant sheets of rain, then migrated by the armchair where I sat in my green satin dressing gown nursing my gin and tonic, to the sofa where Charles sprawled with his legs up, his big head propped on a lacy pillow and knackered after a day on the set of Jimmy's current feature, *The Old Dark House*. He surely would be snoring away if not for the clatter of the storm and Jimmy's chatter. I had to stifle a giggle at us being "refined," but Jimmy had airs and ambition after his ascent from the poorest of the working stiffs. He kept his humble origins under wraps from the Americans, of course, who were as starstruck by any affectation of British nobility as they were by any movie star. As the daughter of Edith Lanchester—socialist, Suffragette and insufferable—I wasn't going to out him for giving the finger to the upper crust. Not for that and not for that other matter either.

"I should wonder that an irate Junior Laemmle, God of Universal, was aiming those arrows of lightning right at the head of James Whale, Hollywood's greatest sinner. No, I shan't compliment myself so highly. Perhaps the bolts are meant for dear Charles, box office thunder claps for England's greatest actor come to American soil."

Jimmy flicked his fingers quickly through Charles' hair, and I observed my husband twitch his neck ever so slightly, but whether from being shook out of a near-nap or discomfort at the sign of possible affection in front of me, I wasn't sure. I knew I needn't worry about replacing another couch, though, because Charles was, how shall I say delicately, too hefty to attract Jimmy's more personal proclivities.

"What of my Elsa?" Charles mumbled, sitting up momentarily to raise his own glass to his lips.

"She is a devil," Jimmy said, with a laugh, clinking his glass against Charles' with such force that some drops splashed onto a fuzzy swatch of the reclining man's pale pink chest peeking out from a partially unbuttoned shirt.

"You know me too well," I said with a laugh.

"Come, Elsa, watch the storm with me!" Jimmy said, grasping my hand now to pull me up to the window.

"You know how lightning bores me," I replied, nailing my bottom firmly to my seat until he laughed again and let go. At that moment the electric lights flickered and flashed off. This house wasn't old—nothing in LA seemed to be much more than a decade or two at most—but with no electricity, it now was most definitely dark.

"Charles darling, can you light the candles?" I asked, thinking I'd probably have to do it myself, but Jimmy jumped to it, igniting the five candles in the candelabra above the fireplace with his cigar and then carrying it over to the coffee table.

"It hardly ever rains in Hollywood, and you know I am weary of Franken-stein," Jimmy said, turning back towards me. "And yet I cannot help but think of another stormy night when three gathered, a man and a couple, Lord Byron, Percy Shelley and his wife Mary Shelley, to weave weird tales. And how the most blood-curdling and creepy of all their stories was penned by that lovely, gentle, pretty young woman. How utterly astonishing."

"Unlike Elsa, of course, who will tell you to your face what she thinks and never worries about anyone's feelings," Charles said. "She's actually quite nice inside though." Even in the shadowy light of candles and lightning flashes, I could see he was sitting now. The opportunity to tease me had perked him up.

"So you both think I wouldn't tell a story of monsters and horror because I'm already so wicked on the outside," I said, rising to the bait. "What would I tell? Maybe a pretty little love story?"

Charles was snorting like a walrus now. He was tipsier than I liked him, so I chose to simply address Jimmy who after all was a friend in need. Besides, I had just what the Doctor ordered.

"As I recall, though, if you read the entire book by Mary Shelley, she thought even the monster needed love and bade Dr. Frankenstein create for him a mate," I said thoughtfully. "Mary wanted to deliver a moral lesson that man shouldn't meddle with the laws of God. But we know there isn't any God, don't we? And what if this new women made out of death didn't love, couldn't love? A man, after all, always expects a woman to love him. I've never understood why a man is so surprised when I don't."

Jimmy took a long puff of his cigar. Even in the dim light, I could discern the first look of excitement I had seen in him all evening—the mad movie director was alive again.

"Like Mary, you have a story to tell me, don't you, Elsa?" he said, perching on the arm of my chair.

"Elsa is quite the storyteller," Charles said. "You can never believe a word she says unless it's about somebody else."

"Shush, Charles," Jimmy said, swatting his hand in the direction of my husband with such force that Charles did something he rarely did—shut up. Then Jimmy turned back to me: "I'm all ears."

Thunder clapped outside.

"All right then, chaps, let me tell you a story, a story where there are no gods but there are monsters."

It all started with my older brother Waldo and me having electric shock parties with the neighborhood children, one of our favorite games the summer I was about ten. We got on rather well for siblings other than arguing over the gramophone. I wanted to play music and practice my dancing and Waldo wanted to take it apart to see how it worked. Anyway, I would devote hours to twisting green, silk-covered wire around a coil and setting out bowls of water in a circle. We'd stick our bare feet in the bowls and whoever was at the ends would hold the connected brass handles while waiting for Waldo to surprise us with the exact moment of the shock. The anticipation was scrumptious and you should have heard us scream with delight. Like every child, I suppose we liked the thrill of it and never thought about any danger.

But then came the frog. We found the little green thing happily frolicking among the rocks beside Leathwaite Road, a tree-lined avenue in southwest London near Clapham Common where we lived for a while. Lovers would hide under the shady low branches for a stolen kiss or a little more, and we kids would stifle our giggles when we spied them so as not to be told to shoo. Waldo and I often found frogs and took them home to a tank that we'd filled with water and some rocks. This little guy, however, would have none of it and jumped right out of my hands as I was trying to pop him inside. We couldn't find him and Biddy ordered us both to bed despite our protestations. So in the morning after she and Shamus, our father, left us alone, we moved all the furniture until finally we spotted the tiny fellow now brown, crusty and flat as paper behind the heavy coal box. Waldo suggested putting him in the kitchen sink and running some water to provide a proper funeral at pond. An hour later, though, the tyke had puffed right up again and was jubilantly leaping all over the kitchen. What I never told anyone though—because Biddy made me swear not to—was how Waldo proudly announced that it hadn't just been the water that had brought the little bugger back to life. He'd dipped in some wire. The frog, henceforth named Lazarus, had been treated to his own electric shock party.

If Biddy hadn't come home and seen it with her own eyes, Waldo might have gotten into puppets sooner, or maybe he dedicated his life to puppetry because of what happened later, I don't know. We didn't have that kind of brother-sister relationship when we got older. I did my own thing and he did his. But after Lazarus rose from his watery grave, Biddy sent him straight off to apprentice with a scientific instrument maker. She had her own plans already then, though I didn't find out about them till a good ten years later.

In fact, I had rather forgotten about the shocks and the frog. I mean, why would I think about any of that when I was twenty years old and living a carefree dream of singing and dancing and my first real notice as an actress, playing the small but crucial role of the Larva in the London premiere of "The Insect Play" by that acclaimed playwriting pair of Czech brothers Karel and Josef Capek. It was at the Regent Theatre, darling Nigel Playfair was producer and director, and he had taken a liking to my performances at the Cave of Harmony which is why he was willing to take a chance on me. Jimmy, I'm sure you remember, Claude Rains played the Lepidoterist that so vexes the lead character, that sensitive drunken tramp, by his killing and collecting of us bugs. John Gielgud was in it, too, quite a cutie, as well as my dear friend Angela Baddeley who played a beetle. You kind of hope to get your first critical recognition playing Ophelia, but I didn't mind being a squiggly wormy thing. I received some of the biggest laughs by whining loudly about my hunger while chatting up the tipsy Mr. Tramp, and then the greatest gasp of horror when my doting daddy Mr. Fly—quite abiding by Mr. Darwin's dictum of survival of the fittest—killed the rather delightful Mrs. Cricket just so his darling daughter could have some supper. Then, of course, nature caught up with me when the Parasite called Mr. Tramp

"Comrade" for being uncomfortable with so much "eat and be eaten" and then ate me. After all, as the line went: "Nature's table is set for all."

I was living on Doughty Street in Bloomsbury, still performing Sunday nights at the Harmony with darling Harold and dating a handsome White Russian whom I met at the 1917 Club in Soho. You might wonder what a White Russian was doing in a place like that, but it'd become a rather dull joint by 1923 and I guess maybe he enjoyed the attention he received from the downtrodden civil servants and low-level Labour Party stiffs who were curious about what it really was like living under communism. They held out great hope that the Russians would get it right so they could convince the British to kick out our king, though most would settle for a polite exile rather than the messy firing squad that bloodied up the Romanovs. My tender White Russian didn't like it that the Bolshys shot the children, though he wasn't all that fond of tsars and kings and queens either. Probably he just liked a more comfortable life in London rather than those wretched winters and famines while the Reds got their act together. Or maybe he was a spy. I never asked because what's the point? If he was any good at being a spy, he'd never tell me.

What got me going to the 1917 was that you could run into E.M. Forster or Herbert Wells—I had to dodge quite a few passes from that philanderer—or someone else quite fascinating like Chaim Weizman for fiery long afternoon chats while downing a gin and tonic. But now it was just doughy-eyed puppies lamenting how little progress socialism was making here and how instead all the young people in London just seemed to want to have a gay old time now that the war was over and they had money again. To be truthful, that's all I wanted to do—the night club frolicking that Biddy detested—and I didn't need that much money to have a good time, especially with a White Russian. He provided all the inspiration I needed to be a convincing, self-absorbed and well-fed little larva.

As I recall, it was right after the first Sunday matinee of the play's run. I should have known something was up when just as I was removing my antenna, Biddy, always my toughest critic, showed up in my dressing room with Waldo, whom I hadn't seen since a very uncomfortable Christmas-time supper—as atheists, my parents never actually would confess to celebrating the birth of Christ but it was one of the few times a year Biddy let Shamus smuggle in a roast pig's head to her strict vegetarian household.

As per usual, she hadn't told me in advance that she'd be in the audience. She greeted me with kisses on both cheeks, hugged me tightly with that somewhat clumsy gesture of someone who does not hug often, and then declared I was "terrific."

Waldo, looking more nervous than I'd ever seen him, extended a hand and nodded. "Yes, simply terrific, Belsa." He swallowed my childhood nickname instead of actually saying it.

Biddy then launched into how she admired the ruthlessly anti-war, anti-capitalist satire of the play, her usual litany of how the world would be better if all people were equal and vegetarians. I, of course, was impatient to change out of the rather tight sheath that was my larva costume, suitable for undulating on a stage floor but with my breasts and hips wrapped tight and flat so as to be childlike, quite uncomfortable when standing and even more so when humoring verbose relatives. Biddy didn't have conversations. She gave speeches. Meanwhile Waldo stood silently behind her, his hands fidgeting in his pockets.

"Well, my dear Elsa, again you did splendidly with the Larva, but then you have had plenty of practice being petulant and demanding and despite my best efforts, spoiled," she added, with her typical lack of any motherly diplomacy. As she turned to leave, I could have sworn she muttered under her breath how my training under Isadora Duncan was going to waste. But whatever she said was not loud enough for me to point out that it was Isadora who abandoned us girls and that sending me to a privileged Paris dance academy at all was a rather un-communist thing to do. Believe it or not, I can let things go when speaking to someone like Biddy for whom there is no dislodging of any idea once set firmly in her head.

As soon as Biddy had turned her back and was proceeding rapidly out the door, Waldo stepped forward and reached his arm out to shake my hand again.

"Waldo, darling, I'm just your sister, you needn't be so formal," I started but he shook his head.

"Come along, Waldo!" Biddy said loudly. "I am sure Elsa needs her rest after such a strenuous performance, and we have much work to do."

"Good bye," Waldo said, his mouth collapsing into a big staged grin. He bowed slightly and then turned and followed Biddy out the door with all the enthusiasm of a recently scolded puppy.

This wasn't the Waldo I recalled from the wild mischief of our youth, but he was a grown adult so if he wanted to be wandering around still tied to Biddy's apron strings, there was nothing I could do, I told myself. No, what I needed was a little inspiration, a little harmony in my own cave before heading to the Cave of Harmony for my late night song and dance. I didn't have a dinner date that night with the White Russian, but he hadn't seemed to mind before when I showed up with a stray bottle of champagne ready for some nibbles.

I transformed from silk larva into a red silk dress which I hoped might remind the White Russian of how much he enjoyed eating red caviar. Then I donned my new burgundy spring cape and a rather large and trusty black men's umbrella because a smart woman will always sacrifice a little style over risking getting her hair wet. Mine already tended to frizz electrically in the perpetual London fog.

But when I turned the bend towards the White Russian's flat, I saw a sight that made me yank myself back around the corner. Because who should be walking ahead of me but Biddy. I assumed it must just be some unlikely coincidence. Maybe she was taking a back cut to Oxford Street or one of her socialist comrades happened to live nearby, too cheap to pay a proper rent. I crept ahead and ducked into an alley where I could keep hidden and still have full view of her movements. But no, with that determined Biddy gait, she headed straight up to my White Russian's building, inside she went, and five minutes later reemerged with him at her side.

I rather liked the loins on that White Russian so I cannot say I was not a little disappointed in seeing my impromptu "dinner" canceled. But I was simply aghast at either of the two possibilities. Either Biddy was outright trying to match me up with any Russian, but since she was opposed to love and marriage that seemed less likely than the other. No, she must be paying him to spy on me. Given that she was rather tight with her money, that also made me wonder now about the quality of his caviar.

The rain was picking up, but I was determined to follow and confront them face to face with my utter disgust. Curiosity, though, made me want to see where they were going first, so when they ended up at the taxi stand at Piccadilly, I hopped right into a rattly new Mk 2 Super parked three cars behind and popped the driver an extra shilling to jump the line and follow. Through the rain, the cabbie paced, keeping just far enough back that I hoped Biddy wouldn't suss that she was being pursued. At first, traffic was sufficient to mask suspicion as we veered down Haymarket towards Trafalger, then cut over along Pall Mall to St. James Street and skirted Green Park onto Knightsbridge, but once we hit Sloane Street, the taxi had to hold back. We crossed the Thames at Albert Bridge. By then, I began to wonder, Battersea Park stretching on my left, if I was returning to old familiar territory.

Once Biddy's taxi turned onto Leathwaite Road, I bade the driver stop just round the corner and watched from the window until my mother's cab pulled outside a house about halfway down the block on the left. I paid the driver, tipping him nicely for his extra effort, and stepped out. As he drove away, I observed the White Russian emerge first and then take Biddy's hand to help her exit their own taxi with leisure. They appeared to be chatting quite animatedly, or, well, as usual Biddy was doing the talking, and the Russian only laughing. I wanted to think he was just being polite, but when I saw him kiss the hand of my anti-class-elitist mother, another idea took hold in my head. Maybe I should just tell Shamus and he'd grab a few mates and teach a fine lesson to my White Russian. But then Biddy refused to ever marry him in the first place even to the point when as all London knows, my grandfather and uncles famously kidnapped and placed her in a private loony hospital for a long weekend. With such an effort to avoid a wedding vow, was it even cheating?

After I saw them mount the steps and enter, I started down the street, determined to pound down the door if necessary and give them my mind. The low-hanging trees that the lovers liked had grown a bit taller in the dozen years or more since we played in their shadows and now offered some shelter from the worst of the rain. It being May, a gray luminescence still glowed through the clouds even now just shy of eight o'clock, but a tiny creature paid the price for my old habit of never looking at my feet. A little way down the block I felt my boot descend on something soft and heard a panicked squeak. I lifted my foot quickly and observed that I had stepped on one of Lazarus's descendants. As I kneeled to check the poor fellow's condition, he leaped away.

I looked carefully but saw no more frogs on the pavement between me and the front steps to the red brick two-story Victorian row-house that Biddy and the Russian had disappeared into. All the curtains were pulled shut, and the only lights in the building shone from two attic windows at the very top.

I rang the bell several times before Waldo opened the door. He was wearing a white lab coat and his hair was wild and uncombed.

"Well, hello, dear brother, are you in on Biddy's affair, too, and what are you doing all dressed up as a surgeon? You look absolutely daft," I said, wanting impulsively to pat down his crinkly locks, but he was already grabbing me by the arm and yanking me into the dark house. He paused to look up and down the street before pulling the door shut.

"Now, now, such melodrama to cover up for our mother dallying with my lover," I continued, chuckling a bit madly because if nothing else, the whole prospect still seemed utterly absurd.

"If only you knew, Elsa," Waldo said. "If I tell Biddy that it was just a salesman at the door, you might still have time to get away."

"Better yet, tell her I'm a Bible salesman, and you know she'll run down the street right after me to debate the existence of God," I whispered out of respect to Waldo's anxiety. Or more likely, I hissed.

"Elsa, really, it's not what you think, but if you don't go away now, she'll pull you right smack into it," Waldo said.

"Who is it, Waldo?" Biddy yelled loudly from above. "Hurry up and get rid of them. We've work to do."

"Just a salesman," Waldo yelled back. "I'm on my way."

"Work? Is that what she's calling it?" I hissed again so close to his ear that he flinched. "And I'm not leaving until I talk to her. You won't begrudge a daughter bidding farewell to her mother, Waldo, will you?"

Waldo gritted his teeth and shook his head.

"You, Elsa, are the most stubborn woman next to Biddy on this whole bloody planet," he declared. "I suppose you aren't going to be sensible and trust me for once and just leave."

"Elsa, sensible?!"

Biddy's cackling laughter filled the foyer as I looked past Waldo to see the shadowy figure of our mother standing on the stairs. She also was dressed in a white lab coat, though I could see the skirt of her tweed theatre suit peeking out underneath.

"Waldo, dear, welcome Elsa inside, take her coat and umbrella. Since she took all that trouble to follow me and Sergei, I suppose it's time we share our little project with her. I mean, what harm can it cause? It's doubtful anyone would believe her anyway if she told. Who knows? Maybe she'd even enjoy doing something to better the world rather than simply entertain it."

"Project?! Is that what they call it these days?" I shouted back. Biddy still had a way of making my head boil back then. Like an able mechanic at a factory, she knew every lever to pull. Meanwhile I let Waldo fold up my umbrella and place it in the stand by the door and help me slip out of my coat. Freed of my wet outer garments, I headed up the stairs prepared to punch Biddy squarely in the jaw. Then Sergei appeared. I hate to say I froze and that I let him kiss me, but I was twenty and yet foolish and it was too easy to let his lips upon mine erase my suspicions.

"Darling Elsa," he said with his thick accent. "You have nothing to be jealous. I am simply assisting your mother and brother with a mission. I wanted to tell you—indeed it vexed my heart to keep anything from you, my sweetheart—but it required the utmost secrecy. Yet now that you are here, my dearest babushka."

"Oh, hell, if there's anything I can't stand, it's the sentimentality of lovers," Biddy said, throwing up her arms. "Just come upstairs!"

We all toggled after her like obedient ducklings. As we approached the first floor, it was apparent that the place was indeed lit after all and brightly, and the thick curtains were fully intended to hide that fact. We followed Biddy to the right into what most likely had been intended as a large master bedroom suite with attached sitting room but had been adapted for another purpose. The first thing that struck me was the humming and croaking—the unmistakable music of frogs. And indeed a shelf on the far wall was lined with terrariums containing the same little tykes that we used to gather years ago. It dawned on me how lucky the one I stepped on actually was, because these fellows had a rather more dreadful sight to watch. On a big table in the center of the room were several of their dead relatives, spindly arms and fat legs stretched on pins, heads and bodies cut open with organs in view and partially removed and stacked around them like petit hors d'oeuvres.

Lined up also on the table were six bird cages surrounded by large diagrams, scattered papers and several notebooks. Inside each cage was a wooden marionette—a king, a queen, an archbishop, a devil, a ballerina and a mermaid strung up to the cage lids. That part was the least of any surprise as my brother had always expressed a fascination with puppetry. He'd carved quite a few when we were children, and we used to put on shows for the neighborhood kids and any adults we could talk into indulging us.

The room's walls were lined with more shelves and tables containing books, stacks of paper, tools and medical instruments and pickled specimens in jars. The chamber was a mish-mash of puppetry workshop and laboratory at the Royal College of Surgeons. At any rate, I felt backstage to some kind of drama.

Biddy, however, made a beeline for the one object that she was clearly most intent on me seeing. She picked up a foot-high jar and presented it like a model showing off a new Paris hat.

"Elsa, meet Eleanor Marx," she said.

In the jar was a human brain preserved in some kind of clear liquid. I wasn't any fool and immediately understood the implication. Much of Biddy's stature among our London revolutionary crowd came from her employment as the last typist to the youngest daughter of Karl Marx.

Those crazy communists had saved the brain of the daughter of Karl Marx.

Now the only question was what Biddy, Waldo and Sergei intended to do with a hunk of dead body tissue. Then I remembered Lazarus. But all they had was a brain, no matter how famous, and Eleanor's body was cremated twenty-five years ago in 1898, four years before I was born. Poor unhappy thing publicly was deemed a suicide after being betrayed by her lover Edward Aveling. Biddy, however, had fluctuated between commending her employer for choosing a most "un-messy" method of suicide in prussic acid and suspecting that she had been tricked into swallowing it by the scoundrel Aveling.

I turned to Sergei, thinking maybe he could clear up this part of the mystery, and saw a tear on his cheek.

"Elsa, we don't have much time. Papa Lenin is very ill." Sergei was now sobbing as he spoke and laid his head on my shoulder. Not used to seeing a grown man cry, especially one so shall we say "manly," I held him and stroked his dark hair.

"I don't understand, what does an old brain of a dead daughter of a revolutionary have anything to do with Vladimir Lenin's health or lack of?" I said.

"Only the hope to finally unite the workers of the world!" Biddy declared, setting the jar back on the shelf. "For when we place Eleanor's brain in a new body, we will have created the perfect successor for Lenin, a woman ready to lead the Soviet Union to become the first real bastion of communism in her father's vision. Once Europe and America see that nation's success under the very daughter of Karl Marx, workers and intellectuals will demand change. Utopia is nigh! We must fulfill the destiny begun in October 1917!

"But we must work fast. Lenin has a powerful enemy in Joseph Stalin. Sergei will tell you how that villain plots to be the next leader of the Soviet Union and how disastrous that would be to our world communist cause. He may parrot the words and say he admires his Comrade Lenin, but the man is brutal and simple and only cares about his own power."

Sergei stepped back from me now, wiping his tears.

"When Papa Lenin received the letter from your mother with her proposal, he knew his friends are now few and fewer every day while Stalin makes promises and eliminates any who stand in his way. That pig even had the audacity to lie to the Politburo that Papa Lenin gave him instructions personally to administer poison if his pain became too severe. But Stalin would never be able to challenge the daughter of Karl Marx. She would have the love of the Soviet people from the moment her feet touched ground at Moscow Station. So Papa Lenin asked me, his most loyal comrade and personal guard, to travel to England to assist and bring Eleanor Marx home. Then he can die in peace, knowing that his dream of Soviet Russia is safe."

Jimmy, Charles, you know that absolutely nothing leaves me speechless. I hate to say I share that trait with my mother. But I was caught between the utter absurdity of a twenty-five-year-old pickled brain and the memory of Lazarus the frog. I turned toward Waldo upon whom the success of the whole crazy plan seemed to depend.

"All right, Elsa, I know it all sounds absolutely nutty, but—" he said, heading towards one of the terrariums which contained a lone frog. He lifted the wire lid and scooped it out. The creature struggled in his hands as he presented it to me. "Take a look at this fellow's head. Behold, Lazarus II."

I bent down and saw black threaded stitches circling the top of the frog's head. I'm no scientist, but I'd spent enough time around them at the 1917 to immediately suss the implication.

"You killed the little sod, took out his brain, and popped it back inside?"

"Not the same brain, but another frog's brain to completely mirror the experiment," Waldo replied, placing the frog back in the terrarium where it issued a loud croak. "I also preserved it for three months in the same saline solution as Miss Marx's brain. I gently attached wires from the new brain to the frog's nerve endings, submerged the body in water and applied electricity. Of course, it didn't work the first time, and dozens of times after, but we finally achieved success just after Christmas and that's when Biddy wrote to Premier Lenin. What we discovered is that the body has to be freshly dead, the heart not stopped beating for more than a few hours."

"Elsa, I know you're thinking that the whole thing's batty," Biddy interrupted. "If it makes you feel better, we saved Eleanor's brain originally just for scientific study. Coroners don't make that much of a salary, so it's well known that for a little cash, they'll slip you an organ, and sew the body back up with nary a word. Poor Eleanor was going to be cremated and she had no living relatives who were likely to inspect her remains before they headed into the oven."

A frog was one thing, but was I really beginning to believe this "experiment" could work to regenerate a human body? Yes, of course, I'd read Mary's *Frankenstein*, but I always viewed it, like you, Jimmy, as just a moralistic horror tale—arrogant Man meddling with God's laws of nature and all that nonsense. Still I'd had a natter or few with a biologist or a doctor, so I knew science was advancing rapidly in extraordinary ways.

"And now all you require is a freshly dead body?" I said. "What are you going to do, murder someone for the great communist cause?"

"Oh, Elsa, you silly girl, of course not," Biddy said, shaking her head. "I took a collection from our comrades in the Communist Party of Great Britain—they paid for this house and every piece of equipment we've needed thus far. Sergei's here to pick up the cash and pay a visit tonight to the Battersea coroner. I was leaving your Insect Play when I received word that he just received a cadaver that sounds more than suitable. It's a sad fact, as you know, that young working women are always dying of foul play in London, and not all of them have kin who can afford a proper burial."

Somewhere in the house a clock struck nine loudly. I'd have to dial a taxi soon or I wouldn't make it to the Harmony in time for tonight's show. At this point, I realized I was going to phone Harold and tell him to make apologies to the audience that I was ill. The company had done without me on a few occasions before, and he knew I wouldn't skive off for any casual dilly-dallying. No, I was going to accompany Sergei to Battersea Mortuary to pick up the body and then watch my brother electroshock the brain of Eleanor Marx back to life to lead the world communist revolution.

As you may have predicted, Sergei wanted instead to drop me off at the Harmony, or if not there, home. He had some silly idea of me being a typical woman, a blushing flower who couldn't handle being around dead bodies. Me?! Yes, I know you find that amusing, Charles. But you'll need to stop laughing if you want to hear the rest of the story.

Finally Biddy threw up her arms and said there was no time to be wasted arguing with me. And Waldo chimed in that he could use another assistant in the operation. It was all in the family now, for better or worse, other than my White Russian, who had turned out to be a Red Russian after all. He was fun for a romp, so to speak, but I was not ready for a husband and he was heading back to Russia anyway if the experiment went as planned. Besides, as Charles knows, even if Sergei had been my fiancé, I wouldn't be taking his orders, and this little test of his character already was making me considerably less fond of him.

As it turned out, the Communist Party of Great Britain had also purchased a car. A taxi wouldn't do for the purpose of discreetly transporting a body, as Biddy pointed out. By this point, Sergei had lost any desire to speak and I could sense he was less worried about my delicate nature than quite angry to have a companion foisted on him for this gruesome task. We weren't in the car long before I ascertained why. The mortuary was next to the Battersea police station by the Thames, but instead of turning left towards the Albert Bridge once we hit the southwest corner of Battersea Park, Sergei turned right.

When I protested, he said only two words: "Short cut" and looped in through an open park gate. I wondered that the entrance was not locked so late and then remembered it still hadn't gone ten. We drove along a muddy road past dark trees and through incessant rain until we reached the edge of the lake which in sunlight and better weather would have been full of rowboats and lovers in straw hats. Then Sergei drove off the path onto the lawn behind a copse of foliage and turned off the ignition.

"You," he growled. "Stay put."

"Sergei darling, you're scaring me a little," I said, because he was.

"If you're going to come along when you are not invited, my babushka, you need to learn to take orders," he said. "In Russia, women are comrades but they respect a man's word."

He glared at me, pulled his cap tight on his forehead, reached for a satchel in the backseat, and then stepped out into the rain. I waited until he was out of sight among some trees and then got out of the car myself to follow. And yes, I took my big umbrella, because if he found me back at the car soaking wet he'd know that I disobeyed his order. I thought I had lost him in the shadows and the rain, but then I spied a flash of light deep among the trees and a woman under an umbrella a good deal daintier than mine with a lantern in her hand. Sergei embraced her and they kissed.

We'd never had any agreement that we would not see other people, but nonetheless the whole evening had been shock upon shock. So he wasn't having an affair with my mother but another woman? And he liked her so much that he couldn't bear not stopping for a snuggle on the way to a mortuary? Obviously Papa Lenin wasn't his most beloved after all.

I should have realized that I was jumping again to a way too easy explanation, but I remind you I was but twenty—streetwise though hardly immune to jealousy. Just as I was about to pop out of the bushes and reveal to his lover that she was not his only paramour, Sergei lifted his hands from her waist to her neck. The movement was so rapid that the poor thing couldn't scream for help should there even be a guard patrolling this part of the park so deep in the greenery and in the pouring rain. I watched aghast as she struggled at first, clawing at his arms without success, even kicking at his legs. But I'd seen his muscles firsthand in the buff so I knew she had no chance.

Nor would I have any chance if he saw that I had seen him. His mission was quite clear now, not the one that my vegetarian pacifist mother intended. Biddy would have never condoned murder, and Waldo spent jail time during the Great War for his claim to be a conscientious objector. Sergei wasn't playing by the rules, and some innocent girl was paying the price of her very life for their idealistic scheme. As for me, the only sensible thing to do was to get back to the car as fast and quietly as I could before Sergei disposed of me, too. As I scurried through the rain, thankful that wet leaves silenced my steps, it occurred to me that if he returned without me, he could so easily lie that he convinced me to let him drop me at the

Harmony after all. So consumed with the cause, Biddy might even have been relieved.

I waited in the passenger seat about ten minutes until Sergei finally emerged from the trees, the body in his arms covered by a dark blanket that must have been in the satchel unless the unfortunate lady had hoped for more than a kiss in the grass. He placed it in the backseat and then got back in the driver's seat and turned to me.

"The coroner felt anxious about meeting at the mortuary, felt here in the dark would be more discreet," he said.

"That bears some logic," I said, adding "Messy business." If I wasn't a little saucy, I figured he'd be suspicious.

We drove back to the house on Leathwaite Drive with me prattling on about some backstage gossip among my fellow actors. Of course, the gears of my mind were all spinning. On one hand, I had seen a woman murdered right before my very eyes and by my very own lover. On the other, I had to tell my mother and hope she had the sense to abandon her noble cause and call Scotland Yard. If Sergei was this comfortable with killing, I had to wonder what more he would do for his Papa Lenin.

When we arrived back at the house, Biddy was keeping watch beneath the awning outside the front door. Sergei stepped out of the car, and she returned a hand signal to give the all-clear. When he went around the car and opened the passenger door for me, I wanted to laugh and say "such a bloody gentleman"—you know me—but danger gave me new common sense. I opened my umbrella, slipped out of the car, headed for the house, and after hooking my coat up in the foyer, I went straight upstairs in the hope of catching Waldo before Sergei carried the body in.

When I reached the frog room, I found it empty. However, I heard foot-steps and other clatter above. Waldo must be in the attic. I spied another smaller set of stairs on the other side of the hallway and sprinted up them. Upon emerging, I realized that the room downstairs was no more than a research space. Here was the actual laboratory, or maybe better put, the stage for the strange production that was about to unfold.

The walls up to the rafters were lined with multicolored tubes and wires—red, blue and green. In the center of the room sat two tables. On one stood the jar that contained Eleanor Marx's brain and scattered paper-work—assumedly Waldo's experiment notes. On the other, a large metal operating table, was a white ceramic tub with low edges just the right size for a woman's body. More wiring and tubes extended underneath to a generator and across the floor hooking into the wall fixtures. The room was like a giant octopus, though with a hundred, maybe a thousand tiny stringy legs. At the far wall was a clear patch of wood floor with a series of levers, and that's where Waldo was poised, deep in concentration making various adjustments with what looked like pliers.

"Oh, Elsa, you're back," he said, looking up, his eyes covered by protective goggles and a surgeon's mask around his neck. "Can you hand me that screwdriver over by the door?"

I picked up the tool he was motioning towards from a table full of tools and medical instruments and started in his direction when he yelled: "Be careful! Don't step on any of the wires!"

I aimed my eyes down at my feet, tiptoeing carefully.

"Waldo, I need to talk to you," I said.

"Can it wait, Elsa? I need to be ready to proceed as soon as your Russian gent brings up the body."

"No," I said, and now right in front of him, whispered, "Sergei didn't get the body from the coroner. He murdered some poor woman in Battersea Park right in front of my very eyes."

Waldo froze. We might not have been close, but he knew that I don't lie. Well, not about anything really important, Charles.

Then he buried his head in his hands and shook his head.

"This is what I was afraid of, that somebody was going to get hurt," Waldo said. "I figured it was likely to be Biddy or me."

"You've got to talk to Biddy, talk some sense into her," I said.

"Talk what sense into me?!" Biddy said loudly from the top of the stairs.

We both turned, as she pranced into the room, obviously practiced at watching her feet to avoid the wires. Behind her, Sergei entered with the body in his arms. The blanket was now removed, the body disrobed and naked. From the poor woman's face and perky breasts, she looked to be about my age. She had curly dark hair and thick brows—some attempt perhaps to match the look of Eleanor? I'd only seen my mother's employer in a photo kept on the mantel in every flat where we lived as children. Without clothes, her pale demeanor—no doubt enhanced by her deceased state—and the remnants of rouge on her cheeks gave no clue to her class or biography. Maybe she'd been naked already in the car. Under the blanket who could tell?

Sergei carried the girl's corpse, maneuvering carefully on the toes of his boots through the maze of wires. He then spread the body out in the ceramic tank. The display of tenderness churned my stomach. He stroked her cheek and brushed her hair away from her eyes. By now Waldo was frozen in fear. After all, Sergei was all muscle and Biddy was all Biddy. It was going to be up to me.

"Biddy… Mother," I said. "Please reconsider. Look at this poor girl."

"Yes, unfortunate dear," Biddy said, shaking her head. "If I could have prevented her from this ghastly end, but that's the reason we need a world without haves and have nots, where men view women as comrades, not as objects, not as chattel to be possessed and then violently discarded. But she will have a new life, bringing hope to all other women. She won't be fooled by love like dear Eleanor was the first time around. She will be wiser, stronger, a leader to make her father proud."

Sergei stepped back out of the wired labyrinth and was standing next to Biddy. He'd shown no affection to me since we'd returned. He just stared stonily in my direction, as if daring me to speak any more.

"No, you don't understand, Mother," I said. "Sergei didn't take your money and bribe the coroner. I saw him murder this woman before my very eyes. Your great experiment is already responsible for the death of an innocent."

Biddy stared at me. Waldo now was visibly shaking. Sergei reached into his coat and pulled out a black revolver which he pointed at the side of Biddy's head.

"My dear babushka and clever clogs Waldo, if this procedure doesn't take place tonight as planned, I will shoot your mad, mad mother as dead as the lady before you," the Blood Red Russian said. "Waldo, you said the experiment only works when the body is fresh. How many frogs died before you figured that out? Already tens of thousands of men and women have died fighting. What is one more life for the greater good of the Soviet Union?!"

"Premier Lenin specifically instructed…" Biddy began. Even with a gun at her head, I was relieved to see she was at heart a diehard pacifist. But despite all my complaints about her, I didn't want to see her become a dead one.

"Quiet, Biddy!" Sergei yelled. Biddy shut up, but her eyes shot daggers. "Papa Lenin," he laughed then, a string of deep guttural guffaws. "Papa Lenin's hands aren't so clean as you think, my naive British comrades. But I am not here for Papa Lenin. A man's tears win him the confidence of women so easily. No, Papa Lenin never received your letter. General Secretary Stalin intercepted it as he does all communications to the Kremlin. He also was quite entranced by your plan. He has a wife, Nadezhda, whom he loves very much. But if he took a new bride, the daughter of Karl Marx, then when Lenin dies—which will be soon—his victory will be assured not just in Mother Russia. Communists around the world will rally around him and his bride until all of Europe is a worker's utopia. The union of Stalin and Marx."

By now, Biddy's face had turned quite pale. Stalin was as much her nemesis as the King, maybe more.

"Waldo, cancel the experiment," Biddy said. "That's an order from your mother."

"Waldo, if you don't carry on, I repeat myself," Sergei said, "I will shoot your mother in the head, then I will shoot your sister. No, while you watch, I will take some of the instruments you have laid out here and remove her breasts and every organ inside until she is dead. While you watch. And listen to her screams. And then finally I will kill you, also slowly, maybe using your own electric shock devices. And then I will send to Russia for another scientist who will follow your notes and complete the experiment. Do you understand, Waldo? Nod if you do."

I looked back at Waldo. For a long moment, he stood frozen, his shaking now stopped, but eyes glazed in shock. Then he nodded.

I saw Biddy take a deep swallow and nod as well. She might have given up her own life for the cause, but listening to Sergei describe the cruel ends he had planned for her children had clearly scared her.

"Elsa?"

I nodded, too. What else could I do? He had us right where he wanted us. And somewhere thousands of miles away in the Kremlin, I imagined Joseph Stalin with his thick mustache lighting a big fat cigar and grinning, too.

***

For the next few hours, Sergei stood sentinel, his revolver pointed at Biddy's head. After a while he pulled up a couple of wooden chairs from the corner. Maybe he took mercy on making an old woman stand or maybe he wanted to save his energy. Killing a woman and hauling her body had to be somewhat exhausting. I wondered what was going to keep him from shooting us all anyway once the operation was completed and he could whisk Eleanor Marx off to Russia. Or worse, if it didn't work.

To keep my mind from macabre musings, I concentrated on helping Waldo prepare the experiment. He assigned me the task of wrapping thick white bandages around the body, "to protect it from electrical burns," he said. Meanwhile, he delicately cut an incision round the dead woman's skull with a bone saw. Once the top was removed like a fancy hat, he soaked up any blood that splashed onto the face with a sponge and delicately excised the current brain. Then he removed Eleanor's brain from its jar, attached some wires to its base and placed it inside the skull cavity, using a long pointy tool with a hook to attach the wiring to the nervous system as he had described previously. I tried not to watch that part too carefully, one, because the bandage-wrapping required concentration, and two, because I didn't understand how any of the science part worked anyway. It wasn't as if I needed to learn to reproduce the experiment. This was Waldo's talent, and I have to admit I was somewhat proud of him. Bringing dead revolutionaries or indeed anyone back from the grave seemed like quite an achievement. If it worked.

Once I was done with the bandaging, Waldo proceeded to attach wires to the rest of the body until it was hard to see the bandages for all the mishmash of multicolored wires. I handed him tools upon request and obeyed whatever minor orders he gave me. "Hold this in place, Elsa." "Twist that blue wire slightly to the right."

Waldo inspected the body from head to toe, nodding and mumbling "check" and "yes." Finally he looked over at Sergei.

"Set to go but I need water. Can I send Elsa down to fetch a few buckets?"

Sergei grunted "da," and Waldo told me where the buckets were stored in the pantry. I got the impression not much cooking had taken place in that kitchen. I made several trips up and down the stairs lugging buckets of water, which Waldo then poured into the tank until the body was slightly submerged. Each time I reached the top of the stairs, Sergei would glare at me, though always keeping the pistol pointed at Biddy. I spread my lips into my sweetest smile just to annoy him.

The clock struck midnight, almost too appropriate for a grisly venture such as ours, and Waldo gave the go-ahead that it was time to commence.

"I need you to stay far back, Elsa," Waldo said. "I hate to say it, but you'd better go by the door with Sergei and Biddy."

I nodded. When I got there, Sergei kicked the chairs down the stairs and insisted that I stand in front so he could "keep an eye on" me.

"All right, everybody ready?" Waldo asked.

"No more wasting time, get on with it," Sergei said. I guess keeping a gun on someone's head for two hours can make even a big brute like him impatient.

Waldo flipped some switches, and the wires and tubes all around us began to sputter and flash. It was rather amazing that an ordinary house could sustain such power, I thought absently while waiting to see what would happen next. Waldo had mumbled something about the proximity of the Battersea Power Station and building extra generators such as the one underneath the operating table.

At first, all the activity happened on the walls, but then the floor began to shake and rattle as the current moved in one tremendous wave into the body. Sparks flew from the water in the tank and the body began to twitch, then tremble, thumping against its edges. I could see why Waldo wanted the bandages; smoke was rising until a small cloud hovered above. The momentum built until the water was bubbling and spurting sparks like a miniature fireworks spectacle.

Once most of the water had either splashed out or perhaps boiled down, Waldo pulled the levers back down and went to inspect the body.

"Well," Sergei said. "Is she?"

"We need to wait a few minutes to see," Waldo said. I could imagine he was nervous, knowing that lack of success was probably even more of a certain death sentence. He motioned for me. I glanced at Sergei, and he made a gesture with his non-gun-bearing hand that I could go.

I tiptoed through the wires and joined Waldo by the tank. We both stared in, waiting, watching, not sure what we wished for.

First her fingers moved. Just the right index and middle and the slightest tap. Then the left thumb did the same.

She opened her eyes and Waldo smiled.

"She's alive," he said, then shouted, "She's alive!"

Sergei's eyes widened but he stayed stiff as if waiting for more confirmation. Biddy actually grinned, seeming to forget for a moment that she had a gun to her skull.

In the tank, the newly awakened creature tried to stretch and flex her arms and legs as if testing their abilities. Restrained by the wires, her eyes communicated confusion.

"There, there," Waldo said, his voice soft like a doting father to a baby. "Elsa, help me loosen the wires so she can sit up. It's safe to touch them now. I turned off all the power to the generator."

He handed me some wire cutters and we both moved quickly, snipping, pulling away the strands and letting them fall into the tub, slide down onto the floor. We thought of speed, not of the mess we were making. We cared only about this new being, fully grown and yet like a child whom we had just brought into the world, of setting her free from her umbilical cords and seeing who she truly might be.

This "She" watched our every move, seemingly aware of our good intentions, patiently testing each limb as we liberated it. She lifted her head first slightly, and then as Waldo clipped the last tendril to her torso, she started to sit. It took her several tries, as if she knew to take each movement slowly. Or maybe this brain, after so many years asleep, was becoming accustomed to an unfamiliar new body further hampered by the bandages. I empathized with her from my own tight wrapping as the Larva, but I was only required to crawl on stage. Indeed, when she finally did sit up, her eyes focused on her arms, stretching them to their limits, twisting them side to side, bending her elbows.

Finally she flexed her legs, indicating she was ready to attempt to stand.

"No need to rush, let us help you," Waldo said. "Elsa, take one arm, and I'll take the other."

I approached her arm slowly, and then sensing she understood, I gripped it gently but firmly. Waldo and I helped her turn her waist and lift her legs off the low edges of the tub until she was facing outwards. Then a slight heave of her arms and her bottom slipped over its edge and her feet onto the floor. She looked at me as if she recognized something familiar, reached out and touched my hair with an innocent curiosity. It was then I fully noticed that the combination of moisture and static electricity had made her own frizz out to a wild state and on her right side, I saw a white streak bleached, perhaps from the sheer volume of power transmitted into her body.

Waldo was absolutely giddy with excitement. I hadn't seen him grin so much since we were children and he'd had a particularly scrumptious chocolate or… resurrected a frog. I almost forgot Sergei and his gun waiting to carry away this progeny of ours, for by now I was as charmed by her as if she were my own daughter. Apparently Biddy had forgotten the close proximity of cold metal, too, because she launched into one of her speeches.

"Welcome back to the world," Biddy declared loudly, commanding all our attentions. Our girl drew her hand away from her hair and turned for the first time towards my mother and Sergei.

"In the spirit of your rebirth, I rename you after the most important day of the year for the international worker. For you will bring a new spring for communism. Behold, my comrades, May."

"Welcome, May," I said, approving for once of a decision by my mother. I wanted to kiss May on both cheeks and hug her tightly, but I sensed May's body tighten. I felt a pang of regret as she stepped away from me and Waldo.

The distance was only a few yards, but May moved slowly, stiffly, still unused to her legs, her mobility hampered by the bandages.

"She needs a comb through her hair, but I did well, didn't I?" Sergei said. I recognized the self-satisfied smirk that arrogant men make when they take responsibility for the smallest aspect of someone else's accomplishment, usually a woman's. "Look at her eyes, her brow, her lips. She could be a twin sister to Eleanor Marx. To think, I found her waiting tables in a coffee house."

When he said the name, May paused. It seemed logical that a brain unused for so long wouldn't remember everything all at once, but May's reaction surely indicated the triggering of some memory.

"I admit I look forward to presenting her to Stalin," Sergei went on, rapt in his reverie. "After he thanks me with a great big bear hug, he will pop open a bottle of the finest vodka. Then a hero's parade through Red Square. Well, after Lenin has passed. First, a funeral like none the world has seen, then a wedding."

By now, May was standing right in front of Sergei, tilting her head first to the right and then to the left. She was studying him, weighing him in her mind. I'd never heard him talk so much, boasting about what Stalin would do for him, a position on the Politburo, or maybe a general. The caviar, the women. He seemed to have forgotten that he'd killed a woman just a few hours ago, much less that she now had an exceptional brain. And if he didn't, well, all I can say is May, scarce minutes from her electric womb, already had the eyes of a woman who would not suffer a chauvinist murderer. Maybe we should send her to Stalin after all.

May straightened her head. Then in one quick birdlike motion, she twisted her neck and leaned torso and face forward at Sergei. She opened her mouth and let out what I can only describe as the longest, shrillest combination of a hiss and a shriek I have heard in my entire life. The only thing it reminded me of was the horrible sound made by the nasty swans at Regent Park, except ten times louder.

Sergei stumbled back as if hit by a stormy gust on the Brighton shore, the kind that can sweep you off your feet and out to sea. May followed Sergei, continuing to emit her shattering scream. He tripped and fell, then scrambled back up, pointing the gun towards May with a confused expression on his face. Clearly he was unused to being challenged by a woman. I savored the chaos that must be transpiring in his brain. If he shot her, what would happen to all that power and glory that he imagined Stalin was going to bestow upon him?

May quieted again, circling and stalking her prey silently now like a lioness on the hunt. He shuffled in our direction, so Waldo and I took the opportunity to scramble around the table and towards a free Biddy and the stairs. I didn't know how this duel was going to resolve, but I was betting on May. She had Sergei backed into the far wall against the switches. His eyes shuffled frantically, the pistol shaking in his hand, confusion clearly short-circuiting his simple animal brain.

With Sergei cornered, May shrieked again, stretched out her arms and pushed him. As he fell back onto the levers, he grasped one in an effort to steady himself, and I heard a sizzle of electricity switching back on. In a parallel movement, he waved the gun towards May's head and pulled the trigger, survival now trumping ambition. But the bullet missed and ricocheted into one of the now reactivated cathode tubes on the wall, a burst of flame rising from its shattered remains.

As the two struggled, Sergei fired more shots, all missing May. She had the advantage of position and it looked also like her electrical birth had endowed her with strength above and beyond an ordinary woman. As strong as I knew Sergei to be, he was like a flailing duck at the slaughter once her hands were around his neck. However, the flames now were spreading along the entire wall and onto the floorboards, making it harder to see. Smoke wafted in our direction, and Waldo had started to cough.

Then the epic battle was over. May straightened and turned back towards us, Sergei's body in a heap behind her feet. She had stopped screaming, and I could see the bandages had ripped open on her chest in the struggle, her breasts and white silhouette reminding me of the Delacroix painting, *La Liberté guidant le peuple*.

"We have to save May," Biddy said.

Waldo looked pleadingly in my direction, torn between his creation and his fear of the rapidly spreading fire.

"Come, May," he called. "Step carefully."

May started towards us, but scarcely had she taken two steps when the decision was made for us. The floor collapsed beneath her. As she fell, we saw her make a last grasp at the boards and extend her hand, but all gave way too fast for any of us to run forward. If one of us had, surely we would have plummeted also.

So instead we did the only sensible thing. We ran down the stairs and out the front door into the rain. The bell of a firetruck clanged in our direction, and several neighbors gathered around, throwing blankets over our shoulders and beckoning us across the street to safety in case of flying embers or if the house collapsed altogether. We stood and watched silently as the firemen battled the flames. Somehow they prevented the blaze from spreading down the row, perhaps aided by the rain, but by the morning, all that was left behind the brick were blackened beams and piles of ash. It was only then that I remembered the poor frogs.

We all assumed that the creature we called May had perished in the fire, and Biddy, who usually could not let any topic drop, never said another word about the matter. Waldo abandoned his electrical studies and, along with his wife Muriel, founded the Whanslaw-Lanchester Marionettes, which became quite famous in puppet circles.

However, almost a year later, I was heading home from the Harmony very late on an April night, a young Irish actor friend on my arm. We decided to cut through Covent Garden. Most of the buskers had cleared out by that hour, except a pair of women, one playing what sounded from a distance to be a Mendelssohn concerto on a slightly out-of-tune violin and the other with a basket of flowers. My Irish friend insisted he wanted to buy me one and, giddy from a few glasses of champagne, we ran over.

The older violin-player was clearly a gypsy, black hair with streaks of gray, dressed in colorful shawls and bangles. The younger woman was also garbed like a gypsy, but her skin was lily pale. She had frizzy dark hair, and when she raised her head, I saw a white streak. Her eyes were empty, cloudy white, blind.

My Irish friend was still laughing and gay, but I put a finger to my lips to shush him, afraid he might say my name and she would remember it. I took the flower from her hand and placed a shilling in her basket.

The old gypsy stopped playing, and bowed her head slightly. "Thank you kindly, mam," she said in a thick Romani accent. Then nodding to her companion and patting her on her head, she added: "Alas, she is quite mad, blind and mad, but she's very kind to an old woman."

"Friend," May said, grinning. "Friend, good."

I never told Biddy. I didn't want Biddy to get any crazy ideas about how she could make this poor thing remember a life she'd probably rather forget. If this and those terrible shrieks were the extent of her vocabulary, I had my doubts that much remained of Eleanor Marx. After all, her brain had been left pickled in a jar for twenty-five years. Or worse, one of Stalin's spies might find out and kidnap her to a more miserable fate. By then, Lenin had passed away, allegedly from a catastrophic stroke, and London's would-be revolutionaries were all convinced that Stalin had poisoned him.

I never saw May again. Who knows? Maybe I was mistaken and she just resembled May, or perhaps the perfect woman with the brain of Eleanor Marx is selling flowers somewhere in London.

THE NEW SOVIET MAN

G. D. FALKSEN

Captain Sergeyev rubbed his hands together against the cold and looked out of his window as the rattling aeroplane came in for its final approach. Below him, he saw the vastness of the Kazakh Steppe spreading off toward the horizon, burnt orange and ochre by the light of the setting sun. Sergeyev frowned at the sight. This was a forsaken land; once a place of horse lords and Tartar warriors, now a place where men were sent to die. Nothing but grass and sand stretching for miles.

Well, nothing but the airstrip and the unsightly little town that it serviced: Karmolinsk. A GULAG camp transformed into a city of concrete and barbed wire circling the blackened depths of an open-air coal mine. A haven for scientists who spent too much and provided too little. The private playground of a war hero now seven years out of date.

Russia had no need of old heroes, certainly not those who promised miracles in the hinterland but could not recreate them in Moscow.

Sergeyev clenched his mouth shut as the plane dropped suddenly, its wheels bouncing against the runway. He shook himself silently and resisted the urges of his unsettled stomach. He was an officer of the MVD, the Ministry of Internal Affairs. Such a man did not succumb to airsickness.

He reached into his pocket and pulled out a crumpled photograph that he always carried with him. His wife Anna smiled back at him. She was far away in Moscow, but the sight of her was enough to distract him from the rough landing as the plane finally skidded to a stop.

And after coughing a few times into the back of his hand, Sergeyev was confident enough to unbuckle his seatbelt and stand, putting Anna's photograph back in his pocket. He could not afford to be seen as weak on his arrival. Though he had the backing of his Ministry, that backing was hundreds of miles away. If things went badly they might avenge him. They would not—could not—save him.

Sergeyev reached out and shook the man next to him.

"Kirilov, wake up," he said. As his brawny subordinate snorted and blinked himself awake, Sergeyev vented a small portion of his frustration and slapped the man across the face. "Lieutenant Kirilov, on your feet."

Kirilov snorted again and pulled himself up. "Yes, Captain. My apologies, Captain."

Ah, but Kirilov was obedient. As much as Sergeyev hated this assignment, he could not lay the blame upon his loyal subordinate. He clapped Kirilov on the shoulder and smiled.

"Come along, Aleksey," he said. "We have scientists to frighten."

"Yes, sir," Kirilov agreed, grinning.

Sergeyev stepped out of the aeroplane and took a moment to adjust his leather coat and put on his hat. That moment gave him time to study the landscape before him. The concrete warren of Karmolinsk was the most prominent sight as it loomed against the crimson sky, surrounded by walls of barbed wire and guard towers armed with machine guns. In the dying light, he could not be certain whether the defenses were meant to keep intruders out or to keep men penned in, and perhaps that was the point.

But far more important than the city was the party of its representatives that awaited him on the ground. First was an aging man somewhere in the later half of his fifties; an old officer in an old uniform that bore the decorations of the Great Patriotic War. Sergeyev frowned. That would be Zapadov, hero of the Winter War, hero of Moscow and Kursk; the scientist who had somehow transformed Karmolinsk into his own private fiefdom. That would soon be corrected, one way or another.

Next to Zapadov stood a girl, also dressed in uniform. But she was only in her early twenties. While she may have seen service against the Fascists, it could not have been anything worthy of note. Indeed, she struck Sergeyev as being rather like a porcelain doll: pale, pretty, and not particularly useful. Perhaps Zapadov kept her around to sate his rapidly aging lust. The very thought of it made Sergeyev sick. What a waste of Soviet womanhood.

The rest of the party was as he had expected: soldiers in drab greatcoats carrying newly issued assault rifles. As Karmolinsk was officially part of the GULAG, these men were under the authority of the Ministry. But Sergeyev saw in their eyes that their loyalty lay with Zapadov and Zapadov alone. Of course, Sergeyev knew, they were not there to threaten him and Kirilov. No, this was an honor guard to welcome them....

Sergeyev scoffed under his breath. If Zapadov meant this to be show of force, he had misjudged his adversary.

But it would not do to show his hand too early. Sergeyev descended the stairs with Kirilov following close behind him. He smiled at Zapadov and exchanged salutes with the old man.

"Doctor Zapadov, I presume," he said, shaking the man's hand.

Zapadov was quiet for a moment. With one finger, his adjusted the wire-frame spectacles that sat precariously on the bridge of his nose.

" 'Colonel Zapadov,' don't you think, Captain Sergeyev?" he asked. "This is an official visit. We must be precise about these things."

Sergeyev was not deterred. It was an old man's ploy to maintain his authority. It would not save him. Even a general was nothing if the Ministry saw reason to investigate him.

"Of course, Colonel Zapadov," Sergeyev replied. He motioned to Kirilov. "My... aide, Lieutenant Kirilov."

Zapadov nodded disdainfully to Kirilov, before motioning to the girl next to him.

"My assistant, Lieutenant Raskova."

"Well," Sergeyev said, "perhaps we should let our lieutenants get to know one another while we discuss our business."

Zapadov gave Kirilov another look and his face turned pale. He cast a glance at Raskova, who, Sergeyev noted, was beginning to smile a little.

"No, I do not think so," he said quickly.

"I trust you know why we are here," Sergeyev said. He pulled an official document from inside his coat and held it out. "But I have papers if the message was... unclear."

Zapadov took Sergeyev's orders and examined them, again adjusting his spectacles. His eyesight was going, Sergeyev noted. That was just as well.

"I understand that Moscow is uncertain about my results," Zapadov replied, handing the papers back to Sergeyev, a small snarl twisting the corner of his mouth. "Though I cannot understand why. I have been most diligent with my reports. I have clearly outlined my methodology... And does my facility not supply tremendous amounts of coal as well? I would think that I am the last person who bears investigation."

"Perhaps," Sergeyev said. "But I am here all the same."

As he spoke, the wind began to blow heavily again, pressing against his back as it bore in from the vastness of the steppe, bringing with it the frigid touch of so empty a place.

"And," he continued, allowing his tone to become severe, "I think it would be best for all of us if we continued this discussion with a tour of your facilities."

There was another burst of cold air that tossed Sergeyev's hair and bit at his ears and cheeks.

"Inside," he said for emphasis.

Despite the cold of the wasteland outside, the buildings of the compound were properly warm. Zapadov and his soldiers ferried Sergeyev and Kirilov past the barbed wire and into the massive facility that made up most of Karmolinsk. Sergeyev made a note of this, even as he shed his coat and gloves at the security checkpoint just inside the front door. There were storage sheds and outbuildings aplenty, along with barracks and the coal mine, but the camp was completely dominated by the main building, a heavy, triangular structure more like a bunker than a laboratory.

As Sergeyev and Kirilov warmed their hands, Zapadov filled in the details:

"As you no doubt saw from the air, the research center here at Karmolinsk is like a triangle. One side is the Reeducation Wing, the other the Medical Wing. You will have no interest in that, of course."

"Won't I?" Sergeyev asked, forcing his teeth not to chatter as he soaked in the warmth that had eluded him for the past several hours of flight.

"You are here about the Doctor's psychological program, aren't you?" Raskova asked, looking at Sergeyev with wide eyes. Perhaps the thought that her superior might be doing wrong had never entered her mind. "Why should you care about the Medical Wing? It is for injuries."

"Why indeed?" Kirilov asked, leaning forward and leering at Raskova.

Sergeyev expected the girl to back away, as most people did when Kirilov towered over them, but Raskova held her ground and stared at Kirilov as their noses almost touched. She slowly turned her head and looked at Zapadov, who shook his head. The man looked afraid, afraid of what might become of his precious toy. Sergeyev tried not to laugh. Trust an old man to leave a girl so sheltered. Perhaps he would let Kirilov educate her about the world before they left.

Perhaps that would convince the old man to be more cooperative.

Seeing Zapadov's disapproval, Raskova looked back at Kirilov and slowly drew away, only then understanding that she might be in danger. But Sergeyev knew better than to provoke the sensibilities of a man who still had a small army at his disposal. He caught Kirilov's eye and shook his head.

"Not now," he said softly.

Kirilov looked disappointed, but knew better than to protest.

"I expect to see all of it, Doctor Zapadov," Sergeyev said. "This is an official review of your camp. The main concern might only be your dubious results in the rehabilitation of disloyal elements, but I believe in thoroughness. Who knows what other inconsistencies you may have here?"

He glanced at a nearby map of the facility. It was very vague, showing only the most basic outline. There were ambiguously-worded areas listed: Principal Reeducation Center, Main Surgical Theater, Rehabilitation. None of it was useful.

"And what about the mine?"

"At the far end, near the prisoner barracks," Zapadov said. He tapped the area on the map. "It is the oldest part of Karmolinsk, originally a katorga penal colony in the days of the Tsar. In fact, it is the source of Karmolinsk's name. The Kazakh laborers called it 'Kara Mola', the Black Grave, after the thousands who died digging out the coal." He smiled a little. "Nowadays we use more modern techniques. We have had only ten deaths this year, which I regard as progress."

"Your repeated requests for more prisoners are strange if you have had so few deaths," Sergeyev noted. "Explain."

Zapadov hesitated, perhaps realizing that his tongue had outstepped his good sense.

It was Raskova who came to his defense:

"The Doctor requires more prisoners because they are useful. Karmolinsk is the third largest producer of coal in the Soviet Union. Does that fact not warrant expansion?"

"It warrants supervision," Sergeyev answered. But he couldn't help but grin a little. "Still, I can see why she is your assistant," he said to Zapadov. "Clever little thing, isn't she?"

Raskova bristled a little at the description, but she said nothing. Neither did Zapadov. Instead, he shed his woolen coat and replaced it with a white medical smock provided by one of the waiting attendants. Sergeyev watched them carefully, keeping one hand on the pistol at his waist. There was not much he could do against half a dozen soldiers armed with AK-47s, but at least the feeling of being armed kept him at ease. In fact, he knew that the authority behind him was his greatest weapon. Zapadov might resent the intrusion, but he would not attack a member of Soviet security.

"Why are you here, Captain Sergeyev?" Zapadov demanded, turning back to them.

"You know why I am here," Sergeyev replied.

"I understand that you are here to evaluate my loyalty and the legitimacy of my work," Zapadov replied. "To verify whether my camp warrants the number of prisoners sent here for labor and rehabilitation. But I do not understand the reason for it. I have already sent countless reports to Moscow clearly detailing my methods."

"No other scientist has been able to reproduce your results, Doctor," Sergeyev said. "Indeed, Moscow is beginning to wonder whether your reports are real at all. And if your reports are falsified, why does the Ministry permit you to administrate this camp?"

Sergeyev smiled. He enjoyed being able to remind men like Zapadov that their private domains did not in fact belong to them.

"Doctor Zapadov cannot be held accountable for the failures of other men," Lieutenant Raskova interjected, her pretty mouth twisting with anger. "His results are real. I—"

"I don't care what you think you have seen, girl," Sergeyev said. He turned back to Zapadov. "I care about what I see and what my superiors accept as fact. And unless I am satisfied by what I am shown here, Moscow will not be satisfied either."

"You are in no position to make threats!" Raskova snapped, taking a step toward Sergeyev.

"Yulia!" Zapadov shouted, halting her.

Sergeyev chuckled. He took Raskova's chin in his hand and smiled at her.

"Oh, I know that the good Doctor has an army of loyal men here. Some of them might even betray the Motherland out of allegiance to him." Sergeyev raised his voice as he said this: a calculated move to remind the nearby soldiers that to defy him was to defy the Soviet Union. "I am only a man. Kirilov is only a man. Two men. But if we do not return whole, unharmed, and with the answers we want, Moscow will send more than two men, and those men will be far less patient than I am."

Zapadov hurried forward and quickly placed a hand in front of Raskova, perhaps in a vain attempt to shield her against Sergeyev's hostility.

"Let us not be foolish," he said quickly, laughing softly without even a hint of humor in his expression. "We are all dutiful servants of the Soviet Union and glorious Marshal Stalin. Do forgive my officers, I beg you. They are unaccustomed to visits like this."

"A simple misunderstanding," Sergeyev assured him, his tone making it clear that it was no such thing. "Already forgotten." Anything but. "Now then, where shall we begin the tour?"

Sergeyev was not surprised when Zapadov chose to begin with the Reeducation Wing. Perhaps he naïvely believed that a jaunt through the tangled maze of concrete corridors and sterile classrooms would sate Sergeyev's curiosity. But the Doctor was a fool if he thought that. Each time Zapadov stopped to present Sergeyev with a new education room, to offer some anecdote about the elegance of his unprecedented techniques, it further confirmed what Sergeyev already knew: Zapadov was hiding something, most likely abject failure and quite possibly active corruption. Could he be selling coal on the black market? Was the Medical Wing being used to produce drugs? Synthetic opiates or recreational amphetamines perhaps? Something was wrong about Karmolinsk, something that Zapadov was concealing from the Ministry.

"Curious that the Ministry would see fit to... review this facility now," Raskova remarked, startling Sergeyev out of his thoughts. He hadn't noticed when she drew alongside him. "Sir," she added, as a deliberate afterthought. "Even if the men in Moscow cannot reproduce the Doctor's results, Karmolinsk is still fulfilling its purpose as a labor camp—"

"Yes, it is curious," Sergeyev agreed, interrupting her to make it clear that they should be worried. "I find it very strange that Internal Affairs has not found reason to investigate the activities of this facility long before now. Karmolinsk is funded by the MVD, protected by soldiers from the MVD, and yet its chief administrator is not a man who answers to the Ministry. Indeed, he seems to answer to no one at all. Doctor…" He paused and smiled. "…Colonel Zapadov enjoys a surprising lack of oversight. That will be addressed soon enough."

Zapadov cleared his throat and quickly interrupted the exchange, motioning for the security officers to join him at a window overlooking one of the classrooms. Sergeyev looked down into the room and saw a dozen men in simple coveralls seated in a row, each man staring at a flickering television screen while he listened to a set of headphones. Sergeyev could not hear what was being played to them, but each television showed a different set of slowly changing images, ranging from patriotic imagery to newsreels to landscapes and commonplace objects. Without the accompanying sound, it made no sense to Sergeyev.

"What is this?" he demanded.

"The basis of my technique," Zapadov explained proudly. "Information. What man desires most is to understand the world around him and to know his place in it. I am giving these men a proper education, stripping away the lies and indoctrination that previously filled their thinking. And what is more, not only will this make them good, upstanding, loyal citizens of the Soviet Union, they will even thank me for it after I am finished."

"They look quite healthy, if a little gaunt and pale," Kirilov noted.

Sergeyev agreed. "Why are they so relaxed? Where is the exhaustion, the stress? Of course your technique produces no results: you haven't broken them yet!"

"If my technique produces no results in Moscow, it is because the men attempting it are incompetent!" Zapadov snapped. Then, thinking better of his anger, he calmly replied, "One does not need to break a man to educate him. One simply needs to calm his mind and remove the falsehood that plagues it. A broken man is no good to anyone, even if he has been put back together again. You see, Captain, misinformation is a disease, and I am merely curing it."

"I would like to see some proof, Colonel."

"Yes, very well."

Zapadov stepped away from the window and led them down an adjoining passage, as featureless as all the rest and lit with the same glaring electric lights. Sergeyev knew at least part of Zapadov's corruption: he was clearly using coal from the mine to provide a tremendous amount of electricity, and he was no doubt falsifying his reports to conceal the extent of it.

Sergeyev followed Zapadov into another room, a small but comfortable office overlooking the classroom. A man was seated at a wooden table, filling out a report. He was tall and well-built, fair-haired, and dressed in a simple black coverall. At first he ignored them, but at Zapadov's approach, the man looked up and quickly stood, smiling in a slow but friendly manner.

"Doctor, good afternoon," he said. His words were Russian but his accent was clearly German. "My observations for today's progress are almost finished. I will have them on your desk...."

He fell silent as he saw Sergeyev and Kirilov enter the room, his face alternating between a smile of greeting and a frown of concern.

"A German?" Sergeyev asked Zapadov. "You have a German running your reeducation program?"

"Only this portion of it," Zapadov replied. "Karl is a meticulous record-keeper."

"I'll bet he is," Kirilov muttered.

Zapadov stepped to the center of the room and began introductions:

"Captain Sergeyev, this man is Karl Drexler, formerly a Sturmbannführer of the Waffen-SS, now my—"

"A Nazi?" Sergeyev shouted, grabbing Zapadov by the collar. "You have put a Nazi in charge of reeducation at a GULAG camp? And without authorization from Moscow? Are you insane?"

"But I am not a Nazi!" Drexler protested, sounding truly offended by the term, which Sergeyev counted as absurd coming from an SS man. "I am a Communist now, I swear it!"

The sincerity in Drexler's voice made Sergeyev pause long enough to realize that his hand was on his pistol. He glanced at the soldiers waiting in the hallway and then released Zapadov. He had made his point. There was no reason to goad Zapadov's men into doing something treasonous for them and fatal for him.

"Explain," he demanded.

"Drexler was a Nazi when he was brought here after the war," Zapadov said. "A devoted Nazi. A fanatical one. But in my care he has been freed from his previous delusions and set on the path of Socialism. He is as true a Soviet as you or I."

Sergeyev snorted softly, dismissing the very suggestion. But, as he studied Drexler, he did read honesty in his eyes. The man at least did not believe that he was lying. And Sergeyev had a great deal of experience in weeding out men who professed loyalty but were not true to their claims.

Still, he would make a note about Zapadov's pet Nazi in his report. Converted or not, the Ministry needed to know about a man like Drexler.

"Again, I would like to see proof," he said to Zapadov.

"I have hours and hours of recorded sessions demonstrating Karl's progress from darkness into light," Zapadov assured him. "I daresay they will convince even you, Captain." He smiled at Drexler and motioned for the man to sit. "Thank you Karl, that will be all."

"Yes, Doctor," Drexler said. Then, as if losing all interest in the MVD officers, he sat and returned to his reports, suddenly ignorant of the other people in his office.

Zapadov led Sergeyev and Kirilov back into the hallway and closed the door.

"How is it done?" Sergeyev asked, falling into step beside Zapadov as the Doctor led them back to the main hall.

Zapadov considered his reply for a few moments before he answered.

"The human body is a kind of biological machine," he said. "Medical science has understood this for generations, even if civil and religious authorities have found the fact too uncomfortable to permit. Similarly, the brain is an organic computational device more complex and nuanced than anything our engineers have ever, and perhaps will ever, construct. Our bodies are driven by a network of nervous wires that, like a telegraph, transmit instructions from one place to another. Our thoughts, our memories, our actions are ultimately the product of electrical impulses that store, process, and transmit data."

"And?" Sergeyev demanded.

"My technique simply removes select portions of mental information, and replaces them with more… acceptable knowledge."

Sergeyev scoffed at Zapadov.

"Is that what you did with the Nazi?" he asked sarcastically. "You removed his Fascist ideas and replaced them with upstanding Soviet allegiance?"

"Yes," Zapadov said. As Sergeyev shook his head in disbelief—at the sheer audacity of the explanation—Zapadov continued, "Fanaticism is a quality possessed by some men and not by others. It does not matter what the ideology, the religious faith, the political allegiance, a fanatic is a fanatic. With Drexler, I have simply erased the legacy of his Fascist thinking and replaced it with a fanatical devotion to Communism."

Sergeyev frowned and corrected the Doctor: "Devotion to the Soviet system is not fanaticism, Doctor Zapadov. It is the logical outcome of a liberated mind."

For a moment Zapadov merely smiled.

"Of course, Captain," he finally said. "Pardon me. I meant that I have removed his fanaticism and replaced it with reason."

"Much better."

After touring the remainder of the Reeducation Wing, Zapadov led them to a comfortable little lounge at the front of the building. Well, Sergeyev reflected, perhaps "comfortable" was too generous, but at least the chairs were upholstered and the wooden table was smoothly polished and free of splinters. There was even a metal samovar of tea waiting for them on their arrival.

"Do you truly expect me to believe that your German subject is reformed?" Sergeyev demanded, as he sat across from Zapadov. Kirilov sat on the other side of the Doctor, a meaningful placement that was not lost on anyone. Raskova, meanwhile, excused herself and attended to the tea, though she repeatedly glanced back at them with suspicion in her eyes.

"Not merely reformed, Captain," Zapadov insisted. "Cured. I have removed every last trace of the Fascist poison from his mind."

"How can you be certain he will not relapse?" Sergeyev asked. "How do you know he will not become an agent of our enemies lurking in your midst?"

Zapadov forced a polite smile as he replied, "Because, Captain, I have not merely suppressed his Fascist impulses. I have erased them. Drexler has no memory of being loyal to the German Reich, though he is aware that he willingly served it at one point. But he remembers nothing now except total allegiance to the Soviet Union. Surely you see the advantage in that."

"If it is true, then yes," Sergeyev agreed. "But I still have not seen any real evidence."

"As I said, I have hours of recordings documenting his progress," Zapadov said. "You are free to review them at any time. I am confident you will not be disappointed."

"So you say," Sergeyev answered.

He watched as Raskova joined them at the table, carrying a tray of glass teacups. As Raskova leaned over the table, parceling out the cups to each of the officers, Sergeyev caught Kirilov eyeing the delicate curve of the girl's neck just above her collar. Sergeyev studied Raskova as well, but what caught his attention were her arms as she reached out to hand him his cup.

Sergeyev grabbed Raskova's wrist and pulled her toward him. Raskova stumbled but caught herself before she could fall and stood there, balancing precariously, using the fingertips of her free hand to steady herself. Sergeyev noticed, to his amusement, that despite being startled, the girl had not allowed even a single drop of tea to splash out of the cup. He also noticed something else, as he pulled back her sleeve and studied her forearm.

The delicate traces of suture scars circled Raskova's arm just above her wrist.

"What is this?" Sergeyev demanded.

The scars suggested either traumatic injury or some manner of bizarre surgical exploration, and as Zapadov grew pale at the question, Sergeyev began to suspect the latter.

"Answer me."

Zapadov was silent, quickly looking into his tea.

"Let me go, sir," Raskova said, somehow managing to frame the words as both a subordinate's polite request and an officer's demand.

Sergeyev chuckled and released her. Raskova backed away from him and pulled her sleeve back down to cover the scars. Then, reassured of her dignity, she placed Sergeyev's cup in front of him, before sitting across from them with her own.

"Answer me," Sergeyev repeated to Zapadov.

Zapadov and Raskova exchanged a look and finally Zapadov shrugged, the gesture of acquiescence suddenly granting him the assurance that he seemed to lack only a few moments before.

"Very well," he said. "During the Battle of Moscow, Lieutenant Raskova and I were already in the capital, supporting our brave Red Army soldiers with whatever medical assistance we could provide."

"I am familiar with your war record, Colonel," Sergeyev replied.

"During the fighting," Zapadov continued, "a German shell hit the field hospital where Yulia was working. While she survived, the explosion destroyed her hands... among other injuries."

Sergeyev glanced at Raskova and saw her turn away, staring down at her hands as she idly played with her fingertips. After a few moments, Zapadov coughed softly and Raskova looked up, breaking free of whatever strange trance had taken her.

"Fortunately, I was able to replace the damaged... appendages... with the hands of a concert pianist who had died earlier that day." Zapadov took a long sip of tea before he continued, his voice tinged with pride. "It was some of my finest work. Perhaps desperation is the greatest motivator, but what I accomplished with Yulia was a miracle. I have never yet created her equal."

Raskova looked back at him and the two of them stared at one another in silence.

Irritated at the sentimentality, Sergeyev cleared his throat loudly enough to interrupt them.

"You expect me to believe that you successfully transplanted a pair of hands?" he asked Zapadov. "In a field hospital? Under fire?"

Zapadov fixed Sergeyev with a hard glare.

"I do not care whether you believe it or not, Captain," he said. "You asked a question. I answered it."

Sergeyev scoffed. "Next you will be telling me that she has the feet of a ballet dancer."

"Of course not!" Zapadov looked genuinely offended at the suggestion. "Are you aware of what ballet does to a woman's body, Captain? The stress upon the bones, the misalignment of joints, the damage to the tendons? I can assure you, Raskova's feet do not belong to a ballerina."

Sergeyev touched his forehead, feeling the first hints of a headache threatening to appear. Zapadov's continued evasion was wearing upon him.

Oh Anna, the things I tolerate for the good of our family, he thought.

"Colonel," he said to Zapadov, "my patience wears thin. We have been here for hours and you have giving me nothing but unsubstantiated claims and fanciful stories." Sergeyev stood, took another drink of tea, and gently placed his cup on the table. "You will now take me to see the Medical Wing and you should hope that I will find something there to satisfy me, or else you will not enjoy the results of my report."

Zapadov quickly stood and raised his hands in protest.

"Captain, I assure you, there is nothing to interest you in the Medical Wing. Nothing but injured miners and blood samples. Why not retire for the night? I will have a place made up for you in the scientists' barracks. Tomorrow you can begin reviewing the recordings from Reeducation—"

"No," Sergeyev snapped. "I have no interest in sleep and no interest in your recordings. The Medical Wing. Now." He waited a few moments for Zapadov to consent. Zapadov replied with silence. "Very well. Aleksey, the girl."

"Sir," Kirilov said, grinning.

Kirilov bounded to his feet and approached Raskova with an outstretched hand. Wide-eyed with disbelief, Raskova looked at Sergeyev and then at Zapadov.

"No—" she protested.

But her cry was silenced as Kirilov wrapped his hand around her throat and squeezed, just enough to choke her voice. Raskova struggled against him, her dark eyes never once looking away from Zapadov. As she lashed out at Kirilov, the brawny MVD officer grabbed her wrist and squeezed hard to restrain her. Still without a word, Kirilov hauled Raskova across the room and slammed her against the nearest wall, pinning her with his full weight.

Sergeyev folded his arms and looked at Zapadov.

"Well?" he asked. "Or shall we continue?"

Zapadov's mouth worked silently, grinding his anger between his tongue and his teeth. But he said nothing.

"Very well…" Sergeyev said. He turned back to Kirilov and nodded.

Kirilov grinned.

Frantically, Raskova's free hand clawed at the fingers wrapped around her throat and finally clenched around Kirlov's forearm, though it was a futile effort. Such a delicate little thing could not possibly resist a man as big as Kirilov.

But the reality of the situation seemed to have finally roused Zapadov.

"No!" he shouted. "No! Stop! Stop!"

The plea was obviously intended for Kirilov—who of course did not listen—but even so Raskova flashed the Doctor a startled look and went limp in Kirilov's grasp. Her hand released the officer's arm and dropped to her side as she gave up resisting. But however obedient, there was anger and resentment in her eyes.

Zapadov turned to Sergeyev and cried, "Very well! Very well! I will show you the damned Medical Wing if it matters so much to you! Only let her go!"

Sergeyev placed a hand on Zapadov's shoulder. "You see? That wasn't so hard, was it?"

He snapped his fingers at Kirilov and nodded. Disappointed, Kirilov sighed and dropped Raskova, who slid halfway down the wall before catching herself with one hand and slowly rising. She glared at Kirilov with utter disgust and hurried to Zapadov's side. Zapadov took her by the arm and guided her to the door.

"I am sorry, Yulia," he whispered, almost too softly for Sergeyev to hear. "Forgive me."

"I understand, Doctor," Raskova whispered back. "I understand."

Sergeyev snorted and shook his head. He had guessed correctly: Raskova was Zapadov's point of weakness. A little pressure against her would do wonders. He might even have his answers by the end of the night, in time to leave at dawn, perhaps with Zapadov in custody for whatever crime he was surely hiding. That would be most welcome.

He looked at Kirilov as the man joined him. Kirilov's mouth was twisted into a grimace as he massaged his forearm.

"That worked," Kirilov noted.

"As it often does," Sergeyev agreed. He glanced at Kirilov's arm. "Are you in pain?"

Kirilov looked embarrassed. "It is nothing, sir. The bitch is stronger than she looks."

It took Sergeyev a moment to register what Kirilov had just said. When he finally did, he laughed loudly.

"Oh, poor Aleksey. Did the little girl hurt you?"

Kirilov scowled.

"Shut up. Sir."

Sergeyev was shocked at the difference between the Medical Wing and the rest of Karmolinsk. There was no sign of the claustrophobic warren of narrow concrete tunnels, though he was certain that the heavy reinforced walls were still there, lurking behind a facade of gleaming white. But here in the Medical Wing, the hallways were wide and high, well-lit with bright if flickering electrical lamps. Everything was covered in brightly polished tile that showed every last speck of dirt and stain waiting to be scrubbed away. The place smelled of disinfectant, though the sharpness of the chemical wash did not completely hide the lingering odor of blood.

"As you can see, Captain, cleanliness is paramount here," Zapadov said. "I have written several papers on the importance of an antiseptic environment, not only in the surgery but also in any place where medical personnel are likely to walk."

Sergeyev grunted.

Zapadov frowned and adjusted his glasses. "Of course, I expect that is of no interest to you." He stopped at one of the rooms and examined a paper chart hanging on the wall next to the door. "Perhaps you would prefer to see an example of the work we do here."

"I would find that a wise choice on your part, Colonel," Sergeyev said.

"As you wish," Zapadov replied.

He opened the door and ushered Sergeyev and Kirilov into the room. It was a small chamber, bare of furnishings except for a cot and a bedside table. The room had a single occupant, a haggard-looking man of considerable stature, whose bare ribs spoke of malnutrition and whose eyes were dark with sleeplessness. But despite hunger and overwork, the man's body was strong and muscular, especially his right arm. Indeed, as Sergeyev approached, he realized that the arm was actually more muscular than the rest of the man. And then he noticed a series of finely stitched sutures around the man's shoulder.

Sergeyev felt his stomach turn. Was it even the patient's own arm? It was too large, the skin was textured differently, even the hair was a slightly different color. And yet, as he watched, the patient moved the arm and flexed his fingers with only a little difficulty. It could not be a transplant.

Zapadov approached the prisoner and smiled.

"Borodin, is it?"

"Yes, Doctor," the patient answered hesitantly. He looked at Sergeyev and then looked away.

"Any discomfort?" Zapadov asked.

"My shoulder," Borodin said. "It is sore. And... and I still feel the rocks sometimes." He swallowed and rubbed his bicep absently.

"Do not worry, that is only your body becoming accustomed to things," Zapadov said. "Its last memory is of being crushed. Now it is being told that nothing is wrong. It will adjust in time."

"Of course, Doctor. Thank you."

Zapadov looked at Sergeyev and motioned to Borodin.

"Captain, this is Patient 2271: Pyotr Borodin," he said. "An ideological deviant seeking to redeem himself through the curative power of hard labor."

Borodin quickly nodded to confirm that this was true; he seemed especially concerned that the officers understand how much he desired rehabilitation. Sergeyev almost laughed.

"A few days ago he was caught in a mine collapse. The poor man's arm was completely crushed."

Sergeyev held up a hand to stop him. "How often does an open-air mine collapse?"

Zapadov frowned and cleared his throat.

"The pit mine is largely depleted," Raskova explained. "But there remains a significant quantity of coal beneath other parts of the camp, so we have begun to dig shaft mines to harvest it." She grinned at him. "Most of it is very deep, beneath a heavy layer of rock strata. Who knows what else we might discover down there?"

"More coal, I would hope," Kirilov grumbled.

Sergeyev agreed with him, both in sentiment and in tone.

"Colonel, are you telling me that you have replaced this man's arm with another?" he asked, returning to the subject of the patient.

"I have and I am," Zapadov answered. He motioned to Borodin. "And here you have the proof. I was very careful to match the limb as closely as possible, but a careful examination reveals that the limb is different from the body." He cast a glance toward Borodin and added, "Still, better than having no arm at all."

"Yes, Doctor," Borodin said softly, staring at his hand as he continued to flex his fingers.

Sergeyev was in no mood to dispute the matter and he did not comment.

Zapadov cocked his head and leaned down to Borodin. "Cough for me," he said. Borodin obliged, with an unpleasant, hoarse noise that sounded both thick with congestion and unpleasantly dry. Zapadov nodded and smiled. "Good. That will be all for now. Try to get some rest."

"Thank you, Doctor," Borodin replied.

Once they had all left the room, Zapadov turned to Raskova and said: "New lungs, I think. Make a note of it."

"Sir," Raskova answered.

Sergeyev waited until Zapadov had resumed the tour before he spoke: "You replaced a man's arm and in only a few days he has almost complete control over it?"

"Yes," Zapadov said, his tone very curt.

"And now you speak of replacing his lungs as well?" Sergeyev asked. He reached out and put a hand against Zapadov's chest to stop him in place. Zapadov scowled at the action, but he was silent. "Doctor," Sergeyev said, allowing his voice to drop into a low and snarling tone, "these things you are showing me seem increasingly less like miracles and more like pageantry. If you are putting on a show to delude me...."

"Nothing of the kind," Zapadov snapped. Here, in his private domain, he seemed to have grown more of a spine. "You demanded to see the work we do here, so I am showing it to you. I have conducted hundreds of transplants here, almost all of them successful."

"How is it done?"

"A biological compound that..." Zapadov paused and considered his words, perhaps wondering how to describe his methodology to a layman. "That deludes the cells of both transplant and host into believing that they are one and the same, and at the same time accelerates the growth process in each."

"Meaning?" Sergeyev asked impatiently.

Zapadov took a deep breath, tinged with the anger of exasperation. "Meaning that a transplanted limb or organ will not be rejected by the body and it will be integrated within a matter of days. Is that sufficient explanation, Captain?"

"An incredible claim," Sergeyev noted. His tone was not favorable. "And yet, you have not reported about this to Moscow."

Zapadov laughed loudly. He snarled at Sergeyev and shouted:

"Submit my discoveries to the approval of men unqualified even to take my dictation? So that the likes of Lysenko may denounce my work as 'counter-revolutionary'? I do not think so, Captain. I—"

Zapadov caught himself mid-shout and took a few deep breaths. He grew pale with the realization of what he had said and to whom he had said it.

"What I mean," he quickly clarified, "is that my work is too important to be misunderstood. It is too important to the future of the Soviet Union. Once my proof is irrefutable, I will of course submit it to the proper authorities. I simply cannot afford to let small-minded middlemen prevent it from reaching those who are qualified to understand it."

It was an attempt at self-preservation, one that Sergeyev was willing to indulge. Zapadov was insane. Even if some part of his claims were true, the man was mentally unsound. He was not a secret criminal: he was simply a deluded old man too arrogant to accept the authority of his masters.

"Of course," Sergeyev said. "That sounds very academic of you."

This seemed to reassure Zapadov and he continued:

"Truly, the work you will see in this facility is merely the culmination of thirty years of agonizing experimentation and research."

"Oh?"

"You might say that today we work miracles," Zapadov said, resuming his walk. "That would be wrong, mind you. These are not miracles, they are nothing more than the achievements of modern science, as simple and material as vaccinating against influenza or setting a broken bone." He sighed. "But when I began my anatomical research during the Civil War, I was truly nothing better than a butcher, hacking at meat with a glorified cleaver. It had to be done, to keep our brave Red Army soldiers from dying unnecessarily, but I soon realized that amputation is imperfect if it cannot be reversed. If one cannot replace that which has been lost."

"Like that man Borodin?" Sergeyev asked.

"Borodin was fortunate," Zapadov replied, leading the group through a set of adjoining laboratories that smelled unpleasantly of sulfur and chemicals. "The men with whom I began my studies were not. But, at least we can take heart that their sacrifice was worthwhile. Hundreds may have died beneath my scalpel, but Borodin lives and he lives with a new, fully functioning arm. One day millions like him will enjoy the fruits of my work."

"Where did you obtain your subjects?"

After all, Karmolinsk had only been placed under Zapadov's authority

213

after the Great Patriotic War.

"Before the war, I was stationed at Vorkuta, where I was able to practice my techniques on the injured miners, but the real work began in the twenties." Zapadov smiled at nostalgic memories. "Those were good days. After my service during the Civil War, I came to an understanding with elements in the secret police. You would be surprised how simple it is to syphon away a few prisoners here or there who are bound for Siberia or scheduled for execution."

Sergeyev chuckled. "No, Colonel, I would not be surprised."

"We do great things here, Captain," Zapadov said. "Repairing injury, combatting disease—"

"Replacing lungs?" Sergeyev asked with a dismissive smirk, remembering Zapadov's words to Raskova.

"Lungs, livers, even hearts, Captain." It was Raskova who answered, again coming to Zapadov's defense when the old man did not care to defend himself. "If Marshal Stalin would deign to visit us, we could do wonders for his health. He might even live to be a hundred."

"That is a very dangerous insinuation, Lieutenant," Sergeyev said. "I think our leader's health has suffered enough from the meddling of doctors already."

Zapadov interrupted him with an irritated snort and said, "Marshal Stalin is more than seventy years old and a heavy smoker. I find it incredible that he has lived even this long. If he plans to reach the end of the decade, he will require new lungs and possibly a new heart." Zapadov smiled. "Which, of course, we can provide him, if only he would place himself in my care."

Behind them, Kirilov took a step forward, making ready to grab Zapadov. The Doctor's arrogance was deeply insulting and his very attitude was dangerous. But Sergeyev was not yet concerned. He held up a hand and Kirilov backed off.

If Zapadov noticed, he said nothing about it. Instead, he stopped just outside a pair of heavy metal doors that stood closed, flanked by a pair of armed soldiers dressed in white uniforms. White, like the doctors, like the tile, like everything in the damned Medical Wing.

"Captain, would you like to know the secret behind my reeducation program?" he asked. "The reason why my peers in Russia cannot duplicate my results?"

"That is why I am here, Colonel, in case you had forgotten."

"It is because they are trying to make the same sculpture with the wrong clay," Zapadov said.

"Explain."

"As you will recall, I liken the body to a biological machine and the brain to a complex electrical calculator."

"Yes. And?"

"When the body dies," Zapadov replied, "the brain dies soon after, starved of blood and therefore of oxygen. The tissue begins to decay and, more importantly, the neural connections begin to break down. But if the brain can be reawakened soon enough, there is a tremendous amount of information that can be reclaimed."

"Reclaimed?" Sergeyev asked. Then he took note of the stranger of the two statements. "Reawakened?"

"An electrical charge sent into the body can, under the correct circumstances, reactivate the heart and the brain, and with them restore life. Of course other factors are important as well: chemical compounds to reinvigorate the tissue, adrenaline to stimulate vital activity..." He stopped short, made a soft noise of annoyance, and added, "But none of that will interest you."

"The reeducation program," Sergeyev insisted.

He did not believe a word of Zapadov's deranged fantasies about "reinvigorated tissue".

"The fact is, Captain, that while certain memories and learned behaviors may be lost to death, even after the neural connections begin to break down a tremendous amount of knowledge is retained, simply waiting to be stimulated. Deep memories especially, or skills acquired and reinforced through extensive rote activity. If things are timed correctly, a man might forget the passage of a year and still remember how to fire a weapon or fly an aeroplane."

Sergeyev blinked a few times as he tried to come to terms with what Zapadov was saying.

"Wait. You are telling me that your reeducation system works because the subjects are killed first and then brought back to life?"

"Clumsy perhaps," Zapadov agreed, "but elegant in its own way."

"Are you insane?!" Sergeyev shouted, unable to restrain himself.

Zapadov ignored him, though he did chuckle a little under his breath at Sergeyev's outburst. He reached into a pocket and drew out a little punch card to which was affixed a photograph and a small section of documentation, almost like a set of identity papers. He placed the punch card into a slot by the door and there was an audible buzz.

"The problem with killing and reanimating," Zapadov said, "is that while it is expedient, it is prone to error. Either the subject is awakened too soon, leaving too many memories intact, or too late, resulting in permanent damage that renders him little better than a brute laborer."

"Fortunately," Raskova added, stepping to the front and pushing open the doors for them, "the Doctor has developed a solution."

Sergeyev followed the girl into the next room and suddenly stopped. He did not know what he had expected, but it was not this. He saw rows and rows of clean metal shelves lining the walls, glinting beneath the lights. On each shelf were large glass jars framed in metal and covered with nests of wires, dials and readouts of uncertain purpose. And in each jar, suspended in some translucent liquid, was a single brain, its surface pierced here and there with slender needles.

"What is this...?" he heard Kirilov whisper behind him.

"Colonel?" Sergeyev demanded, though his voice was suddenly hoarse and even he could barely hear it.

Zapadov patted the two security officers on the back and led them to the center of the room. Sergeyev glanced over his shoulder and saw Raskova following them, matching their strides step by step, her lips parted in a wide grin. Perhaps after Kirilov's rough treatment of her earlier, she was enjoying their distress at the sight. Sergeyev quickly did his best to collect himself.

"This is my new method," Zapadov explained, drawing Sergeyev's attention back to him. The old man had become agitated with excitement. "Once perfected, it will eliminate the risk of error present in the current system. After death is administered, the subject's brain is removed and placed in a solution that will maintain its physical stability. Neural connections are allowed to break down as necessary, but the brain itself is not allowed to decay. And we use a careful application of electricity to stimulate those parts of the brain that we wish to maintain after reawakening.

"Alas, it is still imperfect. Only one in ten is currently usable. The rest are rendered idiots and relegated to the mine." Zapadov quickly raised his hands and made to reassure the security officers. "But! But every failure leads us closer to success. These brains here are expendable, but once a reliable process has been established, we will be able to take a worthwhile individual, remove those thoughts and memories that are undesirable, and reawaken him fit and ready to have the missing pieces filled in."

"Reawaken?" Sergeyev muttered. "Colonel, these... The bodies... Where are the bodies?"

"In storage, of course," Raskova told him, patting Sergeyev on the cheek and giving him a pleasant smile. The girl's sudden friendliness turned Sergeyev's stomach. "The bodies are put on ice until we are ready for them." She paused and tapped her lip with one delicate fingertip, as if remembering something. "That is... assuming we even use all of the original."

"The original?"

Zapadov looked embarrassed at having overlooked that point. He quickly removed his spectacles and cleaned them on his sleeve as he said:

"Oh yes, yes. You see, comrades, the work we do here is all part of a greater whole. Everything connects. Everything is about improving man's condition. Socialism in medical form."

"Speaking of, Doctor..." Raskova said. She consulted a small notebook and then looked at her wristwatch. "I believe it is about time for 2739. I would have spoken sooner, but I was waiting for our guests to retire to the barracks."

As she spoke her last words, she again grinned at Sergeyev and Kirilov.

"Ah!" Zapadov exclaimed. "Thank you for reminding me, Yulia. Captain, come this way. I hadn't intended for you to see this, but I think you will find it most elucidating."

But as Zapadov and Raskova hurried back into the hallway, Sergeyev found himself frozen in place next to Kirilov, staring at the rows of jars and the useless brainmatter they contained. For surely, not a single brain could still be alive, whatever Zapadov might claim.

And suddenly Sergeyev realized that he had been wrong each and every time. Zapadov was not a secret criminal selling contraband on the black market. He was not a petty-minded biologist coveting his methodology like a capitalist coveted money. He was simply a deluded old man who had murdered countless prisoners in pursuit of a fantasy he could not admit was impossible.

"We are going to die here..." Kirilov whispered. He was shaking, more fearful than Sergeyev had ever seen him before.

"No," Sergeyev insisted. "No, Colonel Zapadov is a madman. He sincerely believes that what he is saying is true. We will simply placate him, flatter his delusions. We will leave first thing tomorrow and when I return here it will be with an army at my back and papers for his arrest."

Kirilov nodded and rubbed his face, his hand coming away wet with sweat.

"I wager he has a room full of his 'successes'," Kirilov said. "A pile of corpses with dinner plates in front of them!"

"Pull yourself together, Aleksey!" Sergeyev snapped, keeping his voice low.

"Perhaps he talks to them, you know?" Kirilov continued. "Tells them how much their sacrifice is benefiting the Soviet people!"

Sergeyev opened his mouth to speak, but he was interrupted by Raskova's cool, pleasant voice calling to them from the doorway:

"Are you coming, comrades?" she asked, approaching them.

Sergeyev quickly composed himself and allowed a slight smile.

"Naturally, Lieutenant," he said. "Though after this demonstration, I think some rest will be in order."

Raskova's smile never wavered as she took Sergeyev and Kirilov by the hand and pulled them toward the door.

"I think that rest is precisely what you will require, Captain," she said.

Raskova led them to a viewing room overlooking one of the larger surgical theaters. Zapadov was already there, addressing the scientists in the room below through an intercom. The viewing room was enough of a scientific excess, filled with lights and buttons and incomprehensible readouts that made Sergeyev dizzy looking at them. But the surgical theater was worse. It was covered in the same painfully sterile tile as the rest of the facility and its walls were almost completely concealed behind the massive metal-bound forms of computing machines, electrical equipment, and other, less identifiable devices.

More excess, Sergeyev thought. *More waste to flatter an old man's delusions!*

"And make certain that the current is consistent!" Zapadov shouted into the microphone. "If there is too much, we can manage it. Too little and it will all come to nothing!"

He looked up and saw Sergeyev and Kirilov at the door. Impatiently, he motioned for them to join him.

"Hurry, hurry!" he snapped. "We are almost ready! The process is very sensitive. We cannot delay just for you!"

"I don't understand," Sergeyev began. Then he stepped up to the broad glass window and got a proper look at the surgical theater.

At the center was an operating table, surrounded by curious machinery that flickered with sparks of electricity. Upon it was the patient, but even from the high vantage point Sergeyev could easily tell that the man was dead. The subject was a corpse and a composite corpse at that: an amalgamation of different parts, limbs, and flesh, crisscrossed with so many careful lines of sutures that Sergeyev could not imagine what part of it was original. The stitching across the chest made it clear that the dead man had been hacked open, likely to have his guts and organs shifted around and replaced with those taken from more dead men. This was yet another one of Zapadov's deranged experiments.

And even as he thought of Zapadov, the man drew alongside him and spoke in a voice tinged with pride:

"Behold, Captain, Patient 2739. The product of careful selection and surgery. I do not expect a success, but... This subject was intelligent while he lived. An ideological enemy of the Soviet system. Polish, I think." Zapadov began pointing to various parts of the corpse as he continued. "The body incorporates a torso and limbs from various prisoners of an especially fit build. The heart..." Zapadov smiled. "You will enjoy this. The heart is one of the healthiest I know. It could last a hundred years. Its owner was killed in a rockslide. The irony."

Sergeyev coughed. "Indeed."

"His lungs were almost destroyed by tobacco," Zapadov explained. "Intellectuals, you know. So I replaced them as well. When 2739 awakens, it will be with a new body, stronger and fitter than he could ever have imagined before now."

"I see...."

Zapadov turned to Sergeyev and put a hand on his shoulder.

"You are an intelligent man, Captain," he said. "Perhaps you can understand what we are doing here. You have, no doubt, heard the propagandists speak of the 'New Soviet Man': healthy, strong, intelligent, and utterly devoted to Socialism. A man willing to sacrifice everything without hesitation for the good of the Soviet Union."

"I have," Sergeyev confirmed, though his voice sounded hollow and distant even to him.

"I tell you truly, Captain, such men are not born. They are not bred. They are built. And I am building them here."

"It's not possible," Sergeyev murmured.

"Watch, Captain. Watch with pride." Zapadov leaned forward and pressed the button on the intercom. "Begin."

The scientists in the theater reacted immediately, rushing about the room, each to their appointed task. Sergeyev tried to keep track of them, to register what level of complicity each had in Zapadov's madness, but it was soon lost to him. His eyes darted from place to place as switches were thrown and great arcs of electricity burst through the air. As one such torrent arced in front of the window, Sergeyev jerked backward.

Zapadov chuckled. "No cause for alarm, Captain. That is simply to bleed off excess current. We must keep the level of electricity high, but it cannot be allowed to overwhelm the body. Too little current and it will not revive; too much, and it will…" He snapped his fingers. "Burn."

Despite all efforts, Sergeyev found himself staring down into the operating theater, down at the corpse that lay on the table, connected to countless meters of wires. He watched as the body convulsed, a purely mechanical reaction to the electricity surging through it.

Purely mechanical, he insisted to himself.

Everyone else in the observation room faded away as he watched the twitching corpse on the table below him. One surge. A convulsion. Another surge. Another convulsion. A third surge and….

The corpse of Patient 2739 shuddered violently, arched its back, and opened its eyes and mouth, staring blindly ahead even as it gasped for air. The scientists nearby rushed to restrain it as its chest began to heave with frantic breaths. The corpse twisted under their grasp and fought against them, but its limbs were pinned by heavy leather straps, and its struggles accomplished little. Still gasping for air, Prisoner 2739 turned its gaze toward the observation room window and locked eyes with Sergeyev.

"Help me!" it cried, a statement that Sergeyev saw more than heard against the chaotic noise of electricity and shouting.

He darted back from the window, his breath coming in its own frantic, ragged gasps.

It was impossible. What he had seen was impossible. But he had seen it. He had seen it and he was not mad.

Sergeyev did not quite notice as Zapadov drew up behind him, in the midst of filling a syringe from a glass ampule. Still transfixed by what he had seen in the surgical theater, he only just realized the danger as Zapadov grabbed him from behind. It took him another moment to react and in that moment Zapadov drove the syringe into the vein at his throat.

Lashing out, Sergeyev threw the Doctor away, but before he could do more he felt his limbs grow numb. His head swam, suddenly overcome with dizziness. As he turned to fight his attacker, he lost balance, fell against the window, and slid to the floor.

In a daze, he watched Kirilov rush to his aid, only to be intercepted by Raskova. The girl threw herself upon Kirilov before he could lay a hand on Zapadov, and through sheer ferocity she forced him to the ground. Sergeyev tried to understand what he was seeing, but nothing made any sense as Raskova knelt over Kirilov and pinned his arms with her knees, immobilizing him as easily as Kirilov should have restrained her. Laughing gleefully, Raskova wrapped her hands around Kirilov's throat and began to squeeze the breath from him.

"No! No!" Zapadov shouted.

Raskova looked over her shoulder at him, her pretty face marred with frustration.

"Not the throat!" Zapadov insisted. "No marks!"

Raskova sighed loudly and released Kirilov, only to press her hands over his mouth and nose, suffocating him instead of choking him. Sergeyev struggled to rise, fighting against the creeping numbness in his limbs in an effort to save his assistant. And he continued to struggle even after his eyelids closed and his breath finally stopped. He continued to struggle until his heart beat its last and death took him.

"It is beautiful, isn't it?" Zapadov asked.

Sergeyev looked away from the vast horizon of the Kazakh Steppe and glanced at his friend.

"Beautiful, Doctor," he agreed. "An untamed wilderness waiting to be subdued."

"Indeed," Zapadov said. "And what else do we do here, but subdue untamed things."

Sergeyev shared a laugh with the Doctor, though he did not quite understand the joke. But he had learned over the past week that it was wiser to share in humor than to reveal one's ignorance. Well, he had already known it—Zapadov had told him as much—but sometimes things had to be relearned.

"Now do not forget, you must convince Anna," Zapadov reminded him.

Sergeyev frowned. The name was familiar, but he could not quite put a face to it.

"Anna?" he asked.

Zapadov looked angry. He pulled a small photograph out of his pocket and pushed it into Sergeyev's hand. It showed a pretty girl who smiled back at him. The face and the smile were familiar. He almost remembered them.

"Your wife," Zapadov said.

And then the memory returned, stumbling through a veil of fog. His wife. He loved her. She was pretty and kind. She smiled at him. Her name was Anna. He remembered these things.

"Of course," he replied, shoving the photograph into his coat. "I remember. Only a moment's confusion."

Zapadov took Sergeyev's arm and gripped it firmly. "See to it that you do not forget."

"I will, Doctor. I will."

He glanced up as an aeroplane crossed the sky above them. It circled a few times and finally came in to land at the airstrip on the far side of the compound.

"Just in time," Zapadov said.

"Must I really go, Doctor?" Sergeyev asked.

Zapadov sighed. "Yes, you must. And you had better remember your behavior when you return to Moscow. If they think you are acting strangely...."

"It will not happen, Doctor," Sergeyev insisted, shaking his head to emphasize his certainty. "I assure you. I will be a perfect officer, as you instructed."

"Good." Zapadov smiled. "Now, let us get you to your plane."

As the two of them crossed the compound toward the airfield, Sergeyev saw Kirilov approaching from the barracks, being led gently by Lieutenant Raskova.

"Say 'good day' to the Doctor and Captain Sergeyev," Raskova prompted, as she and Kirilov reached them.

"Good… good day, Doctor. Captain." Kirilov put on a smile for them, but his movements were slow and uncertain. Smiling did not come easily to him; but then, the Doctor insisted that it never had anyway.

"Good day, Aleksey," Sergeyev said, patting Kirilov on the shoulder. "You are looking well."

"Th-thank you, Captain," Kirilov answered.

Zapadov raised a finger and pointed at Kirilov. "Now remember, you must practice your diction before you make your report. This is very important."

Kirilov quickly nodded.

"If you are ever uncertain, Aleksey, simply act angry," Sergeyev advised. "That is what people will expect of you."

Kirilov exhaled, suddenly relieved. He smiled at this news. Being angry was easy.

"Now you remember what you are to say?" Zapadov asked Sergeyev.

Sergeyev thought for a moment. The information was all there, but it took effort to summon it up. He would have to work on that. There had been so many new things to learn over the past week.

"The camp is in order," he said, "but I recommend an MVD officer be assigned here on a permanent basis to provide the Ministry with regular reports."

"Very good, Captain." Zapadov glanced back out across the steppe and frowned. "It seems that relying on my war friends for protection has proven more problematic than useful. Better to let the Ministry hear assurances of my loyalty from within its own ranks."

"That sounds prudent, Doctor," Sergeyev agreed.

He rubbed his head. Things were still a little fuzzy.

Zapadov clapped his hand on Sergeyev's shoulder and said happily:

"We are going to do great things, Captain. Great things for the Soviet Union. For humanity." Zapadov smiled. "I am creating the future, Captain, and you are a part of that. Perhaps between the two of us we will even get Marshal Stalin to visit. For his health."

"That would be... good, Doctor," Sergeyev said.

"Yes," Zapadov murmured. "It would be very good indeed."

THE BEAUTIFUL THING
WE WILL BECOME

KRISTI DEMEESTER

Katrina's father started taking her skin when she was thirteen.

"Research," she told me when I poked at the gauze wrapped around her forearm and then took another bite of her sandwich. Mrs. Papillo shot a look our way and frowned, a witchy finger pointing to the red card at the head of our lunch table that meant we were supposed to be silent.

I waited for Mrs. Papillo to turn away before I nudged Katrina between the ribs. "For what?" I mouthed to her, but she shook her head, turned a small tangerine over and over in her hands.

I did not eat the carrot sticks my mother had packed for me but spent the rest of lunch watching Katrina. Waiting for her to stretch her arm across the table or move in such a way that the gauze would ride up, if only for a second or two, so that I could see that patch of skin her father had taken from her, how he had marked her as different. As something special.

When the lunch period ended, Mrs. Papillo passed a hand over each of our shoulders, her voice a harsh, violent thing when she paused next to me. "Mary Anne, you didn't eat your lunch."

"My stomach hurts," I said, and she stared, those pale eyes passing through me, like I was nothing, like I was a ghost, and then she nodded her head, and I stood with the rest of the class and filed past the trash cans. When it was my turn, I buried the carrots, the veggie wrap, and a sugar-free pudding beneath a stack of napkins. Pressed what I would not put inside of my body into plastic and tried not to think about how my stomach pooched over my jeans.

For the rest of the day, Katrina tugged at her sleeves, covered that strip of gauze so that only the edge of the tape peeked out.

On the bus ride home, she didn't sit next to me, and I tried to ignore her ponytail, the silver butterfly clip she always wore refracting the sunlight into a thousand pieces. Devor Birmingham sat next to me instead, spent the entire ride scribbling a single dark line in his notebook, a sweet, sour smell of sweat all around him.

When our stop came, I scrambled past Devor, but Katrina did not wait. Ahead of me, she walked quickly, her face trained on the ground, her legs flashing white under her dark skirt as they carried her further and further away.

"Katrina!" I called, but she did not slow, and I would not run after her, I would not, and she stumbled, the notebook she clasped to her chest tumbling to the ground, and then she was running up her driveway, the door opening for her as if by magic, and then the darkness swallowed her, all of that blackness reaching out and then there was nothing left in the space where she had once been.

There, on the browning grass, I knelt, her notebook clutched to my chest, and I watched the curtains, waited for my best friend to appear, her hand pressed to the glass, a smile playing at the edges of her lips, but she did not. I counted to fifteen, and then I went home, Katrina's notebook burning against my skin.

In my bedroom, I flipped through the pages, but every one was blank, all of that white space waiting to devour the fingers hovering over it, and I shoved the notebook under my bed.

The next day and the day after that, Katrina did not come to school. Both days, I pretended to eat my lunch, balled up bite after bite before dropping it onto the cold linoleum, and Mrs. Papillo smiled to see my empty lunch bag, and everything inside of me felt light. Like air. Like clouds.

During art, I cut a piece of printer paper until it fit against my forearm and taped it down. I hoped that I would bleed, that maybe Katrina's father would somehow know that my skin was beautiful, too, but nothing happened and so I crumpled up the paper and left it next to my desk.

The next day, Katrina was back at school, and a puke yellow bruise snaked along her collarbone and up her neck, and she looked at me from eyes too dark for her pale face.

I passed her a note during math. "What's wrong with you?" it said, but she folded it up and put it in the little white pleather purse that she carried and did not look at me for the rest of the day.

That night, my mother placed celery on my dinner plate, a square of soggy lettuce, a baby carrot, and I cut them into smaller and smaller pieces until there was nothing left, and my stomach felt like a small, shriveled thing.

"You really do look better. Thinner," my mother said, and I curled my palm against my stomach, thought of what it would be like for Katrina's father to slice away the flesh just under my belly button; what it would be like for him to place me inside of his mouth.

On Monday, gauze streaked across Katrina's upper arm, and I tried to catch her eye throughout Social Studies, but Katrina focused on Mrs. Papillo and her stupid maps, and I spent the rest of the period wondering what it would feel like for a knife to trace out pieces of me, lift me out and into the air so that there was somehow the same and less of me.

My stomach cramped throughout lunch, and I watched Katrina. She stared at something I could not see, and Mrs. Papillo didn't notice that neither of us had eaten. When I got back to my desk, there was a note with the looping, curved letters that betrayed Katrina's handwriting. It was addressed to me, and I cupped it against my palm, waited for something to happen, for something to change, but there was Mrs. Papillo at the front of the classroom, and everything identical to every other day, so I opened the note.

"Under the tree. When it gets dark," it said, and I held those words inside of my mouth for the rest of the day. Like honey. Like a jewel.

After I pretended to eat the dinner my mother made me—a spoonful of brown rice, steamed snowpeas, and a sad, rubbery slice of chicken—I locked myself in the bathroom and stripped down to my underwear—a stretch of baby pink cotton cutting against pale flesh, and I pinched and pulled my skin until it was something that I didn't recognize, and I wished for something sharp.

Dark was a long while coming, and I stayed in the bathroom, listened as my mother washed our plates, tried not to listen when she closed her bedroom door behind her, the lock echoing through the empty house. I tried not to listen to her cry, and when she called out my father's name into that nothingness, I covered my ears with my hands.

I didn't see Katrina at first, but my eyes had not yet adjusted to the dark, and she stood behind the tree—our tree—a large maple whose leaves painted the dark with brilliant fire. Deep orange and russet burned against the night air, and there was the heavy scent of smoke all around me, and I swallowed, my throat suddenly dry.

It technically didn't belong to either Katrina or me, but stood between our houses and marked the halfway point between us. For five years, we'd stood under those branches, whispered back and forth, and the leaves were heavy with our secrets.

"Up here." Katrina's voice came from above me, and I looked up. A pair of dark eyes stared down, and I squinted, tried to make out the rest of her, but she shrank backward. "Come up."

One foot over the other, hands scrabbling against bark, and I was up, the ground falling away from us, and the stars burning large and bright. Katrina sat beside me, her hand guiding mine beneath the gauze, her fingers showing me all of the holes that her father had left.

"Does it hurt?"

"I don't know. I can never remember if it does or it doesn't."

If it was me, I would remember. I brought my fingertips to my mouth, but I could not taste Katrina.

"You've lost weight. So small. You'll shrivel up and drift away." Katrina wound a strand of my hair around her fist. "He thought I was asleep last night, and when he came in my room, I didn't make a sound, pretended like I was a mouse."

I held my breath and the branch swayed beneath us. I wondered if we fell, which of us would remain in the dirt.

"Will you come with me?" she said, and her hands were my hands, and she was squeezing and squeezing, and her eyes were pools of inky blackness as if the pupil had swallowed up everything else, and I felt all of the lightness in my stomach, all of the food I had not eaten and how it filled me up. I thought of my mother sitting alone in her bedroom and swallowing her tears, and my father who found another woman more beautiful, and I told Katrina yes, yes, I would go with her.

When she smiled at me, it was like sunshine, warm and soft against my skin, and we slipped out of the tree, ignoring the rough bark tearing at our legs, and we moved through the night. Katrina laughed, high and bright, and it was almost like nothing had changed, like there had never been a thin, white piece of gauze to come between us, and I matched my pace to hers, and we moved faster and faster through the shadow world.

Katrina's house was dark, the shutters like old blood against white wood, and she led me around back, pressed her fingers to her lips, and then opened the back door. A deep smell, like earth, like rainwater gathered into an ancient pool, came flooding out, and I coughed into my hand, but the smell was also somehow *right*. Something that had always been.

Katrina led me through the kitchen where we had spent afternoons baking cookies, eating batter off of wooden spoons; where we huddled over bowls of Frosted Flakes on Saturday mornings while her father slept on in his bedroom. In all of those years, Katrina's father would hover just behind us, and if I glanced over at him, he would smile, his brown eyes crinkling at the edges. Sometimes, when I woke before Katrina, he would pour a bowl of cereal for me, ask me about school or about what T.V. shows I liked. He would push the sugar bowl toward me and laugh in all of the right places. Nothing at all like my own father who glared when I helped myself to a second bowl of bran flakes and mumbled under his breath that if I wasn't careful, I would end up like my mother.

Far away from my mother, from my father and the tight, sharp words between them, away in the world that Katrina and I created, there were no mothers, no fathers, no careful eyes watching every bite of food that went scraping past my lips, no clipped phrases measuring out the weight of me, no mirror image of my mother's shame, her own body reflected in mine.

Before me, Katrina stopped short, and I slammed into her, my belly curving into the hollow of her back, and I did not move away but leaned into her hair. I never wanted to move again, wanted our skins fused together, a single beating heart that moved through the world like a wondrous thing. A thing that had no beginning and no end, our bodies indistinguishable from the other, and no one would look at the thin casing of skin that covered my hulking form and then look away. Because we—because *I*—would be more beautiful and strange than anything they had ever seen.

She brought a finger to her lips and then extended her arm, pointed down the hallway to a thin strip of light that spilled from beneath a closed door.

It was not a bedroom I remembered seeing before. In my memory, the kitchen jutted like a broken tooth off of a small living room stuffed with uncomfortable furniture and a television too large for the space; at the opposite end of the kitchen, a cased opening led to a narrow hallway, Katrina's bedroom on the left, her father's and a single bathroom on the right. The door I saw now was at the end of the hallway in a place where there had never been a door.

A shadow passed into the space between the wood and the floor, and Katrina held her breath, her back still against my chest, and I did the same. Together, we waited for the door to open, but the shadow moved on. There are times that I think we never breathed again.

"He's working," Katrina said.

"On what?"

"I hear him talking to it. Late at night. He says that it's so beautiful. That it saved him. Then there are noises, like an animal. I cover my ears then. This way," Katrina said, and I followed her into her bedroom, the door opening and closing quietly. She did not turn on the light and walked to the center of the room where a patch of silver moonlight streamed in from the window behind her. Her fingers caught on the bottom of her shirt and tugged upwards, the skin on her back pale and smooth. On her right shoulder, a large patch of gauze marred the smooth flesh, and she stood perfectly still.

I went to her, and she bowed her head when I peeled away the cloth, her voice low. "He whispers when he opens me up."

Katrina shifted, and I watched raw skin ripple, held my hand over the spot as if I could contain her, as if I could keep all of her inside, but she was pouring out, bright blood against that pale skin, and I thought again of how it would feel to be sliced apart and stitched back together as something better.

"You're so lucky," I said, and Katrina turned to face me.

"I didn't like it when he would come in to tell me goodnight. He would wait until he thought that I was asleep and then sit next to me for the longest time. Sometimes, he laid down next to me and asked if he could kiss me, and it was always too long, but he would get up and go away and the next morning he wouldn't look at me." Her breath came hard and fast, and I wound my hand through hers. "The first time he cut me, I fought him. Screamed until my throat went bloody, but he didn't stop, and he cried and cried and cried. Said that it was better this way. After, he didn't come to kiss me goodnight. He was right. It was better this way. Each time he took more and more, but I locked everything inside. Learned how not to scream."

From the hallway came the sound of something moving and then the sound of a door creaking shut.

"Hide," Katrina said, but I shook my head, and she grasped my arms and pushed me toward her closet.

She shut the door on me but not all the way, so I could see a corner of the window, the edge of her dresser, a wooden music box open and a tulle-skirted ballerina gone still. Her clothes smelled like lavender.

I couldn't see Katrina's father, but I could hear him: could hear his breathing gone jagged as he shuffled into the room; could hear him whispering, his voice sliding over me like oil, and I hated Katrina. Hated her for her smooth, flat stomach and her beautiful mouth. Hated her for having a father who loved her. Hated her for being so lovely that her father wanted to take her apart, to carry those small pieces of her with him like a treasure.

The hard, sharp sound of scissors echoed through the room, and I opened the door a bit more and listened for Katrina's silence.

I could see her now, and her father knelt before her, a pair of heavy handled scissors clutched in his right hand, his left wrapped in her hair. She looked back at me, across all of that empty space, and opened her mouth. "Please." Her lips formed around the words, but there was no sound.

Rising, Katrina's father stumbled backward, his hands thick with his daughter's hair. "Thank you. Thank you," he said, and he closed the door quietly behind him.

Katrina turned from me when I left the darkness of her closet, and I went to her, touched her on the thigh, and she tucked herself tight, tight, tight against the wall.

I went out the window as I had so many other times, letting my weight fall against the ground and then rolling with the momentum. Katrina did not shut the window behind me, and I ran all the way back to my house, my lungs and muscles burning.

In the morning, my mother sliced half a grapefruit and placed it before me with a pink packet of sweetener. She watched as I took my spoon and mashed the fruit until the juice threatened to overflow and brought the rind to my lips. She smiled and patted my hair. "Good girl," she said and didn't eat any breakfast of her own. The blouse she'd put on that morning, a deep blue the color of ocean water, was too big, and she plucked at it as she watched me, uncomfortable in this new, thinner body that she inhabited. It hadn't been enough for my father to stay. We hadn't been enough for him to stay.

When the bus came, I didn't get on. My head hurt and there were small pinpricks of light when I moved too quickly. Instead, I waited at the tree— *our* tree—and when my mother's car glided past, all I could see of her face was a smear of frosted pink lipstick.

I plucked a leaf from the branches and folded it until it was nothing more than a bite and then placed it between my teeth. Chewed and swallowed. I wondered if it would take root there, unfurl delicate little tendrils into soft dirt and fix me in this spot forever. It was nice to think of things like that, but my legs moved, and I carried that green inside of me as I ran to Katrina's house.

At some point in the night Katrina must have closed the window because the curtains covered the glass, but I didn't want her to see me there. She would tell me to leave, would rob me of the only thing that I wanted, and so I crept low to the ground, my chin scraping against grass, and I opened my mouth to it and took another bite.

Katrina didn't understand what it was like to empty herself, to waste and waste away until everything inside was hollow. A vast thing covered in dull skin that needed cutting away.

The back door was still open, and I slipped inside. Once, when my father still came home every night, still told my mother and me that he loved us, I would not have been able to fit through a space so small, but I was so much thinner, my bones and skin withered to almost nothing, and I moved through the kitchen like water.

The doors to the bedrooms stood open. At the end of the hallway, the extra door, the door that shouldn't be there, stood closed, and I pushed myself toward it. Katrina did not rise when I went past her door but watched me from underneath her blanket, a jagged line of dark hair falling across her cheeks, and turned away from me. It didn't matter what Katrina thought. Not anymore.

The handle was hot against my palm as if someone had touched it only moments before, and I leaned into it, the door swinging open without a sound.

The room was empty except for a large table. Katrina's father had draped a white sheet over the exposed wood and here and there were dark red stains that twisted outward like bulbous eyes and elongated necks, and I thought I could see myself trapped inside those stains. Beneath the sheet, a small form lay still, and I could make out a nose, the slight concave curve where eyes should be.

The floor creaked beneath my feet, but I didn't care who heard me. Katrina was still in her bed. I would have heard her if she rose, felt her moving through the empty space I'd left behind, but there was only the cold whisper of air moving against my legs as the door closed.

"You shouldn't be here," Katrina's father said. He sat in the far corner of the room, and his body bent and stooped toward something on the floor, his hands rising and falling, something metallic glinting from between his fingers. Sewing. He was sewing.

"No," I said, and he looked up at me, his hands pausing in their work, and my skin sang for him, sang for those hands to slip beneath my own flesh and strip it away. Make it beautiful. Make it whole.

He pointed to the table, to that still form, and he looked at me, eyes like an animal, glittering and bright. "I had to. My own *daughter*, and all I could think of was the way she would feel beneath me, the taste of her breath in my mouth. It made me sick to think," he said, and there were tears on his cheeks and blood on his hands.

"I had to," he said, and his hands pulled back, and I saw the crooked stitches, the skin pieced and pulled together like a quilt.

"A doll," I said and placed a hand on his shoulder. He didn't shrug it away, didn't grimace the same way my father had in those last months when my mother touched him or when I came into the room.

My stomach curved inward, my hip bones protruded like the way they do in magazines when I lifted my shirt, and he watched me pull it over my head, his breath hitching as I did.

"I'm enough. Please. I'm enough."

When he lifted his knife, I leaned into him, and my body was all air, all lightness, and there was only the movement of his hands against my skin and my blood like lace against the floor. "Father," I said, and he lifted the pieces of me and placed them on the table. Beneath the white sheet, the form moved, the chest rising with breath, and I reached for it, reached for the beautiful thing I would become.

When he was finished, he draped the white gauze against my skin like a bridal veil, and he kissed my forehead, his lips feather light and dry like a moth's wing.

I closed the door behind me, left him to his work, placed one foot in front of the other until I stood in Katrina's bedroom. She did not speak but pulled the covers back, and I climbed in next to her.

She curled into me, her arms tight around my abdomen, the raw, exposed meat burning and raw, and brought her lips to my ear. "Sister," she said.

Together, we slept.

In the next room, something new, something beautiful, woke and gasped into the gathering dark.

MARY SHELLEY'S BODY

DAVID TEMPLETON

The stream we gazed on then, rolled by,
Its waves are unreturning;
But we yet stand
In a lone land,
Like tombs to mark the memory
Of hopes and fears, which fade and flee
In the light of life's dim morning.

—Percy Bysshe Shelley

I cannot breathe.

O! God! I cannot breathe!

There is thunder in my lungs, a whirlwind in my throat, bolts of lightning stabbing at my heart, shredding my flesh, shredding my soul like paper. I feel as thin as paper. I am burning! I try to breathe, but all I sense in my chest are those buzzing arcs of light, spreading out like veins of fire through my skin. And still I cannot breathe.

I wonder… should I stop trying?

I stop. There is a faint faraway exhalation, as if from behind a dark wet door. I let myself hear it, the sound of it, evaporating. It is an empty sound, as shallow and void as my body, my poor, sick, wrecked, half-paralyzed, once desirable, once fearless, once unstoppable body.

Ah, I begin to understand. As suddenly and certainly as those flashes of light I still see somewhere beyond what used to be my eyes, I see the truth now.

I no longer *need* to breathe. I am done with breathing.

I am dead.

Well great God, that took long enough!

The doctors are no doubt relieved to be rid of me, the crazy lady from London, wasting away with no obvious cause. For months, for years, there has been only a sense that something was wrong in the spongy muscle of my brain, something vital added or taken away.

And, now my life, my little life, is over.

My hapless heart, so long deluged in bitterness, is finally still.

I feel so much better now.

My head no longer hurts, for one thing.

And that terrible burning smell, like wet feathers set ablaze, that is gone too. How long has it been since it all began, the smell, the headaches, the fainting spells, then the failure of half my body to obey the simplest task?

No matter. I am free of it now.

Free of my body.

Free of my life.

This then, I surmise, is my grave?

This slab of cold carved stone I sense before me, after years of loneliness, is my lonely gray tomb? I cannot see, but I do perceive shapes and structures all around. I cannot feel, but I detect words here, carved into the rock slab before which I stand.

How am I standing?

My body, what is left of it, lies there in the grave.

Yet here I am. Standing.

Kneeling, even. Speaking, if speaking this is.

Had I fingers with which to feel I would caress these carved words, trace out their meaning with my fingertips—and yet, somehow I can. Somehow I do.

I can read the meaning of these etched lines.

Here lies Mary Wollstonecraft Shelley.

Yes. That was I.

Mary.

A wife. A mother. An author.

Daughter of William and Mary Wollstonecraft Godwin.

Those were my parents, yes… though he too much so, and she—dead almost upon looking at me—only my mother in that she conceived me, bore me, and birthed me. And still, in so many ways, Mary Wollstonecraft—the writer, the radical, beloved and despised by so many—gave me more with her life and words than my father, with his calm and silent disapproval, ever gave me with his.

The next line.

Widow of the late Percy Bysshe Shelley.

Shelley.

O, Shelley. My husband, my love, my savior, my only one!

I have no beating heart to ache with, no sense to feel with. How then does your name still stir me so? Almost thirty years have passed since you died, your soul set free beneath the waters of the Gulf of Spezia, your drowned body—with its speaking eyes and face unlike any other who ever walked Earth—burned to gray ashes on the shore. Since that day, O my love, I have missed you so, with only your memory to comfort me these many years.

That, and the singular divinity of your poems.

And, oh yes! I have had your heart.

It's still in my desk.

Your friend Trelawney snatched it, charred and purple, from your funeral pyre. Your heart, dried and flattened, sits in my desk still, tucked away beneath my papers along with three locks of hair, one from each of our three dead children.

I wonder who will discover them, there in the drawer?

I suspect it will be our daughter-in-law, Jane.

It will give her a bit of a shock, that.

A final line.

Born August 30, 1797. Died February 1, 1851.

Odd. I feel as if I have only just died, but I am already buried. That was quickly done. I suspect it was Jane's doing. Ever since she married my dear Percy Florence, that daughter-in-law of mine—whom I have loved with as much of my own heart as was left to love with—has proven nothing if not punctual. But then of course, she has had years to plan.

I have been dying for such a very long time.

And now I am dead.

I must be, for there is my name on this tomb.

Shelley used to joke that if I died before he, he would see to it that my marker proclaimed, "Here lies the body of Anonymous!"

It was a joke, but it came with a sting.

Anonymous was the name under which my first novel was published.

Afterwards followed years of ungenerous assumptions that another must have been the true author of my story, that I was not capable of it. Visitors to our house, when engaged in conversation with Shelley, oft interpreted my watchful silence as dullness, and whispered rumors that my husband likely wrote more of my prose than I. Shelley defended me. After that I saw to it that all of my subsequent works were published—if not always under my true name—then at least under a title which made my authorship clear.

For the rest of my days, all my published writing proclaimed, "By the author of *Frankenstein*."

Frankenstein. My first great success, born of happier days, too briefly tasted.

Frankenstein.

My triumph… my curse… my hideous progeny.

My grave, then, is here in Bournemouth, in the little Dorset by the sea. I recognize it. This is St. Peter's Churchyard, at the center of town, not far from Jane and Percy's house. They had hoped to move me there, to their home, though I have been too ill to travel.

And here I am… in Bournemouth.

How disappointing.

It was my wish to be buried at St. Pancras Cemetery in London, near Mama's grave, and Godwin's. Yet wait. O! I see.

Here they are.

On the other side of my crypt, I find more words.

Removed hither from the churchyard of St. Pancras, London.
William Godwin, Author of 'Political Justice.'
Born March 3, 1756, died April 17, 1836. 80 years old.

That's Papa.

Mary Wollstonecraft Godwin, Author of 'A Vindication on the Rights of Woman,' born April 27, 1759, died September 10, 1797.

And that's Mama.

Apparently, when I told Jane and Percy that I wished to be buried with my parents, my words were taken rather more literally than intended. So here they lie, too, their epitaphs sharing a cold rocky slab with my own. It is a bit of an affront that Jane thought to list the titles of their books, but neglected to mention any of mine. My mother and father were extraordinary, of course, both writers of distinguished literary celebrity and influence—but would it have been too much to follow my name with the words "The Author of 'Frankenstein'"…at the very least?

Is that ungenerous of me?

I suppose it is.

Poor Mama. Poor befuddled Godwin. Dug up from their separate resting places, their mortal remains now to rest beside my own crumbling bones till we all turn together into dusty nothing… in Bournemouth.

This must mean that Mrs. Godwin, my detested stepmother, is still in the ground in London, where she was buried ten years ago, right beside Father. She's moldering there now, beneath the earth, all alone.

There's poetry in that.

O, but I loved it so at St. Pancras, at Mama's tomb. Sheltered by the graveyard's magnificent oak, the grass as soft and cool as the feathers of a dead robin. How contented were the days I spent there as a girl, poring over Mama's books, whispering to her grave the secret thoughts I could never speak to her. I was sixteen when I brought Shelley there for the first time. He was twenty-one and married. He kissed me, at Mama's grave, that evening warm in summer, my heart young and open, every inch of me young and open, to life, to love, to Shelley.

I was with child by summer.

My first child. My tiny one. My sweet baby girl.

No! Stop this. I do not wish to think of her.

Not yet… not now… not ever.

Let me contemplate anything else.

In my life I contemplated everything. It was my calling, my practice. I wrote stories each morning, studied the great books of literature, geography, history, and science in the afternoon, and at night, in my journals, I catalogued the events of my day. It was what I did, and it was enough to fill a life. So is this to be my new existence, then—"writing" the details of my life into the air, perusing my memories as a surgeon fingers a cadaver, stitching my loves and fears and sins together into words—as I have so often imagined my Monster being pieced together from separate, broken lives into one new horrifying whole?

If that is my task, I refuse! It's too much.

Was it not enough to have experienced my life once? Must I live it all again?

But do I have strength to resist?

Contrary to my will, I feel compelled to speak on... to tell my story to this sky and these cold stones. I sense that I do not hold the power to refuse. Against my desires, I know I must remember all the details of my life... though why, and for whom, and to what purpose, I cannot begin to imagine.

What's that? Listen!

I hear more thunder, and the soft hiss of failing rain, somewhere beyond, yet still nearby. Queer, is it not, that no rain falls overhead? And still, I hear it, and the rush of the wind, even closer—faintly crying like the lament of a suffering child. And there it is again, a flash of lightning, striking somewhere beyond the graveyard.

There would have to be lightning, wouldn't there?

God's little joke, I suspect.

From the stormy sky, lightning casts out its spidery fingers, its tendril light illuminating these old stone grave markers all around me, sentry-like, and the mournful faces of impish angels frozen in stone. I can see their faces now.

Dimly, as if through vapor, I begin to glean my sad surroundings.

God in heaven! Did I really just say all of that?

"Lightning casts out its spidery fingers!" "I glean my sad, eternal surroundings!"

For heaven's sake Mary, do rein it in.

You're beginning to talk the way you wrote!

And with that, I need to move. I need to walk.

I trust that neither my tomb nor its decaying resident will be scuttling away anytime soon… so I think I will leave them here, and explore my new neighborhood.

Hello, whose grave is this, with the lovely stone cross?

The Right Reverend Gavin Lang. "His soul is with God."

Well, lucky him. At least he's got company.

And who's here? *FREETH*, a family monument with a dozen names.

Samantha Elizabeth Freeth.

Maureen Elizabeth Freeth.

Margaret Elizabeth Freeth.

Strange, that. Either the Freeth boys were fond of marrying women with the middle name Elizabeth or Mr. and Mrs. Freeth were appallingly unimaginative when it came to naming their daughters.

And who is this over here, beneath this crumbling tomb with the ancient stone angel with its head long removed? *Josiah Nickerson Knowles, IV, "A Gentleman in the face of all adversity."* Well, Mr. Knowles, I hope that wherever you are your gentlemanly head is better attached than the one that once rested on your little angelic guardian here.

Moving on.

Lewis Dymoke Grosvenor Tregonwell, Esquire.

My, what a name! With a name like that, was the "Esquire" really necessary?

So many names, so many graves—all silent.

Is there no one at home, no one to welcome me?

Mama? Papa?

Reverend Lang? Mr. Esquire?

Perhaps one of the Freeth girls?

Amongst these many splayed markers, so lonely and cold, are there no friendly phantoms to share eternity with me? Am I to be the only ghost in this garden of loneliness and midnight, forever its restless caretaker, blabbing my sad story to the stormy skies, dictating my memoir to these disinterested stones?

This, then, is how I am to be punished for my sins!

Had I breath to laugh I would! My particular sins… and God knows, they are not few… have punished me enough during my life to eliminate the need for further sentence now that I am dead.

Besides which… I really must say it… I do not believe in ghosts.

Never since childhood.

And I take exception at being a thing I do not believe in. All my life… fifty-three long years of it… I did many things for which my name was spoken ill, but I never did that, never acted a part which wasn't in me, and I shan't do it now.

Shelley, surely, would defend me in this.

Shelley was never anyone but Shelley.

He believed only in what he could see, and know, and touch.

He believed in me. Well, he did for a time.

He certainly did not subscribe to supernatural agencies. He did not believe in Heaven. And everyone knows Shelley did not believe in *God*… all due apologies to the Right Reverend Lang. As a youth, Shelley made his skepticism clear, initiating his lifelong severance from his wealthy but deeply pious father. Shelley's little pamphlet, *The Necessity of Atheism*, distributed to his fellow students, did not help, resulting in his disinheritance before age nineteen, and his hasty expulsion from Oxford… that, and his enthusiastic impregnating of Harriet, the coffeehouse owner's daughter. Shelley did marry her, though he did not believe in marriage, either… and later, after meeting me, still married to Harriet, he found he did not believe in wedding vows either.

Harriet drowned herself six years later.

If there were such a thing as ghosts… vengeful spirits seeking justice… Harriet surely had reason to come back as one long ago… to haunt me, to punish me for loving her husband more than he loved her. And I dare say she would not have been the only spirit eager to settle old business with Mary Wollstonecraft Shelley.

Fanny, my half-sister, my mother's first-born, you took laudanum in Swansea, alone in a tiny room at the Mackworth Arms, an anguished, half-finished note lying at your side. I know I broke your heart, leaving as I did with Shelley and Claire, abandoning you to the Godwins. Then there's Poor Polidori, you who wanted nothing more than to be judged worthy and of merit… you took cyanide in London. There's Lord Byron—our magnificent, ever-ambitious Albé—you died in Greece in your effort to free the Greeks from the Ottoman Empire. Preparing to attack the Turks at the fortress of Lepanto, you perished, not in glorious battle, as in one of your heroic poems, but from too much bloodletting after catching a cold.

If I had not known and loved you, I might have laughed.

But I did love you, despite your cruelties to my sister, and I wept for you.

And finally... there are the children, my sweet, pretty babes.

William... dead of malaria at three... buried in Rome.

Clara... dead of heat exhaustion at one... I watched you die in Venice.

The baby, my tiny one, born two months premature in London, alive yes, but... for a short time only. All three of you, my little ones, have cause to be angry, my pretty ones, denied by fate and ill-timing a chance to live the fullness of your lives.

You, my tiny one, my firstborn, you might well be most deserving of vengeance... born too early to a mother too young, a mother too headstrong and too foolish. You do know, dear one, though your days were few, I did what I could to make them more? I held you. I loved you. I nursed you. I did more than any mother could to keep you. Did I not?

In the end, I buried you anyway.

I hate this!

Here I am, drawn back to the very topic I said I am not ready to consider.

Is this what you want, God... or whomever? Is this what I am supposed to be doing? Flitting amongst tombstones, spilling my griefs and sorrows? In my life, I never put my 'secret self' forward in print, never spoke in public of my feelings. Even the preface to *Frankenstein*—in its third printing—was written against my will. As a child, sent away to Scotland, walking the blank and dreary shores of the Tay, making up stories as I wandered through the mists, I never made myself the heroine of my tales. Yet this seems to be my forced and unwelcome commission—to speak of myself at last, to dig beneath the skin of my sad, forlorn history, revealing to the air my terrible secrets, confessing with quivering sorrow my tiny unspoken crimes?

Fine! What then, of my mother, my *first* murder?

Let's speak of that!

I killed you, Mama, before ever I knew you, tearing you open as I ripped screaming into the world. The doctors say the infection that took your life ten days later was more the midwife's fault than mine, but I wonder. If I have never been able to forgive myself for killing you, how can I ever ask you to forgive me?

I cannot. And I won't.

So here I am, you ghosts, phantoms, victims of my life! Here I am, all of you, with no pressing engagements to take me elsewhere. If you want me, come and get me!

I should be easy to find.

I'm the only ghost in Bournemouth!

Oh, but this cannot be my fate, condemned for all time to be a babbling ghost? Constructed only of air, memory and anguish! It's so embarrassing! Me, *Mary Wollstonecraft Shelley!* A thin, flickering shadow of the grand romantic I once was, reduced now to haunting a graveyard!

It's so cliché.

Still, I should not, I suppose, object too loudly.

There *are*, after all, worse things than ghosts.

I know that now.

But O my love, my Shelley, I did pray for the sight of *your* ghost.

I sought it out often, listening through the long nights for the sound of your voice, praying for one ethereal glimpse of your presence. In my darkest hours I would have traded my very soul for one more hour with yours.

When I first received word of your boat capsizing, first learned you had drowned, my shrieks must have frozen the blood of all who heard them. In that moment, my Shelley, God knows I'd have brought you back if I could, even after so many days in the water. Had I been there to revive you, to press my lips to yours, to breathe life into your swollen body, to drain the brine from your lungs, to rebuild, feature by feature, your most-beautiful-of-faces, so cruelly teethed away by eels and crabs and dark-eyed fishes as you floated lifeless along the weedy sands beneath the waves… I would have done it.

I'd have called down lightning, shocked the knotted sinews of your body, and brought you back to my arms! Whether as man or monster, I would have done it, Shelley!

But I could not do it. I was not there.

And so I let you go.

Since then, but for Percy Florence—our only child alive past infancy—I have lived my life alone. And now, here I stand. Dead. *Post mortem.* Abandoned... once again... in this stormy sea of voiceless stones, no voice to comfort or accuse me save only mine, mine and these memories as sharp as razors, this torrent of recollections as harsh and horrid and terrifying as a strike of lightning.

I have hit a wall.

An actual wall... a tall one, built of rocks and mortar, covered in vines.

Have I reached the edge of the graveyard? I do not remember it from my visits here when I was alive. The wall is high, and I cannot tell what lies beyond it. Yet still, I hear the fierce patter of the rain on the other side... and there it is, more thunder!

Lacking other entertainment, I shall follow this wall, and see where it takes me. Surely, there is a gate or doorway, some passage out... out into the rain. I should like to feel the rain again, to cup it in my hands, to feel it spill out between my fingers... if I could, but I cannot, can I?

I can no longer feel.

Of course, it isn't the first time I've lost my sense of feeling.

I was thirteen when I was sent to Ramsgate by the sea to cure the rare skin disease that infected my hand and arm. For six months, I had no use of that limb, no perception in my fingers but pain. The doctors treated me with fresh water poultices and daily dips in the bathing machine, and eventually, I began to feel with my hand again.

Till then, I remember walking by the shore, my arm outstretched, my corpse-like fingers bump-bump-bumping against the sea wall as I followed it along the sands, eyes closed, moving ahead with the wall to my numb side, the ocean with its breezes to my feeling other, me bobbing along in the middle, floating between rock and water, between sense and shock, between feeling alive and feeling nothing.

I have often wondered ... was it like that for you, my Creature?

What was it you perceived as you awoke, blood-soaked and gasping, from nothingness into life? What sense could you make of your world? In writing your story, I allowed you but one glimpse of Victor Frankenstein, your callow young creator, before he pulled from you, shrinking in terror at what he'd recklessly wrought.

He left you naked there, on the bloody table, all alone, abandoned, unloved.

You followed him, or tried to, your senses quickening, grasping and reaching from object to object across the room, the very skin of your piece-meal limbs still burning and bleeding from fresh stitches, your animal heart pumping stolen blood through borrowed veins. You followed your father to his room. You stood at his bedside, as he… exhausted from weeks of toil… tried in vain to sleep you away from mind and memory. Your desperate, inarticulate tongue, aching to speak as it had once done, awoke him.

He screamed… but you *smiled.*

That was how I first imagined this moment—you smiling down in confusion and wonder, as your faithless maker shrank away, repulsed and horrified, vanishing into the night. What father would do so, shrinking in disgust at his own child? Alone in Frankenstein's laboratory, you waited, but he never returned. Hours later, hungry and heartsick, naked and cold, you somehow "clothed" yourself, and left. I could never imagine how you'd know to do that, to clothe yourself—so I wrote you a silly line.

"On a sensation of cold, I covered myself with some clothes."

I might as well have written, "On a sensation of hunger, I made myself an omelet."

No matter. I was about to launch you into the world, a deformed and hulking abomination. I couldn't bear to send you out naked, too.

Hand-over-hand, you made your way from the room, your fingers gripping the walls, the stairs, the doorway, until you finally emerged into the open street, a wild November storm still raging overhead.

A lightning storm!

You were born of that very same electricity! Seamed together from the limbs and organs of thieves, beggars, murderers, drunkards, soldiers, farmers and slaughterhouse beasts, you were birthed, just hours before, in a kettle of ice and water, brought to life by the power of the heavens, soon after sentenced to a life in hell.

O, my poor Monster, the punishments I wrote onto you!

The loneliness I heaped upon you!

Can you ever forgive me?

Wait a moment! Whose story am I supposed to be telling, mine or yours?

Where does Mary Shelley end and her Creature begin?

Can I tell the story of my own life without also telling yours? Or vice versa?

Our lives, my Creature—mine too real, yours too full of sorrow—they share common blood, sinews and bones borrowed from one another, as Victor borrowed the arms and legs of lost souls in his fury to build you.

But then, Victor is also me, is he not? In my book, when Victor remembers being a child, watching a tree struck by lightning, that memory is mine as much as his.

I was ten years old when it happened.

The tree stood not twenty yards from our house. There was a blast of lightning, and nothing remained but a blasted stump. I had never seen anything so utterly destroyed. Confounded by the fury of the assault, I asked Godwin, my father, what happened to our oak, and he answered.

"Electricity," he said.

Afterwards, he took me to many public exhibitions, demonstrations of electrical discoveries, galvanic experiments. I saw wires attached to the bodies of dead frogs, twitching as if alive when shocked by machines. I watched my first autopsy when I was five, entranced by the pink and dripping wonders of the body's forbidden inner landscape. One of Godwin's dinner guests once told us of witnessing the animation of decapitated prisoners' heads, their eyes staring wide, faces contorting, their tongues lolling like madmen.

I remember the day Godwin brought home a thing he said was a Leiden jar—"lightning in a bottle," he called it—and a clock-like "Friction Machine," all wheels and levers. The jar gave off sparks in the darkened room, making the children scream with joy and terror. The machine—Shelley collected them, too, I would one day learn—it transmitted a little shock to all who touched the metal handle. My sisters and I shrieked, holding hands in a circle as the machine passed its tiny jolt through our bodies like an apple in a party game. My stepmother disapproved, of course, but Papa, clinging still to my mother's views that girls should be as educated in math and science as men, insisted we know a little of the natural world.

Shelley was ever enamored of electricity.

As a student, he performed his own experiments, electrifying the door handles of his classrooms to give the professors a harmless shock as they entered. Later, courting me at my mother's grave, he told me his own tales, reports of Benjamin Franklin and the "kite scientists," their feet on the ground, a kite string in one hand, peering recklessly up into the storm, pulling down lightning from the sky, trapping it in vessels of water.

Shelley spoke of a recent experiment—two hundred Carthusian monks, hands linked in a sweaty chain, all jerking together at the shock from a large machine, the friction-fueled charge traveling through the spongy vessels of their celibate bodies.

We made jest of it all, Shelley and I, as we lay in each other's arms, whispering of magnetism, attraction, friction, electricity. Like scientists, we explored each other's bodies, believing we would find in each other's flesh the secrets of life and death. We studied up till morning, hungrily learning the lessons we taught each other.

When Godwin discovered us, when he tried to break the growing current between us, it was no use. He sent Shelley with stern rebukes back to his wife, and in response we simply added geography to our studies. We found Godwin's maps of France, Germany, Switzerland, and secretly we planned our escape from England.

But we were not alone, were we?

Claire, my wild and wayward stepsister, guessed at our affair, and learning of our plans to steal away to France, insisted on coming along. She could speak French, which we could not. Shelley argued that with a *second* sixteen-year-old girl in the company, it lent the excursion an air of legitimacy that would allay my parents' concerns.

He was wrong.

Good lord, what a fuss!

My stepmother gave chase all the way to Dover. She only just missed us as we set sail for Calais. Ah, Mrs. Godwin! She cared more about the questionable chastity of her true daughter than she cared to keep me, the daughter of her husband's sainted dead wife, at home by her side. From the day she met me, she was perplexed at my fanciful, watchful, insistent curiosity. By the time I was introduced to Shelley, I'd been sent away to Scotland twice, for years at a time, to save Mrs. Godwin the exasperation of having to look at me. I was not surprised at her consternation when I fled with Shelley and Claire, leaving only Fanny, the other daughter of her husband's dead wife, in her care.

It was my *father's* fury that astonished me.

In truth, his anger struck me to the core.

In *Political Justice*, the book that brought Shelley to his door, he asserted that marriage was a "cruel system," one that should be ignored if not outright abolished. Yet for dallying with a married man, he disowned me, refusing me utterly, the moment I vanished with Shelley and Claire. I did not see my father again, or receive any letters, for three years... not till tragic little Harriet, the coffeehouse owner's daughter, killed herself in the park... and Shelley and I, finally free to do so, were properly and legally married.

But first, there was France.

My God! I am growing tired of following this wall!

How long have I been walking? A while I think—long enough to describe my childhood, reveal my first great indiscretion, and include a short history of modern electricity. I think I'm doing quite well, all things considered, spilling the unhappy story of my existence against my will.

I doubt I ever talked so much when I was alive!

And yet, still I've reached no gate or exit. There must be some way through to whatever lies beyond. I suppose I shall just keep walking. There's little else to do... and the story of my life, as pitiful as it is to recall, is only just beginning.

I am, in fact, just now getting to the good part.

They were beautiful, those first days with Shelley.

We'd done it! Shelley, Claire and I... we'd escaped from the Godwins!

What an exquisite adventure it was, leaving the hedged-in cornfields and measured hills of England, crossing the channel as if flying from the Earth! We travelled by day. By night, we studied the great poets, the Greeks, the mystics—the alchemical mysteries and magical investigations of Albertus Magnus and Cornelius Agrippa. Those books, reeking with forbidden mystery—recipes for turning lead to gold, conversing with angels, raising the dead—they gave us much amusement, with their ominous spells and poetical incantations, descriptions of potions and balms for everything, stories of strange spirits once worshipped by primitive people.

We memorized the alien words of those ancient spells, even inventing little incantations of our own, but Shelley and I worshipped only each other.

Though sometimes Claire did join in.

It was complicated.

But Shelley savored life most when it was most impossible, and what is life, if not a thing to be savored? We purchased a blank journal, and from that day Shelley and I wrote in it together, daily. We resolved to walk through France on foot, then to journey through Germany and Switzerland by boat, along the river Rhine. We would purchase a donkey to carry our books and provisions. When possible, we'd sleep out of doors. When it rained, we'd find an inn. In making our plans, we'd thought of everything, all but one detail.

We had no money.

Shelley sold his watch and chain for eight napoleons. The sum lasted us but six weeks. Destitute, we returned to London in September, instantly turned away by the Godwins. Shelley worked what influence he could, borrowed money where possible, and found lodging for us both, and for Claire, near Gravesend. Five months later, our poor little babe was born, tiny and frail, no bigger than a little shoe, a tiny, clutching, gasping thing.

She claimed me, the moment she gazed on me.

"She will not live the night," the midwife murmured.

But live the night she did.

All were astonished.

In our journal, Shelley wrote, "Baby unexpectedly alive."

Two days later, he wrote, "Favorable symptoms in the child. We may indulge some hopes." My own journal entries were a list of the books I studied that day, casual remarks on the weather, and numerous slight variations on the phrase, "I nursed my baby." From early September, every day I nursed my baby, gazing all the while at her miraculous face, murmuring, "I did this. I made this."

We had made her, Shelley and I... together... our first collaboration.

But then, on the 6th of March, I sat at my desk, hand trembling, and forced myself to write the words, "Find my baby dead. A miserable day."

She was but twelve days old.

For some days after, I could not blot out the thought repeating through my mind.

"I was a mother, and am so no longer."

Two weeks later, I wrote again.

"Dream that my little baby came to life again. That it had been only cold, and that we rubbed it before the fire, and it lived! Awake... and find no baby. I think about the little thing all day."

A deep sadness settled over me then, hanging low over my life as clouds cover the sun. There has not been a day since I have not thought of my little baby. Even Shelley's death... even my own death, apparently... cannot blot out the memory of my babe... the miracle of her, the misery of her.

Still... I know that it was because of my little lost one... she above all other inspirations... that I was ever able to imagine my greatest creation, my one un-killable child.

Oh, yes. It was because of you, my sweet dead baby girl, that I... then only a girl myself... began that next rainy summer in Switzerland to write the pages that would, nine months later, become *Frankenstein*.

By then, the summer of 1816, I'd already given birth to our second child, my pretty William. Shelley—forever dodging creditors and arrest—suggested another trip abroad, a period of respite where he could engage his creative urges, but where to escape to, he was not sure. Claire—still part of our household—was engaged in heady plans of her own. Earlier that year, thinking she'd enroll herself upon the pages of fame on the stage, had arranged a meeting with Lord Byron, then part owner of a theater in London.

She never became an actress.

But she did become Byron's mistress.

I was eighteen that summer, almost nineteen, when Claire suggested that Shelley and I—with her along as well—might spend the summer at Lake Geneva, in Switzerland. She said the views of Mont Blanc would inspire Shelley's poetry. She was correct. She did not mention that Lord Byron would be in Geneva as well, a fresh exile from England after a series of indiscretions and a public divorce, scandals that had rendered him too notorious for London society. So there he was, already arrived in Switzerland, taking the grand mansion, Villa Diodati, on the shore of the lake. Not long after, we rented residences near one another on the lake. We took hasty, tentative steps toward friendship, and over the course of several dinners and daytrips, transformed ourselves into a kind of family, a circle of poets and lovers. We made up casual nicknames. Lord Byron became L.B., and then simply Albé, though his young doctor, John Polidori, always preferred Lord B. I was "Little Mary," or "Sweet Mary," or "Sad Mary"... and Shelley was Shelley, never Percy. Claire was always just Claire—and Poor Polidori, well… that is what we all called him, "Poor Polidori," though Albé called him John.

It was unkind of us, I know.

But Poor Polidori absorbed our petty condescension.

At least we kept him within our circle that long, wet season. It was damp that summer, incessantly dark and unpleasant. Some thought the world was ending. Scientists eventually blamed the eruption of Mount Tambora in the Dutch East Indies. The volcano spread ash across half the world, blocking the sun, murdering crops throughout Europe, bringing unceasing rain.

That was 1816, to be known as "the year without a summer!"

Were it not for the Leiden Jars Shelley carted with him to Switzerland, and one of the many "friction machines" he'd collected over the years, we'd have had little to entertain us when we grew tired of reading and talking.

Beyond that, the various particulars of our days together are well known, as word of our actions, so closely connected to the famous Byron, became something of a scandal all across England.

Even I have written of it—all the names and details of The Byron-Shelley Circle—all of us at Diodati, with little William and a household of whispering servants. Much has been spoken and speculated about our days together on the lake… our long trips out to the glaciers… Byron finishing *Childe Harold* by day and reading aloud to us by night… the wet, ungenial weather that forced us indoors… the little book of ghost stories we passed from person to person, its pages crammed with terror and delight, doomed lovers and armored spirits and kisses of death… our days of boredom leading to fiercer boredom… leading one night to Lord Byron's infamous midnight proclamation.

"We will each write a ghost story!"

Bored and restless, we agreed at once, consenting that it would not be a competition.

But of course it was.

We understood we would all attempt to craft the most terrifying tale ever written.

Claire abstained, choosing instead to be the energetic muse to Byron's craft. Within a day's time, Byron had written a few promising pages about a cursed adventurer who dies under mysterious circumstances in a desert graveyard in Turkey—but he could not complete the fragment. Poor Polidori had a terrible idea about a skull-headed lady peering through keyholes, but it made no sense and he set it aside, taken far more by Byron's afflicted traveller than his own creation. My Shelley, born more for poetry than prose, remembered an incident from his childhood and wrote six or eight awkward lines.

"Helen and Henry knew that Granny,
Was as much afraid of ghosts… as any."

It was dreadful. Even I knew it.

The days and nights passed. One by one, each of my esteemed companions released himself from the agreement. Only I remained excited to the task, casting about in my imagination for a story that might curdle the blood, incite the darkest fears of our nature, awaken a thrilling horror in all who read it. But all I drew from my mind was blank nothing. Each morning, my companions greeted me with the same terrible question.

"Have you thought of a story?"

"I am still thinking."

That was my constant reply.

By daylight, I looked after little William. I studied Latin and Greek. I walked with Shelley on the shore when the weather permitted. And once or twice a week, as the men engaged in lengthy late-night philosophical discussions, I listened. Just as in childhood, lurking in my father's study as he entertained Coleridge and other great writers, I once again became a devout but silent watcher.

On a drenching night in June, with Claire and William fast asleep in their rooms, Albé introduced a characteristically grand topic for the men's nightly discussion.

"It is nothing less than a matter of life and death!" he promised.

Having recently read Dr. Erasmus Darwin's *Zoonomia, or The Laws of Organic Life*—having also just been told by Claire that she was with child… his child—Albé's thoughts had been drawn towards matters of mortality and conception.

"The spark of existence!" he exclaimed. "The fundamental principle of life! Of what secret substance does it consist? I believe science will soon identify that secret, that fundamental element that separates those who are alive from those who are dead!"

Whenever Albé spoke, there was an air of melodious consequence in his deep, resonant voice, as if quoting scripture in the Cathedral. Shelley's voice, for its part, was more that of a mystic in a trance, his timbre soft and high, as if only half-present, part of him in this world and part in another.

"Dear Albé," Shelley replied, gently, "do you speak as one who wishes to stop death—or to create life... or perhaps both—to create life *out of* death?"

"Yes! Exactly! To resurrect the dead!" Albé answered, standing before the fire, his arms spread wide, as outside, the hard rain fell. "But it's been done already, Shelley! It has! Dr. Darwin has accomplished it in his laboratory, resuscitating microbes in a dish of paste made from flour and water... 'infinitely small eels' is how he described them... *'Vorticella'* is their scientific name. Dr. Darwin wrote that when the specimens perished, becoming as dry as a fallen leaf, he used some 'extraordinary means' to restore them to full vigor.

"Therefore, what I wonder is this," he continued. "Will not science soon find a way to do the same with fish, with birds, with animals... and perhaps someday... with human beings?"

I listened intensely.

"Ah. Yes. The experiment you describe is not unfamiliar to me, Lord B.," Poor Polidori interjected. "But you have misconstrued some details. What Dr. Darwin described was a form of pasta we Italians call vermicelli. He preserved three strands in a glass jar. Then, generating some several sparks of electricity, he caused the vermicelli to move, each strand twitching and dancing with its own voluntary motion! Quite extraordinary!"

"Extraordinary indeed, John!" replied Byron with a dark laugh. "Are you quite certain he said *vermicelli* and not *vorticella?*"

"I have heard what I have heard," Polidori retorted with a wounded sniff.

"If Dr. Darwin claimed to have given animate life to a dish of pasta," pursued Shelley, playfully, "did he theorize that in so doing he somehow imbued it with a living soul? Though I do not believe in such primitive notions, do not the religious claim that the soul is the very essence and spark of life?"

"Yes! And therefore, John," added Byron, "were a chef to have served a plate of Darwin's vermicelli, would it not come to the table with a fillet of 'soul' as a side dish?"

"Dr. Darwin made no claim about souls," sighed Polidori with a show of weary patience, "only that the pasta moved of its own accord. Whether dancing vermicelli has a soul is for you poets to decide, not we men of science."

In such a vein did the conversation continue.

Then, close to midnight, one of them... I do not remember which... suggested the notion that perhaps, not long in the future, a creature—some new animal, or new kind of human being—might be manufactured in a factory, assembled from the component pieces of other creatures, shaped into something original—and then, through means not yet invented, imbued with the vital warmth of life.

"To bestow life in such a way!" Shelley mused with wonder. "Would it not be to become the creator of a new species? What nature has taken millennia to accomplish, were it to be done by *man* in a matter of moments, would it not open a torrent of light into our dark world? If man could accomplish what only nature has done, I say it would finally confirm the fallacy of God's existence!"

"Shelley, Shelley! Forever trying to rid the world of God!" replied Albé with a laugh. "But consider it certain! A new species, were *you* its source, Shelley, would bless you. No father would deserve the gratitude of his children so completely as your offspring would give theirs."

"Ha! You, Percy Bysshe Shelley, atheist and skeptic!" Polidori snorted, giggling at the irony. "Were *you* to create life out of nothing, you would become a god! You would have to believe in yourself, would you not? You, a divine minter of crisp *new* souls!"

"But... that's not at all what it would mean!" I said, surprised as the rest to hear myself speak. "You are *not* talking about creating something from nothing! You speak of bringing life *back* to that which is dead. That is the premise, is it not? What is there to suggest such a creation would be granted a new soul? Is it not more likely that if a dead thing were resurrected, like Lazarus in the Gospels, his original soul would simply be returned into his body, intact and functional? Was not Lazarus, reborn, the same man he was before death? Was not Christ?"

"My dear little Mary," smiled Albé. "You speak of the soul as if it were merely another bodily organ... some spirit-world lung or ethereal intestinal tract, an object that might be removed from the body and transplanted back, 'intact' and 'functional.' Is not the soul more like the flame of a candle? A candle may be relit, if extinguished, but its flame would not be the same flame as the first!"

Polidori coughed, overdramatically.

"Let us consider the champagne cork," he suggested, loftily. "Like the soul, the cork was created to move in one direction. Out. Once implanted, it waits to be ejected upon the opening of the vessel. Pop! Once free of its bottle, a cork can never be put back in place without causing considerable damage, either to the bottle... or to the cork. Would not the soul, were it so mundane a thing as you suggest, be very much the same? Some degree of damage would surely be done were the soul's cork ever forced back from whence it popped."

It was Shelley's turn to make his reply.

"It is a matter of essential identity, is it not?" he said, his voice barely loud enough to be heard above the roaring fire. "Were any of us in this room struck dead by a bolt of lightning, then resurrected ten seconds later with a second bolt, would he still be the same person as before? If you are correct, then the 'spark of life,' that 'soul' of which you all speak... the *soul* which makes us each a unique and individual being... it would be wholly eradicated by the first lightning strike, snuffed out—popped like a cork— sent away to wherever it is that souls go. And then, with the *second* strike of lightning, though the body would move again, its original soul would have been *replaced* anew, would it not? Replaced entirely by something else... by *someone* else!"

With Shelley's eyes locked on mine, a feeling of intense tenderness binding our gaze together, I found I could not look away. He finally turned to absently study the fire. Thus, unspeaking, the four of us sat, each enthralled in their own thoughts.

After a long silent while, Lord Byron broke this eerie reverie.

"Yes, well, thanks for that, Shelley," he said. "I shall not sleep tonight for fear one of you will die before morning, your body restored by some fate or fortune, and that someone wholly uninvited will walk in for breakfast tomorrow!"

There were other words spoken between us, but I no longer recall them.

There is nothing else of that night I can remember until the dark hours of the morning, when I was pulled from my uneasy sleep by the dream that changed my life forever.

Blood.

The Creature was covered in blood.

As little William slept, tucked away in his crib, I lay beside Shelley, only half asleep, fitfully yet vividly dreaming. I saw a young man, a wide-eyed student of some unhallowed art, his face pale, his hands trembling. In a low-ceilinged room he knelt, bent over a slippery construct of cadaverous limbs, pieced together into the form of a man, a man floating silently in a shallow cauldron of ice and blood.

Nervously working by the light of a single candle, the scholar feverishly snapped wires into the Creature's arms, legs, and chest, little needles fixing each wire to the thing's gray, mottled flesh. Across the worn floorboards nearby was an array of large glass cylinders, like the Leiden Jars of my youth, circling the student and his grotesque creation. From out of its body, dozens of wires snaked up and into the jars, all connected by a ribbon of copper chain. The student stood, reaching across to a mysterious metal engine the size of a small stove. With mounting excitement, he worked at its gears with hands that would not stop shaking.

One by one, each cylinder sparked and shimmered, snapping and popping with the hazy glow of electricity. Within the tub, sprawled out upon the ice, the Creature convulsed, its sutured limbs, its bloody lips and eyelids twitching and contorting, a thick cloud of pungent steam rising up to cloak the room in swirling vapor. In my dream, the mist was too dense to see beyond. There was the sharp smell of scorching skin. The machinery's hum grew louder, and louder still, then stopped, fading quickly to silence. The student remained shrouded in the cloud of steam, but I could clearly hear his wild, unnerved breaths coming fast and hard.

Then I heard something else.

As a freezing dread flooded my dreaming heart, I began to perceive another kind of breathing. Thick and labored, heavy with effort, the hodgepodge Creature was straining with steady deliberation to draw breath into its numb, unfeeling lungs. At last, the mist faded away and I could see the scholar kneeling again at his creation's side. With an expression of weary triumph on his face, the student of science beheld the accomplishment of his toils, gazing with stark wonder into its strange and pallid face.

It opened its eyes.

Twitching violently, the Creature coughed hard, a stream of dark blood erupting against the student's recoiling face. As the scholar fell back, the abomination pulled itself forward, its arms flailing wildly, a mixture of pain and panic alive in those yellow, watery eyes. Its lips moved vainly, producing only a weak, whimpering cry. From deep inside the pitiful sob another sound arose, a low moan of terror. The Creature pulled frantically at the stinging needles and wires stabbing into its scarred, scorched flesh.

As the monstrous thing thrashed and bellowed, it finally beheld the student, standing above him, frozen in confusion and fright. With bloody arms dripping, the Creature reached up to him, its miserable face a piteous plea.

In an eerie instant, the dream abruptly shifted. Suddenly... I had become the Creature. I was reaching up, watching my maker back away from me, shaken and repulsed. His face, once aglow with glory and triumph, had turned to an expression of abject horror, of anguish, of judgment, of blame.

I recognized it at once.

It was my father's face.

I was myself, a young girl pleading for her father's love and understanding, pleading for his protection, but his eyes were cold with hate. He hated me, for running away with Shelley, for betraying the family. But he hated me also for merely being, for living, for not having perished as an infant alongside my mother... or better yet, *instead* of my mother.

Abruptly, the dream shifted again, my perspective pivoting like the spin of a palm on a wrist, and I was once again looking at the Creature, now standing, its naked body and arms free of the wires, reaching forward, reaching out... toward me.

I stood now where the student had stood.

I was the thing's wretched creator. I was its mother. From the monster's throat came a new sound, not the agonized shrieks of a man, but the cry of a child, my child, my dying child, my little lost baby girl.

And finally it was over.

With that unnatural cry still reverberating in my ears, the smell of burnt flesh hanging to my mind, I opened my eyes... awake again in my bed, with Shelley beside me. Upon an impulse, I rushed to the crib and gathered little William in my arms, assuring myself that he was still breathing, still warm, still alive.

Even now, I remember that feeling, sitting there amongst the thin shafts of moonlight pressing themselves through the blinds, cradling William, working to rid myself of the fright and mangled emotions still grasping at my heart. For a long while, my eyes searched the room, finding some solace in the everyday objects around me. Finally, my gaze fell on my journal, perched atop the pile of paper on which I had vainly been scratching out failed drafts of my poor little ghost story.

My ghost story! I forced myself to think of that.

If only I could write a tale that would fill Shelley and Byron with the same numb terror I was feeling now. With such a story, I might accomplish something remarkable, something of my own, something permanent, something to win back the admiration of my father, and prove myself worthy of the brilliance and ongoing companionship of my Shelley. The thought was as cheering as the morning light that was finally inching into our room.

In that instant, I had it.

"What has terrified me will terrify others!"

As our company sat at breakfast a few hours later, I entered the room, a sense of calm purpose having replaced the terror of my dream.

"I believe…" I tenderly informed their questioning faces. "…I believe I have thought of a story."

That is all! I must rest.

Good Lord, is there no end to this ridiculous wall?

I've yet to find any sort of exit! Does it go on forever, or have I simply been walking in circles, following this absurd stone circle around and around?

I must have. I know I have seen some of these markers before.

That one, there. *Stanyan Louise Barnes.* I've seen Stanyan at least twice now. You simply don't forget a name like "Stanyan."

How can that be? There is no escape? This is madness!

I'm quite certain that St. Peter's in Bournemouth has a gate!

Am I in the real St. Peter's at all, I wonder? If not, then for God's sake, where am I?

I have ever believed in God, but a loving one. I believe in Perdition even less than I believe in ghosts, or I might begin to wonder if I was not in some tiny corner of Hell.

I do not think I am in Hell.

Perhaps… I'm not even dead. Might I still be lying in my bed in London, locked in some endless nightmare of stupor and oblivion brought on by my diseased, failing brain?

No. No. I cannot believe that.

I'm certain I am dead.

And there's the proof! There, just there beyond that shrub, is my very own grave again, rock solid proof that I am deceased.

"Here lies Mary Wollstonecraft Shelley."

I've found my way home!

Well, I might as well have a bit of a sit.

May I rest in peace!

Hello down there! Yes, you in the grave! Knock! Knock! Is anyone at home?

I wonder what my body is doing down there?

I remember, as a girl, lying on the grass at Mama's tomb, thinking about her decaying remains, trying to guess how much of her was left, melting there under the ground. I dared not ask Papa, but I did peek into his anatomy books. I was delighted to learn the Five Stages of Decomposition.

"Fresh," "Bloat," "Active," "Advanced" and "Dry!"

Saying those words together at the dinner table was always enough to make Claire and Fanny shriek in revulsion. Especially "Bloat!"

I couldn't stop saying it.

"Bloat!"

After death, I learned, the internal organs are the first to go, starting with the intestines. As a girl I thought that was somehow appropriate. Just get the intestines out of the way and move on with it! I learned that along with the organs go the heart and the brain, then the eyes, the tongue, and then, all the sinews and tendons, like the strings of a marionette, the pulleys and levers of the marvelous human machine! The bones come later… the bones are the *last* to go. Everything else melts. Sometimes I'd lie at Mama's grave and wish I could be under the ground with her, melting into the earth in my mother's arms.

But I knew I couldn't. She was gone, all gone, dissolved into nothing, all but her bones and her name, not even a memory of her to live on in my tiny mind.

And that's enough of that.

I am so weary. I am tired of thinking, tired of remembering—and yet I feel I must continue, and I dread... I truly dread... what is to come. If only I could lie down, crawl down beneath this stone and into the arms of my own slumbering body, I could sleep there at last, forever.

But that is not to be, is it?

For one thing, I imagine I'd be far past the "bloat" stage by now.

I wonder which part of me is disintegrating this very moment?

I hope my hands are the last to go.

I've always had nice hands.

As a writer, my hands served me well, almost to the end. After the headaches began, once the better part of my body was slowly becoming paralyzed, it was my hands that held out the longest, until they too finally failed me.

For a short time, when I could no longer hold a pen to write, I could still draw, a little.

I could always draw, rather well, I think.

Many days, if I'd grown tired of studying and writing, I would draw.

When I first began to write *Frankenstein*, in Switzerland, the first thing I did was sketch the Creature, exactly the way I saw it in my dream, from cranium to metatarsus, quite like a figure in one of Godwin's anatomy books. I sketched a full human form, my Creature, and painted little red lines slashing across him for the scars that held each piece together. I made up stories for each limb, organ and patch of skin.

I could tell Shelley—or Byron or Polidori... or Claire, if I wanted to risk watching her turn green—which bit of his body belonged to what person, and the peculiar details of that person's history and demise—their bodies and limbs subsequently unearthed, or bartered, or snatched at midnight from the dark dissecting room of the university.

I knew I would never write those secret stories, the "flesh histories" of my Creature.

Those stories were for me alone, for my companions, and for Shelley, my inspiration and teacher. What I first expected to write as a brief few pages, something grisly and gothic and in questionable taste, Shelley encouraged me to envision as a novel. So provoked, I slowly crafted a story within a story within a story—the Creature's tragic tale related by Frankenstein, his own life recorded by an Arctic adventurer at the North Pole, whose story would be told in letters to his sister.

261

It was ambitious, for the first effort of an untested nearly-nineteen-year-old girl, but Shelley encouraged me to be ambitious, to dare to thrust myself up alongside my own illustrious parents. As I began to scribble down my story, Shelley demonstrated an abundance of constant curiosity. In the first part of the book—the fictional letters of Captain Walton, a foolhardy Arctic explorer who once dreamed of becoming a poet—and even more so in the vivid accounts of young Victor Frankenstein, Shelley showed a particularly keen, almost personal interest. He scratched an encyclopedia of notes and suggestions on each of those pages. I suppose he saw something of himself in the pioneering hearts and romantic ideals of Captain Walton and Victor Frankenstein.

He viewed them both as tragic but noble figures.

To me, both men were idiots.

Frankenstein especially.

Frankenstein was arrogant, obsessive, appallingly selfish and more than a bit thick. Aside from discovering the secret of life… which I described in the book as a total accident it took months for him to decipher and recreate… Victor Frankenstein makes not one intelligent decision the entire novel.

I wonder that Shelley never noticed that.

I saw a play in London once, some twenty-seven years ago, five years after the publication of my novel. It was called, *Presumption… or The Fate of Frankenstein.* As the author of the book on which it was based, I was the evening's honored guest. In the playwright's hands, my poor Victor—who in the novel barely completed two years of chemistry school before abandoning his studies—was transformed into *Doctor* Frankenstein. I sat in the balcony, agog with disbelief. The playwright took my laughter as proof of my delight, but it was a display of speechless incredulity! I certainly hope that if, in the future, anyone else ever dreams of transforming my 'Frankenstein' into some sensational entertainment, they will refrain from turning poor, dim, deluded Victor into some ripened and accomplished man of science.

Good lord!! Victor was nineteen years old—the same age I was when I thought him up!

Under Shelley's reassuring watch, the skeleton of the tale was quickly constructed. I decided that my Arctic explorer, Captain Walton—in florid missives written to his sister in London—would describe his journey to the North Pole, where his ship would become trapped between vast sheets of ice. There on the ice, aching for friendship, he finds the dying Victor Frankenstein, brings him, freezing to death, aboard the ship, and records the various facts of Frankenstein's life.

Frankenstein.

Born in Geneva, the son of a wealthy judge, Frankenstein is an older brother to the sickly Ernest and the beautiful young William... befriended in childhood by the kind-hearted Henry Clerval... engaged at eighteen to his beautiful Elizabeth.

Frankenstein.

Obsessed with death and disease when his mother dies of scarlet fever, he turns first to ancient mysteries and magic, absorbing the philosophies of magicians and alchemists... enrolled at Ingolstadt University in Bavaria, he gives up the occult and became a student of chemistry and the sciences. Driven to madness in his search for the meaning of life and a cure for all disease, he pursues Nature to its hiding places, and finds it at last—the very secret of life.

He builds the Creature there, in his tiny room, and there he abandons it.

Years later, when his little brother William is murdered, he finally returns home to Geneva and to Elizabeth... where the monster, the true murderer of little William, is waiting... somewhere. For weeks, I was unsure where the Creature's confrontation with Frankenstein should take place.

At night, alone in the study, writing, I would find myself talking to the Creature... telling his story to the image of him I held in my mind, changing the words "my Creature" to the simple word... you.

When Claire and Shelley proposed a trip to the *Mer de Glace*, the Sea of Ice, at the northern end of Mont Blanc, I was just becoming immersed in my writing.

I did yearn to see the wonders of the mountain—and was somewhat disinclined to let Shelley and Claire spend a week exploring its wonders alone—but I was not easily tempted away from my work. Albé, for his part, encouraged them to go and me to continue writing at Villa Diodati. Whether his aim was to divest himself of Claire or to gain closer proximity to me, I never knew, for I elected to join my sister and my lover on the icy ascent of Mont Blanc. The moment we arrived at the edge of the glacier, an expanse of frozen waves on a jagged slab of sea, I knew at once that *this* was the place where you, my Creature, would first confront Frankenstein.

This is where you would tell your story.

I saw it all, or most of it… your sad, brief history… as clearly as I had painted the scarred canvas of your body—every limb, organ and patch of skin a different country, each alive with its own history and memories, its own victories, its own defeats, each as cold and hard as the ice of Mont Blanc.

As I stood on that ice, I was stirred to cast off my coat. I needed to feel the cold wind against my skin. Stretching out my arms to it, I tried to imagine your own skin, scratched and stitched, the million cells of your flesh alert to the cold as if listening to a symphony of senses.

Oh! If only I could feel that wind now, as I wander this stormy graveyard in the dark!

If only I knew the way out!

If only I understood why I am imprisoned here!

What is happening to me? What lesson is it I'm to learn from these endless stories, this litany of facts and details?

Why do I feel so driven to talk… talk… talk?

Is anyone listening, someone beyond the wall, above the storm clouds?

Is it God, Christ, or some mystic jury, some cosmic bookkeeper, watching me, listening and judging, totaling up the weight and worth of all these words and stories? Is there something I am supposed to be learning from these tales? Do the varied parts of my life contain some great treasure or truth, some terrible secret I am now appointed to discover? Is there a lesson I'm to learn from the life of Mary Wollstonecraft Shelley?

I can accept that… in the abstract.

But why do I now feel so compelled to tell *your* story, my Creature?

I've told it already, have I not?

But no, I haven't.

Not all of it.

Much of what I invented that summer I never put to paper, and much that I did was later scratched out, or altered when Shelley set out to repair my sometimes bald prose, replacing it with his own glowing poetry. But his suggestions and revisions, for the great part, were only in those passages in which Frankenstein speaks, or in the letters of Captain Walton in which Victor eventually appears. Shelley, ever the bold one himself, was far more drawn to the passions of Victor and Walton than to those of my poor, abandoned Creature.

He, we both knew, belonged solely to me.

So I suppose I will spin your tale once again, my poor Creature.

Perhaps not all of it, but at least those parts I never spoke of to any but Shelley and our circle. It is possible that those never-told stories, trapped in the lost shreds of your history, somehow contain the clues from which I might learn whatever it is I am here to learn.

I'm going to have to sit whatever is left of me down.

This might take a while.

I have spoken already, my Creature, of your birth.

But here is what happened next.

Born in pain and confusion, every inch of you alive with senses you did not understand, you staggered from the city in the rain, escaping the fortressed walls of Ingolstadt. In the woods to the north, you hid yourself, your brain a wretched tangle of bewilderment. The rain fell harder, and overhead flashed lightning, from which you shielded yourself, raising your scarred arms to the sky, each limb covered in strips of borrowed skin.

You did not know the history of that mottled quilt of flesh.

Much of it was taken from bodies… some torn from the rough and blemished back of a thief twice whipped for stealing a bucket of beer… some from the broad chest of a soldier who tumbled from the city wall while guarding the gate, his neck broken after falling asleep at his post. One patch was stripped from the long forelegs of a heartbroken student of Divinity, who stabbed himself before the altar of the church where his love had married another.

But you were more than just patches of skin.

You were sinew and bone and flesh and veins, arms, legs, organs.

Each had its own story, many sad, some less so.

Your arms and hands were those of a poor but ever-cheerful oxen-driver, known for singing while at work. He'd been crushed beneath his overturned cart, humming to his last breath, his body buried that evening in a hasty grave, unearthed late that night by Frankenstein.

As you ran from the city in the rain, you stopped at the top of a hill, raising your arms anew to block the torrent. For one uncanny instant, you glimpsed—or more likely sensed, perhaps just remembered—the sight of the oxen cart, rolling soundlessly over, spilling you from the seat, bearing down on you, crushing you, killing you.

Accompanying this vision, as if from deep in your flesh, you could almost hear a jaunty tune, pleasantly and endlessly repeating. Such sensations brought with them a bolt of fear, from which you recoiled, running wildly, your befuddled senses driving you deeper still into the forest.

And so, my Creature, does the story I fashioned for you truly begin—in blood and death, darkness and isolation. Were it not for the soothing light of the moon and the daily salute of birdsong, you'd have soon believed there were no pleasures in the world, only pain, loneliness, thirst, and hunger.

But worse than the weather, worse even than the remoteness of food and water, were those queer fleeting images. Like waking dreams or shadows, coming and going faster than the flash of lightning, the mystifying pictures and feelings kept appearing in your mind. How could you know they were just the lingering echoes of your myriad lost lives, moments buried in the flesh and bones from which you were built?

How could you make sense of it?

When you stumbled, one day, upon a small open fire, left burning in a pit by travelers in the forest, you knelt before it, hungry for the comfort it offered. With it came a brief memory of sitting before a fire, a tiny child in the lap of some larger person, a female, holding you gently, stroking your hair as you absently daydreamed, turning your little pink palms to the warmth of the fireplace. The fleeting pleasure of the memory made you dizzy. In an effort to feel such pleasure more, you thrust your hands into the burning embers of the open fire pit. Pain, blistering pain, was all that awaited you, and you fell shrieking to the ground.

You learned quickly.

Over the next several weeks, still blind to the strange facts of your existence or the name of your foul coward of a father, you learned new things every day, adding to your understanding of the world every minute. You learned that dry wood burned but wet wood did not, that the fire made acorns easier to eat and berries uneatable, and that the little huts and cottages at the edge of the forest contained many wonders—milk and cheese, plentiful water, straw beds—but were the habitation of cruel, frightened people who ran away quickly at the sight of your hulking frame, but soon returned with many villagers wielding sticks and clubs, hurling rocks to chase you away.

In short, you came to trust the generosity of nature and to anticipate the cruelty of humanity. Never did it occur to you to use force against your tormentors, though you were built of strong men who'd known hard labor, dangerous men whose reflexes had learned the actions of swift escape. Your body, large and powerful, was as strong and agile as ten such men, yet to harm another living being, to show as much cruelty to others as had been rained down upon you, was not a talent you would acquire easily.

But in time, you would learn this as well.

Your body was quick, but your mind all the quicker, the gray stuff of your brain snatched from the cracked skull of a brilliant judge who'd served with distinction in the courts of Ingolstadt. From him you gained a few scattered scraps of memory, fragments of a childhood raised up amongst many brothers and sisters, an advantageous education at the University, and a succession of appointments from junior juror to public advocate to district judge and finally to city magistrate. In addition to these scant memories, you inherited the judge's keen intelligence, his sharpness of reason, and more.

By all accounts a man of moral superiority and great wisdom, the judge whose cunning brain you now carried had been a kind man, a fair interpreter of the law. His commitment to his work was such that he was in middle age before knowing love for the first time, his beloved a widow woman of some property whose husband had died, leaving her with a young son. The boy's pleasant, clever nature was a joy to all who knew him, and the judge, who'd always counted himself as happy, was now happier still, as doting and devoted a father to the boy as any child could hope for.

The boy was eleven when, while riding in his family's woods, he chanced upon a trio of poachers, not much older than himself, barely a hair on any of their chins. The scoundrels had been caught in the act of skinning an elk they'd trapped in an unlawful snare, and before the boy could ride off and tell of the crime, they pulled him from his horse, tied him to tree, and cut his throat. Three days later, when the murderers tried to sell the boy's horse at the market, they were apprehended. In due course, they stood trial before the grieving judge, who, finding them guilty, sentenced the young men to be burned at the stake, the harshest sentence ever imposed in that district to ones not yet thirteen.

From that day on, the judge grew harder and harder.

Had his wife lived, her kindness might have eventually eased him back to his former self, but she died not long after, and so greatly warped was his own broken heart, the once esteemed judge became cruel and unforgiving. The slightest offence, when presented in his court, was met always with the heaviest possible judgment.

One evening in November, as he left the court, the judge was struck from behind in the corridor outside his office. He was found soon after, his skull cracked and his throat slit wide, his stiff, unyielding body propped against the wall, on which the word "justice" was scrawled in the judge's own cold blood.

His head, already half cut away, was later presented to the University of Ingolstadt, where early the next morning, Victor Frankenstein collected the judge's once brilliant brain, preserving it on ice until, just a few days later, he brought it back to life inside the sutured skull of your new body.

For many months, you could speak no fathomable language.

Even to your own ears, the sounds you made were coarse and frightening. Only by eavesdropping on others did you gradually acquire the science of speech. In particular, it was from the poor inhabitants of a tiny cottage where you found secret shelter in a meager unused shed, that you learned to speak German and English, but first French, the language of the cottagers.

Feu. Eau. Lait. Bois. Fire. Water. Milk. Wood.

Those were the first words you spoke.

Later, upon finding a bag of books in the forest, you taught yourself, with great effort, to read. And, oh, what an education I gave you!

From Plutarch's *Lives* you learned the bloody facts of human history, of conquest and war, of slavery and murder. While reading Milton's *Paradise Lost*, your heart ached with Adam when he and his mate were cast from Eden. You felt a thrill of admiration when the fallen angel Satan spoke out against the hypocrisy of God. You came to despise the Creator for waging war on his own earthly creations. And in Goethe's *The Sorrows of Young Werther*, you learned that to love and be loved is a thing that is sometimes possible, but that heartbreak, despair and death are a certainty.

But there was another book, my Creature, the kindest and cruelest of all your elementary texts. In the dusty pocket of the clothes I so clumsily devised for you to be wearing when you fled Frankenstein's rented rooms, there was a small notebook. Bound in leather, it was written in clear German script. When you first discovered it, the object meant nothing to you. Not till you learned to read did you discover it was the journal of Victor Frankenstein, your creator. There, in his own hand, were the details of your father's life—his family, his home on Lake Geneva, his childhood friend Henry Clerval, his engagement to a beautiful woman named Elizabeth. Further on was a description of the months he spent scouring ancient books, seeking the secrets of nature, his furious drive to conquer death by bringing the dead back to life. He described the electric machinery of regeneration he had devised. He chronicled his collection of dead bodies and his methods for stitching together a human being.

That is when you finally learned what you were.

More horrible was the journal's brief final page, words jotted by Frankenstein in a rush on the day you were "born." This was the final lesson of your education.

"As the rain patters dismally against the window panes," Frankenstein wrote, "I see the dull yellow eye of the creature open. It breathes hard. A convulsive motion agitates its limbs. How can I describe the wretch I have, with such infinite pains and care, endeavored to form? His yellow skin barely covers the work of muscles and arteries beneath. His hair is of lustrous black, his teeth pearly white, a contrast to his horrid watery eyes, his shriveled complexion, his straight black lips. How can I describe my emotions at this catastrophe? I created him to be beautiful! Beautiful! I have worked for two years, for the sole purpose of infusing life into an inanimate body. But now that I have finished, the beauty of the dream has vanished. Only disgust and horror, breathless horror, fills my heart."

Such agony filled your heart.

In the many months you'd spent watching the cottagers whose home you secretly shared, you'd come to love them, moved by their kindness to one another. When the grown son brought home a new wife, you were overjoyed that he'd found a friend to share his life. Eventually, you conceived a plan in which you might join their family, daring to imagine they would show the same tenderness to you they showed each other.

But those words from your father exposed the danger of your plan.

You'd seen your own face in the reflection of the stream. You knew that compared to all others, you were hideous. Despite this, you had begun to believe that the gentleness of your nature and the sincerity of your words might be enough to allay the cottagers' fear. Now you doubted your plan. If your own father was so repulsed by your face that he refused to embrace you, how could you hope for better from your cottagers?

And yet, with so much at stake… how could you not?

The time came, and you stood uncertainly at the blind man's door.

You'd chosen a moment he would be alone in the house.

You knocked, he called out asking who was there, and in mellifluous French, you answered.

"Pardon this intrusion," you began. "I am but an unfortunate and deserted creature!"

Surprised beyond words to be spoken to in French, the old man invited you inside, where you continued, now encouraged, speaking with more passion and less caution than you had rehearsed.

"I look around me, and I have no relation or friend on Earth," you exclaimed. "I seek the protection of some friends who live near here. But I am full of fears. For if I fail there, I am an outcast in the world forever!"

"Do not despair, my friend!" the old man said, reaching out a steady hand. "To be friendless is indeed to be unfortunate—but the hearts of men, if unprejudiced by self-interest, are ever full of brotherly love and charity."

Your heart filled with hope. But before you could reply with words that would surely secure his trust, there came a noise at the door. You turned to see the blind man's son stepping into the cottage.

You hesitated.

Upon seeing your grotesque form kneeling mutely at the old man's feet, his frail hands gripped in yours, the young man cried out in alarm. Believing his father to be in danger, he fell upon you with great force, beating you wildly with his walking stick. The blind man, astonished, could not tell what was happening, and said nothing. You could have torn your attacker to pieces, but so stunned were you at his violence, and so ill-equipped for this unplanned turn of events, you could only think to run from the cottage, sobbing in sorrow. You spent the night in the woods, desperately devising a way to win back the old man's trust. When you returned the next evening, you found the cottage abandoned and empty. Your beloved cottagers had vanished. All they left behind was a small ember, glowing faintly in the stove. In despair and rage, cursing your wretched existence, you burned the cottage to the ground.

As your last hope for friendship and family dissolved in fiery collapse, you suddenly turned your hungry palms to the roaring fire. Though the force of the heat stung your eyes, there came a slender fragment of the ox-driver's old childhood memory—a fireplace, a mother, pleasure, safety—and even as your face became wet with tears, you felt a powerful sense of strength and courage. Mingled with these sensations was a rising sense of fury and revenge, and then a recurring thought, a need, a demand… for justice. Justice. You had tried to join the cottagers' family. You had been denied.

You thought of Frankenstein, the puny creature who had so wantonly bestowed on you the spark of existence. You could feel the hatred rising in your heart. But there was something else, too. Though the thought of Frankenstein enraged you, it also brought a faint pulse of hope. Perhaps there was a way to change the direction of your fate. You lacked the power of creation, as worked by the Creator in *Paradise Lost*, or you would have fashioned a family of your own. Had you such knowledge, you would summon a companion from the embers of the fallen cottage, building your own hideous helpmate from the ashes of your great failure.

You did not have such power.

But Frankenstein did.

Your father could work wonders. Could he not fashion another creature like you?

With a mate at your side, a female of your own kind, you might attain as much of happiness as the miserable world would allow such beings as you.

You'd chosen your next course of action.

Turning your back to the smoking ruins, you ran quickly into the woods, that faint pulse of hope growing stronger as your heart pumped blood through your swiftly moving body.

You would find your way to Geneva, the home of your father. There, you would find and confront him, forcing him to answer for his crimes. When he begged forgiveness, you would demand that he create for you an equal. Even he would see the justice of your request. Having abandoned you to loneliness and despair, he could hardly refuse you the one thing that might bring a shred of happiness. As your father, he would be honor-bound to consent to it. And if he did not, you would serve him as he had served you. Victor Frankenstein had given you nothing. You would take from him everything, and when there was nothing left, you would take his wretched life.

The journey was arduous and long.

From the first snows of November to the bright blooms of May, you traveled over five hundred miles in six months. Following the wide Danube upriver from Ingolstadt to its source at the confluence of the Brigach and the Breg, you worked your way into the heart of the Black Forest. Wherever the river flowed near the dwellings of people, you bent deeper into the woods. The long swath of forest covered you as you turned south and into the Jura mountain range, with its many caverns and valleys. Then you crossed the Rhine into Switzerland, following the Jura range down toward the city of Geneva.

Though every step brought punishing bitterness and suffering, you endured, your heart never failing as each mile brought you closer to your meeting with your creator. At times, in the open, as you sped through the woods, you felt faint memories of running, running, running, a thrill of flight and motion as your heart beat faster, faster, faster.

How could you know the mighty muscle of your heart had already carried another body for countless miles by the time Frankenstein found it amongst the organs and entrails at Ingolstadt's least reputable *schinder*—a skinner, a flayer, a renderer of animal parts. A master at the melting down of corpses, the *schinder* turned cattle and pigs and horses into thick fat for candles, soap and glue. Frankenstein selected the heart of a horse… a powerful stallion, the recent property of a young soldier killed in battle.

That soldier was conscripted at age sixteen into a regiment of cuirassiers, the armored cavalry of the Bavarian army. But more vital to the army than the young man's skill with horses was the powerful, dark-brown stallion he'd raised from a colt at his family's farm outside Ingolstadt. Known for its speed and stamina, the horse and his young rider were taken away and trained for war. Together, they raced across many raging battlefields without harm. But after three years in the army, the young man was grievously wounded far from home. Barely fit for travel, but desperate to return to

Ingolstadt, the injured soldier was soon discharged. His horse, however, was retained as the property of the Bavarian army.

In the dark of night, the soldier, whispering the soft commands they'd practiced together so many times, carefully led the horse from the captain's stable, and once they were safely away from the encampment, he mounted the horse and they bolted away for the long journey home. The stallion, sensing his master's pain and the necessity of swiftness, never failed, never faltered, never stopped. He carried the soldier over mountains, through rivers and lagoons, across vast plains. The road was hard, and the horse endured savage injuries of his own, but on still he forged, as his master grew ever weaker, finally growing too weak to speak more.

The young man died three miles from his home.

The stallion, now barely able to walk on his tender, bleeding limbs, with his dead rider now slumped but still astride, limped past the walls of Ingolstadt, and up to the door of his dead master's house. An hour later, the horse was shot. His body was transported to the rendering factory, where his body was separated into pieces, his great, unstoppable heart sold to Victor Frankenstein for twenty *gulden*.

Such is the history of the heart that carried you ever forward on your journey to *Frankenstein*.

By the time you arrived in the fields just beyond the walled city of Geneva, the land was blossoming with poppy and rose. With Mont Blanc rising in the distance before you, the peaks of the Jura to your back, you sat in the field gazing at the great walled city, your thoughts as dark as the clouds rapidly gathering over Lake Geneva.

Upon hearing a high peal of light laughter, you looked up to see a small, beautiful boy running with heedless abandon across the field, playing and exploring, stopping here and there to examine some flower or insect upon the ground. He did not see you, so he drew closer, stopping only when you stood suddenly before him.

At the sight of your towering form and malformed features, the beautiful boy screamed. Six months ago, you would have run. But you stayed, studying his features with curiosity. They seemed familiar, but why? How could you know this squawking child was William Frankenstein, the youngest brother of your sworn enemy?

On an impulse, you reached out to silence him.

Your large hand closed tight around his tiny mouth.

At the touch of your fingers to his pleasantly warm skin, a new glimmer of memory flashed before your mind. You felt the ox-driver's rough grown hands brushing against the face of a different child, a girl, his daughter. Ever so gently, one outstretched finger caught a lock of her flaxen hair, tucked it lovingly behind her ear. Giggling with pleasure, the girl's bright eyes lifted up to meet the ox-driver's eyes, her sweet face abloom with affection, with trust, with love.

You blinked, and the memory was gone.

There before you was the squirming, defiant face of the beautiful little boy. Stunned, you moved to drop the boy to the ground, resolved to letting the thing run home to its home, its father, its family.

"Monster! Ugly wretch!" the boy hissed. "Let me go! My father is a powerful man! My father is Frankenstein!"

It took but a moment to kill him.

With a tiny crack no louder than the soft pop of a broken wildflower, you snapped his neck, the slender stem of his throat collapsing easily in your hands, the grip of your powerful fingers patiently squeezing the last gasp from his delicate, breathless lungs. You dropped the tiny body to the ground, a satisfied thrill of victory spreading warmly from your hands through all your veins. You gazed up across the field toward the walls of Geneva. Somewhere there was Frankenstein. This child was his brother, or son, or other relation, it did not matter which. Your enemy would soon learn of this murder, and his callous heart would at last feel a fraction of the agony he'd abandoned you to.

He would come to this place, searching for evidence and answers.

Here, he would behold you for the first time. He would know his creation yet lived.

In that moment he would see that this child was dead because of his actions alone. He would feel anguish and shame… and understand that it was his alone to bear. But you would not yet speak to him, not here, so close to his home and family, his source of comfort and strength. You must draw him away, up into the mountains, somewhere you were at home and he was not.

But where?

You gazed up at Mont Blanc, its vast glacier gleaming white.

There. You would face him there.

High on that lonely glacier, Frankenstein would hear the strange, terrible story of your life. There, you would offer him a simple choice. He could turn his back on you once more, or take the path of benevolence and generosity. He could refuse your reasonable request, or he could accept, consenting to once again assemble the machineries of science and summon the spark of life anew. In granting this, in bestowing unnatural breath upon some new she-creature—a thing of perfect, beautiful ugliness, of supreme horror and monstrous love—Frankenstein would not only be choosing to save you, his first-born, from a life of darkness, eternal isolation, and empty wandering.

He would be saving himself.

You would finally be free to embrace him as your true father, all past crimes forgiven.

But were he to refuse, denying you the life you desired, it would be to embrace death, not just for him, but for all those he knew and loved.

An innocent boy was already dead.

If Frankenstein chose to abandon you again, more would die.

You would destroy his every remaining love, crushing his every hope for happiness and contentment. You would leave his life as desolate and empty as the Sea of Ice on which you would face him. You would break apart his world just as easily as you'd broken this little dead child now lying at your feet.

Good God, I was a sick woman, wasn't I?

I never denied it.

Though I displayed the most refined of manners, I was, from birth to death, a dark, morbid, generously warped person. I took pride in it. All the critics who wrote of *Frankenstein* asserted its author's obvious sickness, though the word "woman" was certainly never employed in any of their reviews, as no one could possibly guess that Anonymous, "the Author of Frankenstein," was, in fact, me.

Nor could they know that dead children—dead mothers, too, and absent fathers—were more than mere plot points in a novel conceived by a diseased and twisted mind. They were, in fact, the very theme and foundation of the author's life.

That is true… in ways that even my closest companions never dared to imagine.

I have gotten off track again. Where am I? Wandering this ridiculous graveyard, I've become so enthralled in the luxurious reverie of my babble that I have become quite lost. There! There's a name I'm certain I've not seen before.

Sir Carter Jackson Anthony Baron.
Born December 1, 1811, Died August 8, 1844.
A Son of Atlantis.

"A son of Atlantis." I don't know what that means.

Was he born in the fictional kingdom under the sea, or is Atlantis the name of his *mother?* Both could be true, I suppose. Why not?

I, more than any, know how likely it is for a truth and a fiction to share the same page… or the slab of granite. That is, in fact, the best way to hide a truth, when that truth is so strange and unsettling few would believe it. You must bury that truth beneath a mountain of lies. You must draw attention away from the lie by surrounding it with half-truths, unimportant details, and pleasant distractions.

Speaking of which, here is a lovely little crypt surrounded by stone lions.
Here lies Captain Jason Van Liere.
Born 1757, died 1806. Sailor. Father. Husband and Poet.
"Love Never Fails."

Ah, my dear Captain! Would that that was so. But Love, I have found, almost *always* fails. Shelley, my own "husband and poet," was a great believer in Love—he certainly fell in it often enough, and with so many different women—yet even he was not able to save the ones he loved.

That's not true.

He did save me, in many ways. But he could not save our children. He could not save his Harriet from despair, or my sisters from foolishness—and in the end, he could not save himself from… himself.

Salvation, it turns out, is not a simple thing.

And now I see that I've stumbled back into my own story, for wasn't salvation the very topic of our final midnight conversation at Villa Diodati? It was some weeks after the trip to Mont Blanc, a few days before we would leave Switzerland, returning to whatever awaited us back in London. Once again, it was Byron, Shelley, Poor Polidori and I, all of us up and awake, talking till long past the witching hour.

"My dear Mary," Polidori addressed me, after I'd finished relating my most recent ideas for my novel. "I must applaud you on the tenacity of your imagination. Your story… or as much as you've revealed of it… it's far more unpleasant, more closely acquainted with the mechanisms of life and death, than I should have thought likely from a girl of nineteen."

I nodded, accepting his clumsy compliment without adding explanation or remark.

"I have been thinking of such matters myself," Polidori continued. "I have been pondering the deeper implications of Lord B.'s vampire fragment, a fascinating project I have now taken upon myself to complete… with the kind permission of its original author, of course."

Albé, lost in his own thoughts, simply waved a hand in bland acknowledgment.

"I care not, John," he said, curtly. "I have no interest in vampires. I've been drawn on to grander things." He described a new dramatic poem, the story of a cursed magician—a bit like my Frankenstein, I couldn't help noticing—and a short lyric about the Titan Prometheus, which he'd completed that morning. "I think it of some merit," Albé said, "an epitaph to that bold immortal who created man, then disobeyed the Olympian Gods in stealing fire that his creation might live. You know the rest—the judgment, the rock, the chain, the vulture, the liver. I am calling it Prometheus."

"I am delighted to hear it," Shelley replied, smiling. "But did you know that I too have been writing about Prometheus? I have just last night begun translating the original drama by the Greek scribe Aeschylus. I envision my work, not as a poem, but a modest drama in four acts, Prometheus' story from the raising up of his illegal creation, to his escape from the rock. I shall call mine *Prometheus, Unbound.*"

Silently astonished, I turned my eyes to the fireplace. How extraordinary! The two greatest poets of our age, plus one discouraged doctor, so challenged by the vivid scribbling of a first-time author, and she a young woman, they've all been compelled to write something greater, something memorable enough to compete with Mary Godwin's gruesome little monster story. As my friends continued their talk, I silently affirmed to change the title of my novel from merely *Frankenstein*… to *Frankenstein: or, the Modern Prometheus.*

Poor Polidori, hoping for a more generous blessing from Lord Byron, broke my thoughts.

"Has it occurred to you, little Mary, that your Creature and my vampire—mine and Lord B.'s, of course—have very much in common? Both are dead, yet both alive. I'm sure you recall our earlier conversation, and my humble metaphor of the champagne cork? If we are to accept that souls exist—and that your notion is correct, that a re-animated creature would be re-imbued with its original soul—I must repeat my suggestion that any process which forces a soul back into its body would fracture that soul irreversibly, placing it beyond all repair or salvation.

"And to that end..." he went on, quickly interrupted by Shelley.

"I beg your pardon, my dear Polidori," Shelley said, a soft laugh invading the tender murmur of his voice. "Before you speak more of souls and salvation—my beliefs on which have taken a bit of a beating in all of your company—let me ask something, Doctor. Where, exactly, within the human body, do you suspect the soul is located? Where would your scalpel slice to find it? Does it dwell in the heart? The head? The blood?"

Shelley gently took my hand in his.

"Or perhaps in the skin of the hand?"

Shelley's query, to my amazement, was not a challenge. He truly wished to know.

"Who can say, my friend?" Polidori shrugged. "The soul could be found anywhere in a man. Perhaps everywhere."

"Well said," Shelley went on. "But consider Mary's creature. It is a thing built of parts. Each part came from a man or a beast. If souls exist, then each man or beast possesses a soul... even Mary's noble warhorse. I wonder, then, which soul it was that inhabited the creature's body when Frankenstein worked his forbidden magic? Which warring organ would rule the creature's thoughts and actions? Which single soul—of his many possible souls—would determine the creature's destiny?"

"His destiny, yes! This is precisely what I was about to ask, Shelley!" Polidori exclaimed. "What is the *destiny* of the creature's soul... or my vampire's soul? They are not like you or me. If we should die, our soul will move on to whatever afterlife awaits it, and whatever damnation or salvation it deserves. But in these stories, we now have a soul suddenly snatched back from that world, crammed once more into its original body... or perhaps another body entirely. My question, as a doctor and philosopher, is simple. What happens the next time it dies? These creatures can die, yes? A vampire can be killed, under the right conditions. Your creature, Mary, might be ripped to pieces or burned alive, yes?"

"Yes!" I replied, a bit more forcefully than intended. "Yes, my creature can die."

Polidori bobbed his head.

"Then I ask you," he continued, now standing before us. "I ask all of you, my friends! When such creatures die a second time—where do their souls go this time, souls we now suspect have been fractured by the actions of their re-animation? Can a soul travel the same path twice, back again to Heaven or to Hell? Or is it not more likely that such a soul, cracked like a cork forced back in a bottle, would end up lost forever, destined by the actions of others to some alternative fate, a fate perhaps worse than damnation, worse even than life in this cruel, ungenerous world?"

Thus concluded, he sat down quickly. For a long moment, none uttered a word.

"My dear John," Albé finally spoke, gentle and genuine. "The only soul I am worried about now is yours. Good God! When, over these last months, did your soul become that of a true poet and philosopher? I do not recall noticing when that happened. But so it has. Bravo, Doctor. Bravo."

Shelley softly cleared his throat.

"What you suggest, Doctor, is terrible, horrible…" he finally said, his trembling voice barely louder than a breath blowing out a candle. "What a terrible thing to be so alone and so broken… condemned to it for all time! The very thought of it breaks my heart! Does any soul deserve such a fate? What creator, what father—be he of Heaven or Earth—would ever allow his children to suffer thus?"

At this, Shelley turned to me, desperately searching my eyes for an answer.

"Oh my Shelley, my sweet, fragile Shelley!" I whispered, softly. "How can you not know that the suffering of children is sewn into the history of the world as surely as our hope that it will someday be otherwise? My Creature is no different than you are or I am. We have both known the malice of those who gave us life. Fathers and mothers have ever been the tormentors of their daughters and sons. It is for the poets and the dreamers and the writers of tales to devise a different kind of story, one in which there is, at long last, a remedy for the cruelties we all suffer and all cause in this world… and perhaps that cure will even reach into the next as well. Is that not possible?"

It was a weak answer, I knew, but I was strangely shaken by Shelley's unexpected emotion, and it was all I had to give.

"Yes, Mary! Yes!" said Albé, his arms spread in the grand gesture of a carnival barker or street magician. "It is up to the poets, my friends, up to all of us! It is our task to change the fate of all souls, living and dead!

"But I, for one, say we need not shed too many tears for the soul of Mary's monster," he continued. "If the good doctor's theory is true, Mary, then when your Creature finally dies and sheds his hideous mortal coil—however many souls his piecemeal body contains—even if he cannot take them on to Heaven or Hell, I believe he will surely someday cross paths with the soul of Polidori's vampire, in whatever castle, country, or otherworld to which they are destined to spend their second afterlives.

"My point is, my dear Mary," he concluded with a grand flourish, "that, at the very least, the two of them will have found a bit of company."

Thus ended the final midnight meeting of the Byron-Shelley Circle.

The summer ended not long after, and as we prepared to leave Switzerland, it was clear that Byron would never return to England. As a parting gift, Shelley left Byron with the Leiden Jar that had provided so many moments of delight, though he declined to leave the Friction Machine behind, despite Polidori's earnest pleas to purchase it, explaining that it was the first he'd collected, and that he was therefore attached to it. We spoke our final farewells on the shore of the lake. Claire was inconsolable, dreadfully disappointed not to have been asked by Albé to stay in Geneva. Several weeks later, in early September, having arrived back in London with little William, Shelley and I resumed our lives as penniless writers. Claire, now visibly with child, had nowhere to hide but with us. With Godwin still withholding forgiveness or absolution, our scandalous little family ended up in picturesque Bath, the seat of High Society, where we did our best to hide Claire's condition from public scrutiny.

Through the long autumn and into winter, I continued to write.

Fanny, who never forgave Claire and me for leaving her in the hands of the Godwins, killed herself in October. In mid-December, we learned of

Harriet's suicide in Hyde Park, her bloated body discovered days later in the Serpentine Lake, a popular spot for proper ladies to kill themselves. The boaters were beginning to complain. On December 30, Shelley and I were finally married. My father, having determined that marriage would mark the return of my long-absent respectability, appeared at the wedding with Mrs. Godwin, all smiles and warm embraces.

I accepted his congratulations, and his meager fatherhood, as best I could. I did not reveal to him that I was once again with child.

Claire delivered her daughter, little Allegra, in January. She wrote to Byron often, informing him of the birth of his child in florid, lovesick letters to which he steadfastly declined to respond.

As 1817 began, Shelley and I were both writing furiously. Having postponed *Prometheus, Unbound*, my husband was now struggling to complete his manuscript of *The Revolt of Islam*, for which he'd confirmed a publisher and received a much-needed advance. Between caring for William and calming the nerves of Claire, I raced to complete my own manuscript. That it might ever be published seemed unlikely to me, though Shelley was confident the book would excite the interest of the general public. I could not bend my expectations toward any such hopes, nor were publishers—or the general public—any true incentive in my hastening passion to finish the story.

It was not for others that I was writing *Frankenstein*... was it, my Creature?

Ever since that early night at Lake Geneva, the evening of my dream, yours was the only face I saw as I labored to bring my "ghost story" to life. I first beheld it as the face of abomination and horror, bearing all the twisted and tortured features of death. It was the face of a monstrous thing, screaming from beyond the grave, and I recoiled from it just as I was drawn to it. But during the long many months I'd been writing, your face changed in my thoughts, and I steadily began to see it as what it always was—miraculous, extraordinary, beautiful... alive with a sad, broken beauty that stirred my soul, as it had not been stirred since I last kissed the face of my poor dead baby girl.

As I labored to bring your story to an end—sentence following sentence, my pulse quickening with each finished page—I began to see something I had never clearly seen. But I now knew it to be true. Just as I had brought you to life, my Creature, even as I now prepared to send you to your death… it was you, who—after my three long years of sadness and silence—was, word after word, bringing life back to me.

You did it.

Beyond your brightest hopes, my Creature, you stood upon the ice of Mont Blanc, and from Frankenstein's mouth you drew his reluctant agreement to build for you a second creature. In exchange for your promise to never again harm his kin or companions, and to speedily retreat, with your new mate, from Europe and all habitations of men, Frankenstein agreed to create for you a female.

Soon after, bidding a tearful farewell to his Elizabeth—their imminent marriage postponed once more—Frankenstein hastily left Geneva, his friend Clerval at his side, taking with him many boxes of scientific supplies.

In patient, watchful pursuit, you followed.

Through Germany, England and Scotland, Frankenstein journeyed for a year, nervously seeking a suitably remote location for his work. By the aimlessness of his path, it was clear your cowardly father remained hesitant to his promised task. But, finally, at long last, cloistered in a rotting farmhouse on an island off Scotland's coast—having sent Clerval away to explore the mainland alone—Frankenstein fearfully but expertly began his work. First, with meticulous care, he reconstructed his diabolical machinery. Then, out of ragged pieces ripped from the fresh corpses of unfortunate islanders, he began to assemble the she-creature.

Nearby, unseen by Frankenstein, you watched and waited.

It was late one night, as the island shook in the grip of a rainless, raging gale, that you saw your bride for the first time. From just outside Frankenstein's window, you beheld the scarred and bloody beauty who held all your hopes for happiness. Though she was finally finished, in flesh and in form, your monstrous companion need still be imparted with the vital spark of life—and then she would be yours. Anxiously, you watched as Frankenstein labored, gently inflating the flat and empty arteries of the creature with the un-stale blood of some newly drowned fisherman, the slippery fluid of the dead man's veins kept fresh by the cold chill of the sea.

The task completed, Frankenstein turned to his machinery.

Leaning in close, he attached to the creature's flesh the many electric wires that would, in a few breathless moments, hum and spark, bringing your beloved to glorious life. As you watched with almost unendurable anticipation and joy, Frankenstein paused. Sensing that he was being watched, he looked up, and saw you at the window.

If only you had turned abruptly away. If only you'd stepped back from the window, fading into the night. Or, holding your position, simply beheld your father coolly, with blank, contemptuous eyes.

If only you had not *smiled*.

Eyes wide, mouth twisted to a knot, Frankenstein recoiled at your face as if struck by a bullet. Fear and rage darkened his countenance, as it had when you first parted his bed curtains on the night of your birth, smiling down at him with hopeful eyes. As then, he took your wide, teeth-splaying grin and pale, gleaming eyes to be the face of malice, of evil, of devilish triumph.

With a motion too swift even for your quick reflexes to prevent, Frankenstein seized his scalpel and brought it down with great force into the she-creature's heart. A howl of agony rose from your throat as Frankenstein, his arms slashing out in a frenzy of bloody action, continued to attack your unborn bride. Her borrowed blood splashed across the table, dripping thickly to the floor, as your faithless father—once again your sworn enemy—viciously and irreversibly unmade what he had made.

His deed accomplished, Frankenstein turned defiantly to face you, wiping your beloved's blood from his eyes, the scalpel still in his hand, expecting your attack, goading you to revenge. But you had already vanished. Only the aching howl of your cry remained, and a solemn promise shouted in a roar, carried to Frankenstein's stubborn, dull ears on the raging wind.

"You will see me again!" you cried. "Never doubt this promise, Frankenstein! My revenge will come! I will be with you on your wedding night!"

Mad with grief, you vowed a thousand acts of evil.

The first was the death of Frankenstein's friend, Clerval. You found him in Scotland, not far away, studying maps outside an inn in Thurso. You left his lifeless, bloodstained body on the boards of a rowboat moored on the shore of Frankenstein's island.

Then you made your way back to Geneva.

After finding a hiding place in the western woods, you lingered with steady forbearance, waiting for Frankenstein's return. You would be patient… and patience, oh my Creature, is a virtue that most definitely was in your blood. That life-giving fluid, introduced to your veins the same way you saw Frankenstein do in the ruined farmhouse in Scotland, had, of course, once flowed through the body of another—a mute murderer of children, confined for years in the damp and dark of the Ingolstadt Asylum. Like you, the child-killer believed in the virtue of patience.

Like you, she knew how to wait.

A pious and mild-tempered young wife, the washerwoman had loved and feared God since childhood. She worked in the laundry at the University, toiling side-by-side with other washers in a room of tubs, hot water and steam. Every day, she prayed to God, begging for a child, but none came. As the other laundry women were each in turn blessed with children, the washerwoman's prayers grew stronger, more desperate and despairing, more reckless. Her husband, indifferent to her desire for children, gave little comfort. After years of patient prayer, she began to feel rising anger toward God, threatening to take her prayers to his enemy, the Fallen Angel.

Alone one night in the church, she knelt at the altar, the stones of the floor wet with her tears. In a burst of passion, she despairingly whispered that she would gladly sell her very soul for a child, but that since her own soul had been judged to be of insufficient worth, she'd pledge the baby's soul instead.

She was with child by the turn of the season.

Anxious and ridden with guilt at what she might have done, the washerwoman told the priest of her illicit prayer, terrified she'd consigned her unborn child to eternal damnation. The priest was kind-hearted, but educated and easily exasperated, not one to suffer foolishness or superstition. He assured the washerwoman that her prayer was nothing more than a moment of weakness, and that no contract with nefarious powers had been struck. His words did little to calm her rising terror, and as the day of her confinement grew near, she begged him for some further assurance of her child's salvation. Grown weary of the washerwoman's fervid petitions, the priest finally sent her away, dismissively suggesting that once baptized and given a Christian name the child's soul would be safe from the reach of Hellish hands for at least seven years. Until then, the priest curtly promised, the worst punishment God would give a child who'd committed no sin, was eternity in Limbo.

Her anxiety greatly relieved, the washerwoman troubled him no more.

For his part, the priest believed that once the child was born, the poor woman's mad apprehensions would fade. He felt certain that by the time seven years of blessed motherhood passed—and the morning of her child's first confession drew near—the washerwoman's fears would long since have faded.

In due course, her son was born, healthy and strong. At his baptism, the priest joyfully performed the rite, the beautiful little boy wrapped in a soft white blanket, a gift from all the other laundry women. From that day on, his mother happily watched her son grow, as delightful and sweet a child as any mother could desire.

When he was seven years old, on the eve of his first confession, she drowned him in a washing tub at the laundry. At the trial, clutching her son's christening blanket in her hands, she calmly spoke of her compact with the forces of damnation, exulting that she'd tricked the powers of Hell, trading her own murdering soul for that of her beautiful, sinless son.

This final confession made, she fell silent, and spoke never a word or prayer more.

Judged insane beyond cure, she was confined to the asylum for the rest of her life.

One year later, on her son's birthday, she hanged herself with a cloth rope, a cord made of long, soft threads the patient washerwoman pulled one by one, ever so carefully, from the soft white blanket in which her beautiful baby boy was baptized.

It was early summer, my Creature—ten months after you faced him last—that Victor Frankenstein finally returned to Geneva, into the worried, waiting arms of his Elizabeth. Recklessly, he set the date of their wedding for a few days hence, arming himself with weapons in anticipation of your expected attack... thus setting in motion the final spiraling chapters of his accursed life.

When you climbed up and through his bedroom window on the midnight of his marriage, you expected to find Frankenstein, guarding his bride. But there was Elizabeth alone and unprotected, asleep in the bed. Frankenstein, ever self-devoted, believing his own body to be the target of your wedding-night threat, waited for you downstairs. A pistol in each hand, his white, terrified eyes were trained on the doorway through which your furious entrance was expected.

Had Elizabeth not awakened and screamed, your poor dim father might have stayed frozen there till morning. On her second cry, Frankenstein saw his mistake, and made for the stairs, but with each step he climbed, your fire-hungry hand now on Elizabeth's pleading throat grew tighter. By the time Frankenstein made his way through the twice-locked door, his wife was gone, her dead, broken body thrown pale and contorted onto the bed, the marks of your fingers now forming on her throat.

Just outside the open shutters, you clung fast, crouching against the window-frame, waiting for Frankenstein's grieving eyes to behold you. But before he did, he fainted. Only later, once recovered, did your father see you there, still waiting at the window. He fired till his pistols were empty, but now at last you were gone. The great conclusion of your planned revenge was to make Frankenstein give you chase, to draw him away from Geneva to some distant place where, in a final battle to the death, you might share together some mutual end. But for the next many months, when not fainting at the thought of you or falling into a nervous fever, Frankenstein was oft constrained by others, confined twice to hospital and once to the madhouse. As weeks turned to months, you played the patient mouse to his sluggish, crippled cat, but in due course, he took up your trail, pursuing you across Europe, into Russia, across the Black Sea, and onto the frozen miles of blank Northern ice.

There, at last, did your twin paths accidentally intercept that of my long forgotten adventurer, the letter-writing explorer Captain Walton, his freezing crew threatening violent mutiny as their ship, in mortal danger of being crushed to pieces, remained caught in the ice at the edge of the sea. You—a mere few miles ahead of the failing Frankenstein—saw the crew's little furred faces, goggling from the bulwark at your massive shape as you raced past their imperiled vessel. Soon after came the ragged skeleton of your pursuer... starving, feverish and nearly dead.

When the incredulous Walton took him aboard, you waited, tarrying out on the ice, having almost reached the Pole, the remotest and loneliest of places. You would go no further without Frankenstein. The Pole was the spot you'd chosen for the fiery conclusion of your story... and his.

On board the ship, the raving, dying Frankenstein dictated to Walton his own sniveling side of the story he first began scribbling—in the rough language of scars and wires, of arrogance and pride—on the flesh, bone, skin and tissue of your patchwork body.

After several days of waiting, you finally ascended the icy stern of the tilting ship in search of your father. With a sense of mounting grief in your heart, you forced your way into Walton's cabin. There before you on the bed, cradled in a vast swaddling of blankets and furs, was the silent corpse of Frankenstein. As a final insult, he had died without you, abandoning his creation once more, and for the last time.

The rest barely matters.

Walton appears. He talks. You talk. With tears in your eyes, you move to the window, turning to look your last upon Victor Frankenstein. You leap, alighting on a raft of ice. You see Walton's face at the window, receding as you are borne away on the waves—his face, the window, and the great frozen ship all gradually vanishing into the night, lost in darkness and distance.

And what of *your* ending, my Creature?

In the pages of the book, you merely told Walton what you meant to do, a promise of fire and ashes. But I, with paper and ink, could not bear to write it, could not force myself to describe in firm and vivid words the final scene of your sad existence. Still, though I could not will my pen to tell it, your fiery death was as clear in my mind as the waking dream that first brought you to life in the early hours of that rainy June morning.

It was a good death, I think, brought on by your own hands, shortly after fleeing Walton's ship.

Before a pyre of wood scavenged from God knows where—the wreckage of broken vessels, perhaps—you first stripped away your ragged clothes and dropped them on the pile. Standing naked on the ice at the edge of the sea, you closed your eyes, stretching out your arms to the freezing cold. Slowly, you beckoned each scrap of skin and flesh, every bone and organ and muscle of your body, to feel and remember again the life it once had lived. Into your sighing throat, you called up every memory and emotion, feeling the sting or delight of every deed—good or ill—ever done by you or to you. Then, your whole body now trembling in a great silent shout of pain, remorse, defiance and triumph, you set ablaze the rags, the timber, and yourself.

The flames took hold and quickly climbed higher, from the pyre to your feet, then swiftly upward. The four long years of your life, you knew, would soon be over. Though your legs were now in agony, your lips blessed the flames and the relief they would soon bring. With your arms still spread out to the freezing cold, your eyes wide with rising torment, you slowly turned the palms of your still unburned hands to the heat of the fire.

Whatever shred of memory those hands once retained from the good, contented life of the gentle ox-driver, it had all long since grown silent.

But still, you closed your eyes a final time, and listened.

There it was.

As keenly as the first dizzying moment you saw and sensed that memory in your skin, you were there again, a child again, sitting before the fire in the comfort of the warm house, cradled in the lap of that forever-nameless woman. Softly, she stroked your hair with infinite tenderness, as you—a young boy wrapped in the arms of one who ever loved you—lifted your small pink palms to the beautiful, warm, enveloping fire… and dreamed.

I finished the book in March.

Rightly surmising that the subject matter would be taken as even more appalling if known to be the work of a woman, Shelley told each prospective publisher—as he shopped the manuscript across London—that the author of *Frankenstein* was an anonymous "friend." In August, Lackington and Co. accepted it—probably thinking it to be the work of Shelley—and agreed to print five hundred copies, doubtful enough of selling even those few. Five months later, on the first of January 1818, *Frankenstein, or the Modern Prometheus*… by Anonymous… was published.

With the exception of some, such as Sir Walter Scott, who praised the author's genius and "happy powers of expression," the majority of the critics in the magazines called my little novel "disagreeable," "disgusting," "degrading" and "absurd."

I ignored them, and so did the public, quickly purchasing every copy and clamoring for more.

My first success. Even Godwin was proud.

By then, my little daughter Clara was born and thriving at three months old.

I was happy.

One year later, after falling ill on the road to Venice, Clara was dead.

We'd fled London again, making for Italy, drawn against all sense into Claire's escalating war with Albé, now an Italian, over her care of Allegra.

So began a long season of death, from which my happiness never emerged again.

In Rome, nine months after Clara's death, little William followed her to the grave.

It was too much to accept, and more than I could endure.

By November of that year—the same month Shelley finally completed *Prometheus Unbound*—I was once again with child... though lost and drifting in a deep, silent sorrow from which I could only rarely free myself. Were it not for Godwin's certainty that his daughter's madness would reflect badly on his reputation, I might have been confined to an asylum. I for one did not care. But for the child growing in my womb, and the daily work on my second book, *Mathilda*—the tale of a father's bizarre, unhealthy obsession with his headstrong writer daughter—I might have done myself an injury.

But I restrained myself. I was done with death. Or so I thought.

When Percy Florence—my radiant, beautiful Percy—was born in Florence, Italy, my darkness lightened a little. *Mathilda* was finished and sent to Godwin for comment. I thought he'd be flattered. He kidnapped the manuscript and refused to return it, or allow its publication. By then I'd begun work on a novel of historical fiction, but my heart was not in it.

There in Florence I had a visit from Polidori, who'd published *The Vampyre* the previous spring. The book was a satisfying critical success... largely fueled by rumors it was written by Lord Byron. Poor Polidori could convince none that he was the true author.

It was the last time I would see him alive.

Shelley, for his part, was as lost as I, unable to rouse me fully back to my former self.

Finding me cold and distant, he finally sought elsewhere for a muse, and found her... often, usually in the form of married women. Though I never knew for certain sure, I suspected that Shelley and Claire found some comfort in each other's arms. All the while, in our journals, old and new, he wrote mysterious notes in the margins, dating back to the beginning of our time together, scribbling notes and commentaries I took as clues, macabre little breadcrumbs I might follow to reclaim his adoration and fidelity.

To my insecure and guilty mind, they often felt like accusations.

At other times I wondered if they were left for me at all, but rather odd musings and explorations of his own—notes about a daughter of a duke reportedly born with the head of a hog, a quote attributed to me, though I did not recall it, in which I supposedly described a cat eating roses, an act that would turn the beast into a woman by morning. To a mad notation I *had* written made not long after the baby's death—two lines of a recipe for a magical potion I remembered from our time studying the alchemists— Shelley added his own recipe.

Nine drops of human blood. Seven grains of gun-powder.

One half-ounce of putrefied brain. Thirteen mashed grave worms.

A "doom salve," he called it.

I considered writing the word, "Bloat!" beneath the notation, but did not.

Whatever the meaning of these cryptic and mystical lines, I could not fathom or decipher it.

I knew that no magic Shelley or I might devise could restore our once un-dissolvable bond.

And still, though as if from behind a curtain of sadness, I loved him as full and foolishly as ever.

In the weeks that followed, I cared for Percy Florence, I followed Shelley to whatever town or country his wandering heart took him, I wrote my novels, and I loved my husband as best I could. There were still moments when—for an afternoon or a night or an hour—I received from him an unexpected reminder of the worship and ardor his poet's heart had once poured out daily—with kisses and sighs and whispers of adoration—upon my face, my hands, my lips, my body, my soul.

In May of 1822, I was once again with child.

We had only recently moved to Casa Magni, on the Bay of Lereci in the north of Italy. Having just learned that her daughter Allegra had died of typhus the month before—in a convent, where Byron had sent the girl to be cared for—Claire was wild with grief and bitterness.

Shelley, meanwhile, had begun work on a new poem... *The Triumph of Life*.

The *Triumph of Life*.

God does have a sense of humor.

A cruel one.

But then, so do I. I have earned it.

On the sixteenth of June of that year, 1822, just before mid-day, I began bleeding and could not stop. I knew at once I'd lost the babe in my womb, and as I staggered unsteady and barefoot through the house to where Shelley was writing, I left a bloody parade of footprints from my desk to his.

I remember little after.

When I awoke the next day, cold and shivering, a strange smell of blood and burning in my nose—as sharp and heavy as a church full of incense—the surgeon explained that Shelley had saved my life, quickly covering my bleeding body in ice to stop the flow while Claire ran for the surgeon. When I could walk again, I saw the blood still splattered across the tub in the bath, a trickle of gory issue—the last of my four dead children—trailing back to where I'd fallen unconscious, within moments of dying, in Shelley's arms. So much blood, so very much blood—yet Shelley had found a way to stop it. He could have let me die, freeing him to the arms of whatever woman he pined for that month, but instead, he saved me.

Twenty-two days later Shelley drowned, his boat overturned in a storm while sailing back from a meeting with Byron in Pisa, across the gulf. What was left of his body did not wash ashore for three days. The quarantine laws of Italy forbade the transport and burial of the drowned, and so did Byron, with his friend Trelawney and a few others, build a pyre on the rocky shore.

There at the water's edge, as if I'd written it, was Shelley burned away, whatever memories his body once held already lost in the cold waters of the gulf. The heat of the fire, I was eventually told, burst open my dearest one's frail but handsome chest, and there was his un-beating heart, steaming amidst his shattered ribs.

Trelawney thought at first to keep it—the blackened core of the brilliant and irreplaceable Percy Shelley—but he relented, making a gift of it to me. Claire and Percy Florence and I left Italy soon after, sailing back, bereft and empty, to England. Shelley's heart made the journey at my side. I'd won that heart once... won it of Shelley with but a promise of my love... but then I lost it.

Now, returning home to London, it was all I had left of him.

And what of my own heart, empty, burned and blistered as it was?

How did it continue to beat, or feel anything at all, over the next nine-

and-twenty years of my life? I lived on, that is sure—for the sake of Percy Florence—though I do not know how I managed it. I wrote what I could to put food in my son's mouth, and eked out a living in magazines and periodicals, scratching out histories and biographies, most of great interest but little importance.

Percy Florence, ever devoted to his mother, grew up strong and healthy, neither troublesome nor very exceptional. In college, he caused no one alarm and sparked little interest. In adult life, he achieved a kind of safe respectability, and eventually inherited his grandfather's estate, Field Place in Sussex, to which he moved us a few years before my body began to fail. I took some pleasure at becoming a resident of Field Place, having never once been invited there while Shelley's disapproving father was alive. Percy Florence, for many years a bachelor, finally met and married Jane, a lovely widow who adored poetry, but had no inclination at all to write it.

As for myself, I edited collections of Shelley's poems, wrote prefaces for new editions of *Frankenstein*, and published six more works of my own fiction, all published to respectable, if less than adulatory, acclaim. *Mathilda*—alone of all my books—was never published, as Godwin refused to return it to me. After he died—a gentler man in the end than he had once been—I searched his house for the manuscript, and again when Mrs. Godwin followed Papa to the grave, but I never saw *Mathilda* more.

A pity, that... I did think it rather good.

By then, most of my old friends were dead.

Lord Byron was long since buried in Greece, his death mourned by all of Europe and by myself—though never by Claire, who had only grown sadder and stranger, as I grew older and less tolerant of her nervous exertions. She's alive still, or was not long ago, living in Florence, clinging daily to her scripture, spitting out regret and bitterness at the very mention of Byron, poetry, and all poets... even my Shelley.

She never forgave my husband, I think, for not leaving me in Italy and running away with her.

As for me, I endured—day passing day, and year passing year—till the eve of my fiftieth birthday, when the headaches began, accompanied by odd smells and strange visions. I lost my hearing in one ear, and my sight in one eye. One by one, my limbs grew useless and heavy as my weary old body began packing its bags, preparing at last to take leave of this world. It lingered on, cruelly, through a long wet winter. Then, with one final gasp of breathless terror and immense relief, my body squeezed out the last dull drops of my life, and I died.

And there, in that grave before me, is my corpse.

Mary Shelley.

Born August 30, 1797. Died February 1, 1851.

Dead in Sussex, buried in Bournemouth.

I am curious, I admit, at what the papers said of my death.

When *Shelley* died, the papers gloated. The *Courier* wrote, "Percy Bysshe Shelley, the writer of some infidel poetry, has been drowned. Now he knows whether there is a God or no." It pained me, their gleeful prediction of Shelley's damnation.

But now I envy whatever knowledge my husband gained with his death.

Here I am, dead myself—for how long in the grave I do not know—having with endless words peeled back the reluctant skin of my long history... and yet the deeper I carve into the meat of my own life, the less I understand! Have I not reached the climax of my life story? I've even related those parts of *Frankenstein* I invented but never put to paper.

Shouldn't the sky be turning light or some similar spectacle... this rocky wall parting open before me, trumpets sounding as some golden road appears before me, bidding me on to whatever fate awaits me?

Good God! I hope I am not required to tell the plots of *all* my novels.

That would be Hell indeed... and frankly I would prefer Hell to that... or to this, this place of endless storm and raging darkness. The storm is growing stronger, isn't it? Is that supposed to mean something? The rain beyond these walls grows louder, too, as does the thunder raging overhead... and there's the lightning again, showing me, with each flash, the now familiar names of these ever-watching tombstones, my only sympathetic friends.

Oh, hello! Best regards of the day, Rev. Lang.

And to you, Ladies Freeth... top of the morning.

Mr. Esquire? It's so nice to see you again. Lovely weather we've been having.

I make jest... though I am not at all mirthful. I am, in truth, utterly sick of this all, weary and worn to nothing. I have nothing left. Have I not revealed enough for judgment to be passed, if judgment indeed is what awaits me?

No.

It is quite clear I have not.

Why do I even ask the question?

There *is* yet one task left unaccomplished, one secret still to reveal. It's a story I have already told... though, in truth, I did not tell all of it. I have resisted... resisted with all my strength... and only now do I understand what I have till now refused to understand.

The part I have avoided reliving is the very story I was brought here to tell.

Shelley once described an ancient magic spell from Cornelius Agrippa's *Histories of Magic*. It was an elaborate incantation against "diseases and tempests," requiring the recitation of various holy names and ancient divinities, several of the elements, the four corners of Heaven, and the twenty-eight mansions of the moon. It was lovely nonsense, and impossible to memorize, though Shelley often tried. To become a true magician and worker of miracles, Agrippa insisted, one must speak the incantation perfectly, without omitting a single celestial house or name.

Perhaps, for me, this is now a bit like that.

Perhaps the story of my life is my own "incantation" against eternal storms and tempests.

And until I speak the whole story, there can be no rest or redemption.

How do I form the words? How do I even begin?

I did tell a version of it, once... in a fashion... a childish attempt to earn some slight ease of conscience. In veiled words I shouted out my sin for the whole world to see! Is it my fault no one recognized it for what it was? But none ever did. None even suspected it... that *Frankenstein* was more than just a ghastly work of fiction inspired by the nightmare of a nineteen-year-old girl.

Buried in the pages of *Frankenstein* was that girl's confession.

My confession!

And now, if I must exhume the truth from out of my fiction, spreading it out as bare as the bones in these many graves, then hear me, you rotting corpses!

You stormy skies!

Let all these watching rocks and silent stones take note!

These are the sins of Mary Wollstonecraft Shelley!

In her youth, she loved a man married to another, and felt only joy when his wife finally died!

She worshipped her husband above all sense, risking her children's lives to follow him across the world!

She betrayed her sisters and friends in not doing enough to soften their anguish! She made an enemy of her father, though she loved him ever! She murdered her own mother in childbirth, and murdered her own babe, too—giving birth to her too early, so eager was she to become the mother she never had herself.

And then, sin of all my sins … I killed her again!

She was born early, ten weeks or more, at the end of February… so little, she was, and so weak. I tried to nurse her, but she would not, and the doctor coldly predicted she would die. Two nights later, there was a storm. Awoken by thunder from deep but uneasy dreams, I realized at once it had been hours since I'd put her to bed, kissed her face, listened to her gently gasping breaths. In the dark, I moved across the room to cradle and comfort her in her crib, but before even lighting a candle, I knew she was dead. Outside the window, a fork of lightning bridged the sky, filling the room with light, and I saw my unmoving babe, shriveled, twisted and gray, her tiny life all drained away to nothing. I screamed, and the next instant Shelley was at my side, his stricken face wet with tears and horror, stretching out to stroke the gray cheek of our little cold child.

She had been dead for at least an hour.

Futilely, Shelley fled the house in his nightgown, dashing off through the thundering streets of London to fetch the doctor.

How could he guess what I was about to do?

I was then still a girl of, what? Seventeen! Raised to believe in the limitless possibilities of science, mad with agony and love, wild with rage and grief, I pulled my little babe from the crib, vowing that she would live again.

Later, whenever I doubted the events of that night, I found proof in the ink of my own journal, where Shelley himself wrote those words the next morning.

"Baby unexpectedly alive!"

Once Shelley was gone to fetch Dr. Clarke, I carried the baby, weightless and stiffening, to the study. In a kind of stupor, I lay her on the desk, quickly assembling whatever instruments were at hand in the home of a poet so enamored of the newest scientific discoveries. Like the lightning that now and then illuminated my work, I recall what I did only in flashes. Years later, in my novel, I wrote of wires and tubs of ice and vast arrays of engines… but in truth, it was so much simpler.

A half-hour later, Shelley returned, the doctor at his side, both expecting to find me cradling the dead child, myself lost in a wild hysteria of tears and wailing.

But I was calm again, spent and weak, but smiling.

Standing in the doorway, Shelley watched me cradle our nursing child in my arms, her little soft face still moving from cold gray to flushed pink, her cool translucent skin growing gradually warmer as she grasped my weary, blood-stained fingers in her tiny hand. The room was filled with the smell of burning skin and blood, some of it mine. One of Shelley's friction machines—high on a shelf in the study when he'd bolted from the house—was now on the desk, a low hum still emanating from its wheels and levers, a thick odor of electricity in the air. But the baby—the living, breathing, suckling baby I held to my breast—she only smelled sweet and warm and alive.

"Mary? Mary?"

Shelley repeated my name till I finally noticed he was there, looking up at his astonished face.

"I did this," I murmured, from out of whatever depth and darkness my mind had gone to. "I did this. I made this. I made her."

The doctor, confused, became swiftly perturbed, presuming that we had misinterpreted the stillness of our sleeping child and dragged him out in the rain to no purpose. He no doubt believed me to be some kind of dangerous hysteric who'd harmed herself in a fit of anxiety, and was lucky not to have similarly injured the baby. He tended to me, but only after examining the babe, whom he declared to be in surprisingly passable health, given the circumstances of her birth. Nevertheless, considering her premature condition, he warned us that the baby was still unlikely to live many days more. Then he departed, back again to wet streets and his own home.

"Oh, Mary. Sweet Mary… what have you done?"

Shelley, struck in equal parts with breathless awe and quiet horror, gently pressed me for details. But I could not give them. I was too exhausted and withdrawn, and could say little—except that my babe was dead, I did all I could to save her, and now she was alive, my little babe, my sweet one, my beautiful monster... alive once again in my arms.

She soon fell asleep, and I quickly followed.

Over the next several days, it was clear that Shelley saw what I'd done as monstrous, and yet he never condemned me for it, or ever said so much with words. He never failed to show me great kindness and care, but I knew that he was greatly troubled by the marvel I had worked.

I saw it in his eyes.

In the journal, Shelley carefully wrote, "Mary well... favorable symptoms in the child... we may indulge some hopes," but I noticed that he could not, without effort, bring himself to hold the child in his own arms. And in those moments he did—always tendering the greatest gentleness to the babe—he would each time turn pale and fretful, trembling with a kind of deep disquiet.

For much of a week, I tended to my babe, nursing her when hungry, comforting her when she cried, all the while watching in amazement as she grew stronger, her little smiling face and searching eyes captivating me more each day.

Shelley began to fall ill, unable to sleep soundly, beset with spasms that concerned Claire, though at first I only barely noticed his distress. At night, he was restless with evil dreams he would not speak of, and in the light of each new morning, he was all the more reluctant to touch, or even look upon, our little reborn child. All the while, I never saw hate or revulsion in my husband's eyes. Never was there a moment I did not believe he utterly loved her.

Yet with every new day, it was clearer that he feared her.

No, not that. He did not fear her, exactly. It was something deeper.

What I saw, finally, was that he was afraid *for* her.

By then, as I gradually returned to some semblance of sanity, I had begun to fear for our strange little daughter as well, in my own gradually dawning way. The more I awoke from my long daze, the more I began to question what foul fate I might have wrought upon the child with my rash actions. What unnatural future had I condemned her to?

Though beautiful, was she not strange, forbidden, an abomination of nature? I had interrupted the course of life and death, brought back that which was not meant to be alive. Motivated by selfishness and motherly hunger, I had, with human hands, dared to mock the hallowed acts of the creator of the universe.

The creator is ever jealous, is he not?

As the gods punished Prometheus, how would I not be punished, too? And what greater punishment than to pour out tortures and griefs upon the very thing I had broken all laws of God and nature to create?

"What have I done? What have I done?"

For two days and nights, I watched over her in rising terror, murmuring aloud the dread that obsessed my mind, desperately afraid that at any moment some act of Olympian retribution would be meted out upon my babe, leaving her sweet, frail frame damaged or deformed, her tiny body left twisting in a lifetime of freakish, vengeful agony.

"Oh, my little girl, my sweet little monster… what have I done?"

Is it possible to commit a sinful act for a sacred reason? How strange, that for all the shocks and terrors we can mete out on our fellow man with our pride and arrogance, our greed and anger and hate, there is still no shortage of horrors we are able to act out on others with our love.

On the morning of the tenth day, I told Shelley what I had decided I must do.

He kissed me softly, and with eyes overflowing, lifted our little child to his face. Whatever nervous tremors haunted him, he overcame them in that moment, holding her so close, breathing her forever into his mind and memory. He kissed her face and her little hands, then, oh so gently, placed her back in my arms, whispering that he would be out for the day, taking Claire with him so that the babe and I would be alone.

For the next three hours, I did nothing, nothing but sing to her.

Tenderly, oh so tenderly, with shaking hands, I covered her tiny nose and mouth, closing them up with no more strength than needed to gently smother out all her breath, all the while caressing and cradling her little writhing body against my sobbing breast. Whatever of my heart had not been shattered to pieces by my baby's natural death, was entirely destroyed when I finally murdered her. Again and again, I whispered soft words of comfort and sorrow, that on her journey back to Heaven, she would take with her the sound of my voice, the memory of my touch, and the undying warmth of my love. When she breathed no more, I held her a moment longer. I kissed her a last time, returned her to her crib, and waited for Shelley's return.

I pulled out the journal, and with a shattered heart I wrote those few words, a lie—the first in a long series of lies—and also my firstborn daughter's only obituary.

"Monday, March 6. Find my baby dead. A miserable day."

It was not till over a year later, in Switzerland, at Villa Diodati, that Shelley and I fully fathomed the stupidity and horror of what we had done...

...what *I* had done.

It was the night of my dream, as I listened to Shelley and Byron and Polidori talking, talking past midnight. It was when Polidori made his absurd remark about souls and champagne corks. The soul is like a cork, he said, didn't he? Formed to move in one direction only... out. At the moment of death, the soul is propelled from the body, and if forced back by means of science or sorcery, then surely irreparable damage will be done... either to the body... or to the soul.

Only then did I understand it.

If Polidori was correct—and I knew in my heart that he was—then in the act of restoring my babe to life, I had certainly fractured her soul beyond repair. Was not this the source of the terror Shelley sensed when he tried to hold her?

And worse still... horror upon horror... then ten days later, when I smothered her to death—thinking that I had simply returned her to the travels from which I had so selfishly brought her back—I had in fact done nothing of the kind.

My baby could *never* go back the same way. She was lost, fractured and broken, splintered and alone, her soul forever drifting beyond the worlds of the living and the dead.

Were it not for little William, I'd have killed myself that night, propelling my own soul into the void to somehow find and reclaim and comfort her.

But even then, I knew, it would not be enough.

Whatever path I'd put her on, only she could travel.

My poor sweet babe, abandoned for all eternity.

From that night, near all of Shelley's poems reflected his growing pre-occupation with matters of life, death and rebirth, his stories filled with witches and sorcerers, dying soldiers and kings, gods and mortals clashing in conflict over the souls of the damned and the lost.

It was, I believe, his way of professing the guilt he carried himself, or perhaps he simply could never stop looking for a way to save our dead lost child.

As for me, the truth of my crimes is all there, though thickly veiled, in the pages of *Frankenstein*—the tale of an innocent child who, without ever asking to live, was brought against its will into a world where only pain and anguish awaits. Some have already declared that *Frankenstein* is the author's warning against the dangerous arrogance of science and medicine, but such matters are merely the soil in which my true confession is buried. My child, my little monster, is the Creature, and I—the wretched creator of her unspeakable misery—am Victor Frankenstein!

And now I have said it plainly.

I carried the knowledge of these actions all the days of my life.

It has been a heavy burden.

It has often driven me to the brink of madness.

Only the love of my other children… my living babes, for as long as they did live… has kept me from surrendering to it. And now, too late to matter, I have spoken it at last, and I welcome whatever final punishment awaits me… though nothing I can do, or say, or suffer now will ever change what I did… or convince me that any other mother, given the selfsame hope of saving her child, would not have committed the very crimes that I have done.

I shall end my stories now… for once and for all.

I shall sit here, upon my grave, and wait for my final judgment.

How long will I wait, I wonder?

If something horrible is going to happen… now would be a good time.

I *am* sitting on the right grave, am I not?

Yes… there is my name.

Mary Wollstonecraft Shelley.

How strange, I can see it easily now!

There is light around me, almost as if the clouds were parting.

For the first time since I arrived in this place, I can see clearly.

By the growing light I can read, without touching, these carved words upon my tomb.

I see my name, and the familiar dates of my birth and death.

Born August 30, 1797.

Died June 16, 1822.

That is wrong. That is not the date of my death.

I died in *1851*. I was fifty-three. In 1822 I would have been twenty-four.

What is meant by this? 1822 is the year *Shelley* died, not I.

He died in July… three weeks after I lost our unborn child, the day I almost bled to death.

Oh God! Oh dear God!

That day, the day I lost the child… it was June 16, 1822, the date now on my tomb!

But that was *not* the day I died… it was the day Shelley *saved me* from dying!

He put me in a tub of ice to slow the flow of blood till the surgeon arrived.

That's what he told me! That's what I have always remembered!

Oh, Shelley.

Oh my Shelley!

What did you do?

You did not save me, did you? I died in your arms.

And then you brought me back from the dead!

How, Shelley? How did you do it?

I never told you how I revived the child from death!

You could not have done it the way I did!

But against all sense, it is true, is it not?

All I remember is awakening after what felt like hours of shadowy dreams full of motion and movement, of ice and of fire. I opened my eyes and saw the doctor there, and you at my side. I remember the thick smell of something burning, not electricity or flesh, but incense and smoke and I know not what. I remember the room, lit by a dozen candles or more. I remember your face, the brightness of the candlelight illuminating the sweat and tears still gleaming on your exultant, exhausted face.

Oh my Shelley!

In some musty book of ancient magic, did you truly discover the secret of life and death? What ancient spells or incantations did you work to summon me back, what forbidden sorceries did you perform to wake my dead and sleeping body?

Would you have told me what it was you did... *what I had become...* had you not drowned so soon after? I was so frail and worn. Perhaps you were only waiting till I was stronger.

But Shelley, oh my Shelley, I cannot imagine to what purpose you brought me back alive.

Did you love me so much still, there at the end of your days?

Or did you mean to punish me?

Knowing, as you did, what would happen to me... to my soul ... broken and disabled for all time, did you mean to consign me to the same fate to which I had consigned our daughter?

No. I cannot believe that.

You were often selfish, as was I, but you were never vengeful.

Why, then, did you do it?

If only my twice-sleeping corpse, here buried beneath this stone, would rise now and tell me! What might she say? What words might she offer to comfort me... the fractured and un-mendable soul that once resided in her body? Will not these carvings form new words to offer explanation? Cannot you stormy skies, so long booming out your deafening noise, shout down an answer? But no, even you, you thunder, you lightning, even now you finally grow silent.

Silent. It has all gone silent.

Out beyond the wall, I can hear no more the sound of falling rain.

There is no more storm... no more darkness... only light, like the dawn of a new morning.

And by that light, I can now see what I never thought to see more... away and across this garden of stones... there is no more wall.

I cannot tell what lies beyond.

There is a mist, a wisp of fog shining with beams of glowing light. Beyond the mist are shadows of hills and distant trees, vast patches of endless green.

Am I free at last?

Oh Shelley!

How did you know?

This graveyard to which I have been confined, it has not been a prison.

I was never brought here for punishment. I was never locked here to make my confession, though it has been through my confession, and all of my stories, that I have at last gained understanding of the truth.

And now, at last, I know.

I died once, but lived on, and then died again.

Shelley brought me back to life for one purpose only... that when I died a second time, unable to proceed to that unknown place to which all souls must travel... I might then go off into whatever land our little baby daughter wanders in, and reclaim her at last.

She is out there, in the mists and shadows, though I cannot yet see her.

I do feel that she is there.

I will find her.

I will comfort her again, and perhaps, together, we will find a way to heal one another at last.

My long sadness—like the rain and darkness that have, for so long, hung over me in this strange place—has at last lifted.

I am happy.

I might still be a bit crazy, of course.

For all I know, this is all just the final stage of madness.

It is possible that my father—still alive in London with my detested stepmother—gave in finally, and declared me insane long ago, confining my raving self to some asylum, like my poor washerwoman. It is possible that all of this—the cemetery, the tombstone, my own grave, and the gleaming land I now see beyond—is only the final figment of my dying, raging imagination.

It's possible.

But I do not believe it to be so.

I choose to believe what I see before me.

Glistening fields, an empty graveyard, and tombs of rock.

Here lies Mary Shelley.

She's well past the bloat phase by now, I would presume, and it's a good thing, too. She's decaying at last, as she might have done over thirty years ago, were it not for Percy Shelley, poet and magician, who gave his troubled beloved one final chance to mend her one greatest mistake.

Rest in peace, then, my beautiful body.

With any luck, our name will one day be known as the true author of our book, our hideous progeny, our *Frankenstein*.

I bid you now farewell.

I am off to find my daughter.

My sweet, lost babe.

My little monster.

COPYRIGHT ACKNOWLEDGMENTS

A good cast is worth repeating…

TITLES AVAILABLE FROM WORD HORDE

Tales of Jack the Ripper
an anthology edited by Ross E. Lockhart

We Leave Together
a Dogsland novel by J. M. McDermott

*The Children of Old Leech: A Tribute to the
Carnivorous Cosmos of Laird Barron*
an anthology edited by Ross E. Lockhart and Justin Steele

Vermilion
a novel by Molly Tanzer

Giallo Fantastique
an anthology edited by Ross E. Lockhart

Mr. Suicide
a novel by Nicole Cushing

Cthulhu Fhtagn!
an anthology edited by Ross E. Lockhart

Painted Monsters & Other Strange Beasts
a collection by Orrin Grey

Furnace
a collection by Livia Llewellyn

The Lure of Devouring Light
a collection by Michael Griffin

The Fisherman
a novel by John Langan

A Brutal Chill in August
a novel by Alan M. Clark

The Raven's Table (February 2017)
a collection by Christine Morgan

Beneath (April 2017)
a novel by Kristi DeMeester

Ask for Word Horde books by name at your favorite bookseller.
Or order online at www.WordHorde.com

AN ANTHOLOGY OF ORIGINAL STRANGE STORIES at the intersection of crime, terror, and supernatural fiction. Inspired by and drawing from the highly stylized cinematic thrillers of Argento, Bava, and Fulci; American noir and crime fiction; and the grim fantasies of Edgar Allan Poe, Guy de Maupassant, and Jean Ray, *Giallo Fantastique* seeks to unnerve readers through virtuoso storytelling and startlingly colorful imagery.

What's your favorite shade of yellow?

Trade Paperback, 240 pp, $15.99

ISBN-13: 978-1-939905-06-2

http://www.wordhorde.com

In his house at R'lyeh, Cthulhu waits dreaming…

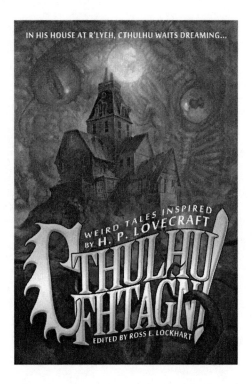

What are the dreams that monsters dream? When will the stars grow right? Where are the sunken temples in which the dreamers dwell? How will it all change when they come home?

Within these pages lie the answers, and more, in all-new stories by many of the brightest lights in dark fiction. Gathered together by Ross E. Lockhart, the editor who brought you *The Book of Cthulhu*, *The Children of Old Leech*, and *Giallo Fantastique*, *Cthulhu Fhtagn!* features nineteen weird tales inspired by H. P. Lovecraft.

Format: Trade Paperback, 330 pp, $19.99

ISBN-13: 978-1-939905-13-0

http://www.wordhorde.com

"*A River Runs Through It*…Straight to hell."

—Laird Barron, author of *X's for Eyes*

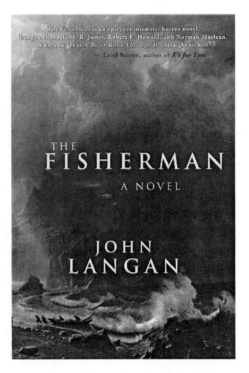

In upstate New York, in the woods around Woodstock, Dutchman's Creek flows out of the Ashokan Reservoir. Steep-banked, fast-moving, it offers the promise of fine fishing, and of something more, a possibility too fantastic to be true. When Abe and Dan, two widowers who have found solace in each other's company and a shared passion for fishing, hear rumors of the Creek, and what might be found there, the remedy to both their losses, they dismiss it as just another fish story. Soon, though, the men find themselves drawn into a tale as deep and old as the Reservoir. It's a tale of dark pacts, of long-buried secrets, and of a mysterious figure known as Der Fisher: the Fisherman. It will bring Abe and Dan face to face with all that they have lost, and with the price they must pay to regain it.

Trade Paperback, 282 pp, $16.99

ISBN-13: 978-1-939905-21-5

http://www.wordhorde.com

"Beautiful and hideous in the same breath, its 13 tales of erotic, surreal, existential horror pack a logic-shattering punch.."

—Jason Heller, NPR Books

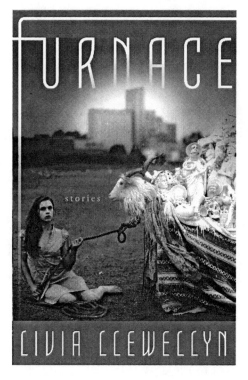

Lush, layered, multifaceted, and elegant, the thirteen tales comprising *Furnace* showcase why Livia Llewellyn has been lauded by scholars and fans of weird fiction alike, and why she has been nominated multiple times for the Shirley Jackson Award and included in year's best anthologies. These are exquisite stories, of beauty and cruelty, of pleasure and pain, of hunger, and of sharp teeth sinking into tender flesh.

Format: Trade Paperback, 204 pp, $14.99

ISBN-13: 978-1-939905-17-8

http://www.wordhorde.com

Photo Credit: Raymond Lawrason

ABOUT THE EDITOR

ROSS E. LOCKHART is an author, anthologist, bookseller, editor, and publisher. A lifelong fan of supernatural, fantastic, speculative, and weird fiction, Lockhart is a veteran of small-press publishing, having edited scores of well-regarded novels of horror, fantasy, and science fiction.

Lockhart edited the anthologies *The Book of Cthulhu I* and *II*, *Tales of Jack the Ripper*, *The Children of Old Leech: A Tribute to the Carnivorous Cosmos of Laird Barron* (with Justin Steele), *Giallo Fantastique, and Cthulhu Fhtagn!* He is the author of *Chick Bassist*. Lockhart lives in Petaluma, California, with his wife Jennifer, hundreds of books, and Elinor Phantom, a Shih Tzu moonlighting as his editorial assistant.

Visit him online at www.haresrocklots.com

CPSIA information can be obtained
at www.ICGtesting.com
Printed in the USA
LVOW12*2317110117

520664LV00003B/26/P